—*Are you worthy?*

The words rang loudly in Teldin's head as the *Spelljammer* seemed to rush toward him at once, like an unstoppable juggernaut. For an instant, Teldin cocked his head and stared at the monstrous ship. He grasped the rail of the deck and whispered, "Am I worthy?"

He knew, then, what the ancient *Spelljammer* was doing.

"Battle stations!" he screamed.

THE CLOAKMASTER CYCLE

• • •

One • Beyond the Moons

Two • Into the Void

Three • The Maelstrom's Eye

Four • The Radiant Dragon

Five • The Broken Sphere

Six • The Ultimate Helm

BOOKS

The Ultimate Helm

Russ T. Howard

The author and editors wish to thank Roger E. Moore
for his contributions to this work.

THE ULTIMATE HELM

Random House and its affiliate companies have worldwide distribution rights in the book trade for English language products of TSR, Inc.

Distributed to the book trade in the United Kingdom by TSR Ltd.

Distributed to the book and hobby trade by regional distributors.

Cover art by Michael Scott.

First Printing: September 1993
Printed in the United States of America.
Library of Congress Catalog Card Number: 92-61099

9 8 7 6 5 4 3 2 1

ISBN: 1-56076-651-4

TSR, Inc.
P.O. Box 756
Lake Geneva, WI 53147
U.S.A.

TSR Ltd.
120 Church End, Cherry Hinton
Cambridge CB1 3LB
United Kingdom

the first, sort of,
for Maria—
for always believing,
for always being there.

. . . pour toujours . . .

and for my parents,
who would have loved this,
no matter what.

Thanks go to George Beahm for the years of encouragement and friendship—and the gracious use of his printer at the last minute—and special thanks go to some *adventurers extraordinaire*: Darin DePaul and Mike Speller, two fine writers and actors who allowed me to help Otis T. Wren save Christmas (with the assistance of Albert Schweitzer), and Jackie, Captain of the Starship McBride, a great friend who helped keep me sane and relatively normal during my exile in Florida.

". . . but always dress for the hunt."

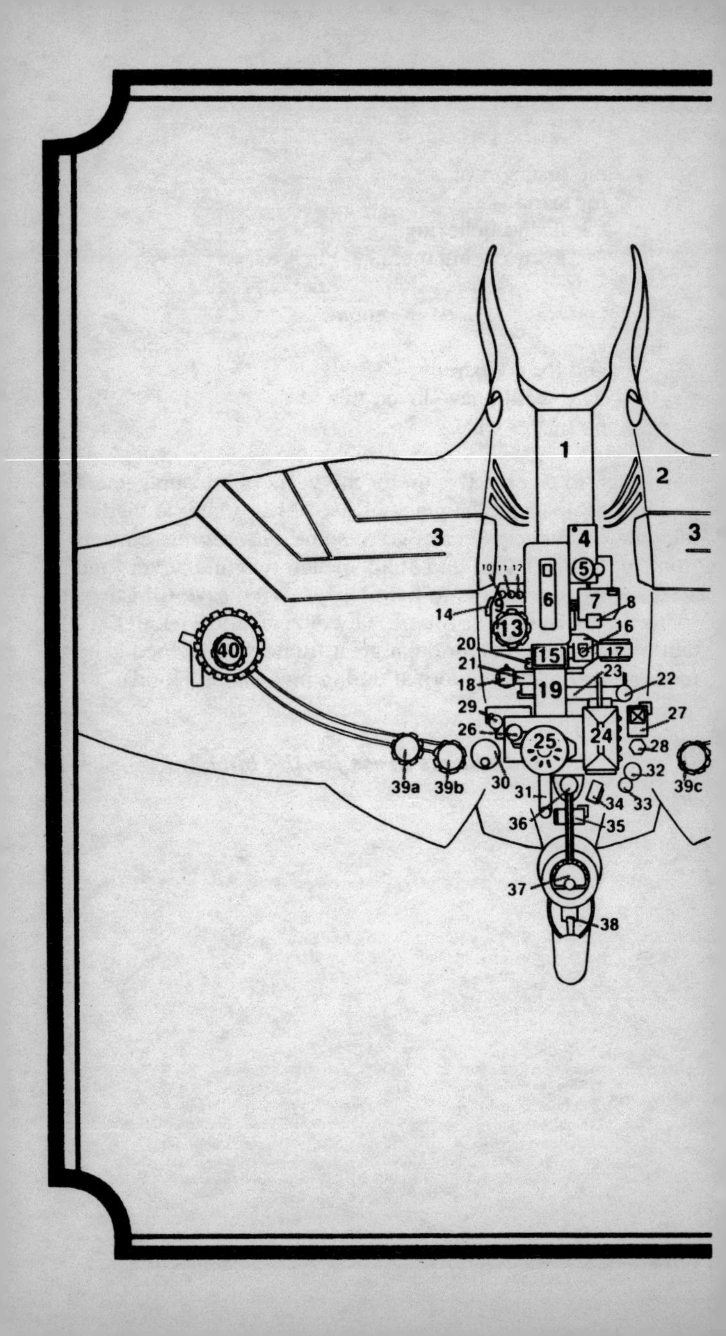
1
2
3
3
4
5
6
7
8
9
10
11
12
13
14
15
16
17
18
19
20
21
22
23
24
25
26
27
28
29
30
31
32
33
34
35
36
37
38
39a
39b
39c
40

The *Spelljammer*

1) Landing Deck
2) Gardens
3) Smalljammer Strips
4) Council Chambers
5) Captain's Quarters
6) Ship's Stores and Market
7) Captain's Tower
8) Library Tower
9) Human Collective
10) Chalice Tower
11) Tower of Thought
12) Tower of Trade
13) Guild Tower
14) Halfling Community
15) Shivak Terminal
16) Illithid Tower
17) Goblin Alliance Quarters
18) Building of the Giff
19) Communal Church
20) Old Wizard's Lair
21) Gnoll Ruins
22) Minotaur Tower
23) Ogre Wizard Quarters
24) Beholder Ruins
25) Dwarven Citadel of Kova
26) Free Dwarves Tower
27) Neogi Tower
28) Hulk Tower
29) Giant Tower
30) Shou Tower
31) Arcane's Tower
32) Tenth Pit
33) Long Fangs' Tower
34) Academy of Human Knowledge
35) Old Elvish Academy
36) Elven High Command
37) Armory
38) Dark Tower
39a) Battery (human contingent)
39b) Battery (dwarven contingent)
39c) Battery (elvish contingent)
39d) Battery (neogi contingent)
40) Dracon Tower
41) Centaur Tower

Our birth is but a sleep and a forgetting:
The Soul that rises with us, our life's Star,
Hath had elsewhere its setting,
And cometh from afar.

Wordsworth

To strive,
To seek,
To find,
And not to yield.

Tennyson

Prologue

• • •

"*. . . which the* Spelljammer *has seen many times before in its ageless travels. It is, instead, the coming of the one called the Cloakmaster that will herald a time of darkness unparalleled by any other. According to the scrolls of the Ancient Ones, war shall be called upon all, and the Cloakmaster's shadow will fall across the spheres.*

"*Alas, the scrolls of the Ancient Ones were lost in the wars after the Blinding Rot, and the sinister purposes of the Cloakmaster are known no longer . . .*"

The journal of Sketh, beholder mage, transcribed by enslaved human scribe, Hofrom; reign of Miark.

He stood on the upper deck of the nautiloid *Julia*, facing into the endless flow, where the course of his destiny had finally led him. The colors, the radiant brilliance of the phlogiston, flared against the ship's protective bubble of air and illuminated his taut features, the square jut of his lightly bearded chin, the corded muscles along his tanned arms. His long brown hair waved in a slight breeze caused by the ship's great speed through the flow. With each eruption of light, his swirling cloak changed its color, from purple, to deep blue, to crimson; and as the nautiloid sailed ever closer to its goal, the cloak grew warmer, more comfortable around his shoulders, as though it had always belonged there. Perhaps this ages-old cloak—which had been worn through the millennia by elves and orcs, reigar and wizards, had been hoarded by a golden dragon, and had been fought over in the Battle of Thrandish, where five thousand humans and unhumans had died for the control of a long-forgotten sphere—had always and ultimately been his alone to bear.

The master of the cloak.

Teldin Moore was sailing to his destiny.

He shivered at the enormity of the sphere before him. He was here! *Finally!* He pulled the cloak around him, gazed out over the prow of his nautiloid, and wondered at the twists of destiny that had started him on a simple quest and had ultimately pulled him to this place, an unimaginable distance from his home on Krynn, and to an unimaginable life for a groundling farm boy.

This was the Broken Sphere.

Teldin took a deep breath and let it out slowly.

It waited for him out there, in the rainbow swirl of the flow: a glimmer of barely reflected light against the cracked, black wall of the sphere.

The *Spelljammer*.

He felt it singing to him, seducing him like a siren, singing a song of wonder, of endless delight and exploration. Of worlds and places uncharted, undreamed of. Of a universe all his own.

Of life.

Why me? he almost said out loud. He looked down at the bronze medallion that the beautiful kender Gaeadrelle Goldring had given him. She had stolen it from an ogre during an attack of the Tarantula Fleet, and had given it to Teldin to help him on his quest for the legendary *Spelljammer*. A gleaming disk of untold power, it now hung around his neck, and he could feel its history, its antiquity, resonating in his fingertips. Who am I to have been called out here? I only wanted answers . . . What is this cloak? Why can't I take the thing off?

And what does it want with me?

He sighed. I only wanted some answers. Now they have led me to a sphere so ancient that it has become only a myth—a legend forgotten even by the races who had lived there.

Teldin sighed. Why me?

He touched the disk and felt its inner warmth humming

through his fingertips. To most, the bronze disk appeared to be just another artifact, a worthless ornament, scratched and dented by the blades of warriors long dead. Its face presented a complicated maze of lines and patterns, intertwined to form geometrical shapes that seemed to flicker and appear when the light fell properly upon its surface. As such, it was simple trickery, an optical illusion: jewelry, perhaps, for a child.

But the amulet had survived for millennia. Its makers had been forgotten by all but the gods, and its inherent powers, weakened as they were by the unimaginable passage of time, were still formidable. If the amulet were clasped in the hand of a brave warrior and turned so that the light of the eternal phlogiston could shine upon it properly, its bearer could make out a secret image, a symbol that had survived the ages, perhaps the symbol of its creators: a three-pointed star, burning fiercely against the night-black maze of lines and curves and angles.

The disk blazed in Teldin's hand. The star was a brilliant pinpoint, filled with the power and light of a million suns. He covered it with one hand and stared into the flow, where a lightning bolt erupted near the *Spelljammer* and flashed against its pale skin.

He gasped involuntarily as the electric power of the amulet coursed up his arm, and the nautiloid disappeared from under his feet to send him swimming alone through the chromatic sea. His mouth hung open as his eyes, the *Spelljammer*'s eyes, were filled with a panoramic vista of the Broken Sphere, an immense black wall extending a billion miles out of his field of vision. Inside, wisps of phlogiston spiraled into the sphere's dying sun and exploded impotently in a reduced image of the sun's nova an eon ago, when the system's shell was shattered and sent hurtling into the flow.

Teldin shuddered. Images came unbidden to his mind: the wave of a mighty wing, the star-bright opening of a portal in a crystal shell; the immeasurable rush of phlogiston into the sphere, then into the sun. Then an immense explosion as worlds rocked, their atmospheres evaporated, their lands scorched, in a single blast of fire. And the crystal sphere blew away like an eggshell.

He fell to his knees and released the amulet. This close to

its bond-mate, the power of the amulet was increased, and its images became more tangible, more visceral, affecting all of his senses. He breathed deeply, taking huge gulps of air as the terror, the remembrance of a million deaths a million years ago, flooded over him, causing him to cry out in pain. His ship sailed ever closer to the *Spelljammer*, an innocent murderer of worlds.

He tasted the wind rushing over a world, a paradise of towering trees and mountain ranges reaching for the sky—

Colurranur, came the name to his mind, an ocean world where saurians and great beasts swam the pure waters, making songs and sealing them in bubbles of air, bound with spells of permanence so that their legacy would live on for their children—

Resanel, came another.

He could smell meat cooking and merchants shouting, selling their wares, in the Citadel of Trekar, on an island of gold on the world of—*BedevanSov*.

He was there, on—*Asveleyn*—as a contingent of armed men swarmed out of the hills of Stog to defeat a screaming band of orcs.

He was Jezperis, a warrior, reveling in the softness of Velina, his woman, as she lay in his arms, sweating and thrusting together under the twin moons of—*Ondora*.

And then, in a searing flash of heat and pain, the worlds were killed.

With an effort of will, Teldin suppressed a cry and pulled himself away from the memories of people long dead, long remembered in the *Spelljammer*'s unconscious self.

The great ship's song still sang through him, a song of blood and loneliness, of a destiny now within his reach. Their lives, like the lines woven on the amulet, were intertwined, forever linked by a pattern set into motion when the universe was young, an insignificant dream of the gods.

It was a pattern of birth and death, of tragedy and heroism. Somehow, he knew that it was ultimately a pattern woven of magic and dreams. Of life.

Teldin stood slowly and leaned against the forward rail of the nautiloid. He was still weak from the powerful images the *Spelljammer* had cast. He grasped the rail with one hand.

The *Spelljammer* was but a ghostly glimmer in the distance, barely visible in the swirling energies of the flow, but he could feel it and nodded to himself. Yes, this was right. He had sailed the endless sea for too long, too far. He had battled neogi and scro, humans and shape-shifters. Friends and lovers had betrayed him, all for what?

A piece of cloth.

He pulled the cloak tighter around him. In response, the cloak turned a deep brown.

"You are wearing an authentic ultimate helm," the giant, sluglike fal known as One Six Nine had told him. "You are the Cloakmaster, Teldin Moore, the future captain of the *Spelljammer*. You need only find your ship to claim it."

An ultimate helm . . .

His enemies were somewhere behind him, he knew, cramped together in battleships and deathspiders, hammerships and armadas. The forces of the enemy, whether orcs or elves or neogi, had followed him across the universe with their lust for power and destruction as motivation. Their forces were seemingly infinite, and not one of them knew a thing about the great ship that waited for him; only that, with his mysterious cloak, they could seize the most powerful weapon of all—a myth, a legend, that spanned the universe. Worlds and spheres would be the victors' spoils. Enemies would be destroyed, bred as cattle by flesh-eaters, enslaved by unhumans and humans alike, . . . and the second Unhuman War would last throughout eternity.

The spheres would never know peace.

Teldin had seen enough war. In the War of the Lance, he had seen friends killed in battle, had stepped over their broken bodies without looking back. He had seen enough hatred; he had seen enough death. His quest—one that had started out simply for knowledge—had become a quest for his own survival, and for what he believed was important: peace throughout the spheres.

I just wanted answers, he thought to himself. But he knew, deep inside, where the soul of a farm boy still hid with fear and wonder at the sights his destiny had shown him, that here he would make his last stand. He and his enemies would meet here, for one last time. No more running, no more chasing legends. Fate had pulled him here for a reason, and if battle is what his enemies wanted, then battle is what they would receive.

But answers would be his. He would find them here, at the Broken Sphere, where his destiny was but a glimmer in the distance.

He found it, a dim speck against a shattered wall of blackness. He could tell neither its shape nor size, but it pulled him with the intensity of a sun, beckoning to him like a siren. His future lay there, he knew, on the decks of a myth; and he would die to keep a simple promise, made what seemed like years ago: *to keep the cloak from the neogi, and to take it to the creators.*

Teldin stared into the distance. The amulet was warm against his palm, and he could feel the lines of its pattern on his fingertips.

One simple promise, he thought. As a favor to a dying alien, I accepted her cloak, the ultimate helm. And it's led to all this.

"I'm coming, *Spelljammer,*" he said out loud. His voice was swallowed in the emptiness of the void. "I'm coming."

* * * * *

The great ship, alive with wonder, swam through the Rainbow Ocean.

The light of the flow seemed to blaze off the citadel of proud towers sprawled upon its back. It flickered across its wide, sweeping wings, scintillating up its mammoth, curled tail, and glimmered brilliantly off a statue of a golden dragon atop a central tower. Its pale underbelly oscillated with color as the energies of the phlogiston flowed around it, an endless river upon which the great ship sailed eternally.

Its song reverberated through the flow, ringing off the crystal shell that had been the great ship's birthplace. Minutes later, a kindori, an immense space whale swimming through the void thousands of leagues away, answered with its own high song, a question wailed between the spheres. The great ship responded with a greeting, which was also a farewell, and sang softly to itself until it sensed that the kindori had swum out of range.

The ship had sailed far on its eternal quest, ranging outward to spheres undreamed of by most spacefarers and their crews. It had sung with the jade insects that dominated the sphere they called C'T'lk'atat. It had swum with the wolf-people of Mefesk, who sailed between the worlds of Lorpulan in ships of ivory and bronze. It had watched a world die as a planet's internal fires wreaked violence upon the surface, and the web-spinners of Hsuun, and their brittle citadels of shimmering silver that stretched across the seas, died as their crystalline castles crumbled into piles of debris, then were forgotten forever beneath layers of black ash and lava.

The peoples of C'T'lk'atat knew the ship as S'Kurl—singer beast.

Lorpulan knew the ship as Zhalabrian, the swimmer.

Hsuun saw the ship as the promised one, a god, Ospilia—redeemer.

The ship had borne many names over the millennia and answered to none. Its name was known only to itself and could not be translated into such primitive concepts as letters or words. Its name was the ignition of new suns, the sound of the flow churning through the universe, of magic opening a window of possibilities, the cry of a mother looking down upon the face of her newborn child.

Its true name was life and death and wonder and awe.

And one name it was known as was *Spelljammer.*

The Broken Sphere and the dying star inside, which had once been named Aeyenna by the eighteen worlds that had comprised the sphere of Ouiyan, were the last remnants of the *Spelljammer*'s birth and deadly escape. Phlogiston flared briefly as it was sucked into the star's fiery depths, and the *Spelljammer* slowly lifted its wing to absorb the sun's weak energy through the pale skin of its underside.

It sensed outward, through the flow. Its sphere of senses, its influence over the universe surrounding it, was subtly increasing, changing, as the man grew nearer. If it had had a mouth, it would have smiled.

The challenger was only seconds away, as the *Spelljammer* measured time, and change had already begun deep inside its body. The temperature in the gardens was subtly warmer, preparing for birth. Its song was louder, stronger; it cried out to the spheres floating anchorless within the flow; it sang of its loss, its loneliness, and the destiny that soon would be attained.

—*The challenger*, it sang.

It saw him then, through the Compass: a simple man searching for answers, for completion. The *Spelljammer* could feel the man's muscles concealed under the helm, could feel the heat in his hands, their strength. His heart was strong, and the man's sense of self, of purpose, was a rush of heat that washed over the great ship and made it feel renewed.

The connection with the man broke suddenly; but in that last instant—and even over the long miles the captain still had to sail—the *Spelljammer* knew that the challenger had mastered the Ultimate Helm. It knew that the challenger was not a raider consumed with an agenda of conquest and violence, as so many others had been, but a simple man confused by fate; a man who had braved all the odds to seek his answers, his destiny, to find them here, where they had forever been.

The *Spelljammer* sang out then. It sang again to the kindori, to the stony contemplators in self-absorbed exile along the Caltassan asteroid belt, to the great dreamers lumbering slowly through the endless sea that was the void; it cried out to all who would listen with their hearts and dream at its song of wonder. The high tones of its songs rang off the spheres, recreating its long journeys through the universe. Each planet was a line, each sphere a stanza. Suns were born and died within a sentence, and the song's last wistful notes stretched out to echo through the void, where perhaps even the challenger would hear, and perhaps understand, and feel a little bit of the *Spelljammer*'s sadness, and the limitless joy, at his approach.

At the consummation of their long-awaited destiny.

For the *Spelljammer* knew that, with the challenger approaching, with change screaming for completion throughout its massive body, this voyage would be its last.

It glanced at the tombstone that was the black, broken sphere, and cried out one last time, a question answered only by the silence of the long-dead, and the *Spelljammer* slowly banked toward the approaching nautiloid. The man had come so far, yet had one last test to complete before the great ship would allow him to take its helm and lead it into its unknown future.

Their fate lay here, forever intertwined, where the *Spelljammer* had been born, where millions had died. The time was now. The cycles were coming back upon themselves, forces converging, blurring the reality between past and present, and turning, perhaps, violence into life.

The man's life song was strong and sang through his bones. The *Spelljammer* answered with the song of its own, and it knew that their songs must soon be sung together, forever.

For life.

—*Are you worthy?* it sang.

It sped toward the challenger.

The ultimate test would now begin.

Chapter One

• • •

"*. . . Newcomers to the* Spelljammer *are generally ignored, but for the interest of the populace. There is a noticeable difference, however, when newcomers approach bearing powerful helms.*

"*From this we can surmise but two things: The ultimate helms borne to the* Spelljammer *are like no other, and somehow entice the* Spelljammer *into aggressive action; or that the* Spelljammer, *as impossible as it seems, is consciously aware that a new helmsman is approaching and wishes to dispatch him before his arrival, for reasons unknown. . . .*"

M'ndora, elf sorceress, *The Book of Lomasun*; reign of JaykEl.

The *Spelljammer* was huge. Even now, at a distance of a few short miles away and closing, the legendary ship blotted out Teldin Moore's view of the void and filled his mind with a sense of unreality, of wonder beyond imagining, even beyond the dreams of the gods. The towers and turrets on the great ship's back gleamed dreamlike—nothing he had ever seen or imagined had prepared him for this sight—and he thought he could barely make out tiny black dots standing and moving along railings and in windows, pointing in the nautiloid's direction.

A welcoming party, he thought. He clasped his hand tightly around the hilt of his sword. Whether they welcome me with steel or with open arms, I'll be ready.

The Broken Sphere was an immeasurable black wall behind the shining spires of the *Spelljammer*. This close, no details were visible in the surface of the crystalline sphere. The great cracks and jagged holes in the sphere were tens of thousands of miles away, on the other side of the universe, as far as Teldin cared, and the Broken Sphere seemed like nothing more than a shimmering obsidian wall, stretching before him endlessly, reflecting only darkness.

Between the nautiloid and the sphere hung the *Spelljammer*.

He turned at gentle footsteps upon the deck of the *Julia*. Beside him, Djan Alantri, the half-elf from Crescent, stared toward the legendary vessel and pointed. The first mate's gray-blue eyes widened with surprise, and his thin blond hair exposed his slightly pointed ears as a gust of cool wind sprang unexpectedly from the bow.

Teldin looked to where Djan pointed. The shadow of the *Spelljammer*'s immense tail was slowly shifting across the towers of the city, and Teldin gasped as he realized that the huge ship was beginning a wide turn away from the cracked globe of black crystal, toward the speeding nautiloid.

Toward them.

Unconsciously, his cloak billowed out at his unbidden surge of emotion, and he felt the *Julia* subtly change its course. He had discovered that he need not be seated at the ship's helm to control its course and speed, and that he could command the vessel without even being on board. But that even his uncontrolled emotions could cause the ship to veer surprised him greatly, especially since the human Corontea was already on the helm. He pulled his cloak around him and mentally straightened the ship's course so that its bow moved in a slow curve and pointed directly at the bow of the *Spelljammer*.

It was as though he could feel the flow of the phlogiston around him, as though he were at one with the universe as his gaze met the blank eyes of the *Spelljammer*. He shivered unconsciously as words rang through his mind. The words were slow and instinctive, blossoming in his mind, not as a voice, either definably male or female, but as raw thoughts and emotions, of half-dreamed images, yearning. It was a cry of need and loneliness, tremulously touching the core of his being and singing through his blood. He slowly formed the cry into barely adequate words.

—worthy . . .

"Are you worthy?" He said them out loud, slowly, testing the weight of each word.

He stared at the *Spelljammer*, his mouth agape. "You," he said softly. "That was you."

He laughed once, a bark of triumph, and his laughter was absorbed into the flow.

The *Spelljammer* was visibly closer. He imagined he could feel its breath as the ship headed toward him, diving into the flow, pushing a tidal wave of wind before it. The shining towers and buildings upon its great back seemed sharper, in clearer focus. Now he could make out a lone figure standing on a squat, round building in the foreground of the ship. It was only a speck, perhaps moving, perhaps gesturing in the *Julia*'s direction.

—Are you worthy?

The words rang louder in his head as the *Spelljammer* seemed to come rushing toward him at once, like an unstoppable juggernaut. For an instant, Teldin cocked his head and stared at the monstrous ship. He grasped the rail of the deck and whispered, "Am I worthy?"

He knew, then, what the ancient *Spelljammer* was doing.

"Battle stations!" he screamed.

The ship came faster, blotting half of the Broken Sphere from his view. Now he could clearly make out the people standing along the railings of the ship's buildings, in windows; positioned among the buildings that somehow resembled sharp spears more than towers. He could imagine his broken, shattered body inside the *Julia*, as it hung impaled upon the *Spelljammer*'s sharpest spire.

His eyes grew wide and he screamed out, "Evasive action!"

But the *Spelljammer* was deaf to his fears. His screams were meaningless, swallowed into the void. Djan shouted behind him, but he could not understand the half-elf's words.

The Cloakmaster backed away and stopped against the hatch leading into the depths of the nautiloid. He reached behind him, took hold of the latch, and stared as the *Spelljammer* loomed closer and closer like a giant, crashing wave.

There was nowhere to run. This fate he could not escape. Cold sweat broke out on his forehead. The damned ship was too big, unstoppable; he knew that. The powers of his cloak were too limited, too—

—Are you worthy?

He shook his head unconsciously. No, he thought, I've come this far, and you're trying to kill me, too—

—Are you worthy?

The words were like thunder in his mind, and he shook his head, realizing exactly what had to be done. They could be saved. This quest was not futile.

They could survive.

Teldin stepped away from the hatch and shook himself out of his fear. "Yes," he whispered to himself. He stared down the great ship, at the towers, their sharp points gleaming fiercely in the fiery light. He shouted into its face, "Yes! Yes! I am worthy!"

Teldin yelled down into the *Julia*. "Corontea! Relinquish the helm!" and he braced his legs and stood firmly on the deck. He closed his eyes and reached out with his thoughts. His skin tingled instantly, raising the hairs along his arms and the back of his neck, and he felt the ancient powers of his mysterious cloak spread through him, infusing him with energy.

He felt it all billowing around him, the flow, the cloak, the untapped pulsations of arcane energies that wove through the cloak like veins. His skin glowed from within as he felt the icy hot powers of the cloak weave around him, a silent cyclone of energy rushing through his body.

His eyes rolled back, and his vision, his mind, was filled with the sight and sound and feel of the *Spelljammer*. He felt people scurry across his back as they saw his ship grow closer. He heard blades shoved into scabbards, heard shouts in unhuman tongues spread over the decks. He felt the flow rush around the *Spelljammer*'s sphere of air. He felt its song ring through each cell of its huge body . . . and in his own mind.

At the same time, he was the *Julia*. He felt the flow rush past the whorls of his hard-bodied shell ship. He felt the nautiloid shudder as he reached out with his mind and plucked the helm away from his helmsman, Corontea, and imagined that both ships were slowing . . .

He saw the forward views from both their bows. He was both ships at once, staring down at each other, measuring the too-quickly decreasing space between them.

He grew calm and closed his eyes. He imagined a whirling ball of air between the two ships, a cyclone of invisible energy, growing, growing, into a storm of power.

The nautiloid moved on, shifting softly, slowing almost imperceptibly. The *Spelljammer*, unstoppable, huge, came on, hurtling toward his flimsy ship.

His cloak, impossibly alive, floated around him, mirroring the manta shape of the *Spelljammer*. Teldin lifted his arms and felt the power flow through him, channeled into magical energy by his ancient cloak. He visualized the windstorm of invisible energy between the ships, and he willed it to grow larger, stronger, into a cushion of raw force to keep the two craft apart.

The nautiloid was slowing, buffeted by the cold winds spinning from Teldin's mind storm; but the *Spelljammer* was too big, too powerful. Its weight collided with his invisible storm of wind and kept plunging on. He pushed out with his mind, summoning the powers of the cloak and willing the energy storm to withstand the impact. At the same time, he visualized the *Julia* and shoved it farther away.

Then he opened his eyes, and the realization hit him without warning. The *Spelljammer* was alive! This great ship was alive. It was sentient. And it knew him. It was coming for him.

For *him*!

—*Are you worthy?*

He wanted to cower, to hide in the protective folds of his cloak and watch as his ship was crushed under the *Spelljammer*'s enormous mass; but the *Spelljammer* was too huge, too purposeful. Teldin could feel that its innate sentience kept it single-minded, determined.

And strong.

Teldin began to sweat with the strain of keeping the ships apart. The *Spelljammer*'s strength was too much; still the huge vessel grew closer, blotting the Broken Sphere completely from his view.

The wedge between the ships grew increasingly small as his

own faith ebbed. He heard himself grunting with the immense strain of keeping the ships apart; he saw a human upon a tower, pointing toward him with a sword, and he shook his head like a caged animal, feeling a hidden strength blossoming within him like a radiant flower.

Live, he thought. I . . . will . . . *live*!

The *Spelljammer* hurtled toward him. It dwarfed his tiny ship and threatened to impale the nautiloid upon its spiraled turrets.

Live!

At his neck, the ancient amulet began to glow. Cold sparks of energy flickered along its mazelike pattern. The chain burst away from the amulet and fell at his feet, and the bronze disk glowed and burned itself into the clasp of his cloak, welding itself as though it had always belonged there.

At once, he felt his feet lift from the wooden planks of the deck. His cloak billowed around him like a thing alive as he floated only inches above the doomed ship. He heard the scream of a woman aboard the *Spelljammer*, the cries of humans running hurriedly away, warning others of the nautiloid's imminent crash. Beneath him, in the belly of the *Julia*, he heard the cries of his own crew members as their impending deaths grew near.

Live!

He stared down at the *Spelljammer* and noticed for the first time the great, empty expanse along its closer wing. He closed his eyes. His hands balled into fists. He pulled his arms together across his chest, and imagined himself as a hand, a giant hand of golden energy forming against the black backdrop of the Broken Sphere, pulsing with the limitless power of the cosmos. He willed the hand to ball into a mighty fist, coalescing beneath the starboard wing of the *Spelljammer*.

He opened his eyes. His cloak flapped like wings in an invisible windstorm. The amulet blazed at his neck like a miniature sun.

With one thought, Teldin willed the *Spelljammer* to bank up at an angle. Instantly, the fist of power swung up and hammered into the great ship's belly. The *Spelljammer* shuddered under the impact, the primal force of Teldin's mind. Its starboard wing tilted up to meet the nautiloid, and Teldin focused on the great empty area along the wing.

In the instant that the nautiloid was pummeled into splinters by the onslaught of the *Spelljammer*'s indestructible wing, Teldin felt himself flung away by the limitless powers of the cloak. It wrapped itself around him in a thick, protective cocoon. Shards of shell and metal and wood shattered around him. Sharp points of debris flung against his cloak as the nautiloid smashed into the wing. The ship almost screamed with the painful groans of metal and wood being ripped apart. The chambered nautiloid blew away like nothing more than ashes, and underneath it all, he could hear only the screams of his terrified crew.

Then, silence.

The Cloakmaster tumbled blindly through the air and landed hard on the great ship's wing. Teldin rolled helplessly as debris from his ship rained upon him. He willed himself to stop, and the cloak shivered, halting his movement. Then he stood on shaky legs, and the cloak unwrapped itself from his body.

The nautiloid's remains stretched before him, a road of twisted metal and broken shell across the *Spelljammer*'s great wing. It was a road he had taken once and could never return along. His fate, his destiny, his future, lay here. He was alive. But his crew lay under the wreckage that had brought them all to their fates, and he turned to shout for help.

There was a scream. One man—Djan!—kicked his way out from under the heavy debris, pulling a limp body behind him. Teldin rushed to help. Djan and his charge—Corontea, Teldin made out—were thirty feet away from the nautiloid when it ruptured in a great gout of heat and flame, spewing fiery wreckage across the *Spelljammer*'s wing.

Spontaneously, the phlogiston that permeated the *Spelljammer*'s air envelope ignited, and Teldin and Djan and the unconscious Corontea were blasted fifty feet away by the explosion.

The Cloakmaster pushed himself off the deck as flaming shards fell around him. He covered his head with the Cloak of the First Pilot and rushed to Djan's side as smaller explosions shuddered around them. He knocked away tiny embers of wood that were sparkling near Djan, and he reached down to help the half-elf pull Corontea away from the flames and to safety.

"She was crushed under a beam," Djan said. He turned to stare at the *Julia*'s blackened remains. The back of his gray clothes were scorched and black. "I—I couldn't reach anyone else," he said, panting. He shook his head as though to clear it, but he sagged down onto the deck, and his voice became barely a whisper. "They're all trapped in there."

"Djan, don't—"

But the half-elf's eyes rolled up, and Djan fell into oblivion.

Teldin placed his fingers upon Djan's neck. Good—there was still a pulse. He looked up. He could still make it over to the crash and tear through the wreckage to find the others—there were thirteen other crewmen trapped under thirty-or-so tons of debris. He stood and had time to take just a single step, then he pulled up short at the shrill cry of hatred that emanated behind him, like the chilling howl of a hungry war wolf.

He spun abruptly. He eyes widened in sudden fear, and he reached for the sword hanging at his waist.

He cried out, "By the gods!"

But an adequate defense was too late. The neogi that had crept up behind him, held tight in the arms of its enslaved umber hulk, screamed an ululating cry of death at the Cloakmaster. The misshapen umber hulk, its mandibles clacking in rage, raised its broadsword high above its head and swiftly brought it down, straight down toward the Cloakmaster's skull.

Chapter Two

• • •

". . . The few scrolls and books that remain from the beginning show that the survivors who sailed the Wanderer were far different from the barbarians I must share the Spelljammer *with today. The early sailors cherished life, cherished diversity, and wished for no better life than to explore and bring peace to all peoples.*

"Today the populace lives in fear of unhumans and even their human brethren, and peace is a forgotten word, replaced by the lust for power and the fear that a particular way of life will be threatened from without. . . ."

Corac, Grandson of Erbur, warrior of Mosabor; reign of Rygosa.

The citadel laid out upon the *Spelljammer*'s broad back rose raggedly at the end of a long landing field, which lay at the ship's bow. The fore buildings held primarily the *Spelljammer*'s human population and were devoted to the ship's politics and social functions. Aft, in the wide shadow of the *Spelljammer*'s great tail, most of the ship's unhumans had formed their individual communities: beholders, illithids, dwarves, goblins, ogres, and dracons. Also aft were the buildings of the Long Fangs and the Tenth Pit, dark dens reserved for the foulest sailors upon the Rainbow Ocean.

Near the tower of the minotaurs and the ruins of the once great palace of the beholders, the squat neogi tower afforded a panoramic view of the *Spelljammer*'s starboard wing. Neogi guards stationed atop the tower saw the Cloakmaster's ship as it rapidly closed with them, and they quickly shouted word—as they had been first ordered to do months ago—that a new vessel was approaching for a landing.

They had no idea that the *Spelljammer*, for reasons known only to itself, would not allow the Cloakmaster's landing to be an easy one.

So when the nautiloid crashed and exploded upon the starboard takeoff strips reserved for the ship's smalljammers, the neogi warriors who their leader, Master Coh, had deployed took advantage of the crash's unexpected proximity and scrambled across the wing like a swarm of black insects, frothing to attack the newcomers and kill anyone who might be the legendary Cloakmaster—the accursed Cloakmaster that had been foretold would soon arrive . . . and bring darkness upon the *Spelljammer*.

In the darkness of the neogi temple, Coh had been taking sinister pleasure in feeding the great old master when Teldin's nautiloid was first sighted. He had instantly ordered his squadron to attack upon landing, then he went on with the great old master's feeding, ordering his personal slave, a towering umber hulk named Orik, to throw in another gnoll slave that had been stolen the week before.

Orik was fully four times Master Coh's height—the largest, most grotesque umber hulk on the *Spelljammer*—and his sharp mandibles clacked with sadistic glee. A symbol of interlocked circles had been tattooed upon the hulk's forehead, symbolizing Master Coh's ownership, and the umber hulk happily bent and lifted a squirming gnoll high above his head.

The gnoll thrashed in Orik's calloused claws. One of its tiny hands beat helplessly against the hulk's thick chest as its screams echoed through the temple. Orik laughed deep in his throat; he loved to hear the cries of the weak ones as they screamed for mercy.

The pit before which Coh and Orik stood was deep, filled with shadows and surrounded by flat tiers upon which Coh's neogi brethren could squat. Inside the stony pit, deep in the darkness and surrounded by the bloody bones of Coh's victims, squatted the bloated, obscene form of the great old master.

Master Coh lifted a claw in a sarcastic wave as Orik tossed

the gnoll high in the air. The slave plummeted into the pit. It screamed once as it disappeared over the lip of the deep pit, then there was a sickening crunch as its bones cracked against the stony floor.

Coh lifted his bulbous, spidery body and scurried to the edge. Orik looked in wonderingly.

The shadows seemed to move in a far corner of the pit. There was yellow glimmer as two glazed eyes blinked open, and the great old master stirred from its nest.

The gnoll's wails of pain shattered the stillness as it tried to drag its broken legs away from the horror inching toward it.

The great old master had been the leader of the *Spelljammer*'s neogi community until Coh had defeated it in a bloody coup. As light fell upon it, Coh grinned mercilessly, baring his yellow fangs in hatred at the master's mutated body.

The transformation into old age wrought horrible changes upon the neogi. Their brown, hairy bodies enlarged to about twenty feet long, and their minds slowly wasted away until only feeding was important: the taste of raw meat, the heat of pulsing blood, were their only obsessions.

The great old master's shadow fell upon the disabled gnoll. The neogi's long black neck towered over him. Foul spittle oozed from the master's wide, gaping mouth, and light glimmered wickedly off its poisonous teeth. With one ferocious lunge, the master's eellike head snapped forward and took the gnoll into its mouth. Bones crunched under the strength of its mutated jaws, and the gnoll's screams faded like smoke on the wind.

Coh laughed and brushed back a tuft of its multicolored fur with one claw. His brown coat was resplendent with all the colors of the spectrum, paints and tattoos in shapes and symbols that signified his rank as a superior neogi. He absently thought, as he watched the shape of the gnoll slowly slide down the great old master's long black throat, that there was at least one patch of fur that could use another design. He was the natural leader of the *Spelljammer*'s neogi; who else could claim that title?

Master Coh was a natural mage, though of limited magical abilities, and he felt the newcomer's presence behind him before a word could be spoken. "B'Laath'a, speak," he said, and he kept his eyes studiously upon the great old master.

B'Laath'a approached. In the dim light of the temple, no ornamental pigments were discernable on his squat, furred body, save for a line of arcane patterns splashed in bright scarlet, painted along the back of his neck and reaching to a point just above his eyes.

B'Laath'a was an enigma to his fellow neogi: a powerful, spiteful wizard who eschewed the more typical trappings of neogi culture, such as the body paints that proudly signified rank and status among his brethren. He was proud of his muscular, hairy body, pruning it regularly with his long, sharp teeth and feeding off the lice that infested the soft fur of his abdomen. He refused to cover his body with military sigils; his vanity would not allow it. Instead his fur was dyed a permanent, deep black, symbolizing to him all of his secret powers, his hidden strengths—for black was all the colors of the spectrum merged into one.

He held back a snarl of hatred. Coh. Coh was a joke, a pretender, as far as B'Laath'a was concerned, barely worthy of being leader. Coh was nothing more than a militaristic thug.

Now, as to himself, . . .

B'Laath'a feigned a respectful bow. "Master Coh, squadron attacked a nautiloid, have we. Cloakmaster it is come who has."

Coh turned around quickly. "Cloakmaster? Foretold you the one?"

"Yes, lord. Numbers half dead are. Mighty the cloak is. Destroyed Sketh and slavemeat by magic are."

"So, come the Cloakmaster is. Dead he is?"

B'Laath'a slowly shook his smooth black head. "No, lord. Forces returning speak as we are."

Anger glinted deep in Coh's small eyes. "Dark Times not will neogi harm! Stopped Cloakmeat must be! Ours Cloakmeat will be!"

B'Laath'a bowed his head as Coh scurried past him. Then the leader turned. "Prepared are you. The agent prepared is?"

"Of course," B'Laath'a said. "My assassinmeat ready has been since arrival. Meat smuggled to the tower has been . . . time for one last."

Coh smiled evilly. "Plan of ours action must be put to. Now time is!" He raised a claw to the series of colorful, interlocked circles tattooed on his forehead and concentrated. *Come*, he commanded silently.

In a few moments, the door to the temple opened and closed silently. The agent stepped quietly forward on bare feet, a ritual of neogi enslavement.

"Here your precious Cloakmaster almost is, meat," the neogi master said. His black, hairy body was a proud swirl of colors and designs, radiating his power and status among his slithering brethren, and he puffed out his chest to impress the slave. "Well it may not go killing the Cloakmeat during our initial attempt. You will, of course, if caught as we have commanded do. Correct." It was not a question.

The agent seemed to stammer, as though B'Laath'a's spells and mind-wiping were being fought. Coh grunted in anger, and a sharp pinprick of white-hot pain erupted in the agent's mind. The agent fell to the floor.

"Correct," Coh said. B'Laath'a stood over the agent and spoke a spell of pain. The agent's skin grew bright red with fiery pain. "Correct," B'Laath'a said.

"Y—yes," the agent stammered. "Yes—the Cloakmaster will be yours, Master . . . Teldin Moore must d—die . . . "

* * * * *

The neogi, clasped in the arms of its umber hulk, snapped out at the Cloakmaster with its needle-sharp teeth.

Teldin's hand went to the hilt of his short sword at the neogi's scream, but the blade of its enslaved umber hulk was a silver, deadly arc, curving down toward Teldin's head, and Teldin realized in a flash that he had no time to deflect the blow.

The Cloakmaster lunged forward, angrily grabbed the snapping neogi by its long, eellike throat, and wrenched it from the umber hulk's grasp. The hulk's sword hurtled down in an unstoppable arc and neatly sliced through one of the neogi's legs.

Teldin stomped on the flat of the umber hulk's blade and threw a powerful kick into its chest. The hulk stumbled backward, hardly affected, as it was protected by thick layers of hide. With a shout, Teldin slammed the neogi to the ground and drove his foot into its fat neck. The neogi gurgled a cry of pain. Its claws scrabbled the air, vainly attempting to block Teldin's assault. Its needle-sharp teeth bit at the air, coming far short of injecting their sickly venom deep into Teldin's veins.

The Cloakmaster's sword was a blur as it arced high, then dropped swiftly down, deep through the neogi's skull and into its evil brain.

Teldin jerked out the sword. Great gouts of blood spurted from the wound. The dead neogi's umber hulk stood and stared as its master's blood pooled around its feet. Teldin wasted no time. He leaped forward and sliced into the umber hulk's thick shoulder.

It fell to one knee and screamed in rage. One great arm went up to block a second blow, and the arm was cleaved away at the shoulder with an eruption of hot, ugly blood.

The umber hulk collapsed at Teldin's feet. He spun to face squarely the oncoming horde of neogi, but a series of loud shouts echoed behind him, and the neogi horde was met from behind by an angry band of human warriors, which rushed from across the landing field at the *Spelljammer*'s bow.

There were at least twenty of them, Teldin thought, a motley assortment of humans in armor, wielding weapons that had been collected from all the known crystal spheres. Armed with huge broadswords and battle-axes, the humans swarmed over the reptilian hordes and engaged them fiercely.

Teldin dove into the fray, swinging his sword from side to side and carving a path through the waves of black neogi flesh. The reptiles chattered and snatched out at him with their razor teeth. His sword cleaved their heads from their necks; his cloak swatted at them unconsciously, protecting his limbs from sword cuts and blows, and even the tiniest scratch from a venomous neogi fang.

Around him, the swarm of humans broke the neogi line. One small male, clad in a long, plaid cloak, shot barbed projectiles at the neogi from a deadly silver slingshot. When a neogi was hit, even with a minor scratch, within a minute it would begin to twitch horribly, then collapse into a spasmodic heap, screaming in searing pain.

Other humans were not so lucky. One warrior went down, trapped between the sharp axes of two umber hulks. Another fighter battled back-to-back with a female warrior. The woman was the first to fall, caught in a thigh by the snapping jaws of an angry neogi. The man was left to fend off two more of the venomous beasts, then was pulled down as the woman's murderer leaped upon him from behind. Another woman kept the neogi at bay with wide swings of her battle-axe, but one of the umber hulks cast a heavy spear with ease and impaled the woman through the chest.

The battle shifted without warning. As their comrades began to fall, the surviving humans became determined to win and pressed on with increasing fury. Teldin heard the neogi scream in pain and rage, and he watched as umber hulks staggered away without guidance, their masters lying dead in their own dark blood.

A human behind him shouted "Cloakmaster!" and Teldin spun around.

A ferocious neogi had crouched and sprung from the deck and was rushing down at him from midair.

Teldin brought up his sword and thrust the blade deep into the neogi fighter's pulsing heart, then slammed the spiderlike body to the ground and kicked it off his sword.

He turned to spy a huge man, almost broader across his shoulders than he was tall, swing his broadsword in a huge arc to slice through the thick necks of two advancing umber hulks. They fell at his feet, and as their blood sprayed onto his legs and boots, he laughed loudly at the reptilian hordes and their slaves.

"Thanks," Teldin said. The warrior kicked one of the hulks in the side. His foot bounced harmlessly off the thing's thick carapace.

The man's long, thick beard was tied in a cord that dangled to his waist. He bent and lifted one of the hulks' swords, and Teldin could see that this man, though small in stature, was barrel-chested and muscular, and his armor had seen a lot of damage.

The warrior turned. "So, you're the Cloakmaster?" he asked, panting.

"I—" Teldin did not know how to react. "Well, yes, I suppose I am. How did you—"

He was cut off as a huge umber hulk ran up behind the warrior and grabbed him from behind. The human's swords clattered to the deck, and the warrior squirmed to get away. The hulk's grip was like an iron vise, and as its sharp, clacking mandibles moved inches closer to the warrior's neck, a fat neogi scurried out of the surrounding battle and bared its fangs, preparing to sink them deep into the human's flesh.

Teldin balanced his short sword in his hand, then aimed quickly and hurled it at the ugly neogi. The umber hulk lashed out with one hand, caught the sword, and cast it to the deck. The human lashed out with one, thick hand, but the hulk swatted it away and quickly replaced its hold on him. Its mesmerizing eyes seemed to glimmer with dull amusement.

The neogi laughed at Teldin as it bared its yellow, needle-like fangs. Venom dripped from its mouth and spattered the deck. The neogi turned to the warrior again.

It raised its blunt head, ready to lunge.

Teldin felt his rage building, and his skin began to shiver with energy. The cloak whipped wildly about him. He felt its warm energies pulsing through his veins. He cried out "*No*!" and twin bolts of blue, magical lightning lanced out from the folds of the cloak and speared the neogi and its hard-skinned servant.

Arcs of mystical energy pulsed from the cloak to engulf the unhuman enemies. The warrior fell from the hulk's arms and scrambled away.

The neogi screamed in white-hot pain. The umber hulk fell to its knees, covering its beady eyes with its thick claws. At once, fingers of crackling energy erupted from the assailants' eyes and mouths. Their bodies seemed to blaze blue from within.

Their screams were high-pitched wails of pain and seemed to echo in Teldin's ears long after they had stopped. In an instant, the unhumans were nothing more than lifeless, burned-out husks, and their charred black bodies crumbled to the ground like the broken, blackened hull of Teldin's nautiloid.

The bearded warrior stood slowly. The fighting had stopped around them as Teldin's cloak had fought back, and as their brother fell to the Cloakmaster's magic, the remaining neogi started running for the safety of their tower. One female warrior carefully leveled her crossbow and nailed a scurrying neogi through its neck. She screamed a triumphant battle cry, and soon the unhumans were gone.

The burly warrior picked up Teldin's short sword and handed it to him. His eyes twinkled with the exhilaration of a battle well fought.

"Yes, I guess you are the Cloakmaster," he said.

Teldin shrugged, smiling. "My name is Teldin Moore. How do you know me?"

The warrior stroked his long beard. "I suppose you could say we've all been expecting you. I'm CassaRoc. CassaRoc the Mighty, they call me. And I think you can say . . ." He paused to appraise Teldin with his clear, cool eyes, then nodded once and smiled back. "I'm a friend," he said.

Teldin stared after the retreating neogi. In the distance, they were clambering off the wing, up the *Spelljammer*'s side, toward the protection of their tower. "Thanks," Teldin said. "I need all the friends I can get."

"Don't we all, boy?" CassaRoc said. "Don't we all."

CassaRoc ordered his warriors to help move Djan and the fallen Corontea. As a dozen ran to help, the remaining humans gathered around the two warriors, sheathing their swords. CassaRoc shouted, making sure he could be heard by all. "Well, that should teach those damned neogi not to mess with the collective, at least for a while. All right," CassaRoc yelled. "Who's up for a round of ale?"

The humans laughed and shouted agreement. Many stood with their weapons poised, waiting for another possible attack. CassaRoc placed a hand on Teldin's shoulder. "Come on," CassaRoc said. "Your people will be well taken care of. We should leave now, before somebody else decides they want a piece of you."

A tall man strode up to them, neatly outfitted in shining armor of silver and white. A heavy white cloak billowed behind him, and the warrior wore his thick, reddish blond hair in a wild mane that suggested to Teldin that the man was far less tame than his paladin armor suggested. "The centaur tower," the warrior said, casting his gaze over the others' heads. "Mostias can protect us there for a while. We can smuggle the newcomer into the Chalice tower after things settle down."

CassaRoc nodded approvingly. "You're right, Chaladar," he said. He leaned to Teldin and winked. "Besides, the centaurs make some excellent ales."

The woman armed with the crossbow came up beside CassaRoc. Her curly brown hair was held back with a band of shining steel, and she held herself proudly, like a self-assured warrior. "What about Chel? And Gar? Do you want to just leave them here?"

CassaRoc frowned and looked toward the bodies of his fallen comrades. "I know they were friends of yours, Na'Shee," he said. "They were friends to us all, but we have to worry about the living now. Let's get the Cloakmaster here to the tower first. You can round up some men later and bring the bodies to the Tower of Thought." He laid a hand on her shoulder and smiled softly. "Don't worry. They won't be forgotten."

Na'Shee nodded silently and looked back at her friends' bodies.

Chaladar called out "Let's go!" and the group started jogging toward the outermost tower on the *Spelljammer*'s right wing, with Djan and Corontea each carried by four warriors in the center of the group. Chaladar, the paladin, took point, while CassaRoc ran at the rear. Teldin ran protected in the center, and continually glanced over his shoulders at the tall spires of the citadel sprawled across the *Spelljammer*'s back.

As they ran, CassaRoc pointed out some of the towers and explained a little of the ship's layout. The light of the flow flickered gold and violet across the variegated collection of towers and turrets. Multipatterned flags flew at the pinnacles of several buildings, and the ship's tail, towering above the rooftops and battlements, was a constant reminder of the majesty of the vessel, of the wonder of a living myth. To Teldin, the gleaming towers, the graceful sweep of the *Spelljammer*'s hull, represented nothing but the fulfillment of a dream—a dream of extraordinary adventure that he never could have conceived while a simple melon farmer on Krynn.

But the simple life of Krynn was a lifetime ago and a universe away—or at least it seemed like that to Teldin. Krynn was now little more than a memory, both good and bad. The nights on his land had been sweet, especially in summers, when the hidaglia blossoms were in full bloom and the air was scented with their perfumed musk. But there were bad times that he could never forget, no matter how hard he tried . . . the things he had seen during his treks in the War of the Lance, and the oppressive abuse heaped upon him by his father.

A gleaming glint of gold caught his eye, high atop the Elven High Command. He focused on it and smiled at the sight, realizing that his long quest was now at an end, that his answers were here, and nowhere else—especially not on Krynn. Krynn was forever gone, for him; it was a way of life to which he could never return, and now did not want to.

The centaur tower was low and asymmetrical, a guardian twin to the dracon tower strategically situated on the port wing. The centaurs were the ostensible wardens and gunnery officers for the tower's fifteen huge catapults, but to Teldin, the building seemed dark and in terrible disrepair, and he wondered if the centaurs should hold the great responsibility for manning the *Spelljammer*'s starboard weapons.

CassaRoc closed and bolted the main doors of the tower behind the humans. His band of warriors instantly relaxed inside the safety of the tower and started unbuckling their tight, heavy armor. Some told jokes and insulted the neogi hordes, calling their eellike mothers "beholder whores" and their fathers "Torilian maggot lovers" (though neogi had neither mothers nor fathers). A few centaurs popped their heads out from their stables and joined in the good humor, wondering if beer would later be poured for free.

CassaRoc ordered Djan and the female helmsman taken to a healer. Teldin stopped them as they carried Djan away. The half-elf was still unconscious, and Teldin placed his hand upon Djan's breast. "They'll take care of you," Teldin said. Then he turned to Corontea. She was bleeding heavily from a nasty gash to her forehead, and her legs and arms were seriously burned.

He closed his eyes. CassaRoc said, "Go on, now," and the warriors took Teldin's people away.

CassaRoc said, "You can't do anything for them, now, Cloakmaster. There's no sense in feeling guilty. We all know the risks of spelljamming. So did they."

CassaRoc and the others started off, and Teldin turned to survey his surroundings. His nose was filled with the underlying scents of farm odors that he had grown up with: of hay and sweat, of earth, and above that, the heavy aroma of horse manure. But here in the dim light—he could see that even light panels in this section of the tower were faulty and fading—the stables seemed cramped and unkempt. Wooden walls were rotting, some with ragged holes where angry centaurs had kicked them out, perhaps in drunken rage. Teldin could also make out the sweet, cloying scent of old ale permeating the walls and floor, almost like fermented honey.

"These are their quarters," CassaRoc told him. The two of them walked side by side through the stable common, then entered a cramped garden, somewhere in the central portion of the tower, Teldin decided. The feeble light panels in the walls and ceilings made what few grains the centaurs were cultivating seem pale and sickly. Gray mushrooms sprouted from the other half of the garden, some growing in rows, others in natural rings. "If they offer you any of the fungus, just say you're not hungry. It wasn't made for human consumption."

Teldin nodded. One large mushroom was mottled with splotches of purple. Teldin thought it quivered as the humans filed past.

"I see what you mean," he said.

CassaRoc kept his voice low. "The damned centaurs are right enough, but they've grown soft. They just don't care about anything. This tower could be impenetrable, if only they kept it up. The collective would hire on to fix things up for them, but they just don't care. All the centaurs really care about are their brews." He elbowed Teldin in the side. "By the Gods, I can understand that." He smacked his lips. "The leader here, Mostias—big centaur. Big. You'll like him—he makes this one ale that—"

A loud, hearty shout greeted them as they entered a large dining area. The humans went to mingle with a troop of centaurs, grabbing goblets of ale at a long, wooden bar stretched along one wall. The small warrior cloaked in plaid ordered a mug of fruit juice. The massive centaur behind the bar scowled at him, then poured him the mug and slammed it on the bar. The small man lifted it in salute and grinned lopsidedly at Teldin. "Nice to meet you, Mr. Cloakmaster, sir," he said happily.

Na'Shee approached Teldin, cutting off his view of the small fighter. Her eyes seemed strong and determined, but they glinted with gentle humor. "You did well out there."

"Thanks," Teldin said, "you're a great shot. I'm sorry about your friends. I owe you all."

She shrugged it off and looked away sadly. She changed the subject abruptly. "I've seen magic artifacts before, masks that speak, a tempest in a bottle; but that cloak—"

Teldin grinned. "I'm just glad CassaRoc is all right."

"She held out her hand, and Teldin shook it. "I'm Na'Shee. Sometimes I work behind CassaRoc's bar. You may find it a little tougher around here than you think. If you need anything, you let me know."

"Sure," Teldin thanked her, and he slowly realized that he had somehow made a new friend. Then he turned as a huge centaur strode from behind the bar and trotted up to CassaRoc, towering at least three feet over the warrior's head. The centaur held a huge, crystal tankard in one great hand; the mug was shaped like a giant boot and filled to the brim with golden ale. He handed it to the human and laughed. "Well fought, little one," the centaur said. "Sorry we couldn't meet you fast enough to help with the battle." CassaRoc forced a smile while the centaur went on. "Damned neogi are an infernal lot. Can't trust a one of them."

"Never have," CassaRoc said. He took a long pull of his brew, then belched. "Never will. The only good neogi—"

"—is a dead neogi!" cried the other humans. They raised their drinks to each other.

"I think they've heard your tirade a little too often, my friend," said the centaur.

"I see that," CassaRoc agreed, laughing. "But I'm not wrong, am I?"

The centaur shook his head. "My friend here needs one of your brews," CassaRoc told the huge centaur. He clapped Teldin's shoulder. "Teldin Moore, meet the finest centaur brewmaster in all the known spheres: Mostias."

"Ahhh," said the centaur, "the fabled Cloakmaster." He bowed his head. "Come on. I'll draw you an ale."

Teldin shook his head. "Just some water, if you will," he said. "After the crash and that fight, all I'd like is a mug of water and a place to sleep."

Mostias nodded and clapped a heavy hand on his back. "Coming right up." Teldin stared as the fat centaur shambled to the row of taps lined up behind the bar. He could not believe the centaur's size: his thighs were as big as tree trunks, and his bulbous stomach seemed as large as a cow's. His thick mane shook as he walked.

CassaRoc whispered to Teldin, "Lazy creatures. 'Sorry we couldn't meet you fast enough,' " he mimicked. "Right."

They bellied up to the bar as Mostias finished pouring Teldin a tankard of cool water. "On the other hand," CassaRoc said, "these centaurs are second only to myself at the refined art of brewing."

Teldin finished his water in several gulps. CassaRoc grasped his glass boot in both hands and opened his mouth wide. Twin streams of ale flowed messily down his chin. He slammed the boot down on the bar and wiped his sleeve across his mouth. "Ahh, Mostias, that's good!" he cried.

CassaRoc turned around and spoke to the company. "Now don't go quaffing all the ale you can. Leth, Spokaad, you, too, Hertek. Finish your ales and take positions along the tower. We have a guest—" he glanced at Teldin "—who a lot of our enemies would love to sink their diseased teeth into. Now, drink up! And take your posts!"

His warriors readily agreed and quickly finished their drinks. They nodded at Teldin as they filed out, and CassaRoc gestured Teldin over to an old, wooden table near the center of the room.

Chaladar, the grand knight, casually bowed his head to Teldin. He straightened the ends of his thick, reddish moustache with his fingers, and he said to CassaRoc, "I'll take the door. I've already placed two men at the entrance to the tower. We should leave within the hour. The neogi may have time to regroup, or even ally themselves with the Long Fangs." Chaladar gritted his teeth. "This could be more trouble than we expected."

CassaRoc nodded. "Very well," he said. "Be on your guard, paladin."

Chaladar opened the door and stepped just outside the entrance. His broadsword gleamed with a pure silver light, and he ran a hand appreciatively down a flat side. "Scaleslicer and I are always careful."

He turned his back to the room and stood watch with his shining sword unsheathed. CassaRoc leaned close to Teldin. "A good man," CassaRoc whispered. "A holy fanatic, of course, but a good man nonetheless."

Mostias poured Teldin another tankard of water, and CassaRoc led him to a table where they could sit and talk.

"Sorry about your men, and your ship," CassaRoc said.

In his mind Teldin saw the mountain of flames engulfing the *Julia*, the explosion that had spewed shards of debris across the great ship's wing, and the empty silence that followed, signifying the sudden death that had fallen upon his crew. "I wish things had been different. I promised them a quest, journeys to spheres no one has ever before seen. They didn't sign on with me simply to die a few months later."

CassaRoc nodded knowingly and watched him. "So you're really the Cloakmaster?"

Teldin chuckled ruefully. "Either I am the Cloakmaster, or the cloak is the master of me. No matter the case, this cloak is what brought me here."

"Well, we're grateful you're here. I'm grateful you're one of us. And don't worry. Your people will be taken care of."

"Thanks. Quite a welcome," Teldin said. "We would have been killed if it wasn't for you and your men. I had no idea that word had reached you of our approach. To be honest, I never thought anybody here would even know who I was. Or would care."

CassaRoc took a slow sip of his ale. "You don't know how long we've been expecting you. There are wizards all over the *Spelljammer* who have been foretelling the coming of the Cloakmaster for years. But, lately, a lot of rumors have been spreading, especially an ancient beholder myth about the coming of the Cloakmaster. It has the whole *Spelljammer* on edge. That's why you were attacked. The neogi didn't know—

gods, nobody knew—who the Cloakmaster was going to be, and they didn't care. They only know the beholder myth: that the coming of the Cloakmaster will herald the start of the Dark Times.

"They're not taking any chances. The older races know what happens during the Dark Times, and they don't want it to happen again. They're killing all the newcomers to the *Spelljammer*—to make sure they get the Cloakmaster, and the Dark Times will never come.

"Right now," he said, "you can bet that word is spreading across the ship that you are here, and that we've got you. You are going to have a fiendish time here. Everybody wants you . . . and, I guess, that cloak of yours."

Teldin had no reply and quietly sipped his water. CassaRoc lowered his voice. "That's a mighty powerful weapon you got there, son. You know, I don't take easily to a lot of people, but you're all right, Moore. You've been through a lot, and you're ready to take on more. And you saved my life. I owe you."

"It wasn't me," Teldin said. "My cloak—"

"The gods it wasn't! That cloak wouldn't have done a thing if you hadn't willed it. I saw you."

Teldin thought back. He had learned to control the cloak somewhat, tapping into hidden energies and abilities that only months before he never would have thought existed. He still was not exactly sure what he was doing and what the cloak was responsible for, but he could command its awesome energies for the most part, especially when he let the control come naturally, without concentrating too hard. At least, he figured, if he was not now the compleat master of the cloak, he was well on his way.

"Perhaps," he said.

"Perhaps. I had no chance against that ignorant umber hulk, not without a decent weapon. *Perhaps.* Right."

Teldin looked around at CassaRoc's assemblage. As he spoke, centaurs entered the room, carrying bandages and poultices for CassaRoc's wounded fighters. "We were lucky out there. Hardly anyone was hurt."

"I've got good fighters. Those neogi can't compare to a human on a rescue mission. Or on a quest." He finished the tall boot of ale and slammed it again on the table. "It's time, Teldin Moore," he said. "What's your story?"

With the crash and the immediate battle for his life behind him, Teldin was beginning to feel light-headed and tired, and he was becoming desperate for a soft bunk for the night. Or the day. Whatever they have in the phlogiston, he thought. But a story?

"My story? I don't have a story."

CassaRoc watched him skeptically. "You said you were on a quest. What brings you across the Rainbow Ocean, Cloakmaster?"

Teldin's eyes felt heavy from exhaustion. When he looked up, all the humans who had helped battle the neogi were expectantly watching him.

"Well?" CassaRoc said.

"Well," Teldin began, taking a gulp of water. "Very well. From the beginning." He cleared his throat. "I've come here because the neogi shot down a spelljammer that destroyed my farm on Krynn, and I was entrusted with some kind of magical cloak that I haven't been able to take off, even for a bath, for about a year."

The humans stared at him. Somewhere behind him, a centaur whinnied for another flagon of ale.

"You asked," Teldin said.

"That I did," CassaRoc said, smiling. He turned to his companions. "It's going to be a long one, friends, but I think it's going to be good."

Teldin took a deep breath and started in, explaining the crash of the reigar craft on his farm, and his subsequent quest to remove the ancient cloak that the captain had given him. At first, the warriors listened as would any dubious group: laughing, making jokes and, occasionally, loud, sarcastic remarks. But by the time Teldin recounted his vicious fight with General Vorr and the almost accidental acquisition of the bronze amulet by Gaeadrelle Goldring, not a single warrior interrupted him, nor did they even march back to the centaurs' bar for more of ale.

Teldin told his tale in a calm, even voice, looking back honestly at his own foibles and mistakes, even admitting his misguided trust toward Aelfred Silverhorn and his initial distrust of the giff Herphan Gomja—a mistake for which he felt he would never forgive himself. Frankly, it was all a little embarrassing to Teldin, revealing the chain of events that seemed now to be a life long past, perhaps even a childhood of sorts. Here, today, on the *Spelljammer*, he felt he was finally grown up, in charge of his fate and his life; and the people around him made him feel comfortable in their attentive silence, accepted, as though he truly belonged—a feeling he had never really had before, not even on Krynn.

When he was finished, the warriors nodded and talked quietly among themselves. At the door, Chaladar was nodding approvingly. Teldin had recognized the style of the paladin's armor, and knew that he also hailed from Krynn.

Behind Teldin, Na'Shee touched his shoulder softly and said, "Men would die for a mission such as yours. Be proud of yourself. You have achieved your quest."

Teldin raised his water mug in a mock salute. "Thanks to you."

A shadow darkened the bar's doorway, and Chaladar stepped aside to let another human in. He turned to watch the woman as she paused inside the doorway and stared at Teldin Moore.

"The Cloakmaster," she said. "I knew it would be you."

Her words were like the gentle flow of a mountain stream, and Teldin instantly recognized her voice. His mouth fell open as he stared at the elven maiden, her long silver hair flowing like a river over her shoulders. Her eyes sparkled with flakes of gold, perhaps a little more dimly than when Teldin had seen them last, but she was still beautiful, still radiant, and he felt a pit open up deep in his stomach.

He leaped up from the table and took the elf into his arms. One hand ran slowly down the length of her luxurious silver hair.

"Cwelanas," Teldin whispered into her lips. "Cwelanas, is it really you?"

Chapter Three

• • •

". . . Destiny is not to be toyed with or ignored. In my crystals I have seen the destiny of the Sphere Chaser an eon from now. I have seen that it begins with an act of innocent kindness and will end once destiny has brought answers to all those with the courage—or the naiveté—to seek them. . . ."

Corost, mage, *The Scroll of the First Seeing*; reign of the First Pilot.

The beholder ruins stood in the shadow of the *Spelljammer*'s mammoth tail, the once-proud columns broken and cracked after two years of the fearful onslaught by the mysterious disease called the Blinding Rot, and the eye tyrants' subsequent internecine wars.

The disease had decimated the beholder population, sending the survivors into a mad, xenophobic rage of destruction against their own race. No matter how much they hated all other races, they saved their true hatred for themselves: for all other beholder clans, and for any brethren who were different, or sick, or injured at all.

Still, the ruins stood, their tyrannical population diminished to barely a dozen beholders who craved the destruction of their enemies and, as did their most hated enemies, the neogi, the total enslavement of inferior races.

To the clans of the beholders, inferior meant everyone but themselves.

Inside the dimly lit ruins, the ancient tyrant Gray Eye held council with the remainder of his beholder brethren. His huge, milky white eye stared at each of the eleven beholders in turn. His smaller eyes waved stealthily on their thin stalks, like snakes targeting their prey, and the scales overlapping his round body were tinged pink in anger. Four powerful *ioun* stones circled his body in frenetic orbits that mirrored his evil mood, granting him safety against attack.

Gray Eye had considered the situation aboard the *Spelljammer* for a long time, ever since word had first reached the ship that the Cloakmaster was on his way.

The Cloakmaster. Gray Eye had bristled at the term when he had first heard it from one of his brothers. At the time, he had been floating along the roof of their ruins with three of his guard, and had been focused on the defensive capabilities of the nearby neogi tower. When word first came of the Cloakmaster's approach, Gray Eye had been so infuriated that one of his smaller eyes had narrowed its focus on a neogi guard standing along the neogi tower. Within seconds, a scarlet beam of light erupted from the eye and took the neogi unawares. The guard thrashed and screamed in agony as its brown flesh disintegrated into smoke and ash.

The Cloakmaster. So many people had borne that cloak, Gray Eye knew; so many had commanded their own spelljamming ships across the universe, wearing that same vestment of illusion. *The Cloak of the Damned First Pilot.* Who was this, one insignificant human, to dare wear the cloak upon his shoulders and claim himself its ultimate master?

It should belong to a beholder.

Gray Eye knew more of the history of this cloak, and its bearer, Teldin Moore, than most others. This human was much different, he knew: stronger, more determined than any cloak bearer before him. Perhaps the human was even linked to the *Spelljammer* in some subtle, intrinsic way—a way that might mean failure to the eye tyrants' plans.

And to myself, Gray Eye thought. If the Cloak of the First Pilot belongs to anyone, it should belong to a beholder . . . and that eye tyrant is me.

And so, Teldin Moore must be destroyed.

"War," the leader of the beholders began. His brethren watched him unblinkingly, their great eyes focused and glaring red in the gloom of their ruins. "War. This must be our goal. For too long, peace has reigned supreme upon this ship. We must focus our efforts on one goal—conquest!"

His fellow beholders hovered lazily above the floor of their sanctuary, waiting, smiling evilly, their great central eyes focused on their leader.

Long veins pulsed in anger under the surface of Gray Eye's huge, ocular body. His scales rippled as a wave of fury washed over him. "The damned Cloakmaster has finally arrived," he said. "The prophecy of darkness is coming true, even as we speak. The Dark Times will be upon us all if we are not swift."

He paused in thought. "I almost wish that this human had been killed earlier by the neogi. Now the burden falls upon us, and it is one in which we should rejoice. The humans have decimated the neogi forces. The time to strike is now, to take the cloak from the Cloakmaster and destroy the damned neogi, all in one concentrated attack.

"We must form strategic alliances with others—those who also wish to take command of this vessel, perhaps the ogres, and the minotaurs—they will be easy to enslave—and then—" the beholder laughed maniacally "—*break* those alliances, and use the inferior species for our own purposes, for *cattle*."

His beholder brethren laughed among themselves, the sound of hoarse coughing. Gray Eye looked out among them and hesitated. When last the Dark Times fell upon the *Spelljammer* and the ship's food-producing gardens closed upon themselves, Gray Eye had taken full advantage of the chaos and the weaknesses of others to assume the leadership of the beholder community. Cannibalism, looting, and murdering of his own kind—these crimes had kept Gray Eye alive and in power. His brethren were young and knew nothing of the last Dark Times.

Gray Eye would commit the same crimes today to take control of the *Spelljammer*.

"When the Dark Times soon fall upon the ship, we will be compelled to barbarism that almost destroyed our species here many years ago and will surely devastate our numbers today. We cannot afford that. We cannot afford to wait for the human to come to us. We must leave the confines of this ruined palace and attack. We must take control now!"

The veins in his pale, round body throbbed in rage. His great, milky eye was rimmed with crimson. The cloak, he believed, would soon be his.

Let the Dark Times come, he thought. What will it matter to Gray Eye, the new Cloakmaster?

He laughed, and the other beholders joined in. But he was laughing at them.

"We must destroy Teldin Moore," Gray Eye said with finality. "We must destroy the Cloakmaster *now*!"

* * * * *

High in the horned tower of the illithid empire of the *Spelljammer*, a black-clad mind flayer climbed the last few, dark steps to the level where the illithids' brain mold was carefully cultivated. Its pungent aroma caused the tentacles on Drikka's large, octopuslike head to twitch unconsciously, and he hungered for the sweet sentience that the mold offered.

The mind flayer bending over the brain mold, like its junior officer, wore only black. The only noticeable differences, to a human observer, would be the leader's proud bearing and the intricate field of stars decoratively woven into its long black cape. Mind flayers otherwise appeared genderless, almost clonelike, though humans found it useful to label them male or female.

The leader did not look up with its milky white, pupilless eyes. *What is it, Drikka?* the mind flayer thought impatiently.

Lord Trebek, we have word.

The Cloakmaster, Trebek guessed.

Yes, my lord.

Speak.

Drikka told Lord Trebek of the nautiloid's crash upon the *Spelljammer*, and the destruction of the neogi forces by the Human Collective.

The leader of the illithids rose from the brain mold garden and brushed off his reptilian hands. *So it is true*, Trebek thought calmly. *So the beholder myth is true . . . Have you notified our guest?* he asked coldly.

Drikka hissed in anger. Like Trebek, Drikka did not think

much of their guest, the newcomer. If Drikka could have his way, the newcomer would be killed as a traitor to its race. *No, my lord. If you wish, I shall do so now.* Drikka turned to leave.

Trebek held up a purplish, three-fingered hand. *No, Drikka, I shall do it. The* phlbasta *is in my study as my guest. I will handle it.*

Drikka took a step back. *Phlbasta* was perhaps the worst thing that could be spoken in the mental language of the illithids—especially in reference to another illithid. It called the mind flayer in question a traitor, a dung eater, a lover of humans, and it challenged its racial purity. *Very well, lord,* Drikka thought, and he turned and went downstairs.

Trebek thought in silence for a moment, then strode up the stairs to the highest level. Scowling, he knocked twice on the door to his own private study. He opened the door without waiting.

The mind flayer seated at the desk was poring over thick, leather-bound books stacked high on Trebek's desk and in the bookcases affixed to the walls. He rapidly made notes in a book of his own and referred back to one huge volume, detailed on the pages with ancient drawings of the *Spelljammer*, its towers, and some of its mysteries.

How goes your research? Trebek thought.

The researcher looked up absently. The mind flayer's milky white eyes seemed tired and weak and did not reflect the normal cunning of the illithid mind. *Hmm? Oh, Lord Trebek, my apologies. Yes, yes, everything is fine. Much of your information is highly valuable.*

It seems your information was valuable as well.

What do you mean?

The Cloakmaster has arrived, as you predicted. It seems the beholder myth was true.

The Cloak— The illithid closed the book he was reading. *You mean Teldin Moore is finally here? Where is he?*

With the humans, Trebek said scornfully. *They are currently secure in the centaur tower. They will probably try to make their way to the human area very soon.*

Good. Good. The illithid rose from the desk. His long purple robes seemed ill-fitting, and he stood inches shorter than Trebek, clasping his unhuman hands together in peaceful thought. *Thank you, Lord Trebek, for the use of your study. It has been most illuminating. If you will be kind enough to continue to allow me access . . .*

Of course, Estriss, the leader said. His words were filled with a sarcasm that he hoped Estriss would not perceive. *For as long as you wish. My only hope is that my few resources will help lead you to your answers. This ship holds many secrets, and I'm afraid that my humble research has gleaned but a few of them.*

Your library is most extensive, Lord Trebek, more than I could have hoped for, Estriss said.

Trebek nodded and closed the door behind him. Estriss turned and stared out a small window, watching the colors of the flow play like fire along the buildings around him.

Perhaps now, he thought, the *Spelljammer* will yield all of its secrets. Perhaps Teldin Moore, and the cloak, will bring me all the answers I will ever need.

Outside, in the hall, Trebek stood silently at the door, deep in his own thoughts. He took a clump of brain mold from a pocket and chewed it slowly, silently, until the mold's being washed through him with a sweet, intoxicating hum.

Estriss, he thought, you consort with humans. You cannot be trusted.

Trebek started down the stairs and paused between floors of the horned tower. Estriss could be a problem, he thought. He was a friend to this human, this inferior Cloakmaster. Trebek shivered in disgust. You are a liability. I will see you dead before you get in the way of true illithids and our power on the *Spelljammer.*

Phlbasta, Trebek thought, you are not a true mind flayer to me.

Chapter Four

• • •

"*. . . It was decreed that there be two artifacts that shall bring the Chosen One to complete the Cycle of All. The Compass, imbued with the very soul of Egrestarrian itself, and the Cloak, which shall protect the Pilot as it had the First, and give to him the ability to end that which we inadvertently begat. It is not penance that shall be paid, but the price of destiny*—Tru'vaer.

"*It was with our spells and invocations that the Cloak was banished and left on the island of Gol on the world known as Westrelon; and the Compass was taken to an unnamed sphere uncounted thousands of leagues distant, where it was left to be discovered in the center of a natural ring of dormant volcanoes.*

"*May destiny call the artifacts together once again. May destiny call the Cloakmaster to the Renewal of the Dream. . . .*"

The Mage of the Owls, journal; reign of Velina, the Second Pilot.

"Cwelanas?" CassaRoc said, turning toward the newcomer. "Teldin, you know our elven friend?"

But Teldin had already gone to her. He held the lithe Cwelanas tightly in his strong arms, his lips pressed hard against hers. Her arms curled around his neck and her body slowly molded against his.

"Yes," CassaRoc muttered, "I suppose you *do*."

She had hardly changed since Teldin had last seen her. Cwelanas's long silver hair spilled over her shoulders and hung seductively over one side of her slim face to hint at hidden beauty. Her eyes glimmered a pale gold, and her smooth, soft skin was almost alabaster, tinged pink with the heat of the kiss.

Cwelanas, Teldin thought. It had been so long since they had been together, but hardly a day had gone by without his thoughts turning to the elven woman he had left behind on Krynn—the woman he had never dared hope to see again.

He held her close in a long embrace, until Chaladar very obviously, very loudly, cleared his throat. Teldin slowly pulled his lips from hers and looked up sheepishly.

"We really should hurry things up," Chaladar told him.

Teldin smiled and nodded, then led Cwelanas over to CassaRoc's table. "You know each other?" Teldin asked.

CassaRoc nodded, smiling, and shoved a stool out with his foot. "Sit down, woman. We have a few minutes, eh, Chaladar?"

Chaladar's face was stern. "We should leave before anyone discovers he's—"

"That's what I said," CassaRoc interrupted. "We have a few minutes. Mostias . . . "

The immense centaur closed off the tap and placed three tankards of ale on the bar. "Well ahead of you, little man." He took the tankards in one huge hand, brought them around to the table, and placed one in front of each warrior. "Anything for a friend of the Cloakmaster," he said, smiling at Cwelanas. He then bent down and whispered to CassaRoc, "There is the matter of a certain tab . . . "

"Not now," CassaRoc whispered hurriedly, "not now." He waved Mostias away.

Teldin and Cwelanas left their ales untouched, and instead sat staring into each other's eyes. CassaRoc watched them both for a moment, then took a long draft of his ale. "Women," he said under his breath.

"I thought I'd never see you again," said Teldin, breaking the awkward silence between them. "I thought you were out of my life forever."

"And I, yours," Cwelanas said. Her red lips glistened, and her eyes sparkled with gold. "I felt lost without you after you left me on Krynn. I've been through so much since we saw each other last—you don't know how much I've thought about you."

Teldin could focus only on Cwelanas, on the light playing over her soft, silken hair and the cool smoothness of her skin. He had been alone for so long on this seemingly endless quest that true companionship—even love, he thought—had become barely a consideration. But Cwelanas had stirred his heart from the moment he had first encountered her aboard the *Silver Spray*, her father's elven ship, docked at the quays of Palanthas.

Since his last day on Krynn, Teldin had eventually fallen under the guile of Rianna, who had betrayed him; and had come to love Gaeadrelle Goldring, whom he still loved as a friend; and Julia, whom he had lost to the gods. After Julia's death, he did not know for sure if there would ever again be room in his heart for love.

He looked into Cwelanas's sparkling eyes. Perhaps, through all his adventures on his haphazard quest, this was the woman that he truly wanted. She had been there for him at the beginning, and as he gazed into her eyes, he realized that his feelings for Cwelanas were strong, and that they had been there since the start, and he had been too dense to understand them.

Something opened in him then, a warm flicker of hope deep within his chest. If there could be room that had not been destroyed by the fear of his friends and lovers turning against him, betraying him for the power of the cloak, then there was room only for one . . . room enough for Cwelanas.

"How did you come here?" Teldin asked simply.

Something flickered behind Cwelanas's golden eyes. To Teldin, they seemed wide and beautiful, two enchanted wells that he could drown in; but he noticed that their luster was slightly dimmed, and she kept her eyes averted from him as she talked.

"It was shortly after we left you at Sancrist," Cwelanas began, "when we were attacked by pirate ships that swooped down on us from wildspace.

"My father was injured in the attack. I saw him go down under the blade of a buccaneer, and that was the last I saw of him."

"Why did they attack?"

"Oh, Teldin." Cwelanas hesitated, and her eyes filled with tears. "Oh, Teldin, because of you, because they wanted that cloak of yours."

Teldin stared into his memories, recalling his long-ago conversation at Crescent with Julia and Djan, of Teldin's way with *verenthestae*—what Djan had described as a force exhibited in people whose very existence seemed to sow the patterns of destiny and fortune for themselves and others.

Cwelanas wiped her eyes with the back of her hand and took a gulp of ale. She touched Teldin's hand. "It's not your fault, Teldin. I didn't mean that. They somehow found out about your cloak, and they finally tracked us down on Krynn. They kidnapped me. They tried to get it out of me . . . where you were heading, what the purpose was for your quest.

"I told them nothing, Teldin. I could not betray you. Even—even though they tortured me. . . . "

She lifted one sleeve. Teldin grimaced at the long burn scars running up one arm. "Cwelanas, . . . " he said.

She shook her head and rolled down her sleeve. She held her arm tight against her. "I—I wouldn't tell them anything, Teldin. I would not have them kill you, not after they killed my father."

The room was silent. Some of the warriors had heard Cwelanas's tale before, but it was still a tale of tragedy and dishonor, and all respected her for what she had been through.

"I was on board their ship for weeks, I think, perhaps even months. I was kept locked in a cargo hold, and when I was not being questioned, or assigned slave duties throughout the ship, they . . . they shared me . . . with the crew."

Her eyes grew distant. Teldin's jaw clenched tightly and his hand unconsciously gripped the hilt of his sword. "They finally made a mistake," she continued, "and I escaped from my chains in the hold. On deck, I overpowered the second mate and killed him with his own dagger. I went through the ship carefully and slit the throats of all those who had . . .

"They finally caught me, just as I was about to kill the captain. They threw me overboard, into the phlogiston. I cannot describe the sensation when I finally succumbed to the flow. I floated there for I don't know how long, until I was found by the *Spelljammer.*

"They tell me I'm lucky. Once they brought me aboard—I have CassaRoc to thank for that—I thawed out quickly. I must not have been out there for very long. I don't feel very lucky. I still see them in here." She rubbed her forehead. "I still hate them. And my father . . . I can't ever be sure what happened to him."

Teldin glanced at CassaRoc. "We intercepted a report from a neogi messenger," CassaRoc said. "One of their mages had spotted something in the flow. It wasn't long before our own scouts made out her shape not far off the port bow. We intercepted her before the neogi could, and we took her to the Tower of Thought." He laughed. "A few of my ales brought her around soon enough."

Teldin watched Cwelanas and felt pride, mingling with awe, at her strength during the trials she had lived through. Something nagged at him, though, the sheer coincidence of her reappearance as his quest was coming to an end. Coincidence? he wondered. Cwelanas was stronger than he had ever known, and he knew now that she was *supposed* to be here, at journey's end, to help fulfill his still unknown destiny.

No. It was not coincidence. It was *verenthestae.*

He pulled her to him and held her gently in his arms. "I will get you out of this, Cwelanas," he said. "We will get out of this together."

Chaladar again cleared his throat, this time louder. CassaRoc stood. "All right, we get the point, paladin." To Teldin he said, "Sorry, Cloakmaster, but it looks like your reunion will have to wait. We have to get you out of here. It would be best if we could smuggle you out, but it looks like we'll have to take our chances outside, and probably make a run for it." He turned to his companions. "Any ideas?"

No one answered the warrior. He looked questioningly around the room. Suddenly, the little warrior with the slingshot stepped away from the bar, sloshing his ale onto the floor. His mouth agape, he pointed toward Teldin.

"Emil?" CassaRoc said. "Emil, are you bewitched, son?"

Emil blinked and scratched his head. His eyes were wide with confusion. "CassaRoc, sir, look at him. Look!"

CassaRoc turned and faced Teldin. "What in the name of

the gods . . . !"

The Cloakmaster was standing beside Cwelanas, and as the warriors in the room watched silently, his face shifted its features. He became shorter, thinner, and his apparel changed hues and texture to resemble a plaid cloak and ill-fitting clothes.

Emil jabbed his finger toward Teldin. "He's me, sir! He's j-j-just like me!"

CassaRoc, suspicious, scrunched up his face and looked Teldin over. "Is this a spell of some kind?" he asked. "Are you a magic-user?"

Teldin smiled and looked at his now puny body. He had deliberately chosen the least dangerous warrior in the room in order to appear unthreatening. He knew that his shape-shifting ability was sometimes feared, but he hoped that this display would prove his good intentions, his trust in CassaRoc's people. And he hoped it wasn't misguided.

"No, it is not a spell," Teldin said. "It is merely another property of the cloak. I show this to you to prove my trust, for I am grateful for your rescue today. Now, if your friend Emil here doesn't mind—"

"Emil the Fierce!" Emil said, a wide grin on his face. "Oh, I am honored you chose me to imitate, Mr. Cloakmaster, sir. You don't know what this means to me, you really—"

CassaRoc quieted him with a gesture. "You're talking like one of those gnomes, son. Now slow down."

"Okay, sir, okay."

"Now, Teldin, what do you suggest?"

Teldin thought for a moment. "It might be best if we stagger this, try not to call attention to ourselves in one large group. Let's try to get to the tower in threes and fours. I'll go out as Emil—"

"Oh, yessir, yessir, you bet, this sure is—"

Teldin and CassaRoc exchanged a glance. CassaRoc rolled his eyes at Emil and said softly, "Don't ask."

Teldin continued. "I'll go out in the first group, with you, CassaRoc. A larger group will follow, tightly protecting someone in the middle, someone with my build. Chaladar can lead them, and maybe make those who are watching us believe that I'm with them. Perhaps a little subterfuge will confuse them."

"The neogi aren't that smart," CassaRoc said.

Teldin adjusted his cloak, now a duplicate of Emil's brown, plaid cloak, around his neck and wondered if he looked as ugly as he felt. He turned to Cwelanas. "How do I look?" he asked.

Cwelanas smiled softly. "It might work, Teldin. You better stay low, though. Even with your cloak concealed, its magic can still be detected."

"Rest assured," Chaladar said, "the scum will be out looking for you."

CassaRoc said, "Cwelanas, go on ahead. Let my boys in the Tower of Thought know we're coming. They'll be ready for us."

Cwelanas nodded sharply and faced Teldin again. She kissed his cheek. Across the room, Emil blushed. "Be careful," Cwelanas said, and she hurried out the door.

Mostias murmured to CassaRoc, "Now, about that tab . . . "

* * * * *

Cwelanas reported as she had been told, and the first group from the centaur tower, including the disguised Teldin Moore, made it safely across the great starboard wing of the *Spelljammer* to rendezvous with three of CassaRoc's men at the edge of the ship's long landing field.

The group crossed in front of the council chambers and entered the great open market beneath the ship's stores. Here merchants hawked their meager wares and curios; weapons and armor were made and repaired; clothing and footwear were tailored to order.

The market was neither as extensive nor as bustling as had been most markets Teldin had toured, but it was certainly more friendly than most. At least a half dozen humans waved to him, greeting him as Emil or "little adventurer"—a term Teldin quickly came to despise, and he wondered just how Emil could put up with it. But, knowing Emil, he mused, how could they put up with him?

Then he remembered how valiantly Emil had fought against the neogi, and he realized that, though Emil's body was small, his courage and honor more than made up for it.

The band of warriors passed a booth full of charms and crystals. The men hardly noticed an old woman sitting in the stall who gasped as they walked by. They did not know that Teldin had been spotted, and quite easily, at that; the magical qualities emanating invisibly from his cloak had been detected by the old woman, who had seen the cloak's energies fanning out behind him in the shape of a great manta, glowing with all the colors of the spectrum.

As Teldin's company left the market and headed straight for the Tower of Thought, Teldin was also identified by an elf loitering near a stall that sold exotic desserts. "Did you see that?" the elf said. The shopkeeper, a stout man used to eating a large percentage of his own wares, twisted his fat bulk out of the booth to watch the warriors turn toward the tower. "What? I don't see anything."

The thief ran off with an armful of pastries and sweets, and he headed straight for his quarters at the Elven High Command. It's true. It's true! he thought. The Cloakmaster legend is true! The Dark Times are almost upon us! The elf knew he had to report to Lothian Stardawn that he had seen the one called the Cloakmaster enter CassaRoc's tower, and that the stories about the cloak were true: for with a simple magical charm that he had stolen from his grandmother two decades earlier, the elven thief had seen a cape of energy swirling around Teldin Moore as though it were a thing alive.

Oblivious to all this, Teldin paused as CassaRoc opened the great door to the Tower of Thought and invited him in.

The thick door closed behind the party, and CassaRoc led them all up to a great dining area, where most of CassaRoc's fifty men waited for their leader. As they entered, the group clapped him on the back, while Teldin strayed around the room, secure in his disguise. He found Cwelanas at the bar, and he sidled up to her. "So far, so good," he whispered.

"That's what you think," she said.

"What do you mean?"

"You were spotted out there by someone," Cwelanas said. "Count on it. If you weren't seen by a neogi mage, or a beholder, then someone else with magical abilities found you out."

"Perhaps . . . an elf?" Teldin asked, instantly suspicious.

Cwelanas glanced up. For a moment, she appeared almost sad. "Perhaps."

"I'll be on my guard."

CassaRoc came over and pulled Teldin an ale from a long line of taps behind the bar. He sipped at it until the larger group finally came in, led by Chaladar. Emil had been kept hidden tightly in the center.

When Emil was revealed, the disbelieving humans stared between him and Teldin. Finally, Teldin imagined himself wearing his own features, his own musculature, and his own clothes. His body seemed to grow warm, tingling with energy, and he heard the warriors gasping and talking among themselves as his features reshaped into his own natural appearance. The plaid cloak metamorphosed into a dark band at his throat, clasped in front by his amulet, which had shrunk to the size of a coin.

There was silence for a moment, until Emil said, "Boy, that sure was something, Mr. Moore, sir. I sure would be honored to help you out even more—hah! *more*, get it, sir? hah!—you just let me know if I can help you out at all, Mr. Cloakmaster, sir—"

Teldin patted him on the shoulder. "I appreciate the offer, Emil—"

"Emil the Fierce!" Emil said.

Teldin smiled. "Yes, yes. Thanks."

CassaRoc stood up on a table in the center of the room and motioned Teldin to come over. He looked down at all his warriors and nodded appreciatively.

"Fellows of the Pragmatic Order of Thought," CassaRoc began, "we have a very important guest with us—more important than even he knows, I think. This is Teldin Moore. He's come a long way to rendezvous with the *Spelljammer*. And he's not a mage or anything like that. He's the one we've heard all the rumors about. He's the Cloakmaster."

The crowd turned toward Teldin, who really did not know what to say. He had not expected a reception such as this, nor a formal introduction to the Human Collective by its leader.

"I know, it's hard to believe, but you all saw it here, and the ancient rumors about the cloak are true. And with it, Teldin here saved my life and routed the cursed neogi."

CassaRoc paused for effect. "Now, I think the *Spelljammer* is at a turning point, and I think things are going to be a lot different now that Teldin is on board. Chaladar and I have talked about this a lot, lately, once we all heard the rumors. And we're pretty much agreed: Teldin here is the Cloakmaster, and it is his destiny to be here with us, whether we like it or not.

"We've all heard the legends of the Dark Times. Now, it seems to me that if the legend of the Cloakmaster is true, then the legend of the Dark Times is probably true as well.

"But we are humans, here, and Teldin is one of us. His cloak has brought him here for a purpose, whatever that purpose may be. I, for one, think we have to stand behind him. Now, I'll let him speak to you, and you can judge for yourselves the truth of his words."

CassaRoc climbed down and placed his hand on Teldin's shoulder. "Go ahead, boy. Don't you worry. They're good people." He left and walked around to the bar.

"CassaRoc is very kind," Teldin stammered. "Honestly, I don't know what all this means. I don't know anything about the Dark Times. I don't even know what they are."

As he spoke, his confidence grew and his voice became stronger. "Please don't think that I've come here to do you harm. I've been trying to reach the *Spelljammer* for a very long time—it seems like forever. I always thought I'd been called out here for a reason. I thought at first that it was the curse of my cloak, but now I think maybe it's more than that."

The words came easily, and he knew that these thoughts were honest, things he had been considering for a long time.

"I'm here for some great purpose, whatever that is. And so, I think, is the *Spelljammer* itself. I have been called across the spheres for a reason. I have a lot of enemies who want my cloak—neogi, illithids, even elves—" He glanced at Cwelanas, who smiled thinly at him. "And I believe they want this so they can somehow control the *Spelljammer* and make it a force of evil across the spheres."

This gained Chaladar's full attention. The paladin stood up straight and focused his gaze on Teldin. The zeal for punishing evil was strong in Chaladar, and he would do anything to thwart the plans of those who dared to embrace chaos.

"I won't allow this," Teldin proclaimed.

Chaladar agreed loudly, shouting, "Go on, Cloakmaster."

Teldin looked out into the warriors' eyes and realized they were listening to him. Their trust was incomplete, he knew; he could see that in some of their expressions. He knew he had to prove himself to them, as he had already proved himself to CassaRoc, and now Chaladar. "If I am here for a reason, somehow bound together with this cloak and with the *Spelljammer*, then it is a purpose for good, not evil. It is a purpose for life, and for honor—not conquest and death."

The warriors began murmuring their agreement. The dark band at his throat began to grow warm, but he did not notice.

"I will need your help. If my enemies—our enemies—want this cloak, then that means they want me. That means that we'll have a fight on our hands, another fight to the death, probably, but a fight for good, a battle for the *Spelljammer*'s destiny. There is a war raging right now, perhaps a second Unhuman War. When this is over on the *Spelljammer*, maybe we will all be able to live in peace and explore the universe, without fear of dark magic and unhuman enemies. But I'll need your help."

The crowd was silent, staring at Teldin. Chaladar came up and said quietly, "Teldin, your cloak."

Teldin looked down. On its own, the cloak had unfurled and grown, softly flaring out behind him in the approximate shape of the *Spelljammer*. Its colors flared brightly, seemingly infused with the energies of the flow, and, as he watched, the inner lining grew dark and the light of stars appeared within, as though the cloak were a vista upon some distant wildspace.

Chaladar said, "I told Teldin that I believed he could unite the collective into a force for good. I now believe that was his destiny all along. Teldin Moore . . . Cloakmaster . . . I will be honored to stand with you—and all the warriors of the Chalice tower will stand with you as well."

CassaRoc's warriors shouted agreement with the grand knight. From the bar, CassaRoc shouted, "And we're with you as well, Teldin. Aren't we, lads?"

At that, all the warriors in the room cheered. Teldin looked upon them and smiled, at CassaRoc, at Chaladar, at Emil and Cwelanas. But there was a frown on her face, and before he could question it, hands were reaching for him, clapping his back, shaking his hand. From around the room he heard cries of "To Teldin Cloakmaster!" Toasts were made, and the warriors introduced themselves for so long that, by the end, he could remember only a handful of their names. His doubts slowly drowned in an overwhelming sea of friendship.

Through it all, no one noticed a small, dark shape crawling on the floor, poking its black, furred snout from around the bar. No one noticed its faint sweet smell, the stench of something long dead.

And no one noticed its white, burning eyes.

* * * * *

There was no warmth, no friendship, in the oppressive silence that lay deep within the secret warrens that veined the mighty *Spelljammer*. The dark world hidden beneath the citadel, the tunnels that stretched mazelike from tip to tip throughout the *Spelljammer*'s body, were cold and reeked with the stench of ancient evil. Only the dead and the undead walked in the warrens. Silence was spoken here, broken only by the shudder of a death rattle, the screams of souls, the whisper of black winds from the worlds beyond the grave.

The tunnels wove unevenly through the *Spelljammer*, ending at only a few points with concealed entrances at the lowest levels of the citadel. Where the living made their homes above, in chambers of light and air, surrounded by mementoes of their accomplishments and the items they needed to live happily among their brothers, the undead of the warrens lay quietly in nests of dry straw, moldy furs, and torn tapestries. Their existence was one of unquiet hatred, existing against their wills between the planes of light and dark, in lairs where the endless warrens intersected or widened enough to afford room for nests.

The dead enjoy their own company.

In one dark, secret lair, hidden deep within the ship so that even the *Spelljammer*'s magic could not detect his evil, exiled to a chamber carpeted with spongy layers of black mold, hung with fineries of moss and green fungi, and furnished with the bones of the long dead, the Fool watched.

His eye sockets were black pits of darkness burning deep inside with bright pinpoints of silver light. He watched through the eyes of his undead vermin as the warriors far above, in the Tower of Thought, surrounded the Cloakmaster and accepted him as one of them.

The Fool rose from his throne, a bleached chair formed from the spines of orcs and the skulls of elves, and he paced the chamber. Where he walked, cold black smoke rose from his footprints.

His gray skin was shrunken, pulled tightly, like parchment, across his undead bones. His eyes glared fiercely, and his skull-like face was contorted in an eternal rictus of hatred. His long, skeletal fingers absently rubbed the length of a crimson amulet at his neck, and the long, rectangular crystal swirled with an unnatural, inner fire.

Long ago his name had been Romar. Now he was simply the Fool. A library of legends had grown around him over the decades. Some believed he was merely a zombie. Some believed he was a skeletal worm that fed on the heart of the *Spelljammer*. Others believed he was the *Spelljammer*'s secret captain. Few had ever seen him; most believed he was a myth, a shadow creature used to scare children.

But the few who had had dealings with the Fool were never the same again. Master Coh believed the Fool was an ally— Hah! The neogi had much to learn, and would learn it soon. The Fool brooked friendship with no one and was ally only to the dark gods. Coh was not a master, but a puppet.

The Fool laughed. He was not called "the Fool" because he was stupid, like his "allies," but because he had fooled everyone—even the *Spelljammer* itself—about his secret existence within the ship's warrens.

But things, the Fool foretold, will soon change.

Through the eyes of his undead rat, he could see the contemptible respect on the human warriors' faces, the sickening strength with which the Cloakmaster carried himself—oh, the arrogance of this human pest!—and the Fool whispered to himself of the things he would do to Teldin Moore, Teldin *Cloakmaster*, of how delicious it would be to command this mortal's undead body like a marionette, once the cloak and the *Spelljammer* were his.

He knew the cloak. He had followed the signs and had bonded long enough with the *Spelljammer* for knowledge of the cloak's history to become his. He knew what was the legend and what was the truth; he knew the course of the *Spelljammer's* destiny, and what the coming of the Cloakmaster truly meant.

For the Cloak of the First Pilot had been returned, and the Compass was the key that would guide the Cloakmaster and the *Spelljammer* to their unseen fate.

Unless he could take the cloak, and the *Spelljammer*, for himself . . . one last time.

The Fool hissed, the laughter of the dead.

"Spellllljammerrrrrr . . ." he said, licking his taut lips with a desiccated tongue.

The Fool's whispering was the sound of the cold wind whistling through dead trees; the sound of worms burrowing through bones nestled deep within the ground. His ways of thinking were far different from those of the living. His ways were the madness of death, the joy of destruction, the sweet perfection of utter despair.

As he whispered dementedly to himself, he ran his hands over the mildewed doll's head atop his long conjuring wand, and he imagined his darkest fantasies, his secret desires, his long-hated memories: of the *Spelljammer*, of his failure as captain of the great ship many years ago—Failure! Because the *Spelljammer* was not worthy of me!—of his death-long quest for revenge.

His whispers were broken and rambling, the rasping of the dying. They echoed off the cold, slimy walls, a perverted reflection of Teldin Moore's own promises of life, of peace.

"Yesss," the Fool uttered to the darkness. He could see it all now, his last stand before the Dark Times began. "Yesssss. A mighty fight. Many battles . . . and blood . . . the blood . . ."

The Fool shuddered in ecstasy, his twisted mind filled with visions of death and revenge against the *Spelljammer*.

"Many will die at my hands. War and blood, to the death . . .

"A fight . . . for evil. For souls . . . for death . . . for the *Spelljammer's* final destiny . . .

"Its . . . *death*!"

The master lich laughed to himself for a long time. Above, in the market of the *Spelljammer*, shopkeepers shivered for no reason, and children began to cry.

Chapter Five

• • •

". . . *Of course, we had heard the legends of a fabulous cloak of untold power. It was even written that the Architects themselves had no conception of its powers when the cloak was first transformed. It appears to protect and answer its bearer eccentrically, but in ways entirely appropriate to the situation. . . .*

". . . *The fight was over within mere seconds. We never saw Lekashta, the mind flayer, again. . . .*"

Journal of Steelbender, dwarf of the Rock of Bral.

Several hours later, after Teldin had bathed and eaten a hearty meal of cold meats in CassaRoc's galley—for fires were forbidden while the *Spelljammer* was sailing in the phlogiston—he felt relaxed and ready to take on the duty of convincing the leaders of the halflings, the dwarves, and the giff that his coming was not a promise of doom. He was here only to fulfill his quest, to discover why he had been called out to find the most legendary spelljamming craft of all time. The cloak, an ultimate helm, he knew, was too valuable to fall into the hands of the evil neogi or any other unhuman race. If it did, then the Dark Times would truly come, for the unhumans would use the cloak to subjugate all others. These things would serve as his argument to win allies.

Their only hope of success against the unhumans was to ally themselves behind Teldin, the Cloakmaster, and help him end his quest—before the forces of evil could take control and wreak destruction across the known spheres.

CassaRoc had provided him private quarters in the Tower of Thought, and he had quickly fallen into a deep, restful sleep for several hours. He woke refreshed, though still a little weary from the day's events. He bathed and put on fresh, comfortable clothes, which CassaRoc had provided, then lay down for a while in his quarters, trying to relax before his meeting with his potential allies.

He put an arm across his eyes and felt his heart beating fast, too hard. Things had happened too fast since he had reached the *Spelljammer*, and it was hard for him to conceive that he, a simple farm boy from a backwater world such as Krynn, was finally aboard a legendary ship—almost a god-ship—that sailed between the spheres as easily as a fish could swim across a pond.

The *Spelljammer*! It was almost too much to believe. The magic amulet felt warm against his chest, and he sighed, happy that he was finally where he belonged—*Yes! I belong here!* he suddenly realized—but he had no idea what he should do next, or how he had to end his quest. His heart beat faster. He wanted this over with, soon; he wanted to finish what he had come here for, whatever that was. . . .

He sat up and rubbed his eyes. Rest would do him no good now; he was too excited, and, though he felt strong after his bath, he knew that the events of the long day would catch up with him in a few hours. Already he felt light-headed, but he did not know if that was from the day's battle or simply exhilaration at his journey's end. Or . . .

Cwelanas. No matter what he thought about, her face appeared to interrupt his concentration. It had been so long since they had last seen each other, but the emotions he felt for her were strong, perhaps stronger than when they had parted at Sancrist.

Not long after his impromptu speech before CassaRoc's warriors, Cwelanas had begged off to perform a few errands for CassaRoc. She had given Teldin a gentle kiss and let her hand linger on his arm. " 'Teldin Cloakmaster.' I like the sound of that. They'll rally around you with a title like that." She looked into his eyes. "I never thought you would find me," she had whispered to him, a hint of sadness in her golden eyes.

Then she had left, and Teldin had been pulled by CassaRoc to meet some of his fighters.

Now he could not get her out of his mind. She had been lost to him long before he had even met Gaeadrelle Goldring, the kender. He wanted to believe that Cwelanas's presence here was more of a distraction than anything else, pulling him from his purpose. He hated to admit it: he could not deny a very obvious attraction to the silver-haired elf. But his mission on the *Spelljammer* was paramount, he thought, and a romance was not at all what he had planned, not at all.

Still, her face would not disappear from his mind.

Teldin was lost in thought when CassaRoc's messenger knocked on his door, and he did not even look up until the messenger loudly called out his name. He recognized the voice and sighed softly.

He opened the door, and Emil stepped in quickly. The short little warrior threw back his plaid cape and exclaimed, "Hi, Mr. Cloakmaster, sir. CassaRoc the Mighty sent me to get you. He said the leaders of the halflings and the giff and somebody else are here to see you. Boy, I tell you, you and that cloak of yours sure are impressive. You don't know how much I'd love to—"

"Okay, okay," Teldin said, "calm down." Then he added, "You remind me of some gnomes I once shipped with."

This sent Emil into a fit of high-pitched laughter. "Oh, no, no, sir, I'm not a gnome, not at all. I just get excited and get carried away sometimes. You just let me know if I start bothering you, sir," he said, grinning. "Everybody else does. Oh, yeah, you bet, I can be a pain." He laughed.

Teldin patted his shoulder, wondering why Emil smelled vaguely of cheese, and together they went down to the tower's meeting hall, Emil chattering incessantly along the way. Teldin tuned him out eventually, since Emil really needed only himself to carry on a conversation, and spoke to him only when they reached the great hall's door.

"Thank you, Emil. You've been a great help."

Emil blushed and squirmed happily, wringing his hands. "Boy, Mr. Teldin Cloakmaster, sir, I sure do—"

"Thank you. That's fine, Emil. You go on now. I don't want to keep you from your duties."

"Oh, oh, oh, oh, okay, sir," he said happily, and he scurried away.

Teldin opened the door and heard CassaRoc call out, "Here he is now."

He stopped and stared at the huge giff rising from the table, convinced that what he was seeing was impossible. "Gomja?" he almost asked. But Gomja, the giff that had become his friend while still on Krynn, was far away. He was with the gnomes now, the leader of the entire gnomish military, and he knew he would probably never see his large friend again.

The broad-shouldered giff that stood before him now was fully Gomja's height, maybe taller. He boasted an odd, triangular plate that seemed to have been bolted onto his snout, and it was overlaid with ivory and decorated with scintillating diamonds. His uniform was the full dress of the giff military, and his barrel chest seemed ready to burst the uniform at its seams.

Teldin shook the giff's mammoth, outstretched hand, which seemed surprisingly gentle. The giff introduced himself with a slight bow of his head. "Lord High Gunsman Rexan Hojson," he said.

"We call him Diamondtip, for short," said CassaRoc, touching the tip of his nose.

Teldin smiled and tried not to stare at the giff's ornate snout, but he found it quite difficult. "I see. It's a pleasure to meet you, Lord Hojson." Teldin introduced himself, and the others around the table stood.

"Agate Ironlord Kova," said the leader of the Citadel of Kova, thudding the handle of his battle-axe once on the floor.

Teldin nodded. The proud dwarf barely stood as tall as Teldin's waist, but he shook hands regally, and his closely cropped gray beard gave Kova an appearance of quiet dignity.

Another dwarf came around the table, his hand outstretched, his red hair so bright that it almost seemed aflame. "Vagner Firespitter, of the Free Dwarves," he said loudly. His wild, bushy beard was painted with the colors of a rainbow, and his mane of bright, scarlet hair did nothing to detract from his motley assortment of clothing, a brilliant blue tunic and pants of yellow and black.

Two halflings came around the table to shake hands. Teldin

looked down. "Kristobar Brewdoc," said the younger halfling. He was thin for one of his kind, with barely an ounce of fat around his thick torso. "Hancherback Scuttlebay," the other halfling said. He was shorter and heavier than Kristobar, and he wore a black vest bearing mystical patterns and runes.

"Gentlemen, we're glad you could come so quickly." CassaRoc said, "Now, if you'll allow me a word with the Cloakmaster before we begin . . . "

The leaders nodded and waited as CassaRoc pulled Teldin over to the bar. He kept his voice low. "Chaladar the Holy is being righteous again."

"Where is he?" Teldin asked.

CassaRoc scowled. "He knew this meeting was important, but he refused to sit in the same room with the halfling Hancherback. He's a thief, just like half the other beings on board this ship, and His Holiness wouldn't be caught undead here with somebody like him."

Teldin nodded. "That's unfortunate. His backing here would have helped us a great deal. But the two of us will make do, I'm sure."

CassaRoc nodded.

"Don't worry," Teldin said, trying to import more assurance than he felt. "We'll do fine."

"One more thing," CassaRoc said. "The elves and the Shou have not responded. Probably to be expected, but I don't like the sound of it. We may have a problem with them. You can trust an elf only so far. "

Teldin shrugged. "Yes, I know elves well. There is nothing we can do. We'll discuss this later."

Teldin gestured for his guests to sit. The giff, Diamondtip, squatted upon a metal keg of CassaRoc's, the only seat in the meeting room sturdy enough to bear the beast's weight. The others pulled their chairs around the scarred wooden table.

"Sorry for the delay," Teldin said, deliberately turning to each as he spoke and looking into each one's eyes. "By now, I'm sure you've heard various versions of my arrival and the reasons for my coming. Let me tell you the honest truth and try to clear up any misconceptions you may have.

"They're calling me Teldin Cloakmaster. I've discovered that the cloak that I bear is an ultimate helm—perhaps, if I am correct, *the* ultimate helm," he said without thinking, wondering where the words had come from. "And with it I've been searching the universe for the answers to my questions.

"My answer is here, I know now. My answer is the *Spelljammer* itself, though I still don't know what it all means. I am not here to harm anyone, nor am I here to bring on the Dark Times, as you have probably heard. I don't even know what the Dark Times are."

The huge giff nodded slowly and scratched under his bulbous chin. He scrutinized the Cloakmaster with his small, dark eyes. Kova, the dwarf, laughed. "You're going to have a hard time getting along with all the others," Kova said easily. "We all know the beholder myth. If you truly are the Cloakmaster of legend, believe me, you are in for an uphill battle. You'll be lucky if you live the night. If the Dark Times do come, all the races will be at war with each other for power, and for the food in the stores.

"Besides, if you are the Cloakmaster that has been foretold, I believe you will not fare well in a battle with the elder dwarves."

"The elder dwarves?"

"Aye," the dwarf said. "The true captains of the *Spelljammer*. I fear they will not look kindly upon your arrival and the threat of the Dark Times."

Teldin said it quickly. It came unbidden, from his heart, and he knew the words were true. "There is no captain of the *Spelljammer*. Not now."

CassaRoc stared at him. "Teldin, how do you know this?"

Kristobar said, "The captains are secret, hidden. Everyone knows this."

"We believe the ship is ruled by the dwarven gods," said Firespitter.

Hancherback stifled a laugh. His eyes twinkled in merriment. He loved a good scuffle.

Teldin said, "The *Spelljammer* has sailed for a long time, and many stories have arisen to explain its history and who captains it." He absently ran a finger along the edge of the amulet. The metal was warm to the touch, welcoming, and when he spoke again, he knew the words were true. "This I know: With our forces combined, we will defeat the evil armies on board the *Spelljammer*, and all of its enemies.

"I do not want war at all. I want nothing more than to end this quest and let everyone get on with their lives. But I will defend myself when attacked, for any reason. I have no desire to harm anyone or bring these Dark Times about. I just want to live.

"I need you to help me. I believe Lord Kova is absolutely correct: I present some danger to the populations here—at least, that is how they perceive it. My coming was foretold by your beholder nation, and I did not even know that I was coming here. Your legend may well be true. Perhaps, without my conscious will, my mere presence here will bring about the Dark Times. I hope not.

"But I need to resolve my quest. We need to protect our interests on the *Spelljammer*, with as little bloodshed or human lives lost as possible. Without each other, this ship will become a curse throughout the known spheres, piloted by our enemies."

CassaRoc turned and waved for attention, and a steward came over with tall mugs of ale for everybody, and water for Teldin. Vagner Firespitter held the steward's arm and drained his tankard, then handed it back for another. "Fine brew, CassaRoc," he said.

"Perhaps we should start at the beginning," CassaRoc said. That might make things a bit easier to understand. And I can get everyone another mug of ale."

"I think that's a good idea," Kova said.

"Both very good ideas," said Firespitter.

Teldin told the story of his quest once again, as he had earlier told CassaRoc's warriors, and he emphasized his friendship with Gomja, the giff, and his heroic acts on Teldin's behalf. He spoke of their powerful fellowship and the allies he had made on his journey to the *Spelljammer*. CassaRoc related how Teldin's nautiloid had crashed on the wing, and told of the vicious melee with the neogi that had greeted the Cloakmaster upon his arrival. He relished the story of how Teldin's cloak had rescued him with a dozen or more bolts of magical energy; then he finally brought them to the present, to focus on the purpose of the meeting.

"So we need allies," CassaRoc said. "Once word gets around

that the Cloakmaster is here, every foe on the ship will be after him and his cloak. We need to combine our forces for good, to protect the *Spelljammer*—and our existence here."

Teldin felt that his and CassaRoc's speeches had allayed some of their potential allies' fears, but he could feel that they still did not trust him entirely. Who could? Indeed, if anyone else held the power they believed he held, he too would be afraid.

He would almost be a god. . . .

Hancherback Scuttlebay cleared his throat. "All this is well and good, human, but I've seen nothing to prove that Teldin Moore is the Cloakmaster. If we're going to put the entire halfling population on the battle lines, we'll need—"

He stopped, for right before him Teldin's face was changing shape, metamorphosing into that of Hancherback's fellow halfling, Kristobar Brewdoc.

The halflings watched silently and reached for their ales at the same time. Diamondtip and the dwarves laughed.

"This is but one power of the cloak," Teldin began to explain, "to assume the shape—"

Kristobar interrupted sharply, sputtering, "This could be but a simple spell, a spell for children. We need more proof, Teldin Moore. Much more than this simple parlor trick."

Teldin quickly resumed his true features. His body felt warm, and he could feel the energies of the cloak building in a powerful surge. The hair on the back of his neck stood on end as the cloak's power tingled through him.

The cloak billowed around him. The halflings scattered backward from the table, and at once the cloak elongated, reaching out for Kristobar with its edge. The inner lining had turned a deep blue, like the sky at sunset, and suddenly the cloak enveloped the halfling in its folds.

Teldin's cloak unfurled, and the halfling was gone.

* * * * *

He floated among the stars of wildspace. Below him hung the sun of his home sphere, and he could feel the coldness of space on his bare arms, in the hollows of his bones, chilling him with the emptiness of death and eternity. The stars, cold and piercing, almost close enough to touch, blazed around him, and Kristobar felt that he would float here forever, forgotten, abandoned.

Loneliness washed over him, and he knew that he was lost.

He was cold and alone, isolated in his own empty universe. He felt a cold sharper than on the wastes of Artalla, a cold he could imagine was more severe than the embrace of the dark gods themselves.

Still he was alone. He screamed out his need, his fear, but his voice was plucked away, impotent in the cold emptiness of space.

Totally . . . alone . . .

* * * * *

"Where is he?" shouted Hancherback. "Bring him back!"

Teldin stood silently, as amazed as the others in the room. He closed his eyes and concentrated on Kristobar's face.

The cloak swirled around him. The colors inside shifted to a shade more dense than any black those assembled had ever seen. At once, the cloak curled out, and Kristobar was expelled from the dark lining. He huddled in a fetal position on the floor, shivering. "N-n-no one," he said. "So c-cold . . ."

He was helped to the table and swaddled in blankets, and the cold inside Teldin's cloak soon dissipated. Teldin apologized for any inconvenience. "Sometimes it does things on its own," he said. "Sometimes I wonder exactly who the master really is."

"Cloakmaster, CassaRoc," Diamondtip said finally, "we all have reasons for a strategic alliance." His voice was a deep rumble tinged with quiet dignity. "I believe you are a man of peace, and, although we must all defend ourselves at times, I think none of us here wants war. We simply want to survive in happiness.

"You may count on the two dozen warriors of the giff to stand by you when battle calls. Cloakmaster, you have convinced me, at least, with your magic cloak . . . but especially with the honesty I sense behind the story of your quest, and behind your eyes. My only wish is that your friend, Gomja, could be here to share in our victories. He is a credit to the giff. To fight beside him here would honor me."

"Thank you, Lord Hojson," Teldin said. He looked at the others. "Can we count on your support as well, gentlemen?"

Kristobar cast a wary glance at Teldin, then leaned over to Hancherback. They talked among themselves for a moment. Lord Kova took the opportunity to speak. "I have seen enough. The Citadel of Kova will side with the Cloakmaster—though it is still hard for me to believe that the *Spelljammer*'s captains are not dwarves. I do not know how you know this, but your cloak is powerful, and I feel that destiny is somehow being woven here today, as the threads of your cloak are somehow woven tightly with your own.

"The dwarves of Kova number three hundred. We will fight by you, Teldin Cloakmaster, or we will die."

Firespitter agreed. "We number only about a hundred in the Free Dwarves' tower, Cloakmaster, but we will gladly fight by your side, for life and for peace throughout the spheres."

"Good," Teldin said. "Excellent." He faced the halflings.

Hancherback stood proudly. "We're with you, Cloakmaster, all two hundred of us. We're small, but we'll give those neogi—and anybody else—a run for their money."

Firespitter lifted his ale in a toast. The others rose and lifted their mugs. "To Teldin Cloakmaster," Firespitter said, "to peace, and to—" he thought, stroking his decorated beard "—to the Alliance of the Cloak!"

Chapter Six

• • •

"*. . . We are naturally superior. No one shall escape the fury of our righteousness . . .*"

Beholder mage Kronosh; reign of Jos Dragonrider.

Death came to the minotaur tower quickly and mercilessly.

The minotaur guard at the tower door was initially shocked to see three of the xenophobic beholders floating past his post. He was even more surprised when one turned toward him and grinned, baring its ugly, misshapen teeth in a feral smile. A small eye on one of its ten eyestalks turned toward the guard. A yellow beam of intense light flared, and instantly the minotaur staggered back, no longer in control of its own mind.

The beholder turned to its companions. "Our first slave of the war," it said, laughing.

They proceeded into the tower stealthily, the enslaved minotaur leading the way through the narrow corridors. At each door, the minotaur would enter and the beholders would charm other minotaurs with beams from their eyes.

Most of the tower's forty minotaurs were their slaves by the time the beholders reached the quarters of the minotaur leader, Hammerstun Breakox. One minotaur knocked on the door and said, woodenly, "Lord Breakox, we must speak with you."

The answer from inside was swift. "Come!"

The beholders ordered nine minotaurs to enter and surreptitiously surround their leader.

Breakox was huge, more than sixteen feet tall—twice as tall as the other minotaurs and four times as fierce. When the minotaurs did not speak, Breakox stood and said, "What is this?"

The minotaurs were silent.

In an instant, Breakox knew that something was wrong with his warriors, and he lunged for the mammoth axe that leaned against the wall.

The minotaurs jumped him. Breakox struggled blindly, kicking with his mighty hooves, crushing a warrior's nose. But their numbers were too strong. They pinned him to the floor, his huge arms pulled back and held by minotaurs on each side.

Breakox bellowed loudly for his warriors to attack, but when he heard the beholders laughing coarsely as they entered the room, he knew that the cause was lost, that all of his warriors must be enslaved.

The three beholders approached. A minotaur pulled back Breakox's shaggy head so that its masters could fully see the great minotaur's submission.

As one, the beholders stared at Breakox with their eyes of charm. Three yellow beams lanced from their deadly eyes.

Breakox squirmed against the minotaurs who held him. He felt the magic working its way into his eyes. He closed them tightly and screamed defiantly.

The power of their eye beams flared back toward them. The beholders flinched and floated back, their charm spells ineffective against the minotaur leader. They blinked in pain; no one had ever held his own against even one beholder's powerful eyes. Beneath them, Breakox laughed. "You will never enslave me, monsters! I will forever be free!"

The beholders huddled among themselves and whispered together. They parted and approached the captive leader. "You are, perhaps, correct, minotaur. We doubt that you could ever serve the beholder empire in any capacity. Therefore, you must die. Your head will be carried by our armies as a warning to others. In death, you will serve."

The beholders focused on a tall minotaur warrior who bore a broken horn. Stiffly, he walked over to Breakox's great axe and picked it up. Sweat broke out on the minotaur's snout; Breakox could see that his warrior was struggling to break the beholder's unhuman control, and, inside, he smiled, for his warriors were courageous, even in defeat.

The one-horned minotaur gripped the axe with two hands and brought it above his head.

Breakox struggled suddenly and threw one warrior off his shoulder. The others pounced on him; he could see the horror of what they were doing reflected in their eyes.

They held him down. His chin was pressed hard against the floor.

He bellowed, one last scream of hatred and defiance. He could see in the eyes of his minotaurs their great fear, their useless struggle against the beholders' mind control.

The great axe swung down.

A beholder gestured a thin eyestalk and ordered a minotaur downstairs. At the base of the tower, the minotaur opened the huge door and allowed Gray Eye to float in, his glimmering *ioun* stones whirling around his scaly body. Behind him, ShiCaga, the chieftess of the ogres, strode in, towering a good four feet above the minotaurs. An evil smile flickered across her craggy face. "This is good," she said to Gray Eye. "Very, very good."

In the chambers of the slain minotaur leader, ShiCaga and Gray Eye agreed to an unholy alliance. Together, with the combined forces of the ogre and beholder communities—and with their numerous slaves—they would destroy the neogi and mind flayers. And with the ogre chieftess's sons at the lead of forty ogre warriors, the human forces would later be destroyed—in revenge for the death of ShiCaga's husband, and to secure the ship's stores for their unholy alliance.

Gray Eye wanted something else. He wanted the cloak, and the ogres were just stupid enough to help him take it.

Then the ship would be his.

The rasping, sinister laughter of the beholders rang throughout the tower.

Chapter Seven

• • •

". . . I have had visions, mother, visions of worlds beyond this one. I know that I must be hallucinating, or dreaming, but they are so real. I have seen suns born and whole worlds spin on their axes. And I saw a black pearl as it cracked, from the inside out. I do not understand these things, but I know that I must leave here to seek something more, something wondrous, and something that is better than the life I have here. . . ."

Letter to Meranna, mother of Jokarin.

Teldin, CassaRoc, and the giff, dwarf, and halfling leaders talked among themselves for an hour after their agreement to become allies, making broad, preliminary plans for defense and explaining to Teldin the multifaceted—and sometimes highly confusing—political situations aboard the *Spelljammer.* The ship was more crowded than he had originally thought, holding whole communities of illithids, goblins, neogi, dracons, ogres, beholders, elves—it was all too much, and Teldin finally decided that it just did not really matter, as long as he could get the answers he needed.

Privately Teldin and his allies were all worried that no word had been sent from the elves or the Shou. The Shou were largely unknown to Teldin, but he had had enough untrustworthy dealings with the elves to last him a lifetime, and he decided it would be best to consider them both, for the present, as potential enemies.

They briefly talked about some of the legends concerning

the *Spelljammer*, in order for Teldin to get an idea of the great ship's history—what they actually knew of it—and the power structures and hierarchies on board. No one had ever heard of Teldin's cloak before the beholder myth had started to circulate months earlier. Neither could they elaborate on the Dark Times and what they meant to the ship. "All we know," Diamondtip explained slowly, "is that the Dark Times herald war for us all. Food will be in short supply, though we don't really know why. Most of the communities have food supplies and even grow some themselves. Our primary food comes from the *Spelljammer*'s gardens, and I can think of no reason why that should ever stop. The gardens are open to all, and the harvests are plentiful. We go completely without want."

Talk eventually turned from there to the nature of Teldin's cloak. All, of course, knew of ultimate helms, but they could not be sure of the peculiar qualities the cloak had displayed. "That could be what pulled you out here," Lord Kova said, stroking his trim beard. "But if the cloak is truly an ultimate helm, it is the strangest helm I've ever heard of."

"Perhaps it is something special," said Kristobar Brewdoc. "That would explain why the evil ones consider you dangerous—perhaps it is some kind of device whose magic is uncontrollable, or even limitless. A charm like that could destroy all your enemies."

"Aye," CassaRoc said, "even . . ." He took a draft of ale. "Even the Fool."

"The Fool? Who is that?" Teldin asked.

"No one," Brewdoc said hurriedly. "Make-believe, to keep children in line."

Hancherback snorted loudly. "Not hardly. He's real, I tell you, but he is less than human—far less." He turned to the Cloakmaster. "Evil incarnate, he is. A serpent in the belly of the *Spelljammer*."

"Aye," Kova said. "We mortals brought the monster to the *Spelljammer*. And we mortals must destroy it."

Firespitter was silent through this, glaring occasionally at Lord Kova. He believed that the Fool was a myth created by the Kovans for some unknown purpose—only the dwarves under Kova would be so stupid as to fashion such a ridiculous bogeyman. A worm. Hah!

"No one knows who the Fool really is," Diamondtip said, "or if he really exists. Some say he is the secret captain, some say he was the captain once, now deposed. Others say he is a being formed by the violent deaths of others, a being of soulless energy. Others don't believe in him at all."

A blank look fell across Teldin's face. There was something there with them, he could feel, something cold and empty gnawing at the pit of his soul.

CassaRoc was watching him and said, "Teldin, are you all right?"

Silently Teldin reached across the table and plucked the dagger from CassaRoc's belt. He held it between his fingers and hefted it, then turned slowly, as if in a trance. In one strong, swift motion, he slung it toward the base of CassaRoc's bar.

"What in the name of the gods do you think you're—"

CassaRoc stopped when he saw what Teldin had done. The dagger vibrated, its point embedded in the wood, and a huge black rat was impaled upon the blade. The knife had speared the rat straight through, yet it still squirmed, scrabbling with its sharp claws against the floor and the wooden bar. There was no blood.

"How?" asked Hancherback.

"It was already dead," Teldin said. He pulled the knife from the wood and held up the squirming rat.

Firespitter said, "Undead?"

Teldin nodded. His eyes glazed over and he held his hand close to the rat. The amulet at his neck grew warm. "Someone had to control this rat. He sees through their eyes."

"Who?" CassaRoc asked.

Kova answered. "The Fool, that's who. That's been a legend, too, that he sees through the eyes of others."

"No," Teldin said. "Only the undead, I think."

"It looks as if we've got one more enemy than we planned on," Diamondtip said. "Well, my guns will be ready for him."

Teldin crushed the rat's head beneath the heel of his boot. Blackness stained the old floor, and the rat died its true, final death. The Fool, Teldin thought. Perhaps the legends about him are true. Teldin nodded. It seems as if the battle lines have been drawn. If I've been called here to become the

Fool's enemy, then I am right about my quest.

I'm here to fight for life, and the Fool fights only for death. . . .

The alliance soon adjourned so that its members could take the news back to their respective communities, and to prepare for the eventual war with the evil unhumans. When the allies were gone, CassaRoc closed the door and pulled Teldin over to the table.

"I'm weary," Teldin told the warrior. "I am so tired of fighting and death."

"I don't blame you at all, Teldin. You've been through a lot today."

Teldin yawned. His eyes felt scratchy, and he rubbed his face to keep himself alert. "It is catching up with me, I think. Still, I feel as though there is much to be done. I couldn't sleep earlier. I don't know if I could now."

"You look as tired as you sound. Go on to your quarters. You'll sleep just fine."

CassaRoc watched him silently as the Cloakmaster stared away. "There's just so much to do."

"So, what is it with you and that cloak?" CassaRoc asked.

"What?"

"You're . . . seeing things, aren't you? You knew that undead rat was here."

Teldin thought. Yes, he had been seeing things and hearing things, and knowing things that he had no knowledge of before he had landed on the *Spelljammer*.

"I'm not sure," Teldin finally said. "I did know the rat was here, but I'm not sure how." He thought for a moment. "I think it's a combination of things. The amulet and the cloak, working together, perhaps. The fact that I'm here on the *Spelljammer*, where its magic is more powerful, may help. Perhaps the powers of the cloak are getting stronger as well."

"Or perhaps you are," CassaRoc said.

Teldin nodded. "Yes, you may be right. It may be me, but I don't know everything about this ship. Actually, I know very little. I don't think I'll know everything until I become—"

He stopped himself. Until I become . . . what? He did not know, but it was there, flickering like energy through the cloak, through his being. Somewhere inside him, his reason for being here was locked away like an ancient treasure. And the key was somewhere upon the *Spelljammer.*

Someone knocked loudly on the door to the meeting hall, then opened it. One of CassaRoc's warriors, a tall, gangly fighter named Hath, stuck his head in. "CassaRoc, a word with you."

CassaRoc grunted and stepped into the hall. Hath closed the door. Teldin heard voices behind the thick wood, but could not make out any words, then CassaRoc came back in.

"Teldin, I'm sorry. My man just gave me word that your helmsman—"

Teldin stood. "Corontea?"

CassaRoc frowned. He seemed to sag slightly, and he took a deep breath. "Teldin—"

"Don't," Teldin said. "Corontea didn't make it."

The survivors from the crash of the *Julia* had been sneaked over soon after Teldin and CassaRoc had made their way to the Tower of Thought. At that time, Djan had been administered medicines and healing spells for superficial cuts and burns. The healer had placed a sleep spell on him, to give his injuries time to heal.

Corontea, however, had been a different matter. The *Julia*'s female helmsman had far too many internal injuries, and the healers knew that there was nothing they could do for her except relieve her pain.

CassaRoc sighed. "I'm sorry, son. My healers tried everything, but they claim she was hurt too badly. One healer would cast a spell and heal one wound, and it seems like another injury would pop up. There was nothing they could do except ease the pain. They cast a spell of numbness over her. She died in peace, at least."

"At peace," Teldin said. He scowled. "She died because of me." Teldin shook his head at the irony. "Sixteen other people on board the *Julia*, and only two survive, all because of me." He looked up. "What about Djan?"

CassaRoc shrugged. "Same as before. He'll be fine tomorrow, they say. My healer does wonders with burn salves and poultices."

"Good." Teldin pulled his cloak around him. "I think I'll head to my quarters soon. I'm going to stop in on Djan first, and see how he's feeling."

CassaRoc smiled. "Good man. Sleep well, Teldin. You need a good night's sleep after all you've been through."

Teldin left the meeting room as CassaRoc joined his band of warriors in drinks. He climbed the tower stairs to Djan's tiny room, which seemed only slightly larger than a storage closet and held only a narrow bunk and a small table, where half-empty vials of potions and creams had been left by CassaRoc's healers. Dim light from the phlogiston was the room's only illumination, glowing through a small window in one wall.

Teldin could see that his half-elf friend was in pain. Sweat beaded across Djan's pale brow, and his sheets, tangled uncomfortably around his body, were stained with sweat.

Teldin drew the sheets free and pulled them carefully up to Djan's neck. His friend's eyes flickered as Teldin bent over him, then slowly opened. "Teldin . . . " he whispered.

"I'm here."

"How . . . the crash . . . "

"Don't talk now," Teldin said. "We survived, and the healers say you're going to be fine by tomorrow. You'll be a little stiff, but you'll be up and fighting." He smiled, hoping that his friend would not see through his bravado.

Djan's eyes closed. Teldin thought he had gone to sleep again, but suddenly Djan's eyes snapped open again.

He whispered, "Corontea . . . ?"

Teldin turned away. Djan and Corontea had become close friends on the journey to the Broken Sphere, and he did not want to hurt Djan again with news of Corontea's death. "The healers say you have to sleep. That's the only way these potions will work. That's an order, first mate. Now, you have to rest."

Djan grabbed Teldin's arm. The grip was weak, and his normally pale flesh seemed white, almost translucent. Teldin looked down. Their eyes met for a moment, then Djan's face seemed to sag, as though in defeat, and the half-elf turned away.

Teldin felt he could say nothing. They sat in silence until Djan said softly, "I heard the guards as I was brought here."

Teldin watched him.

"Our coming was foretold. The Cloakmaster."

"I've heard it," Teldin said. "Now, get to—"

"They said, 'The Cloakmaster brings death. The legends of

the beholders are true.' "

The Cloakmaster placed his hand on his friend's. "Never place much faith in legends. People have a tendency of making their own fears come true."

Djan faced him with teary eyes. "I don't listen to legends such as that. It is the fact they knew you were coming. The Cloakmaster. And coming for a reason."

"And?"

"Teldin. Can't you feel it? This is your destiny. This is your purpose. We are supposed to be here. *Verenthestae.*"

Djan's eyes flickered shut, and Teldin sat on the edge of the bed as Djan fell asleep. He then rose and opened the door. In the light angling from the corridor, he saw Djan's chest rising evenly in peaceful sleep.

Teldin closed the door. "Damn," he said. "Damn."

He climbed the tower steps to his meager quarters, where he commanded his cloak to shrink to a thin necklace, and he removed his clothes and prepared for bed. CassaRoc was right. The day had been damned hard and exceedingly strange. His quest had taken him farther than he had ever expected, and it had forced him to grow in directions that had before seemed inconceivable.

He lay across his bunk and pulled a light blanket over him. The glimmer from the phlogiston flickered through his single small porthole, across the opposite wall. It was just dim enough to let him fall asleep quickly and easily.

* * * * *

He was standing, naked, looking down at the bunk, where his body lay sleeping. He saw the line of the cloak wrapped at the base of his neck, the amulet a dark talisman below that.

The amulet.

He realized that his chest was glowing, and he looked down at his astral body. The outline of the amulet, pulsating with golden light, was imprinted on his chest. The three-pointed symbol burned coldly and flickered against the darker image of the amulet's mysterious pattern, woven like veins across Teldin's ethereal flesh.

His dream self traced one of the lines of the amulet, and he heard the Spelljammer*'s voice in his head, a high, keening song that echoed with immense age, immense sorrow.*

His quarters disappeared from around him. He was floating in the cold blackness of wildspace, in a sphere he had never before seen. Here the stars burned with their own inner fires around the circumference of the sphere, and he could feel the eighteen planets lazily circling the huge yellow star at the center.

—Aeyenna.

He knew the star's name as though he had been born there, and he knew that he was looking untold millennia into the past, at the One Egg, the Cosmic Egg, the Broken Sphere.

—Ouiyan.

He laughed out loud; he could feel the echoes of his own voice, laughing in his sleep, somewhere in a bunk yet to be dreamed of. He laughed, for the wildspace of the sphere known long ago as Ouiyan was filled with a million swimmers, singing high, sweet songs of peace and freedom. Teldin swam among them, pushing himself through space with his small wings, and he knew he was one with them, seeing through their eyes.

The spaakiil *migrated from planet to planet, star to star, living in harmony with the humans and other creatures inhabiting the planets below. The manta race was looked upon as something holy, and their sentience was revered among the people of Ouiyan, who respected the swimmers' intelligence and their simple philosophy of benevolence and love.*

Then a great shadow fell across the worlds and the spaakiil *scattered across the sphere in horror. He felt their terror screaming through his bones as, one by one, his brethren were butchered, and the peoples of Ouiyan were decimated by forces they could not understand.*

The spaakiil *met together between the stars. A fleet of ships sailed with them, and in a thunderous explosion of unharnessed, magical energy . . .*

Someone called him. The amulet shone at his neck, calling . . .

He was running. The floor was the maze engraved in the amulet, and he twisted around corners, following the narrow walls and the fleeting shadow that hovered just out of his vision.

Teldin!

He stopped suddenly. Cwelanas stood nude before him. She was radiant, her silver hair flowing down her shoulders. She beckoned to him. He took one step—Teldin!—*and stopped.*

Cwelanas came to him, reached for him with one soft hand, and ran a finger down his chest.

Her hair caught fire. Her finger glowed where she touched the sigil imprinted on his chest, and her face, her body, was seared away in a blast of light.

Then it was Gaye standing before him, the kender who loved him, whom he had left with the fal One Six Nine millions of miles away. She glowed with an inner fire, like a being of raw power. Her dark eyes danced with golden fire, and her youthful appearance seemed infused with a new awareness, one of newly found purpose. Her long black hair swam around her head as though it were alive, and her robes, tied at her waist with a belt woven with golden symbols, flowed about her.

His love for her washed over him in a warm embrace, and he saw for the first time how much she resembled Cwelanas. Then she spoke, but her words were distant, a whisper on the winds of dream.

He cocked his head. Gaye shouted, but the dream wind scattered her words as though they were pieces of broken feathers.

She floated before him and stretched out her hand. She placed her palm upon the design on his chest, and he heard her words in his head, though she did not speak.

Three things you must understand, Cloakmaster, three things that I cannot explain.

The closest are not what they seem.

Follow the woven heart.

The mark will show the trust.

Then Gaye faded from his view, a beatific smile lit like fire behind her eyes. He called out for her, reached out to her with his strong, bare arms, but she was gone.

* * * * *

He was awake then, alone in his bunk in the Tower of Thought. Gaye's name was but an echo in his ears.

In the dim light from the flow, he climbed out of bed and dipped his hands in a water basin and splashed away the cold sweat that had formed on his face and neck. The water trickled down his chest, and he touched his skin, looking for the mark that had burned there in the dream.

She had been so close, and Teldin had no idea what the dream was all about, why he had seen Gaye so clearly, so differently. She had changed, he saw, if that was really she who had come to him. He shook his head. No, it was a stupid dream. Gaye was long gone, just a kender, a friend. She did not have the power to travel through the realm of dream.

He could feel he was still weary from the day's adventures, but he had been asleep for four or five hours—usually enough for him. It was probably almost day watch on the great ship, anyway, and he was sure he wouldn't be able to get back to sleep. He felt anxious and suddenly wanted to get out of his room and explore.

He turned and reached for his clothes, and he noticed that his door was open, just a crack. He pulled on his pants and reached for his short sword.

Slowly, he pulled open the door.

It was Cwelanas. She faced away from the door, her back to him. She was weeping into her hand.

"Cwelanas?" he said.

She shook her head. "I heard you call out—"

And Teldin realized she must have heard him call for Gaye while he had been dreaming. He smiled and turned around, tossing his sword across his bed. He reached forward to take her in his arms. "Cwelanas, I was just dreaming—"

She turned. Her eyes were wide and crazed, rimmed with red. Tears streamed down her face. Her mouth was contorted in a grotesque expression of inner agony, and she jerked her hand out from underneath her dark cloak.

Something glimmered in her hand. Her knuckles were white and taut, her fingers tightly gripped around a wicked, snakelike dagger. Her lips quivered with terror. She raised the weapon above her head. "I—I love you, Teldin!" she screamed. "I love you!" And she swung the silver point down toward Teldin's heart.

Chapter Eight

• • •

". . . There is justice in the fact that the Cloak, portent of evil to many races across the spheres, invariably brings destruction only to those who deserve it. . . ."
Linedozer, mage, *XXVII Scroll of Richmon*

The woman who stood proudly inside the entrance to the beholder ruins was beautiful by human standards. She was tall and muscular, and her deep red hair cascaded like a river over her shoulders and shone crimson in the dim light of the ruins' faltering light panels. The patch over her left eye added an exotic quality to her lean face, and the sharp silver symbol in its center gleamed like a polished blade.

A beholder of a lower caste floated toward her. Four tiny eyes, unblinking, stared at her. "Lord Gray Eye will see you now," it said, and it led her toward the leader's chamber. On the way, they passed minotaur guards, positioned at doorways and carrying out orders for their new masters.

Selura Killcrow smiled. She could feel the excitement of the upcoming war already vibrating in her bones, and she licked her ruby lips in anticipation.

The beholder stopped beside a great door and motioned with an eyestalk. The minotaur guard opened the door, and Selura stepped in.

The eye tyrant floated leisurely above his dais, his *ioun* crystals slowly orbiting around him. Gray Eye smiled. A line of blood oozed from between his sharp teeth, and Selura saw the spattered mess of raw meat that the beholder was eating from a large plate beneath it. Large rib bones poked out, dripping with dark blood.

"Ahh," Gray Eye said. Its voice was low, emanating scratchily. "Welcome to the once proud Kingdom of the Beholders," the great eye said. "The once proud, and soon to be proud again." The creature laughed, and its laughter was the coarse sound of grinding bones.

Selura forced a smile and approached. The stench of the raw meat was overpowering, and she wondered how long it had sat rotting. "I see you have done well in your first conquest," she said. "Congratulations."

The beholder dismissed her. "Bah. We should have done it years ago. They're so simple. Minotaurs. Stupid, ugly creatures."

"But good slaves," Selura offered.

"Excellent," Gray Eye agreed. He gestured to the plate below him. "Better meat." He laughed.

Selura suppressed a shudder. As leader of the Long Fangs and the proprietor of the Sharptooth Common Room, she had to deal with the vilest members of all the *Spelljammer*'s races. The eye tyrant was no less and no greater an evil than anyone else who patronized her tavern; but the sight of the rancid meat, and its stench, curdled her stomach, and she wondered what type of being could willingly, happily eat that.

It doesn't matter, she thought. He'll be dead soon. They'll all be dead.

"What do you want, human?" Gray Eye asked abruptly. A huge piece of meat hung from between two ragged teeth.

"I have something I think you might want," she said.

The beholder's tongue flicked out and sucked the chunk of meat back into its mouth. "What might you possibly have that would be of interest to the beholders?" he said around the flesh in his mouth.

Selura walked slowly around the room, pretending to admire the torn and rotting tapestries, the obvious signs of violence and war that scarred the chamber. Gray Eye watched her, then sighed. "Enough theatrics, woman. What do you have?"

Selura fingered a faded, ancient tapestry depicting a victory of the beholders in a battle on Legadda, a planet located in Icespace. She knew nothing of its history, nor of the crystal sphere in which the original battle had taken place.

"Ruins," she said to the beholder. "Everything here is in ruins."

Gray Eye grunted. "You speak the obvious, human." His voice was like the crunch of gravel. "What are you getting at?"

She smiled a seductive human smile, one that had sent men willingly to their deaths, and hoped it would work on the beholder. "Revenge, Gray Eye. You want revenge."

The beholder watched her with its large, milky eye. "So. You want to sell me revenge. For what?"

"Revenge," she said sweetly, "for the Blinding Rot."

Gray Eye floated silently. All his eyes turned to watch Selura.

Yes, he wanted revenge. They all wanted revenge. The onslaught of the Blinding Rot had decimated the beholder population on board the *Spelljammer* years ago. There had been more than a hundred of them; they had been the most powerful nation aboard the great ship, stronger than even the elves. Then the disease had come: the Blinding Rot.

One by one, the beholders' eyestalks withered, then fell off like dried twigs. Death followed soon thereafter, either naturally, or at another beholder's eyes.

The xenophobic beholders hated differences in their race and despised deformities so much that they would kill. After the Blinding Rot had destroyed half the population on the *Spelljammer*, most of the handicapped survivors were slaughtered by their brethren, for fear of the Rot and for hatred of the unfit. A handful survived, mostly on hatred and dreams of revenge against those who had brought this doom to their race.

And, of course, there were the . . . unspeakables . . .

Until now, they had only suspicions about who had infected the race with the Rot. Now an opportunity for blood revenge was at hand.

"You have proof?" Gray Eye asked.

Selura nodded.

"What do you want?"

"Only one thing," she said. "Your word that the beholder

nation will not harm the Long Fangs in any way during the coming war. You will leave us alone, in peace."

Gray Eye considered. "That can be done," he said. "It is agreed. Tell me."

She approached the dais and said softly, "The neogi."

The large, milky eye glared at her. "The neogi. We have long suspected that. What proof do you have?"

"A renegade neogi is with us at the Long Fangs' tower. He admitted the neogi plot to a confederate of mine not long ago."

"The neogi . . ." Gray Eye said. "How?"

"They infected a small portion of your food. The Rot was so contagious that it took only a few days to pass among you. By the time you learned of it, it was already too late."

Gray Eye nodded his huge body. "There shall be a truce between us during the war for the *Spelljammer*. The neogi bastards will be ours." He smiled. Light flickered off the shards that were his teeth.

Later, outside, in the warm light of the flow, Selura breathed deeply and relaxed. That went well, she thought. That went perfectly.

Soon war will break throughout the ship, and in all the chaos and lovely death, the Long Fangs will remain untouched. The fighting will be over, and the other forces will be ravaged when we finally reveal ourselves.

The ship will easily belong to the Long Fangs.

To me.

Chapter Nine

• • •

"*. . . None shall be untouched by violence. The coming of the Cloakmaster shall end the cycle began by Egrestarrian, continued by Drestarin, Wrycanion, Ysaallian, Trisilliar, and the others. The end shall belong only to Creannon—the* Spelljammer—*and the end, as foretold, shall herald a new beginning, and a new birth, and life shall be as it always was. . . .*"

Scrying log of Sunholder, elf mage; reign of Dwir.

The slim, curved blade was a flash of cruel light as it arced toward his chest. Teldin had just enough time to shout "No!" when a gray blur whizzed between them and struck Cwelanas's arm with a loud crack. The elf cried out as the dagger was slung against the wall.

The gray shield rang sharply against the stone wall and clattered to the floor. Na'Shee ran past Teldin and took up her shield, then slipped the elf's dagger into her belt.

"How . . . ?" Teldin asked her.

"It's broken," Na'Shee said to Teldin. Cwelanas was gripping her wrist, and blood oozed between her fingers. "She won't be killing anybody for a while." The female warrior pressed Cwelanas against the wall with one foot, and the elf moaned in pain. Na'Shee drew her short sword and pressed the tip of the blade against the elf's throat. "We better get CassaRoc," Na'Shee said, and she shouted down the corridor.

"What are you doing here?" Teldin asked.

"CassaRoc is no fool. You have too many enemies on this

ship," the warrior woman said. "He's assigned you guards for as long as you're with us." She stepped back and called again for more guards. Within a minute, Teldin heard the rumble of feet rushing up the tower stairs, then CassaRoc was there, panting. His eyes were half closed; Teldin could tell he had been sleeping.

CassaRoc nodded once at Na'Shee. "What happened?"

Na'Shee adjusted the shield on her arm. "She wanted to see Teldin. I was stationed at the end of the corridor, and I let her pass, since I knew they were friends. I heard his door open, but I never heard her knock first. So I came up and watched from around the corner of the stairs. I heard Teldin call out a name, and she came running out. She started crying outside the door when Teldin came out. She turned around, and her eyes were . . . crazed, possessed. She pulled out a dagger and went for him." Na'Shee grinned an angry, righteous smile. "I took care of her."

CassaRoc smiled. "Good work. I knew this would happen. Didn't think it would be so soon, though." He turned to Teldin. "Are you hurt?"

Teldin shook his head. He could not take his gaze from Cwelanas. She sat huddled on the floor, crying, rubbing her shattered wrist. Her eyes looked hollow, fixed on some point in oblivion that only she could see.

CassaRoc's warriors lifted her from the floor and tightly gripped her arms. "We'll lock her up, you can count on that," CassaRoc said.

Teldin went to her. Her eyes were empty; she could not see him, but focused instead on some point behind him, or somewhere else in her mind.

"Cwelanas . . ." he said.

He grasped her shoulders and tightened his grip. "Cwelanas, why?"

She blinked and slowly moved her head around, as though she were just awakening. Her eyes met Teldin's. At first, they were blank with incomprehension; to Teldin, it looked as though she recognized no one around her, even him. Then her eyes widened as she focused on his face. Her mouth opened in a silent scream, then she thrashed violently against her guards and pulled her good arm away. Her arm went up, her fist clutching an imaginary dagger, and over and over she brought the dagger down into Teldin's chest, moaning, "Teldin, Teldin . . . I love . . . no, Teldin—*Noooo*!"

She screamed as though the agony of killing Teldin was more than she could bear. The Cloakmaster grabbed her wrist and held her hand to her side. She screamed again and struggled hard against the guards. Na'Shee grabbed her from behind, pulling Cwelanas's shirt tightly against her body. The material stretched and exposed her flesh. The top button snapped off, pinging as it hit the floor.

Teldin, curious, stared at Cwelanas. "Stop her," he ordered the guards. "Hold her still."

The guards clutched her tightly, and slowly her fighting subsided. He came forward and lifted her tear-streaked face in his hand. "Teldin," she said unconsciously. She did not see him or anyone else; she was alone and adrift in the empty world of her mind. "Teldin . . ."

He reached up and gently pulled aside the collar of her shirt. He took a deep breath.

"What is it?" CassaRoc asked.

"Come look."

The warrior craned his neck forward. Above Cwelanas's right breast a spiked, colorful symbol had been tattooed.

"Recognize it?" asked CassaRoc.

Teldin nodded slowly. To the guards he said, "Take her somewhere safe and have the healers examine her wrist." To CassaRoc he said, "You have a wizard? Clerics?"

He nodded. "Leoster. We can get King Leoster to come from the Guild tower. But what is it? What does that mean?"

"She has been bewitched somehow," Teldin said. "She tried to kill me, but she didn't want to. Someone has forced her." He gestured, and the guards took Cwelanas down the hall toward a cell. Teldin turned, his face grim.

"It's a mark of bondage," the Cloakmaster said. "I've seen something like it before . . . on the slaves of the neogi."

Cwelanas was taken to a spare room, and guards were placed on her door. A healer tended her broken wrist with bandages and strong spells, while CassaRoc, in the absence of clerics who could help, sent immediately for His Royal Majesty, the Puissant and Sage Leoster IV, also known as the

Silver Lion to his community in the Guild tower. "Leoster is the best," CassaRoc told Teldin as they closed Cwelanas in the room. "If he cannot save her, then she cannot be saved."

Within half an hour, Leoster came. The king of the Guild tower was little more than a frail old man whose life, like those of the Guild's other nobles, revolved around wizardry and hobbies. Leoster's was a large coin collection, which spanned the riches of the spheres.

But he was still a king and still a mage of considerable power, and CassaRoc knew that if Cwelanas could be cured of her mind control and an explanation discovered, Leoster was the wizard to do just that.

With his urns and potions, Leoster set to work. Cwelanas was pale and feverish, muttering incomprehensible sentences in her delirium, when Teldin and CassaRoc adjourned to the common room. The mage told them he needed time to work the poisons out of her.

Poisons, Teldin thought.

Killing.

"Everyone wants the *Spelljammer*! Everyone wants this damned cloak! And everyone wants to kill me because of some ancient legend I have never even heard of!" Teldin slammed his fist on the table. CassaRoc's tankard of ale shuddered, spilling over the rim. "When is it going to stop?"

CassaRoc blotted up the ale with a cloth. "Calm down, Cloakmaster," he said. "Save your energy for your enemies."

Teldin glared at him silently from across the table, then sat down and stared at the wall. CassaRoc quaffed his ale.

Teldin seldom became angry like this; usually he was too even tempered to explode in front of his friends, or to get carried away by strong emotion. But the anger had been building in him since they had come down to the common room, and the Cloakmaster's frustration at the attempts on his life over the past year or so—all for a gods-damned piece of cloth!—was boiling over.

"Why?" Teldin shouted. He slammed his fist down again. "Why?"

"I don't know why!" CassaRoc shouted. "Fear! Your enemies all want what you've got, so the Dark Times will not fall on them."

Teldin settled back in the wooden chair and glared at the floor. "I'm just so sick of it all," he said to no one. "I didn't come rushing into the flow because I wanted to. It was this!" He fingered the cloak. "You know, it's not like I had much of a choice." He paused and picked up a glass of cool water, drinking half of it in a single gulp. "I've had friends betray me, friends die on me. Enemies have tried to kill me—people I didn't know and had never heard of. When is it going to stop?"

"It's not going to stop," CassaRoc remarked. "It's going to get worse."

Teldin stared at him silently.

"Everybody knows you're here now. Everybody knows you're the Cloakmaster. And everybody wants your power. From what you've told me, it's been like this ever since you started your quest, and it won't end until you . . . well, do whatever you have to do on the *Spelljammer*."

Teldin looked away. "You're right." he said. "But how? What do I have to do? Is there anyone or anything that could help me, point me in the right direction? I need this quest over with. I need answers, and I need them before anyone else dies."

"Or before you do." CassaRoc shook his head and took a drink. Well, there is one place I can think of."

"Where?"

CassaRoc grunted. "The library tower. No one has been in there in my memory. There are a lot of stories built up about the place."

"Such as?"

"Supposedly, all the accumulated journals and logs of the *Spelljammer*'s captains and mages are collected there. They say the tower is protected, though."

"Protected by whom?"

The warrior laughed. "Not who. *What.* The story goes that Neridox, a wizard, sealed himself up in the library years ago. If anyone breaks in to plunder, Neridox's spirit is supposed to rise and attack all who enter."

Teldin scratched his beard. "But this is just a story, isn't it? You don't know any of this for sure?"

"Aye, just a story, but the library has remained sealed for as long as I remember. I wish there were a map we could use, instead, and follow that."

Teldin stared off again. There was something he knew he should remember, something important . . .

The dream! He had dreamt in the night. Disjointed images of beings, like the *Spelljammer*, but much, much smaller; a burst of magic and energy; and she, Gaye Goldring, had come to him. The amulet had burned on his bare chest. She had given him a message . . . What was it?

The closest are not what they seem.

Cwelanas, he knew in a flash of insight. Gaye was warning me about Cwelanas.

The mark will show the trust.

Yes. Cwelanas, again, he believed. The mark proved to him that she was not acting with her own will, but was under the insidious command of the neogi. She could be trusted, he knew now, and he was instantly relieved that his love, this time, had not been misplaced.

There was a third message. What was it Gaye had said?

CassaRoc had said something about a map to follow.

Follow the woven heart.

"Follow the woven heart," Teldin said. CassaRoc looked at him. "Follow the woven heart," he repeated.

"What in the hells of Arcas does that mean?"

Teldin said, "I'm not sure. I had a dream last night, before Cwelanas attacked me."

"And?"

"I knew a kender once, long ago. She's the one who found this amulet. I dreamt about her. I think she was trying to give me a message. Two of the things she said have already come true. She tried to warn me of the attack, and she spoke of the slave tattoo. And she told me, 'Follow the woven heart.' "

CassaRoc grunted. "Dreams can be powerful things. What do you think it means, a woven heart? Like sewing?"

Teldin shrugged. "I don't know. The cloak, perhaps?" He ran the material through his fingers. "I don't know all its properties. Maybe it could lead me to the ship's helm."

"How? How do you use the cloak normally?"

"Usually I concentrate on what I need done. Other times, it works for me unconsciously."

"Try to use it now. See if that's what she meant."

Teldin pulled the cloak around him. He concentrated on the ship, and an image of a ship's helm: a sturdy chair facing into the flow. He waited for the familiar tingle of energy that was both warm and cool, but he could tell he was trying too hard. The powers of the cloak remained dormant.

He shifted in the hard chair and clasped the cloak's edges in his hands. He let his mind go free, allowing the magic to enter his being. . . .

He opened his eyes and sighed. "Nothing."

"All right," CassaRoc said. "So we wait. We'll figure it out eventually. It has to mean something, right?"

Teldin stared off, trying again to summon the energies of the cloak, then he gave up for the night.

A guard entered the common room and walked straight to CassaRoc. "Sir," he said, then he nodded to Teldin. "Cloakmaster, there are two visitors at the tower gate who wish to see you."

"Together?" asked CassaRoc.

"No," said the guard. "One is a mind flayer." Teldin and CassaRoc both looked alarmed. Illithids were dangerous enemies. "He asked for the Cloakmaster by name. He says his name is Estriss, and he wishes to see the Cloakmaster. The other is Stardawn, of the elves, who wishes to speak with you both. I have them separated."

"Good," CassaRoc said. "We don't need mortal enemies going at each other in my tower."

"Estriss?" Teldin said. "Estriss is here?"

CassaRoc smiled. "You know him? Well, now we're getting somewhere," he said. "Send them up to my quarters. Escort them together. We'll meet them up there."

The guard hurried out, and the warriors stood and stretched.

"Estriss may be able to help me. He's been searching the spheres for the Juna—the supposed creators of the *Spelljammer*. If anyone aboard can answer my questions, it is he."

"I hope so, Teldin," CassaRoc said. "For if you don't get this quest of yours over with, I fear you may not survive another day."

* * * * *

"The war for the *Spelljammer* has begun," said Lothian Stardawn, leader of the Elven High Command, "and you, Teldin Cloakmaster, are solely responsible."

Stardawn was a haughty, ambitious elf who took care to appear impressive and commanding at all times. His armor was highly polished, and his apparel was made of the finest elven cloth. His long hair was swept back from a sharp widow's peak above his forehead. He stared at the Cloakmaster, the elf's sparkling gray eyes glinting like tempered steel. They seemed to pierce Teldin's bravado; the Cloakmaster instinctively wanted to take a step back from the aggressive elf, but he forced himself to hold his ground and stare the elf down in return.

In the doorway, a mind flayer appeared. Teldin's face involuntarily broke into a smile. "Estriss," he said, holding out his hand. "Our meeting again seems more than circumstance."

Estriss was shorter than the typical mind flayer, or perhaps his bearing was merely less alarming. His black and purple robes flowed about him, and he made an effort to overcome the shock that CassaRoc wore on his face. The illithid took Teldin's hand in his clawed mauve appendage. His voice rang softly in Teldin's mind. *So, Cloakmaster, you have arrived at last.*

"You've been expecting me?"

Indeed, Estriss said. *I have been here for some time now, and I feel the end of your journey is at hand.*

"You do not fear the Dark Times?"

Teldin, Teldin. You bear the Cloak of the First Pilot, the Ultimate Helm, the legacy of the lost Juna. Your coming here was foretold by the beholders. No, I do not fear a man's destiny. And your destiny, tied in with the legacy of the Juna, is meant to be great. Of that, I am sure.

CassaRoc welcomed the strangers and held out chairs for them. His quarters were more expansive than most of the rooms in the Tower of Thought, but just as spartan. Except for the small bar set up in one corner, the room contained only CassaRoc's small bunk, a wooden wardrobe, a trunk, and a round table, where fewer conferences had taken place than all-night card games broken only by periodic trips to the bar.

"Can we get on with this discussion?" Stardawn requested. He took a seat opposite Estriss and folded his hands on the tabletop. Estriss looked at Teldin. Teldin looked at CassaRoc. CassaRoc said, "Sit. I'll get us some ales."

Estriss said, *Not for me.* CassaRoc looked at him as though he were crazy, then nodded once, remembering that illithids preferred brains to beer.

CassaRoc shuddered.

"I'm here as the ambassador of the Elven High Command," Stardawn said. "We have heard the rumor of the Cloakmaster's coming. I am here to ensure that elven concerns are duly considered during the Dark Times, in case this human is truly the Cloakmaster we have heard about."

CassaRoc brought over the ales and sat down. "We sent for you in order to allay your fears. Teldin has no desire to harm anyone on the *Spelljammer*. The Dark Times are the furthest thing from his mind."

You may rest assured that Teldin is the Cloakmaster of legend, Estriss said. *He bears the Ultimate Helm.*

Stardawn scowled. "Speak not to me, illithid. I will have nothing to do with you. My concerns are with the alleged Cloakmaster." He turned to Teldin. "An ultimate helm is nothing," he said. "Helmsmen have come and gone, and they all bore ultimate helms." He paused. "The elves have no argument if you wish to claim to be the Cloakmaster of myth . . . if, indeed, you can. We simply wish to ensure that our concerns are met.

"Already battles are breaking out across the ship. As we speak, my brothers are fighting those of the goblin alliance, an age-old feud that will finally result in the destruction of the disgusting goblin hordes." The elf took a breath and pointed a finger at Teldin. "Your powers are many. We need assurance that the elves will be offered protection against all its enemies."

Teldin considered his words. "What can I do for you?"

Cloakmaster, Estriss said, *your duties, and your abilities, will soon become clear. Through all my research, at least one line of information has become clear: I believe it is your duty to ensure peace throughout the* Spelljammer, *for the elves and all the races. Minor skirmishes and feuds are inevitable, but war and wanton murder are things that no race must be allowed to commit.*

Teldin looked Stardawn in the eyes. "I've spent too much time and come too far on my quest to allow atrocities such as this to take place under my authority."

Stardawn said, "That has not stopped the beholders from conquering the minotaurs—"

"And it hasn't stopped you from engaging the goblins," CassaRoc commented.

The two warriors glared at each other over the table.

"I do not yet have all my answers," Teldin said. "I have been called to the *Spelljammer*, and now it seems I must wait, but I know not for what. The battles seem to have begun without me, or because of me. If I can, I'll stop them all. Already I've seen too much death and devastation, and I still can't get many clear answers why.

"But I have had enough. This cloak is more than an ultimate helm. It is the Ultimate Helm, I believe. I can't tell you how I know, or why this helm is different. It just is. But if it is my destiny to take the helm of the *Spelljammer*, I will see it through to the end.

"If the Elven High Command wants peace, then it shall have it. A ship as wondrous as the *Spelljammer* should preserve and cherish life, not destroy it.

"If you demand a guarantee, then you have it." Teldin stretched out his hand to the elf.

Stardawn rose from the table, ignoring Teldin's proffered hand. "Your words are noble, human, but I have no proof that you are the Cloakmaster foretold by legend, nor that your word is any better than that of any Long Fang."

Teldin took back his hand and shrugged. He briefly explained to Stardawn and Estriss how the cloak had become his and how he had found the *Spelljammer*. He finished by recounting the attacks on him as soon as he had arrived. He offered a demonstration of the cloak's powers, but the elf shook his head.

Stardawn was silent for a moment, then he said, "I must take this information to the high command. The decision will be ours together."

He nodded once, then left.

CassaRoc commented, "He didn't touch his drink." He pulled it over to him.

That did not go well. The mind flayer's voice was loud in Teldin's mind.

"No, Estriss, it didn't," said Teldin. "In my previous dealings with elves, I've found them to be nothing but contradictory in all their affairs. First they're trying to kill me, then they're my best friends."

"You can say that about everyone," CassaRoc said.

They have their own agenda, Estriss said, *whatever that is. I would be cautious of that one, though. There is a fire inside him that burns almost uncontrollably. I would not trust Stardawn for all the gold in Realmspace.*

Teldin looked at his friend and smiled. He thought, I'm not always sure I trust you either. What he said was, "I should have known you would arrive here before me."

I was lucky. The arcane I traveled with already knew of the Spelljammer*'s position. I have since been accepted by the illithid community as a friend and an advisor.*

"And your research?" Teldin inquired. "What can you tell me?"

With the cloak, you may know more than I. What do you need to know?

"First," CassaRoc interrupted, "where do the mind flayers stand?"

Estriss was silent at first. *I have spoken with Lord Trebek, and he wished me to express his regrets that the illithid community can do nothing at this time. He is taking the all-too-human attitude of 'wait and see.'*

However, I will place my trust in Teldin. I have no loyalty to the Spelljammer's illithids. My loyalty is to knowledge. You and I . . . Well, he said mentally, *I will help you all I can.*

"Good," Teldin said. "I respect that, my friend." He leaned across the table. "Now, what can you tell me? I need to become the captain of the *Spelljammer*, and I don't even know how."

Ahhh. Estriss's facial tentacles twitched with interest. *This is one of the first things I discovered in the books of Lord Trebek. Your first task is to find what is called the* adytum.

"*Adytum*? How do I find that? What is it?"

Estriss made a curious sucking sound, the equivalent of illithid laughter. *You don't find it. It finds you.*

"What does that mean?"

The adytum *is a chamber of some kind, hidden from all but those who are worthy. Now, let me ask you, have you felt any odd yearnings while on board, a feeling to get out and explore the* Spelljammer*?*

Teldin considered. "No, not really. Well—" The dream. When he had awakened from the dream, he had gotten out of bed and wanted to get out, to explore. "Yes," he said. "Yes. Once, but—"

Excellent. This is what you are to do: Listen to your feelings. When you are called, you must answer. The end of your quest lies there, in the adytum.

Soon, it will call you, and you will hear.

Estriss stayed and talked for another hour, going over his research. Teldin was overwhelmed, forgetting much of it, hoping that it would come to him later, when he needed it. The growing of brain mold was not all that interesting, nor was an examination of the Guild tower's patterns in hobbying.

Estriss's research was best when it touched on the truths or near truths of the *Spelljammer*'s legends. Estriss was especially interested in Teldin's account of his journey to Nex, and his confrontation with the devolved Juna and their protective world-mind. He was disappointed to hear of their regression to the primitive, but was fascinated by the concept of a living planet.

"I have discovered something else," Teldin said, "but without the benefit of hard facts. I am receiving images, feelings of some sort, of events long ago that had to do with the *Spelljammer*. I do not pretend to understand all that I have seen, but I have been shown that the *Spelljammer* was not created by solely the Juna. I believe they were but one race that helped in its creation."

Estriss stared at him curiously. *How do you know this?*

Teldin wondered if the mind flayer would take him seriously. "The amulet. It is a guide to the *Spelljammer*. It has shown me much, and since I've been here, I have seen even more, visions of the past, I believe. The *Spelljammer* was created, yes, but I don't know why. It is a living thing, and I believe it was created through the combination of magic and life—a life-form that has long been extinct. And it was here, at the Broken Sphere."

Estriss watched him closely. *There's something else, isn't there?* Estriss queried.

Teldin nodded. "The *Spelljammer*. It did this."

CassaRoc stared silently, his ale frozen halfway to his mouth.

"Did what?" he asked.

"The Broken Sphere. Thousands of thousands of years ago, it was known as . . . Ouiyan. Then, in the throes of the *Spelljammer*'s creation, the great ship itself destroyed the sphere. There were—" Teldin had to think. The number came to him. "There were eighteen planets here. All are dead now." He paused. "All dead. The *Spelljammer* is a murderer of worlds."

* * * * *

Stardawn paused in the open market to examine game pieces of molded pewter. He had found out what he needed to know. The Cloakmaster—for he was indeed the Cloakmaster—had no idea of his own power. There was still time to kill the simpleton and steal the cloak. Stardawn, alone among so many, knew that with the helm, all the *Spelljammer*'s secrets would be his.

No more rumors. No more gossip. With Teldin Moore dead, all his theories about magical items brought to the ship would be proven correct. If they were, the greatest ship in all the spheres would soon be his, and his elven brethren would reign over the universe.

Lothian Stardawn would be their lord.

Humans, he thought, they're all so gullible.

Chapter Ten

• • •

"Amid the death,
Amid the hatred,
One shall come
To honor the ages.
Blood will run
From bow to stern;
Destiny calls,
And all will learn
That Life is not
To be torn asunder.
Life is wisdom
And visions of wonder. . . ."

Excerpt, "A Chant Between Two Worlds" by an anonymous bard; reign of Elad.

The main level of the beholder ruins was uncommonly bright. Usually the beholders disdained such light, preferring instead the comfortable coolness of the shadows.

But, for their honored guests, they were more than willing to make an exception.

Amid the toppled columns and the ruined statuary, ShiCaga the Enchantress, chieftess of the ogre population, stood surrounded by her towering sons, HiRotu and AziKash, and ten of her misshapen ogre warriors. ShiCaga was beautiful by ogre standards, and her face was decorated with white powders and lotions that made her appear like an ugly, towering ghost.

Opposite the ogres, waiting near one of the broad staircases spiraling up to the beholder quarters, stood a dozen representatives of the minotaur race. Onehorn, their newly elected leader, snorted angrily at the head of the group. His was the mark of the broken horn; and his was the shame of murdering his own king under thrall of the beholders' hypnotic powers. The eye tyrants had released the minotaurs from their spells, knowing well that the charms would shortly wear off anyway, and that the minotaurs could not be charmed forever. A treaty, Gray Eye had decided, would keep the minotaurs on the beholders' leash and send a powerful signal to the *Spelljammer*'s general population.

Then the minotaurs could be disposed of when the time was right.

Onehorn groused at the beholders' rule, but he also knew that a treaty would keep the minotaurs alive—long enough, at least, until they could plan a suitable revenge—and from under the eye tyrants' spells of subservience. He shuddered with anger, remembering how Breakox had been slaughtered by his own uncontrollable hand. *Breakox's blood was on his hands*! Now, though, the protection of the minotaurs was most important. Vengeance, he determined, would most definitely come later, but his shame would last forever.

The final group arrived through the ruins' huge doors. Each standing more than twenty feet tall, the seven hill giants stooped to enter the ruins, then stretched to their full heights inside. As they came to a stop in the center of the room, the colony of beholders, led by their ancient leader, Gray Eye, floated down through the circular entrance in the ceiling.

The beholders, surrounded by their invited guests, hovered a few feet off the floor. On a table behind them lay a long piece of parchment detailing a series of agreements.

"Welcome," Gray Eye said, "to the first treaty of the beholders, and to the beginning of the end of the neogi."

The hill giants, a family of renegades from the giant tower who felt stifled under Taja Deeplunder's rule, grunted their approval. Their substitute leader, Torg Stoneater, rested his hand on the hilt of his mammoth battle-axe. "We welcome the chance to fight with our allies, the minotaurs. The giants have been lazy for too long under the rule of Taja Deeplunder. She is more neutral in matters of war than we prefer. We crave battle. We crave the spilling of our enemies' blood."

Gray Eye watched the giant with its opaque eye. "You will have your chance soon, Stoneater. The battles have already begun across the ship, and we must strike against the neogi before the Cloakmaster brings about the Dark Times. If we hesitate, our forces will be the first to feel starvation under the rule of the humans."

The assembled forces nodded in agreement. ShiCaga of the ogres stepped forward and said, "Let's get on with it, then. Let's sign the damned thing."

Gray Eye stared at her balefully. "That, chieftess, is precisely what you shall do. You have all read the treaty." The eye tyrant asked the ogre, "Do you wish the honors?"

ShiCaga took the quill from the inkwell on the table and hurriedly signed her name. "There," she said, "now let's draw some blood."

Onehorn strode to the table and signed the treaty, then turned to Stoneater and handed him the quill. "You honor us," the minotaur said.

"Your leader was strong," Stoneater remarked. "He was originally of the hill giants, as you probably know. We respected his strength, as we respect yours." The giant cast a quick glance at the beholders. "There will be time later . . ." he whispered.

Onehorn nodded briskly and walked away. The giant signed the treaty, then threw the pen onto the table.

"We are done," said Gray Eye. "We are now the Beholder Alliance, and I promise you unconditional victory in our war against the neogi.

"Our resources are great, our blades are sharp, and our forces are mighty. Now . . . we must plan for battle. By the end of the day, our swords will be red with the cold blood of our enemies, and then our prize will be laid out before us and our forces will be unbeatable.

"The neogi will be dead. We will have nothing to fear from the Cloakmaster, and the Dark Times will never come."

* * * * *

Building by building, Gaye explored the great ship. Her astral body floated unseen among the humans and the dwarves, the illithids and the halflings; through the open market she went, and above, through the ship's stores, and through all the floors and rooms of Leoster's Guild tower. She passed silently through the walls of the shivak terminal and the illithid tower and stayed for a while in the Citadel of Kova and studied the actions of the dwarves.

Although she had commanded invisibility to the people of the *Spelljammer*, she could see her own innate energies flowing about her, permeating her being with soft, golden light. Her robes, the robes of an acolyte, whispered around her as though in a spectral wind, and the belt that was her badge of accomplishment glowed from within the ancient symbols that had been affixed there.

Her psionics training was complete. Under the tutelage of the fal One Six Nine, she had become a master of psionics, of mental powers that seemed, to some, to be magical. She had long been apart from Teldin, a man she had come to love, and then had to leave. With One Six Nine, she had decided to seek her own destiny, as had the Cloakmaster, and it was then, in her final days of training, that her psionic abilities had shown her that their destinies were intertwined, that her trial by fire would take place, not by the fal's side, but millions of miles away, on a ship called the *Spelljammer*, and by the side of the Cloakmaster . . .

Where she had always wanted to be.

Invisible, she saw the battle begin between the ship's elves and goblins, as an imperious elf named Carrara, who bore a shield emblazoned with an elven eagle, ran her broadsword through a goblin named Kral. Then the forces were met on both sides, and she could sense the pain and the souls as blood was spilled; she took her leave and vanished through the walls of the goblin quarters, then back, into the *Spelljammer*'s tail.

On her journey through the ship, she saw armies readying for battle, warriors practicing sword thrusts before mirrors. In meeting halls and in taverns she heard whispers of treachery, threats of war. She overheard words of hatred and watched weapons being sharpened and prepared. Over and over she heard talk of a myth, foretelling the coming of the Cloakmaster. In the chambers of the elves, the illithids, all the longest-lived races that populated the great ship, those who remembered the last Dark Times were filled with fear, for the Dark Times meant nothing but a long period of starvation for the weak, of interminable battles over food and supplies.

It was the coming of the Cloakmaster, she knew, that would bring war once again. Soon the decks of the *Spelljammer* would run red as the ship's various factions killed to take the cloak before the Cloakmaster could achieve his destiny.

From somewhere across the universe, she shuddered.

Soon her search through the *Spelljammer* would be complete. The astral form of Gaeadrelle Goldring, whose body lay in a deep trance several million miles away, in Herdspace, would soon return to the *Spelljammer* and to Teldin Moore, to Teldin the Cloakmaster, and help guide him to his destiny . . .

A destiny she was not sure he would survive.

Chapter Eleven

• • •

". . . It is not the answers that are important. It is the quest itself that defines its own significance. It is the courage to follow the course dictated by your most secret, innermost needs, and not a course directed by your base desires or follies. When you complete a quest, you have found yourself. . . ."

Bestwick, adventurer; reign of InDar.

Leoster IV, king of the Guild tower, stayed with Cwelanas for more than three hours—time spent purging the noxious evils that had been twisted throughout Cwelanas's mind.

The damage to her mind was undeniably the work of a powerful neogi mage; the bright tattoo was proof enough of neogi handiwork, but its placement was unnecessary; the tattoo was nonfunctional, simply a sign of the black mage's sadistic ego and his hatred for humanity.

At first, Cwelanas was restrained to the bed with ropes, and her injured arm was strapped to her stomach. Later, Leoster kept her calm with spells and absorbed some of her pain with his own considerable empathic skills. He felt her horror blossom like a blood-red pinpoint of fire as he saw what the neogi had put Cwelanas through, as he felt her mind being raped by the neogi and twisted to murder the man she loved.

Leoster screamed out with her once, tied by her pain and fear. The guards rushed in, thinking the neogi spy had done something horrible to the old man, and they gaped at the arcane sigils drawn upon the walls in what looked like blood and chalk, at the intricate patterns etched in saltpeter and ground bones upon the floor, at the flickering balls of light floating brightly at her head and hands and feet. Leoster, drenched with sweat, seemed feral, no longer a man born of nobility, the head of a royal house. His body was taut and shivering with the strain of sucking the evils from Cwelanas's soul. He stared at the guards and shouted through bared teeth, "Get out! Get out now, or she will be lost to us!"

The guards backed out slowly, staring at the elf's half-closed eyes, swirling inside with a pale blue mist. They closed the door behind them, and stood outside with their swords ready. Never again would they consider Leoster anything less than a true king.

Leoster came out a long time later. His face was drawn and pale, seemingly a decade older than when he had gone into her room. But he stood proudly, confident that the elf had been saved. Under his care, her seizures of murderous rage had been quelled, and he had put her under a spell of sleep, so that his magic could more easily work its way through her mind and cleanse her of all evil influence.

Teldin paced outside the door. Leoster shook his head, beaded with sweat. "They did their work on her, I grant you, Cloakmaster. For a while there, I thought she would be lost forever."

He looked into Teldin's face. "Part of her didn't want to live, not after what she tried to do to you. You'll need to take care of that, I think. I've done all I can do, all anyone can do. Her elven strength helped her. If she had been human, I doubt she would have survived the neogi magic."

He placed a hand on Teldin's shoulder. "Now, if you love her—and if these old eyes of mine can still see right, I think you do—*you* have to bring her back. Show her you care, that you understand it wasn't her. That's what she's afraid of: that you won't forgive her."

Teldin nodded silently, then thanked the king for coming. Leoster quickly admonished him to let Cwelanas sleep for a while. "Don't go in just yet. She needs her rest," Leoster said. "She needs to heal. There will be time enough for reconciliations."

Teldin let her sleep for several hours before his concern for her got the better of him. He left a meeting with CassaRoc and Chaladar and climbed the stairs to her quarters.

Two armed guards stood outside in the corridor. Teldin thought they were unnecessary, but CassaRoc had insisted, as a precaution. "Look what happened last time," he had said.

Teldin reached for the door.

The room smelled of incense and medicine. He closed the door behind him and stood over her, watching her face in the light from the flow.

Her hair was damp and stringy, where she had perspired heavily during her struggles against Leoster's magic. Her face seemed thinner, paler, and she breathed peacefully in her sleep.

Her wrist bones had been healed by CassaRoc's healers, but her arm was heavily bandaged as a precaution, and had been salved with a numbing potion. The sheets had fallen to reveal her shoulders, the swell of her breasts. He reached to cover her, then stared in rising anger at the brand that would forever mar her once-perfect flesh.

Teldin knew he would kill the neogi bastard who had marked her. For once, Teldin wanted blood on his hands.

He brought the sheets around her neck and sat down in a wooden chair near the bunk. He watched Cwelanas for a few minutes, then let his eyes close as he rested. Far too much had happened to him already, and he had been aboard the *Spelljammer* for only a day. Now he felt it in his bones, and the soft light and the smells relaxed him, washed over him like a spell.

He woke to a gentle touch on his knee. He pulled himself up and smiled at Cwelanas, who had reached out and awakened him. He held her hand in his, felt her cool, soft skin against his calloused palm.

They spoke simultaneously.

"How do you feel?" he said.

"Are you all right?" said she.

Cwelanas smiled weakly. "I'm sorry," she whispered. A tear formed in the corner of her eye.

Teldin bent over and kissed her hand. "You didn't do anything, you know that. It was the neogi."

He could see in her golden eyes that, yes, she knew that,

but she still held herself responsible.

He ran his hand along her face. "You have to stop blaming yourself. You had no control over what they did to you."

She wept softly then, into Teldin's hand. He wiped her face with a cool, damp cloth.

"You don't know how I fought them," she said quietly. "You don't know what they did to me."

Teldin looked into her eyes and said nothing. What could he say? He had been through a neogi torture session himself, not long after his quest had begun. He knew first-hand their innate hatred of other races, their inbred egotism that labeled other lives simply as "meat."

He knew the pain he heard when his bones had cracked, when he had tasted the warm tang of his own blood.

He knew.

He held her in his arms. There was nothing to say.

After a while, she told him what had really happened to her after their parting at Sancrist. Her voice was flat and emotionless, toneless, as though the telling were merely mechanical, a way of purging herself of the black neogi poisons. But it was more than that. She felt drained, empty, worthless. She could feel nothing, right now, except shame. How could Teldin feel anything for her if she could feel nothing herself?

"I told the truth about the wildspace pirates," she began, "of Krynnspace. But not all of it.

"They captured me not long after you left. They wanted your cloak, and somehow—I never found out how—they tracked me down. They thought I knew where you went, and why.

"They kept me for several days, until we were overtaken by a squadron of neogi ships outside Krynnspace—deathspiders and a mindspider. The pirates had no chance. The neogi forces were larger and stronger, and the pirates were easily killed.

"The neogi wanted me, too, to hunt down the cloak. I was tortured." She choked up. Teldin handed her a mug of cold water. "I told them nothing, for I had no idea where you were. Then their commander, B'Laath'a, decided to . . . make me a slave . . . mentally.

"He went inside my mind for information. Then he planted

things there. He tried to subvert me. He wanted you dead, to get the cloak. The neogi know all about ultimate helms, and how they guide their bearers out into space. They knew it was only a matter of time until you reached the *Spelljammer.* It was your destiny, even they could see that.

"I was their last chance to seize the *Spelljammer.* One neogi ship brought me here, just myself and B'Laath'a. I don't know how he found the *Spelljammer* from so far away, but B'Laath'a is an evil mage, and I know he made sacrifices to get the gods to give him information.

"He deliberately set me adrift in the phlogiston, right in the *Spelljammer*'s path. B'Laath'a landed here. After he ingratiated himself with Master Coh, the two of them made sure that the humans discovered me in the flow. He knew they would try to rescue me, and then I'd be planted in the community where you would first be accepted.

"I lost track of how long we waited for you to arrive. They used to smuggle me through a secret passage into Coh's quarters in the neogi tower. They never let up, pushing themselves into my mind with their spells . . .

"I fought against them, Teldin. I did, I swear I did. Even as I was trying to kill you, I was struggling inside to control myself, to take control of my actions. I've never felt so powerless. And all that time, I was trying to scream at you, to warn you, to make myself just let go of the dagger . . ."

She was quiet for so long then that Teldin thought she had fallen asleep in his arms. Then she said, "He marked me."

Her eyes glazed over. "He kept me awake while he did it, to make sure I understood that I was property, his property." She paused. "It burned. He laughed at me as he marked me. He made a joke about how it would make my flesh tender, tastier."

"I think our mages can take it off," Teldin said softly.

Cwelanas was silent, then she shifted away from him and turned to face the wall.

"What is it?" Teldin asked.

He heard her sniffle into the sheets. "How can you even stand to be with me, after what I did?"

"You didn't do it. In all of this, you are innocent. You've just been another pawn of the neogi, and, believe me, they will pay for hurting you."

He knew when he said it that his feelings for her were more than friendship, even more than simple attraction. He wanted revenge against the black-hearted creatures, because he had cared for Cwelanas for a long time, had cared for her more than he had ever known. Now, seeing her huddled beside him and so vulnerable, marked with her shame both mentally and physically, he realized he truly loved her.

He chided himself for being so dense, so caught up in his quest, that he had not immediately recognized it as love. And he wondered if he would be feeling this way now if it hadn't been for his dream of Gaye Goldring and her cryptic messages. Yes, the trust for Cwelanas was there, and he knew it was not misplaced; but he was not sure he could have acknowledged his emotions if the dream had not slapped him awake.

Or had it been a dream?

No, he realized, it was not a dream. It had been Gaye, calling to him, he knew, but from where? All the way from Herdspace? And how? He shook his head, wondering if he would ever understand the true meaning of his journey, the simple "why" that had pulled him out into the endless sea of the flow.

Still, Gaye's thoughts had been of him, and of those he cared for. *The mark will show the trust.*

Aside from proving Cwelanas's innocence, did that also mean that Cwelanas cared for him? That he could trust in her love as well as her loyalty?

He was not sure, and he hated that; he had been too trustful in the past, and, although he wanted to trust Cwelanas with his life, after Rianna's treachery, and that of Aelfred Silverhorn, he knew he was scared, perhaps too scared, to fully trust anyone again.

He fought down his feelings of distrust and fear. He watched Cwelanas, lying on her side. Her chest was rising slowly, softly, and he knew that she had fallen asleep again. Cwelanas had suffered torture and mental rape and had gone through what would have been too much for him, more than he could have expected of anyone. Now he knew he must go through the fire for her.

He smiled and gently disentangled himself from her. He tucked her in and kissed the side of her head.

He watched her for another minute, then he whispered, in a voice so soft that he could hardly hear it himself, "I love you."

He closed the door behind him.

But Cwelanas had not been asleep at all, and her heart had thudded like thunder when she had heard him confess his love.

She wanted to spin around and reach out for him, shouting his name, and have him take her up in his arms and hold her tight, so the pain, the memories of the sharp instruments of the neogi, would all go away.

She heard the metallic click of the door latch. She turned as she heard his feet echo down the corridor. But she could not reach out, she could not cry his name. She had hurt him too much; and now, no matter what he had said, she knew that he belonged here, fulfilling his quest on the *Spelljammer*, and that anything he once felt for her would be better left forgotten.

For how could he really love someone who had tried to kill him?

Forget him, she thought. He'll never be yours. You don't deserve him.

When she finally fell back to sleep, her pillows were dark with her tears.

Chapter Twelve

• • •

". . . Why is it that most of us have never considered leaving? Do we not have the free will granted to us by the gods? Why are so many of us ignorant—or uninterested—in the Spelljammer*'s true nature? Most of us do not realize that the* Spelljammer *is a ship: it is believed by some to be a floating city, or a living beast upon which we live, or even a god. Even now, I am not sure that my perception of things is correct. . . .*

". . . This absence of curiosity among the populace is itself most curious. . . ."

Nab Featherley, gnome; reign of the Shrouded Man

In the moist darkness of the horned tower, Drikka and Lord Trebek of the illithids walked silently down the tower stairs to the audience chamber on the main level. Drikka opened the door for the leader and Trebek made a grand, silent entrance, swirling his long black cape dramatically around him.

The walls of the horned tower were hung with long red draperies, highlighting ancient tapestries and sculptures that portrayed the history of the illithid community on board the *Spelljammer.* Light rods cast a pale glow from golden sconces set in the walls, creating deep shadows in the corners of the room and behind the aged tapestries of silk and golden thread.

It was in such a shadow that Estriss hid, safe from the suspicious eyes of his brethren. He knew well the hateful nature of illithids, and he knew well that Lord Trebek had been scornful of him from the start.

This address had been kept secret from Estriss; it had been only through a barely overheard conversation between two mind flayers that Estriss had learned of Trebek's proclamation, so he hid in an alcove behind a tapestry in the audience chamber and waited.

The great audience chamber was crowded with the *Spelljammer*'s entire illithid community. Dressed in their traditional gowns of black or gray, the mind flayers turned as one upon Trebek's entrance, then bowed their heads as he took his seat upon the royal dais. Drikka bowed as well and stood with the other illithids to Trebek's right.

There is much to discuss, Trebek announced in the hissing thought-speech of the mind flayers, *much that concerns the future of the illithids.*

The mass of seventy illithids stood in silent respect for Lord Trebek. Although he was a relative newcomer to the *Spelljammer*, Trebek had wisely stayed out of clan politics and had enjoyed a neutral position among his people, garnering friends on all sides who had eventually recognized him as their leader.

Breakox is dead. He let that sink in for a moment as the mind flayers shifted uneasily. *Breakox is dead, murdered by the beholders. Our plans to take control of the minotaurs must be abandoned, as they appear to be under beholder control.*

Trebek rested his elbows on the arms of his chair and steepled his claws before him. *We are not warriors,* he thought to the mind flayers. *We are illithids—we control. There is much we can do to wrest the* Spelljammer *from the hands of our enemies—and much we can do to foster war among the other races, while keeping ourselves well protected.*

He stood and paced before the mind flayers. Estriss watched Trebek silently from his hiding place. Enemies, Trebek had said. Estriss knew how illithids thought: everyone was a potential enemy, especially if they were not of the mind flayers.

The Cloakmaster has come. Battles have been fought between the minotaurs and the beholders, between the elves and the goblins. As our enemies destroy themselves, we will be in the perfect position to swoop down upon the remaining forces and enslave them. The needs of the illithids are of paramount concern. When the Dark Times fall upon the ship, we will need more than our tasteless brain mold to survive. We will need the brains of our enemies.

The assembled mind flayers began to hiss in expectation. Trebek knew precisely what words to use, what promises to make, what strings to pull. Like any good politician, he knew to promise them everything, then deny it all later.

I have worked hard to keep our enemies on edge with each other. Our position now is highly . . . tentative. He stopped at the front of the dais and looked deliberately into their midst. *Our ultimate enemies are the elves. They are perhaps the strongest community on board, and I believe that any battles in which we become involved should directly affect the downfall of the elves.*

The mind flayers hissed agreement.

Our position is one of mental and sociological superiority. I will not allow our race to become sullied by the warlike emotions of the other races.

We must stay out of this war for the Spelljammer *until it is clear that we can win. It is only by fostering enmity between the elves and the goblins that our enemies will be decimated to the point that we will become victorious. Let us antagonize the elves, and then attack, so that the* Spelljammer *will be ours!*

The assemblage applauded its leader, and Trebek went on to detail his plans for insurrection among the races aboard the *Spelljammer.*

Alone among the illithids, hidden from the eyes of his evil brethren, Estriss watched and listened silently, holding counsel with himself. Only Estriss considered the *Spelljammer* an intrinsic force in the universe, as something more than an object of conquest.

Only he, of all the mind flayers, had a friend who was human.

With all the others of his own kind surrounding him, he felt completely, utterly alone.

Enemies, Trebek had said.

Estriss listened and watched and wondered who the enemies really were.

Chapter Thirteen

• • •

"*. . . Racial warfare will be ignored and will lead to unity whenever a threat is made to the* Spelljammer. *Then the races will come together and fight as brothers to preserve their cherished home. I myself have seen the lords of the illithids and elves, pitched in glorious battle, drop their arms as the* Spelljammer *was attacked from the Rainbow Ocean and fight side by side . . .*"

Bernard, scribe of the Guild; *Scroll of the Seven Suns.*

After speaking with Cwelanas in her quarters, Teldin went downstairs to watch CassaRoc and Chaladar, the paladin, put their warriors through sword practice and hand-to-hand combat. Then they went to the tower's armory and checked the condition of the weapons. A feeling of anxiety had come upon him suddenly, as soon as word had reached the tower of the meeting going on in the beholder ruins. The possible alliance of the beholders with the minotaurs, ogres, and hill giants meant only trouble for the humans under the flag of the Cloakmaster.

"Nothing good can come of this," CassaRoc said.

Chaladar grunted once, and his hand settled on the hilt of his sword. "They are preparing for war. All of them, the unhumans."

CassaRoc smiled. "Ah, well. What does it matter? With the warriors of all the Human Collective, and our unhuman allies, they will not stand a chance. Ahh, I like a good fight."

Teldin's chest suddenly grew tight and warm. He stopped in midstride.

"What's wrong?" Chaladar asked.

"This is wrong," Teldin said, clutching his chest. CassaRoc came up and looked him over.

Chaladar said, "Are you well?"

"I have to do something," Teldin said, "get out. We're doing nothing here but talking. I need to—to roam. The *adytum.* I need to find the *Spelljammer*'s *adytum.*"

They went to the common room and sat at a table. "Perhaps its time you did some exploring," CassaRoc said. "A few of our warriors, with you in disguise . . ."

Teldin said abruptly, "It's in that direction."

CassaRoc turned from the tap. Teldin was standing, pointing a finger at the tower wall.

"That's toward the stern," Chaladar said slowly. "How do you know?"

Teldin shook his head. "I don't know. It's just a feeling . . ." He looked down at the amulet, where he clutched his chest, and felt a shock ripple across his skin. "Paladine's blood! What . . . ?"

He ripped open his shirt.

Above his heart, his skin glowed in the shape of the amulet. The flesh was warm, pulsating with a tingle of gentle heat.

"The design!" Teldin said.

A pattern, a maze inside the circular ring, glowed on his chest. He remembered the message from Gaye: *Follow the woven heart.*

"This is how I find it," he said. " 'Follow the woven heart.' Somehow, this is a map . . . no, a compass, that will lead me to the *adytum.*"

CassaRoc came over and placed his finger on the glowing pattern. "I don't feel a thing."

"It's warm," Teldin said.

"Not to me. Is it always like this?"

"This is the first time I've seen it." He thought for a moment. "No. I saw it in a dream. But I don't think it was really a dream."

CassaRoc looked questioningly at Chaladar, then back to Teldin. "Maybe it's time to go looking for this . . . *adytum* of yours."

"Maybe," Teldin said, "but I don't know what to do once I

get there. Perhaps a visit to the library tower would be best."

A guard then entered the room and told CassaRoc that an elven messenger had arrived with a decision. The leaders decided to go down and receive the elf alone, as he had been ordered to hurry back to the Elven High Command and assist in the battle against the goblins.

Several minutes later, Teldin nervously paced the confines of CassaRoc's common room, waiting for CassaRoc and Chaladar to return.

Despite his host's generosity and the increasing trust and loyalty of his warriors, Teldin was growing increasingly claustrophobic inside the Tower of Thought. It had been hours since his conversation with Cwelanas, and the uncertainty of the entire situation on board the *Spelljammer* had begun to gnaw at him.

He did not crave action or bloodshed; he simply wanted to get out of the damned tower and explore, to search, to finally do what he had come here for.

He touched his amulet and watched the light reflect off its engraved surface. Is this the feeling Estriss had asked about? The yearning to be active, to search for his answers out there, among the others?

Is this the call?

He walked behind the bar and poured himself a mug of cold water, then gulped down half the mug and filled it up again.

The desire to leave, to get something done, burned at him like the sign of the amulet upon his chest.

He looked up suddenly and cocked his head. There had been a noise from somewhere outside, like a clap of thunder, or an explosion. Out in the hall he heard shouting and the sound of the warriors' feet as they rushed to their positions throughout the tower.

He flung open the door. "What's going on?" he shouted.

There were cries from above, then a warrior rushed by. Teldin reached out and grabbed his arm. "Wait. What's happening?"

The fighter gasped, then managed, "The neogi. They've started fighting the neogi." Then he turned and ran up the tower stairs.

Teldin heard more warriors rushing up the stairs, then CassaRoc and Chaladar ran up beside him. "The war has definitely begun," CassaRoc said. "Chaladar's scouts spied the start of the battle not five minutes ago. The beholders, the minotaurs, and the ogres just couldn't wait. They're all in it together."

"They're in the neogi tower now," Chaladar said. "They may not be able to hold it. Already a fire has started. The explosion blackened the face of the beholder ruins. The minotaurs are struggling to put it out, but who knows what will happen with this war? Their pointless battles may destroy us all."

"What are we going to do?" Teldin asked.

"Nothing," CassaRoc said. "Absolutely nothing . . . yet." He held up a folded piece of paper, decorated with a broken seal of red wax. "A communique from our friends, the elves."

He cleared his throat. " 'We, the Elven High Command of the Sphere Wanderer *Spelljammer*, do hereby promise all aid and assistance during the coming times of war to the Cloakmaster, Teldin Moore. We do hereby sign in treaty with the Cloakmaster and his allies, the Human Collective, to fight to the death our mortal enemies, and to ensure the safety and purity of the elven race.' "

"And it's signed by Stardawn and the elven leader himself, Admiral Drova Highstar."

Teldin took it from CassaRoc and read it, though slowly. Teldin had never read very much, nor very well. "Can we believe this?"

Chaladar shrugged. "Personally, I trust very few people. These elves think they're needed everywhere, or nothing would get done. Frankly, I'd rather have them with us than against us, but I don't want them at all.

"Ah, well. The Human Collective will never fall, even if the elves fight against us."

"And Stardawn?" Teldin said.

"Trust your mind flayer friend on that," CassaRoc said. "Stardawn is his own man. He has his own agenda."

"What does that mean?" Chaladar inquired.

"'Means I wouldn't trust him farther than I could spit," CassaRoc said.

" `He's mad that trusts in the honor of an elf.' "

They both stared at Chaladar.

He shrugged. "Poetry. I read it somewhere."

The Cloakmaster spoke to himself. "They're all so formal and proper, the elves, but in the end," he said, crumpling the message, "it's just a piece of paper."

Chaladar nodded. "Well said."

CassaRoc finished the ale he had earlier left on the table. He made a face; it had grown too warm. "Come on," he said. "Why don't we go up to the Guild tower and take a look?"

Teldin said, "At what?"

CassaRoc smiled. "The battle with the neogi. We can see over the ship from the top of the Guild. With luck, the neogi and the others will kill each other off. Maybe we won't have to fight them at all."

"Too bad," Chaladar said, smiling grimly. "Too bad."

CassaRoc led the way down into the lower floors of the tower. There, a series of passages led to the other human towers, and across into the cavernous Human Collective.

Leoster's guards recognized CassaRoc and Chaladar and let the three men pass. Within the Guild tower, Teldin saw many of King Leoster's fellow nobles going about their daily duties; but many more were occupied with activities that clearly fell beyond their chores as noble warriors: gardening, researching such topics as the temperatures of differing wildspace and the tooth sizes of unhuman races, and collecting games and ancient books. One noble, a council member named Charnom, even boasted an extensive collection of jokes from across the known spheres . . . most of which were off-color, and had to do with buxom females of all the known races.

At the top of the Guild tower, six guards had been posted, keeping watch on all sides. The Rainbow Ocean was a flare of brilliant colors, a swirling chaos surrounding the *Spelljammer* on all sides. Teldin, CassaRoc, and Chaladar went to the starboard side and peered over the roofs of the other buildings, toward the neogi tower.

CassaRoc pointed. "There. Do you see?"

Teldin was instead looking for the trail of wreckage left by the *Julia* across the *Spelljammer*'s wing. He felt a sense of loss, of innocence left behind, but he could not find the wreckage on the wing; it appeared that some great hand had swooped down and cleared away the charred debris.

"There!" Chaladar cried. Teldin turned and saw a plume of black smoke rising into the ship's huge air bubble from a thick, round tower at the stern. A band of minotaurs was struggling to put out what was left of the fire before the resulting explosions of phlogiston brought the tower down upon their heads.

"They better get that out soon," CassaRoc said. "The *Spelljammer* could be in trouble if the flow were to explode too much."

The warriors watched for a while, but the real battle had been pushed into the tower. One of Chaladar's guards said that the ogres had forced their way inside, cutting senselessly through a flank of about twenty neogi and their umber hulks. The reptilian neogi had retreated into their tower, followed quickly by the attacking ogres and their monstrous allies. Even from this great distance, Teldin could easily make out pools of blood spattering the deck.

For the first time, Teldin had a chance to admire the spiraling towers and the mixture of architecture spread out along the *Spelljammer*'s immense back. The flow played like fire along the golden spires and glistened off the winged statue atop the horned tower. He felt the amulet calling him, pushing him toward the tail of the ship. The symbol burned at his chest; now that he could see his goal, the *Spelljammer*'s call seemed even stronger.

They decided they had had enough, and they made their way back through the Guild tower, then into the collective and into the lowest level of the Tower of Thought. HarKenn, one of CassaRoc's guards, nodded as they entered. He bore several large weapons upon his leather belt and had smaller weapons hidden under his cloak and in his boots. His helmet was of an odd design, and the light shone off it in multicolored flashes.

The warriors passed and were near the doorway to the second level when they heard screams from below. They instantly wheeled about and ran back the way they had come.

The screams and shouts grew louder, and they stopped HarKenn as he stumbled up the stairs, and fell into the Cloakmaster's arms, bleeding from almost a hundred tiny wounds along his thick legs.

Teldin shook him while Chaladar reached for a light rod fastened to the wall. "HarKenn, what is it man? What happened to you?" Then Chaladar held up the light rod, and CassaRoc saw all the blood, painting the warrior's legs so that his wounds were nearly invisible.

HarKenn's eyes were wide with fear. Teldin held the light up and peered the way HarKenn had come, up from the shadows.

CassaRoc slapped the guard. His whimpering stopped. "HarKenn, tell us! Who did this to you?"

In Chaladar's light, they could see black movement on the stairs below, moving rapidly toward them like a rippling sea of fur. Sparks of white light glared at them angrily.

Teldin said, "CassaRoc, . . ."

HarKenn began to mumble. Spittle bubbled in the corner of his mouth. Without warning, he reached out and grabbed Teldin's tunic. His grip was like that of a vise, and he pulled Teldin into his face.

"The rats!" HarKenn shouted. His eyes gleamed with the pure light of madness. "The rats in the walls! They're chewing their way out!"

Chapter Fourteen

• • •

"*. . . Does not the creation of a thing wondrous also imply that a thing fearsome has been born? These things may be one and the same; they may be separate, individual entities.*

"*Something evil lives here, I sense: a lamprey of evil, surviving on the* Spelljammer*'s wastes. . . .*"

Leoster III; reign of Jokarin.

The maze that was the *Spelljammer*'s marketplace was alive with sounds and exotic aromas, with the pungent tastes of foods and spices from Oerth and Edill, of liquors from Toril and spiced vegetables from Coliar. Merchants shouted for attention, proclaiming that their wares were far better than any other's. The populace chattered, livestock and domestic animals lowed and barked, and from all over the *Spelljammer* Gaeadrelle Goldring felt the ship's life force pulsing like energy, with the latent powers of a sun.

She walked the deck invisibly, her astral body projected from a sphere that many of the *Spelljammer*'s inhabitants had never heard of, and she took in all the sensations of life that she could discover: the wail of an infant, the taste of *charraka* from mermen of Conatha, the scent of a perfume from Krynn.

And she smiled at the wonder of the life force that was the *Spelljammer*, the force that had called to Teldin Moore in answer to his own quest: for adventure, for purpose, for life.

She turned as a cool breeze rushed through her silently, like a dark, psychic wind. It does not belong here, she thought suddenly, and she shivered once, feeling her body in Herd-space shiver in immediate response.

She concentrated, and her psionic senses spread out before her in an invisible web of psionic energy. The cold comes from there, she thought, looking out over the *Spelljammer*'s landing field and toward its bow, and brings with it the taste of darkness.

The feelers of the gargantuan ship stretched out into the phlogiston like twin battering rams. Gaye reached out with her arms and let her psionic senses play over the bow, and she felt the evil wind pass through her like ice, blowing from starboard.

Inside the cavernous tear duct hidden below the ship's starboard eye Gaye discovered one of the unknown entrances to the ship's secret warrens, which ran like veins through the body of the *Spelljammer*. The breeze, a cold, dark wind tinged with the cold scent of death, sang through the tunnel. She took a step back, assaulted by the unnatural taint to the putrid air, then she forced herself forward into the organic tunnel, down into the ship's body.

Phosphorescent lichen and moonwort grew in patches along the smooth, porous walls, affording just enough pale light for Gaye to explore. Using the foul breeze as a compass, she felt her way through the warrens by following the steadily increasing stench of death. Several times she took wrong turns onto branching paths, then doubled back within seconds, realizing her mistakes.

Deep within the *Spelljammer*'s port wing, Gaye stumbled upon a source of the psychic odor she was following. The chamber she discovered was hollow, like an air bubble, and strewn with gnawed bones and dried, brittle hay. The hay had been piled to form nests, and on seven of these piles lay the corpses of human warriors. The still bodies of black rats lay along the walls and in heaps on the floor. She sensed outward and felt the chilling death force that lay dormant inside the bodies, and she knew that these were the undead, and that this was their hidden lair. The sense of evil was pervasive. It was too much for just a handful of zombies, and she realized that there were many undead hiding in the warrens, far more than anyone had ever guessed.

She wondered who their master was.

As she examined the long-dead humans, the bodies of the rats twitched as one, jerking as though they were waking up. They massed and started toward her. She gasped in fear and jumped back instinctively, thinking they were attacking; then they passed harmlessly through her invisible essence and continued on through the tunnel in a black, slithering mass of undead vermin. She laughed nervously.

Where are they going? she wondered. What call do they answer? She willed herself forward and followed them. Their sharp claws clacked hollowly against the tunnel floor. Their black eyes gleamed with pinpricks of unholy light.

At an intersection of six tunnels beneath the *Spelljammer*'s citadel district, the rats converged with other armies of rats, swarming from the other tunnels. Here, at this junction, the smell of death and coldness grew much stronger. As the undead rats squirmed deeper into the ship, Gaye stayed behind and reached out with her psionic senses. In her mind, one tunnel loomed darker, more claustrophobic than the others. It smelled foully of ancient evil.

Her senses led her to the tunnel closest to her left. The trail of magic was strong inside the tunnel, and the path took her to a curtain of darkness that seemed almost solid. It curled like black smoke at her feet, at the touch of her ethereal hands, and she knew that the chamber beyond was the source of all the undeath in the warrens. The power emanating from within was considerable, tingling coldly against her intangible form. It was a force that seemed to permeate from the very walls, infecting the *Spelljammer* like a disease.

She stepped through the black wall of mist and gazed in silent terror.

Gaye had never seen an undead creature such as the one before her now. It resembled a lich of some kind, she thought, some form of which she had no knowledge. Its flesh was not rotted, but rather incredibly corrupt, stretched taut, like mummified skin, over its prominent bones. Its eyes were bright stars hidden deep inside shadowed eye sockets, and its black, hooded cloak kept its skeletal body in the concealment of cold, soothing darkness. A heavy ruby amulet, burning with a fierce red fire, hung at its chest. And as she watched it, her psionic senses were overwhelmed, and feelings and images and tastes and smells flooded through her uncontrollably, chilling her with their very touch. She tasted blood on her tongue, the cold sensation of raw evil coursing through her veins. She wanted to scream.

The lich spoke in low tones, an evil hiss that seemed to resonate throughout the organic chamber. His fingers twitched with the clack of dried bones as he wove a spell of forgotten antiquity. The words were ancient, unknown to her; but in them she could feel the ring of history, of chanting voices long stilled, of gods long ago desecrated.

Gaye realized it was the rats he was controlling, and at once she could feel that he could see through the eyes of his vermin.

Then she was seeing through his eyes, the dead eyes of his rats, as well: the dark passageways, the dim light panels on the walls, the guard posted at the entrance. She realized that the rats were winding their way through the Human Collective and into the Tower of Thought.

She saw the wave of rats as they swarmed over the lone human guard, their yellow teeth snapping hungrily into flesh as he stumbled and ran, bleeding, up the stairs, toward—

Gaye screamed in her mind. *Noooooo!*

—toward Teldin . . .

The master lich turned toward her. His spell was a forgotten whisper on his thin, translucent lips. "Ehhh?" he said. "Someone is there . . ."

With a wave of his hand, an aura of shimmering energy erupted around Gaye, revealing her form to the master lich.

His eyes sparkled with the color of blood. The skull-like face seemed to smile. *A guest,* he said telepathically. *I have a guest.* He beckoned once with a skeletal arm, and Gaye was jerked forward, toward him.

Welcome to my palace, he said. *My palace. A palace of the dead . . . and the undead.*

He laughed, and his laughter was the sound of a soul screaming in torment. Gaye's blood went cold. *I do not know who you are,* he said, *but I . . . I am called . . . the Fool.*

Chapter Fifteen

• • •

"*. . . In response, I say that the design of the* Spelljammer *is obviously deliberate, and that the citadel has a secret, more far-reaching purpose than man can understand. Perhaps each tower has some larger purpose than to simply house the individual races. Who can say, since only the lower floors of the Armory are ever open to us? Who can say until we gain entry into the Dark Tower?*

"*We may never know. The* Spelljammer *tends to hoard its secrets like a jealous dragon. . . .*"

Rambergius, cleric of the Tower of Thought; reign of Coronas.

The rats were a black carpet, swarming up the tower stairs in a sea of rotted fur and gnashing yellow teeth. The stairway was hidden by their solid black mass, and they moved up the tower in an undulating wave, their ragged claws scraping the stone steps.

"Get him up!" Teldin shouted. CassaRoc and Chaladar lifted HarKenn from the stairs. "Get him inside!" he said. "It's rats! Gods! I've never seen so many rats."

Teldin backed up the stairs and rushed through the open door with the warriors. He slammed the door behind them and bolted it. Still, the gap under the door seemed too wide to him, too vulnerable; as Teldin watched, a long black snout appeared under the door. Claws and teeth ripped at the wood.

Teldin lashed out with his boot and crunched the rat's snout under his foot. Black blood trickled from its shattered jaws. The rat was still for a moment, then twitched back to unlife and started clawing at the door in increasing fury.

"Undead," Teldin said. "The rats are all undead."

CassaRoc stared at him in surprise. Chaladar said, "It can be only the Fool."

Teldin nodded unconsciously. Chaladar's words rang true. Instinctively, he knew the paladin was right.

They were trapped in the common room. The bolted door was their only exit, and, as they watched, the gap at the bottom was gnawed larger under the fury of the rats' yellow fangs.

CassaRoc hefted HarKenn in his arms and laid him out at one end of the bar. The guard moaned once, then fell unconscious. Blood oozed from his wounds and dripped onto the bar.

The warriors drew their swords and waited. They knew the blades were virtually helpless against the undead swarms, unless they could somehow sever the rats' spines or chop them until they truly died; but they had no other weapons, and the rats were attacking in too large numbers.

"Fire would do it," CassaRoc said.

"If we could have a fire in the flow. You saw what happened at the neogi tower," Teldin said. "It would bring the tower down on us all—right where the Fool wants us."

Chaladar said, "No. I believe he wants you."

CassaRoc nodded. "This is another assassination attempt, Teldin. He doesn't care about us. It's you he wants."

"Because of the Dark Times?"

"No," Chaladar said. "He would have no concern of the Dark Times, since he lives in darkness. He wants you for some other reason."

Teldin placed the light rod on a table and stared down at his amulet. The rats had chewed ragged the bottom of the wooden door. "Me . . ."

Teldin sagged and let the amulet fall against his chest. He looked over to the rats. Their claws and teeth were flashes of dull ivory, and splinters of wood were spewed across the floor by their razorlike teeth. Then one was squealing, squirming its fat body through a chewed-out gap along the floor. It leaped straight at Teldin.

Chaladar cried out. The paladin's sword was a silver flash as it swung down and sliced the rat in two. Its hind legs scrabbled to move forward; its jaws snapped at Teldin's booted feet. Then it ceased, finding true death at last.

"We're going to have to do something," CassaRoc said.

Chaladar frowned at the oily blood smeared on his sword. From outside they could hear CassaRoc's warriors shouting for them, warning others of the rats. CassaRoc yelled back, "We're trapped in here! Call a mage! We need help!"

Then another rat was inside with them, and another, and another. Within minutes, the floor was strewn with the severed torsos of the black vermin, and more were streaming through the widening gap in the door.

The trio kicked and sliced their way through the rats and climbed up on the bar. Three rodents leaped up and were killed instantly by the grand knight's swift sword. Some scrambled up the wooden bar using their sharp, dead claws, and were crunched under Teldin's heavy boots or skewered by CassaRoc's blade.

The floor was a slimy mass of dark blood, of dead and undead vermin. Teldin paused and focused, concentrating on his cloak and its powers, but its hidden energies refused to be summoned. The powers of the cloak seemed to be exhausted, and Teldin considered if its magic did not work on the undead . . . and if it would work on the Fool.

The undead rats came on.

Teldin said, "The cloak will not help us, and we can't stay here and try to chop them all in half. There are just too many." As he said this, two rats leaped onto the bar and dove for his legs. He lashed out and kicked one across the room; the other drove its fangs into his flesh, and he screamed in pain. CassaRoc reached down and tore it away, then bent it back in his bare hands until its spine snapped with a loud crack.

"We might have to make a run for it," Teldin said.

"Where do we go then?" CassaRoc asked. "They'll just come after you again."

"The Fool is the one we have to stop," Chaladar said

angrily. "He is the one controlling this evil."

The rats leaped and scrambled over each other in their frenzy to reach the Cloakmaster. The warriors lashed out with their swords and their heavy boots, but the rats swarmed from under the door with increasing ferocity, spitting chunks of wood from their bleeding mouths. Sweat ran from the warriors' faces as they speared the vermin on their blades, and CassaRoc's bar ran with the rats' black blood.

Then the wooden door rocked under the impact of a great weight. Again the door shuddered in its frame. The heavy iron bolt squealed as the weight hammered the door again and again.

Then the bolt sprang out of its braces and the wooden door shot open. A wave of rats poured into the room, chattering with unnatural hunger, and, from the corridor beyond, a large black creature crawled in on eight clawed legs. Its long yellow teeth gleamed in the light, and it focused its eellike eyes on Teldin and smiled. Gray drool oozed from its lips.

"A neogi," CassaRoc said.

"No, look!" Teldin said, pointing. "It's the one Na'Shee shot when I crashed on board."

The neogi hissed at Teldin, focusing its black eyes on him. A bloody crossbow bolt protruded straight through its neck.

Teldin said, "It's undead."

* * * * *

"Distracted are they," said one squat lieutenant, crouching in the shadows at the bottom of the Tower of Thought.

"Undead of the rats because."

"Guards all main level on. This way follow."

The two furry shapes scurried up the tower's back stairs. Their black claws clacked against the stone. Behind them, two tall, muscular shapes followed, lumbering blindly up the stairs.

On the upper level, they paused to listen through the wooden door. At the leader's command, the tallest of the huge shapes opened the door and stepped into the dimly lit corridor.

The guards at the door stared openly and quickly whipped out their swords, but the giant intruders reached them in seconds. One guard went down from a single hammering blow to his forehead. The other managed one lunge at his grotesque attacker, then was gripped from behind. His attacker's mandibles quickly closed on the guard's soft neck, and he died as his blood spilled onto the floor.

The intruders opened the door to Cwelanas's quarters. She lay in the bed, in restful sleep.

The furred black leader grinned. "Now . . . now, ours the shemeat is. Soon, soon, cloak perhaps ours will be."

Silently, the unhuman intruders approached Cwelanas.

Chapter Sixteen

• • •

". . . Many obstacles the Cloakmaster must overcome, for enemies many he will find, chief among them the unreason and hatred that unhumans generate for all others. It is this hatred, many believe, that has created a being which leeches off the soul of the Spelljammer, *whose desire is nothing less than the* Spelljammer*'s destruction. Revenge is its heart; evil, its soul.*

"Was this evil once human? Doubtful is that, according to the legends that have circulated for years. . . .

"But that is all we have: legends, rumors—no facts. . . .

"Of but one thing we can be certain: great evil walks these decks . . ."

Prince Arastor of the Human Collective, *The White Book of Knowledge*, reign of Brother Darke.

The undead neogi glared at Teldin with its black, empty eyes. Pinpricks of bright light shone from deep in its sockets—*the Fool's eyes*, Teldin knew. The neogi bared its needle-sharp teeth and waded through the undead rats toward the Cloakmaster.

Teldin raised his sword. Rats snapped at his boots as he leaped from the bar, diving for the neogi.

The neogi snarled as Teldin fell full upon it. They went down together, into the onrush of rats. Teldin wrapped his legs around the neogi's bulbous torso and held back its snapping face with his forearm. His sword plunged deep into its round belly. Black blood gushed from the wound.

The rats around them scratched at Teldin's face and arms, gnashing their yellow teeth. He winced as he felt long fangs sink into his thigh, others in the back of his leg.

The neogi rolled through the rats, trying to shake Teldin off. His grip on it was tight. His sword slashed down and down, countless times into the fat, undead flesh, and the neogi still snapped at Teldin's face and neck, seeking his warm blood. Teldin felt the sting of rat bites across his legs, across his arms, and several in his sides. His blood was warm and sticky, oozing from dozens of small wounds, and he could tell that the scent of his blood was driving the undead rats into a frenzy of hunger.

Teldin pressed hard against the neogi's neck, bending back its head. He kicked out with his bloody legs, feeling his feet sink deep into its cold flesh. With one mighty lunge, a bone in its neck cracked, and Teldin hurled the neogi away. It fell against the wall with a wet, sickening crunch.

The Cloakmaster struggled to stand upright, panting with exhaustion. The rats scrambled up his cloak, leaping for his arms and neck. The neogi rose across from him, its head lolling on a hideously broken neck. Its black eyes watched him ferally, and with a tortured scream, the neogi leaped over the rats.

It gnashed its teeth at him in the air. Teldin swung his sword in one swift motion, and the blade sliced cleanly through the neogi's neck. Blood twirled through the air in an arc. The undead neogi's head dropped into the wave of rats. Its jaws snapped once, then stopped. It took a single, involuntary step forward on its sharp claws; then, as if sensing that some vital part of it was missing, the neogi body staggered, then fell over onto the floor, instantly smothered by the undead rats.

Rats were covering Teldin's arms, his back. He tore them off with a swipe of his hand, then could feel them jumping, replacing their brothers, on his shoulders, his legs. CassaRoc screamed for him, but the rats were leaping at his face, drawing blood on his cheeks. He felt teeth at his neck and wrenched two rats away with his bloody hands.

Then a furry snout dove into his cheek. He heard the clack

of teeth snapping for his eyes, and he flung himself away, squeezing his eyes tight. He stumbled onto the floor. He felt the rats scurrying beneath him, then over him, over his legs, closing their jaws in his flesh. He felt dizzy. He knew he was bleeding from countless tiny wounds, and he blindly waved his sword defiantly through the rats' midst.

But the undead came on, seething toward him in an unstoppable mass. He jerked himself up from the floor and spun, trying to shake off the rats, squeezing them in his hands until their bones snapped beneath his fingers.

Then the room spun. His head tingled with cold: not with the power of the cloak, but from the numbness of losing blood, from the physical shock of countless wounds.

He fell to the floor as he heard his friends shouting his name. But his sight went black as the rats fell upon him, and he could hear only the snapping of their teeth.

* * * * *

Gaye involuntarily took a step back. She could feel the immensity of the Fool's evil wash over her in a cold black wave. Her astral body stood revealed in a pale silver light.

She could still see through the eyes of the Fool's undead rats as they followed the Cloakmaster through the Tower of Thought. Then he ran into the common room and slammed the door on the vermin.

Darkness. Gaye shuddered and willed her own vision to return.

The undead master watched her, clucking his tongue almost in laughter. *What have we here?* he said. *An impudent kender, who pretends command over powers she knows nothing of.*

Gaye searched her memory. He was a lich, she was sure, but what kind?

They circled each other slowly, warily. She reached out with her psionic senses to test his strengths and weaknesses, feeling a tickle on her skin as she realized he was doing the same to her.

She felt the blackness that permeated each cell of his body, the corruption that had laid claim to his once-human form. She could feel the enormous powers contained within him, the absence of life, the hatred for love. She focused on the pinpricks of energy that served as his eyes. They grew in her mind, until they were blazing like suns . . . twin suns of cold, dark fire.

She staggered under their fury, the boiling heat of his hatred for all life, especially for the being-ship that he once commanded and now wanted dead.

. . . *once commanded* . . .

In a single blaze of brilliant icefire, her mindsight was open. Their senses were linked as each reached out to assess the other's power, and her mind was filled with visions of the past; she saw and felt and *was* the Fool—

Romar

—and saw the power of the ship's sting destroying cities and lands—Romar's unstoppable quest for power, spreading a path of destruction across the spheres—his fall from the captaincy, and his insatiable lust for revenge—and his transformation at the hands of gods from the darkness, from outcast to master lich—

Gaye gasped. A *master* lich!

Then she knew everything, just as the Fool had likewise absorbed all knowledge of her newly learned psionic powers.

She knew his goals.

And he knew her limitations.

From across the chamber, he laughed at her, a rasping laugh that echoed of the grave. *Nothing*, he said. *Your powers are nothing. You are but an insect, a speck blotting my plans for revenge*. He swatted a skeletal hand in the air. Her head jerked violently to the side with the impact from an invisible hand. Her cheek glowed warm where his magic had slapped her.

She lowered her head and glowered at him from under her eyebrows. Her hands lifted into the air, her fingers jutting outward in stiff, awkward positions that reflected the strict discipline of her mind. Circles of glowing power slowly formed around her hands.

A challenge . . . The master lich laughed. *I do so love a challenge* . . .

There is no way I will let you kill Teldin, she replied telepathically. Bolts of blue energy erupted from her hands and hit the master lich squarely in the chest. He stumbled back and stared at her with his piercing eyes. They narrowed in focus. Without warning, a powerful force slammed into her and threw her into a wall.

She gasped for breath as her shoulders rang with the impact. The lich's fingers glowed with yellow energy. She crossed her wrists in front of her. A flare of power flew toward her from the lich's fingers, only to be dispersed by a sudden shield of psionic force shimmering around her like a diamond.

The Fool laughed hollowly. *Good. That's very good.*

Then she was bombarded by cold winds that sang from the lich's throat. She was pummeled by crackling balls of power that flickered soundlessly from the lich's eyes. She was struck by bolts of black energy that seemed to absorb the light. Her psionic shield wavered unsteadily, shimmering dully as it was weakened by the Fool's assault.

She raised her arms high. The air in the chamber began to swirl, forming a tornado of bones and black smoke that surrounded the Fool and sent him spinning.

Over it all, the Fool laughed.

The wind stopped upon a single gesture of his bony hand. His eyes burned red, and Gaye's body jerked suddenly, under his mental control. He opened his arms wide for her, and she jerked forward like a puppet. Through her psionics, she felt his plans for her, the delicious taste of her death at his hands, and his scheme for her long undeath under his command.

She concentrated and bolstered her psionic strength and regained control of her fingers. "Mental discipline is enhanced by physical discipline," the fal One Six Nine had told her. "The proper positions of your body will complement and increase the focusing of your mind."

She crooked her fingers in complicated configurations. There! Her right arm was free.

She took another step forward, toward the Fool and his deadly embrace. She held her arm up and thrust out with her mind.

The Fool suddenly staggered back under a psionic blow that exploded against him with incredible force.

Gaye was free.

She gasped for breath. The Fool was far stronger, more practiced, than she. Gaye knew she could not stop him, not now, as weak as she was; perhaps she could stun him momentarily, just long enough to escape his lair and somehow help Teldin . . .

The Fool bellowed with anger. His howl echoed through the warrens like the wail of the wind. He kneeled and raised his arms high above his head and called out, *Ygsykhan! Turollabak! Hear me!*

Gaye focused and realized what she had to do. She drew a deep breath and tapped all the psychic energies she had left. She felt the energies swirling within her, flickering through her veins like fire.

The Fool stood up. He waved his hands above his head in an intricate pattern. Black smoke curled around his feet, spreading its deadly tendrils toward Gaye.

She screamed in her mind. The power coursed through her like holy fire, and the chamber was seared with the unyielding white light of a nova, coursing, pulsing from her flesh in a fountain of energy.

The Fool staggered back and collided with the wall. She felt the chamber instantly cleansed of his foul evil and felt the Fool's consciousness dwindling away in the purifying light of her soul.

She knew he would revive in just a few seconds. She drew back her energies and focused once more. Slowly, a stasis bubble formed around the Fool, a hindrance just powerful enough to slow time within the bubble, enough to afford Gaye time to escape.

She sagged, exhausted, but knew she had to go on. With her remaining energies, she visualized the deadly vermin attacking the Tower of Thought. *Teldin*, she called weakly, *Teldin . . .*

Her astral form faded away, swirling into a glowing, green miasma.

* * * * *

The bones of an undead rat were shattered beneath Teldin's pounding fist. Their teeth dug into his sides, his arms, his legs.

Blood ran copiously from tiny, ragged wounds, and still the rats came on, swarming over him, piercing his skin, seeking the hot taste of living blood.

He fought them, ripping them away like leeches, then he realized that they were no longer attacking. In his mindless rage, he had thrown off at least twenty rats that had simply ceased to move, to attack. He tried to stand and felt dizzy, but most of the rats that had scrambled upon his body fell off dazedly, moving sluggishly, yet without purpose.

Chaladar yelled, "Teldin! Look!"

He wavered on unsteady legs.

The room slowly filled with a green mist, emanating from the jagged hole under the door. Where the mist touched the undead rats, they began jerking spasmodically, violently. Their angry eyes, glowing with unnatural white light, slowly changed, burned with green fire, and their mouths were flecked with bloody spittle. They squealed as the mist entered them and burned its way through their rotted bodies, until their eyeballs sank inside their heads and the mist curled from their empty eye sockets.

In minutes, the floor was littered with the bodies of truly dead rats, layered over with a carpet of swirling green mist.

CassaRoc and Chaladar jumped off the bar. Rat corpses crunched under their weight. They helped Teldin up to the bar, where he could sit away from the vermin. "You need attention," CassaRoc said. "You are bleeding like mad."

"The Guild tower," Chaladar said. "Leoster can take care of you there."

Teldin looked beyond them and said simply, "Wait."

The green light from the corridor brightened, then the doorway seemed to glow, filled with emerald light, and inside the light was the dim shape of a woman.

"Do you see that?" CassaRoc said.

Chaladar nodded.

"Good," CassaRoc said.

She passed through the door and stopped. The green energies that had destroyed the undead rats faded away, and her form was enveloped in a soft, golden glow that radiated a feeling of peace.

Teldin said, "It—it's Gaye."

Gaeadrelle Goldring floated directly to Teldin and smiled. His expression was one of shock—gape-mouthed, wide-eyed shock. She could tell he had never expected this.

"Gaye? Are you real?"

He reached out, and her energies fluttered with warmth on his fingertips. "It was you," he understood then. "It wasn't a dream I had. But how? How are you doing this?"

Gaeadrelle Goldring's lips moved. Although her words were inaudible, her voice echoed within all their minds.

The Fool wants you dead, Teldin. I have stopped him for now, but it is only temporary. The undead will do his bidding. Follow the woven heart. Do not hesitate any longer.

Gaye seemed to sigh, flickering like a dying torch. Teldin reached out for her, but his hand passed harmlessly through the gold mist.

"How did you come here?" he said.

Teldin, I do this for you. Listen to me. I must go now. I am weary and must rest. Her voice became loud in his head. *Follow the woven heart. Your destiny must be fulfilled, and the Fool must be destroyed.*

She started to fade, then her eyes widened, as though she had seen something invisible to all others. *Teldin, you must beware. Others seek your . . .* She faltered, then her form faded from view. Her last words were a whisper inside his mind. *You are a target . . . of the bushi . . .*

Then she was gone.

Blood seeped through Teldin's torn clothes, over his skin. The cloak was pure and untouched. The blood seemed to bead off it, as though magically repelled.

CassaRoc cleared a path through the rats bodies, kicking them away. Blood was smeared thickly over his boots. He jerked aside the door and shouted into the corridor. "Come on, now! We've got to get this place cleaned up!" Then he looked around and shook his head. To the Cloakmaster he said, "This is bad business, Teldin. Bad business."

Teldin nodded. His cloak hung heavy across his shoulders. He felt perhaps more tired, more exhausted, than he had ever felt before.

CassaRoc's men stopped in the doorway and craned their necks to look in. No one really wanted to come in and wade ankle-deep in rat carcasses, but after CassaRoc explained to them the attack on Teldin, they were more than willing to haul HarKenn to his quarters. A healer was called for the guard and for Teldin, and other warriors went to get shovels and barrels from the basement, in order to dispose of the rat carcasses. Emil even came up and inspected the room on his own. "I'll get the mops," he said happily.

After most of the warriors had charged off, Chaladar excused himself. "I must check on the Chalice tower," the grand knight said to CassaRoc. "His wounds are more numerous than I thought. I'll send Leoster over again, in case he is needed. In the meantime, I suggest you double your guards on duty."

CassaRoc agreed, and, as the paladin left, he shouted up the tower for his healer. In a few moments, a priestess known as J'Kai stepped carefully into the room and examined Teldin. She took him behind the bar and bathed his wounds with fresh water.

First she dried his wounds, then took a jar of white lotion from a pouch at her waist and lathered the medicine into the bites. "I count almost a hundred wounds," she said, then she told him not to move very much. "Leoster will be here soon. This will take care of superficial infections, but this is the work of the undead. Leoster will be better able to heal you than I."

Teldin thanked her and drew his cloak around him. His wounds felt hot and stinging—purified, in a way, he thought—but he felt as though more than blood had been drained from him from today's events.

CassaRoc's warriors filed in then, bearing implements to clear the room of the dead vermin. Another of his guards ran in, spied CassaRoc helping with the clean-up, and spoke with him for a few minutes.

CassaRoc came over to Teldin as the guard hurriedly left. "It doesn't seem like it's going to stop," he said.

Teldin was too tired to talk. CassaRoc said simply, "Our allies are itching to get into battle with the neogi. With the attacks organized by the beholders and their allies, our alliance thinks the time is right, when the neogi forces are weakened." He paused. "If they don't hear from us soon, they'll start without us."

Teldin almost wanted to laugh. "The beholders. Our allies realize, don't they, that we'll have the beholders to battle after we defeat the neogi."

CassaRoc shrugged. "Not everyone is known for using their brains in the heat of battle."

CassaRoc and Teldin started when they heard shouts echoing from the level above. "What now?" CassaRoc said.

CassaRoc stepped into the corridor and started for the stairs, when a guard almost rushed into him in his flight down the stairs. The guard gasped for breath. "CassaRoc, we don't know how it happened."

"How *what* happened?"

The warrior shook his head in regret. "Somehow, they overpowered Hath. They have the lady Cwelanas."

CassaRoc turned in the doorway, but Teldin had overheard and had already jumped from his seat at the bar. The three of them ran up the stairs, three steps at a time. Teldin felt as though he were surging with energy, and all he could imagine was Cwelanas's sleeping face.

The inside of Cwelanas's room was dark and smelled strangely of the secret potions of the mage Leoster. In Cwelanas's place, the guard, Hath, lay quietly on the bed, staring at the ceiling with blank eyes.

Teldin scanned the room, then stood above the guard for a moment before speaking.

"Hath, what happened here?"

The man neither heard nor saw him. His eyes stayed at some invisible vista, seen only by him. His face was blank and gaunt, and his white eyes seemed as though they would burst from his head.

Teldin bent down and gripped the man's shoulders. He was filled with anger, with worry over the fate of Cwelanas. He placed his face in plain sight before Hath's eyes. "Hath, we have to know. What happened here?"

Teldin's shape eclipsed the light from the corridor. The guard's eyes blinked once, then slowly swiveled to look Teldin in the eyes. "C—Cloakmaster?"

Teldin nodded. "Yes, yes, it's—"

Then the guard's eyes rolled up to expose only the whites.

His back arched in sudden, violent pain, bending him like a bow above the bunk, and thick black smoke roiled from his mouth and nose. Teldin released his grasp, feeling the intense heat building within the man's flesh.

"*Cloakmaster*," Hath said, but his voice was a hiss, the telltale rasp and the broken syntax of a neogi.

"*Cloakmaster, . . . elf hostage have we in place you find cannot. Save you must Cwelanassss, shemeat . . . precious is your cloak we need. Barter no. One chance only: cloak for meat. Find us you will. Soon do, before shared meat is by brood . . .*"

Then Hath collapsed onto the bed, his eyes gray with the heat of the black fire churning out of him. The smoke stopped as suddenly as it had started. His body caved in with a sickening sigh. CassaRoc felt the guard's wrist, then jerked his hand away from the intense heat.

He looked at Teldin and shook his head.

Teldin stood silently, then grunted and kicked the end table across the room. CassaRoc and the others watched him, almost sharing his loss. "Neogi bastards!" Teldin shouted.

"I recognized the voice from council meetings. That was Master Coh. He's the one that's taken her," informed CassaRoc.

He stroked his long beard and thought about it. "I tell you, he has something to do with the attack. Coh is a black mage. I'd wager that he and the Fool are plotting something together."

Teldin took a deep breath. He faced CassaRoc. "No damned neogi is going to harm Cwelanas again," he said. He placed his hand on the hilt of his sword. "Alert Chaladar, Leoster, and our allies. Start getting the warriors together and arm them—arm them well.

"Break out the catapults. We're getting into this war far sooner than I had intended—but I'll be damned if I let Cwelanas die under the claws of the neogi."

Chapter Seventeen

• • •

"*. . . Many are the servants of evil. They are drawn to the flame of goodness like moths in the dark, and their mistress is the Queen of the Abyss. . . .*"

Admiral Loquestor Hellfire VI, elf lord; reign of Blacksteed

Far beneath the inhabited citadel that stretched across the back of the *Spelljammer*, the being once known as Romar, who was once a captain of the great ship many years ago, sat upon his bleached throne of bones. In a globe of sight floating above the floor the Fool watched the neogi community being attacked by the beholders and their vicious allies. He watched as the neogi were chased into their tower like the sadistic cowards he knew they were.

He gestured with a skeletal hand. The globe's view shifted, and he watched as the Cloakmaster shook an enchanted human in the Tower of Thought, and the guard erupted in black flame.

"Coh." The Fool hated the sound of that disgusting neogi name.

He should not have been surprised, but he had had no idea that Coh could possibly have been that cunning. "He has his own agenda," the Fool spoke to himself. "And he has nowhere else to run but to sanctuary." He laughed. "Here."

His laughter echoed off the walls. "But I have my own sweet agenda," he said, "and it does not call for a further alliance with a trained neogi. The woman will be mine, whether he knows it or not, and Coh . . ." He giggled madly, mocking the neogi master. "And mine will neogi master be. Coh meat will be."

The Fool rose from his throne, laughed, and kicked out at an undead rat, laid flat on its back. The corpse bounced off the wall. The Fool was still weak from the fledgling's psionic attack, but she would not be given a second chance to defeat him at his own work.

Oh, no.

"Gaeadrelle Goldring, the kender . . . oh, she will die, too. Oh, yes . . . a glorious, painful death, one especially suited for hurting me—*me!*—the one true captain . . ."

The Fool glowered angrily and screamed to himself.

"She will return . . . if only to help her precious Cloakmaster . . . and I will be ready to taste her fear . . ." He pondered a moment and grinned. "Perhaps my . . . servants would enjoy the taste of her soft, raw flesh . . . her cold terror . . ."

He decided. "The kender will be dealt with. But first, the neogi.

"Then, death for all . . . as I take the *Spelljammer* to its ultimate destiny . . . inside the fiery depths of the Broken Sphere."

Even in his humiliation, the Fool laughed and laughed and laughed.

The Fool knew that Death, ultimately, was a cosmic comedian. And who better to be court jester to Death than the Fool?

Chapter Eighteen

• • •

"One shall come under the auspices of shadow.
One shall come to deliver the darkness.
One shall come whom all have wronged.
One shall come without purpose.
One shall find purpose.
One shall be the Redeemer.
All are One."

Prophecies of Bama, pirate bard of Duval; reign of Fausto.

"Ships ahoy!"

The shout from the roof echoed down through the Tower of Thought, and Teldin thought he could hear the cry repeated loudly from the other nearby towers of the Human Collective.

He stepped out of the tower's weapons room and started up the stone stairs to the roof. Outside he found CassaRoc and Chaladar staring up into the sky. CassaRoc raised a cylindrical tube to one eye and stared through it. He squinted against the bright light of the flow. "I don't know," he said to the paladin. "Never seen their like before."

Chaladar held out his hand. "Let me see."

CassaRoc handed him the tube, rimmed in brass. Chaladar aimed and peered through it for a long time. "Vaguely Shou design, I think. The wings, or fins, are like those of dragons. I'm not sure, though. They're some of the largest vessels I've ever seen."

Teldin came up behind them. "The spyglass. Is it gnomish work?"

CassaRoc turned, surprised. "We didn't hear you come up." He nodded. "Yep. Bought it off a gnome a few years back, around Evermeet. The only thing a gnome has ever designed that has a practical use, I'd say. Well worth the silver I paid."

Teldin took the glass and hefted it. He had used one before, in another sphere. This one seemed more streamlined and advanced, a tube carved of wood, about a foot long, with glass disks affixed to both ends by rings of brass. He aimed at a distant tower and looked once, marveling at the device's seemingly magical ability to bring far objects into clear focus; then he aimed it toward the speck in the phlogiston where the two leaders had been looking.

In seconds, he spotted them. CassaRoc pointed out five other areas in the flow, where only distant specks could be seen against the swirling chaos.

Teldin whistled.

In all, nineteen ships were closing on the *Spelljammer*. Six were deadly deathspiders and a mindspider—probably planning to rendezvous with B'Laath'a, Teldin surmised—and, far in the distance, were two incredibly huge vessels that Teldin could not identify, ships that resembled giant, finned centipedes. As they sailed, the ships' segmented hulls twisted as though worming their way through the flow. Beyond them, Teldin picked out three hammerships, an elven man-o-war, a squid ship, two nautiloids, a galleon, and three wasps.

"The deathspiders," he said. "I could be wrong, but I have a hunch that the neogi will try to take advantage of B'Laath'a, the neogi mage who assaulted Cwelanas. They'll be sure to join the neogi in their fight against us, and they'll probably try to kill me again as well."

Chaladar nodded. "Vicious, evil beings."

CassaRoc said, "Be sure to expect other assassination attempts, too."

"The other ships nearby," Teldin continued, "I've never seen before. They remind me of dragon ships with the colors, and the ornamentation, but much larger. And I'll tell you this: they don't look friendly."

"They're still a few hours away. We still have time to get to the neogi and get Cwelanas back," CassaRoc said.

Teldin was silent.

Cwelanas. Yes, we will get her back.

They stared into the flow for a while, keeping track of the converging ships. Even at this great distance, they could tell that some ships were already battling among themselves. Ballistae were firing from the deathspiders, and missiles were sent hurtling into a deck of a hammership. Catapults aboard the hammership rained boulders upon the swifter deathspiders, but they turned away before they could take much damage.

Teldin looked down upon the *Spelljammer* with CassaRoc's gnomish spyglass. From the tower, he could see that the open market had closed, probably for fear of war, and that sporadic fighting among the races had already broken out across the ship. A better view could be had from the pinnacle of the Guild tower, Teldin knew.

"What does the watch atop the Guild tower report?" he asked.

Chaladar leaned back against the tower railing and removed his helmet. He ran his fingers through his long hair. "The fighting has increased at the neogi tower," he said. "The bastards seem to be rallying, perhaps because they know their allies are on the way. And look." Chaladar pointed down. "The neogi are starting skirmishes all over the ship. They're using their slaves and umber hulks to terrorize the humans."

The paladin replaced the helmet and looked at Teldin seriously. "We can't wait much longer. We'll have to strike soon, Cloakmaster, or we humans will be worn down. Just give me the order."

"The others will be here soon," Teldin said. He looked at Chaladar, standing tall in his gleaming armor, and CassaRoc, ready to throw his men into a good fight. He had been on the *Spelljammer* for only a short time, and these men were ready to lay their lives down for him. He glanced away, at the fighting below. Somehow I have already become their leader, he thought.

And he felt, in his soul, that this was how it was supposed to be.

"Let's go down," Teldin said. They followed him to Cassa-

Roc's common room, now clear of rat corpses, and they waited for the arrival of the allied leaders.

It had been almost three hours since the discovery that Cwelanas had been kidnapped by the neogi, and Teldin had used that time well.

He had been healed by King Leoster and could walk and fight very well, though he was still a little stiff. Then, together, he and CassaRoc had organized the fifty or so warriors of the Pragmatic Order of Thought into four squadrons and had armed each with two short swords, a dagger, and whatever other weapons they could carry. In addition, all the leaders of the alliance had been informed of the humans' intentions, and the giff, dwarves, and halflings had all started preparing for war. Lord Diamondtip had even come over for a short while to assure the Cloakmaster that all was going well in the giff's smoke tower.

The collective and their allies had more powerful weapons than Teldin had initially believed. The Human Collective itself had twenty ballistae ready and armed. The Chalice was ready with one armed ballista and a catapult, and their fifty fighters were more than ready to spill a little—or a lot—of neogi blood. CassaRoc's two catapults were in perfect working order, and the Guild tower was readying five ballistae and five catapults, which had been kept in storage.

Unfortunately, the halflings were armed only individually. The two dwarf communities, however, shared nine catapults and fifteen ballistae between them. The giff were extraordinarily enthusiastic about the battle and had kept their weapons in total readiness. Lord Diamondtip had even mentioned a surprise, a giff specialty, that he thought the Cloakmaster would appreciate.

Secretly, Teldin hoped the surprise was not very dangerous. The giff were well known on the *Spelljammer* for their inventiveness with explosives, but even CassaRoc and Chaladar were surprised when Diamondtip described to them the giff's secret weapon: four bombards bound together at the pinnacle of the giff tower. Manned by eight giff, the bombards could rotate 360 degrees on a single, circular platform.

Teldin hoped the war would not get so desperate as to use the giff's guns in the phlogiston. With the giff's joy for explosives combined with the combustive nature of the flow itself, he had wondered if this war would engender an explosive force as powerful as that which had destroyed the Broken Sphere. Then Diamondtip had explained to him that the explosion could not harm the *Spelljammer*. "Sure, the *Spelljammer* would be shaken up, and the giff's tower would be taken out," Diamondtip had shrugged, "but so would the towers of many of our enemies."

"I'm relieved," Teldin had said weakly.

Although the Elven High Command contained ten ballistae, spaced throughout at various entrances in defensive positions, Teldin and the others were more concerned about the elves' promise of alliance. The elves had been informed of the upcoming attack and had been asked to join in a planning session, but Teldin was not convinced of the elves' sincerity and guessed that they probably would not show up for the meeting.

For three hours, the humans prepared their weaponry and made preliminary plans to attack the neogi. Scouts watched from the roof of the Guild tower, the tallest of the human buildings, and sent word of the battles at the neogi tower, and of the fighting breaking out across the great ship.

Diamondtip finally left to check on preparations at his own tower, and the human leaders went to CassaRoc's weapons room to double-check the armament. Then the approaching ships had been spotted by the watch, and Teldin knew that the war would soon begin, a war he did not know how to prevent.

In the common room, Teldin and the two leaders discussed Cwelanas's kidnapping. It had all boiled down to only one conceivable possibility: neogi, probably Coh himself, had sneaked over into the Tower of Thought. The violence done to the guards indicated that large umber hulks had been with them, and they must have taken Cwelanas down the same, little-used stairway that they had sneaked up.

"Tell me more about Coh," Teldin said.

CassaRoc and Chaladar shared what little information they had that Teldin had not yet been told, of the rumored connection between Coh and the Fool, of his devoted slave, Orik, the ship's most dangerous umber hulk. Teldin knew that Cwelanas had told him the truth of Coh's partnership with the neogi who had brainwashed her, and he was convinced that Cwelanas was now his hostage—if not worse.

"Shemeat," the guard had spoken in the tongue of the neogi.

The sign of Coh was a series of interlocking circles, tattooed on the neogi master's forehead. When Teldin found him, the tattoo would be the first thing to be cut from Coh's body.

The layout of the neogi tower was unknown to everyone in the Human Collective. The neogi were so despised by all the races on the ship that few, other than neogi slaves, had ever been inside. Teldin decided that a swift assault upon the tower would be best, and then to swarm through the tower and take back Cwelanas as quickly as possible. Perhaps then they would find the neogi at their least defensible, when their strength was weak after the attacks by the beholders and their unhuman allies.

It was rumored that there were only fifty neogi in the tower—about forty, now, counting their losses in the skirmish that had occurred when Teldin's ship had crashed—and about thirty umber hulks and slaves. The human forces would overpower them easily—unless they were to engage other unhumans in the process of the assault.

And that possibility could not lightly be ignored.

The discussion was interrupted when Lord Diamondtip and the elf Lothian Stardawn finally arrived to the Tower of Thought, followed shortly thereafter by the halfling leaders, Hancherback and Kristobar, and the dwarf king, Lord Kova. With CassaRoc and Chaladar, Teldin quickly sketched out his plans to cut through the sporadic skirmishes between the collective, on the *Spelljammer*'s port side, and the starboard communities, to eventually reach the neogi tower en masse.

It was while their plans were being laid that a newcomer appeared and inadvertently interrupted the meeting. The discussion stopped suddenly as his shadow darkened the doorway. CassaRoc's hand went to his sword, for he feared another assassination attempt on the Cloakmaster.

Teldin looked up and instantly rose from his seat. "Djan," he said warmly.

Djan, the half-elf and the only other survivor of the crash of the *Julia*, stepped into the room. He held his left arm stiffly at his side, but he smiled as Teldin approached. His thin face had been brought back to its normal hue, and his eyes sparkled with the cold glint of steel.

"CassaRoc's healers have assured me that I am well," Djan said. "I cannot let you get into this fight alone."

"Djan," Teldin said, "I think you should wait until you're much better."

"I can't wait any longer, Teldin. I've always hated being sick. I feel totally useless in that bed." He placed his hand on Teldin's shoulder. "I did not sail across the known universe with you to stay asleep and miss the events that called us here. Besides, you need all the able men you can get."

Teldin grinned and pulled Djan around to face the assemblage at the table. "This is my first mate, late of the *Julia*," Teldin said. "Djan will be with us on all decisions regarding the war for the *Spelljammer*. We've come a long way to find the *Spelljammer* and discover my destiny—"

"—Our destiny," Djan said quickly.

Teldin nodded. "And Djan here deserves a lot of the credit."

Teldin made the introductions and pulled a chair over for Djan. The half-elf sat, and together the Alliance of the Cloak finalized its strategies to rescue the stolen Cwelanas.

* * * * *

The humans of the Tower of Thought volunteered to go first and cut a vicious swath through the fighting around the collective. In the hour that the leaders spent talking and preparing, minor assaults had broken out threefold across the ship as the neogi spread their attacks: dwarf was now battling neogi, elf was battling neogi—almost no race was spared from violence, and soon the blood of all the races would be spilled at the murderous claws of the neogi.

Teldin laced up his leather armor and slipped on his vest of mail. He had shrunk his cloak to the size of a necklace as he pulled on his armor, and he commanded it to lengthen over his shoulders, just to see how he looked. Presently, his cloak filled out, and he was the image of the valiant, broad-shouldered warrior, ready to die for a cause. He tested the feel of his sword in his hands.

Behind him, Djan and CassaRoc examined their weapons and their armor. CassaRoc's had obviously seen a lot of action. His armor was dented across his chest and scarred from many sword thrusts. Djan had borrowed light armor from CassaRoc's cache and finished tugging it over his lithe frame just as CassaRoc snapped a heavy cloak around his neck. They looked at each other in silent appraisal then turned to the Cloakmaster as though they were saying, "We're ready."

Teldin turned. "Almost time," he said.

Djan nodded.

Teldin concentrated. Slowly, his cloak and amulet shrank again into a thin necklace, which he covered with the collar of his shirt. Then, before his companions' staring eyes, the contours of his face shifted. His hair changed color, his shoulders widened, and his form shrank by several inches. For the charge to the neogi tower, it would not do to have the Cloakmaster be seen by all of his enemies.

"No matter how much you do that, I'm never going to get used to it," Djan said.

Teldin asked, "How do I look?"

"Look for yourself," CassaRoc said. He held up a small piece of polished steel.

Teldin stared at the familiar face in the mirror. The craggy features, the angry light behind his eyes—just looking at himself made the old feelings churn inside, fear and hatred mingling with love.

"You look quite good," Djan said. "Anyone in particular?"

Teldin remembered the stern lessons of his father, his heavy hand, and how he had practically chased a young Teldin off the farm to find peace, the only peace he could truly find: alone, on the dangerous, bloody fields of the War of the Lance.

He looked up from the mirror. "No one important."

He led them from the room to the tower entrance. CassaRoc's warriors waited anxiously along the walls of the corridor, adjusting scabbards and cloaks, nodding as the leaders passed, and barely casting a glance at Teldin. They had been told of Teldin's planned strategy to cross the ship; despite his disguise, they recognized him by the hastily painted insignia above his left breast, the mantalike outline of the cloak unfurled, or perhaps even the *Spelljammer*, with a yellow circle at the neck, signifying the amulet.

Djan took his place beside Teldin. "You don't have to do this," Teldin said. "You should probably stay in bed, like I said."

The half-elf secured his short sword on his belt. "You're here for a reason, Teldin, a reason more important than the life of a half-elf. Remember: *verenthestae*. You're here for a reason that is far more complex—possibly predestined—than you truly know. I am here because I'm with you. *Verenthestae*. I must be here for a reason, too."

Teldin accepted the explanation with a grin, then handed Djan an extra dagger from his belt. "Just in case. Take care of that arm."

Djan smiled.

At the prearranged time, CassaRoc led his warriors out of the tower in a furious charge toward the open market. The human warriors swarmed through the market, careening into stalls and accidentally spilling wares across the deck. Teldin was just another warrior in the rear flanks, which, when the human and halfling armies united, would take the lead and invade the tower in search of Cwelanas. Behind them, a squad of men carried between them a huge battering ram, ready for the tower invasion. The warriors of the giff, elves, and dwarves would meet them after word was sent that the neogi tower was taken.

The clang of steel rang out as the humans engaged a couple of umber hulks that had cornered a stray halfling in the market. With their massive battle-axes, the hulks easily parried the warriors' sword thrusts. Then, with a shrill scream, a huge shadow lumbered around the corner of the market. A tiny warrior sat atop a giant beast, which Teldin finally recognized as an example of an extremely rare species, the giant space hamster.

The warrior was Emil. His plaid cloak flowed proudly behind him as the small fighter charged the umber hulks, shouting, "For the Cloakmaster!" Flashes of steel flew from his sling and his poisoned barbs struck the umber hulks in each of their chests, their long points embedded in the flesh beneath their armored carapaces. Again, twin barbs of steel were slung with uncanny accuracy. One struck an umber hulk just above its miniature eye and pierced its skull; the other found its target in the thick flesh of the other hulk's neck.

The hamster bared its sharpened teeth and slashed out at the misshapen giants. Blood spurted from deep gashes across the hulks' chests and dripped from the hamster's mouth.

As one, the umber hulks wavered on their flat feet. The loss of blood and the speed of Emil's poison sent them weakly to their knees. They fell to the deck, their arms and legs flailing helplessly, white foam bubbling rapidly from their gaping mouths.

Then they were still.

The warriors erupted with a cheer for their first victory of the War of the Cloakmaster. Emil waved gleefully at Teldin. "This is GhoTaa," he said, quickly, laughing. "I trained him myself."

Teldin shook his head, amazed at the little warrior's prowess, and smiled. "Good work, Emil," he shouted. "You keep surprising me."

Emil grinned broadly, and his face turned a bright red. "You should see what I can do with pigeons and weasel bats."

The hamster snorted and spat umber hulk blood onto the deck. Teldin stepped away, remembering the giant hamster that had once tried to eat him.

Emil laughed, but he and the warriors found they had no more time to congratulate themselves. The fighters of the halfling community rounded the open market and joined the human ranks.

As a combined army, they charged across the landing field at the *Spelljammer*'s bow and passed around the council chambers, turning toward the neogi tower in the distance. The fighting had increased since their last report from the tower watch. Here on the starboard side, the skirmishes had broken out in full. The warriors ran past the bloody corpses of human and neogi alike, and helped defend several lone warriors who had been ambushed by neogi slaves and umber hulks.

They rounded the corner of the captain's tower. Teldin looked up briefly and wondered what, if anything, he could find inside to help him discover his answers. Then they were in the street between the tower and the goblin quarters.

Teldin ordered his squad to take the lead, and he and Djan sprinted for the squat neogi tower, visible in the near distance.

Something small and silver whistled through the air. The warrior to Teldin's left fell, a star of steel embedded in his head.

Then the street echoed with a high-pitched war cry, and Teldin's squad was surrounded by warriors clad from head to toe in red silk. There were about thirty of them. The remainder of CassaRoc's fighters were not far behind, but the strange combatants engaged Teldin's men immediately, baring wicked, curved blades and razor-sharp *shurikens* of steel. One of Teldin's warriors cried out "Shou!" then was struck down by the powerful kick of a red-garbed fighter. A single sword thrust quieted Teldin's man permanently.

Teldin knew little about the Shou, only that they were a race of oriental humans whose religious adherence to the Path made them deadly to anyone they considered an infidel. It was no wonder that they had never responded to Teldin's request of a treaty: they wanted the *Spelljammer* for themselves, to prove across the spheres that the holy Shou path was the true Path.

Djan quickly jumped into the fray, his sword singing through the air as he brought it down toward a Shou fighter. The shou's blade came up, and sparks flew as steel met steel.

Teldin whipped out his sword and started forward to aid his friend. Then his head buzzed with a warm feeling, a sense of urgency. Instinctively, he jerked back his head, and a *shuriken* whizzed just an inch past his face.

He spun around.

His antagonist wore a suit of black silk and a hood of scarlet. His sword gleamed in the chaotic light, and the man approached him cautiously. "You are the one," he said. The man's accent was strange, clipped as though the Common tongue were awkward to him. "Cloakmaster. You are not invisible to our wu jen."

Teldin knew that his disguise was then pointless. As the fighter's sword went up, Teldin took a defensive stance with his sword, and he felt his features return involuntarily to their original shapes. The Shou, he thought. They had the chance to be our allies. Now this. Just another obstacle keeping me from Cwelanas.

"Come on," Teldin said. "Let's get this over with. I have neogi to kill."

"Don't count on it," the masked fighter said, and he leaped toward Teldin, his sword a rapid blur of flashing steel.

As Djan locked into combat with his own assailant, Teldin parried and thrust up, blocking the Shou fighter's overhead thrust. The two warriors met with a ringing of steel, their blades locked together above their heads. The Shou lashed out with a foot and knocked one leg out from under Teldin. The blades disengaged. Teldin ducked under the Shou's blade and swung his sword out, to be thrust aside effortlessly. The Shou laughed.

Around him, Teldin's warriors were battered by the onslaught of the Shou. Djan successfully blocked the efforts of his opponent, but the contest was evenly matched between them. Despite the arrival of CassaRoc's lead warriors, the Shou fighters were expert in hand-to-hand combat and fought with a speed that Teldin found amazing. Half of his squad was already unconscious or bleeding, and the remaining Shou doubled up on his other warriors.

The leader, it appeared, had reserved Teldin for himself.

The Shou danced around Teldin with the practiced air of a panther toying with its prey. His sword flicked out to nick Teldin countless times on his cheeks and arms.

Anger built within Teldin like the white-hot flames of a gnomish furnace. His companions were falling around him, even as more of CassaRoc's warriors arrived.

He felt the familiar, cold-hot tingle of energy surround him like an enveloping blanket. Time seemed to slow; the fighter swung his sword with ever-decreasing speed, until it seemed to almost stop just a few inches from Teldin's face.

Then Teldin swung up with his sword. A shower of sparks erupted from the weapons' impact, then Teldin kicked out and sent the Shou fighter sprawling across the deck.

Slowly, the fighter sprang up, fury glinting in his dark eyes.

The cloak whipped around Teldin like a thing alive. The fighter pounced, his hands and feet cocked in positions of attack.

Then Teldin screamed inside. The cloak spread out, and whirling *shurikens* of pure energy shot out from the coruscating lining of the cloak. One star impaled the Shou in the palm of a hand; another burned deep into a thigh. The *shurikens* found their targets all across the fighter's body, in his torso, his arms. Wherever they hit, his flesh and clothes burned with the white heat of a sun.

The final *shuriken* shot out from the cloak like a blazing comet. The Shou assassin went down, a burning crater of smoking, cauterized flesh centered in his forehead. His eyes stared blankly into the endless flow. The energy of the cloak's *shurikens* faded into wisps of white smoke.

The remaining Shou fighters paused in midattack as their leader dropped stone dead to the deck. With renewed energy, CassaRoc's men pressed the attack and quickly felled half of them. Djan's opponent fell as a misplaced sword thrust was knocked aside by Djan's practiced block and the sharp point of Djan's blade tasted for the first time the blood of the Shou. Within a minute, the other Shou backed away individually, then decided to make an escape for the comparative safety between the close towers of the citadel region.

In retreat, the Shou threw their remaining *shurikens* at Teldin and his men and called out with angry, impotent threats of revenge. The humans' shields effortlessly knocked away the razor-sharp weapons. A dozen bolts shot from the warriors' crossbows, mostly missing their targets as the Shou wove singly through the buildings and disappeared. Two Shou were dropped with clean shots by a pair of Hancherback's halflings.

The alliance warriors quickly assessed themselves, then started again for the neogi tower. Only a handful of men were lost in the skirmish with the Shou, and Teldin knew—as did CassaRoc the Mighty—that before the war was over, much more Shou blood would be spilled, if not to gain the *Spelljammer*, then in simple revenge for the ambush upon Teldin and the loss of CassaRoc's men.

At the entrance to the neogi tower, the humans quickly dispatched the small squad of minotaurs left behind to secure the doors. Then the entrance was pummeled by CassaRoc's heavy battering ram. With a splintering groan, the doors broke open to reveal the darkness inside the neogi tower.

The fighting became furious as the humans swarmed inside

and pressed their foes. The towering ogres inside the entrance chamber numbered about five, the minotaurs about ten. The butchered corpses of neogi and umber hulks littered the floor, together in death with the less numerous corpses of their enemies. Behind them, directing the fighting throughout the building, were five angry beholders. At sight of the assembled humans, the beholders floated quickly through the inner door and disappeared into the central corridor.

The entrance chamber was taken quickly, as the enemies were dispatched simply by the human alliance's strong numbers. Teldin pressed the attack into the tower's central hallway and ordered squads into each of the tower's six other chambers. "Find the elf!" Teldin shouted. "Bring her to me!"

The grimy walls, already dark with the spattering of neogi blood, became redder as the humans sliced into the battle between their enemies. Neogi blood pooled innocently with minotaur and ogre, and, inevitably, human.

Teldin crashed into the tower's most opulent chamber, Coh's study, by kicking open the door with his powerful legs. Inside, four neogi were torturing a beholder, one of the eye tyrants that had fled when the humans attacked the tower.

Teldin was a blur as he raced between the neogi, lashing out with his sharp sword to cleanly slice through their bony legs, to skewer one neogi through its round belly. The anger was hot in him, and his sword cut through the reptiles with unseen ferocity. Within minutes, three neogi lay dead in pools of their own black blood. The fourth huddled against the wall, blood oozing from twenty shallow wounds across its squat body, one segmented leg dangling helplessly by a shred. The tortured beholder lay dead on the floor, its great eye staring emptily up at its withered eyestalks.

The Cloakmaster's sword sliced through the air in front of the neogi. The eellike head snapped back in fear. "Coh," Teldin said. "I want him. Where is he?"

The hostage shot a furtive glance to a large, ornate box resting on a stone pedestal. The neogi began to laugh. "Coh is here not, meat. Shemeat you want taken is. Never will find her you, unless cloak is—

With a scream of rage, Teldin's sword plunged into the neogi's black neck. It's pointed tongue quivered as the beast gurgled in death and fell limply to the blood-stained floor.

Teldin examined the beholder the neogi had killed. Its huge eye was glazed over in death, and behind it was an open trapdoor. The Cloakmaster put it together instantly: the other beholders had used the trapdoor to escape—the same secret door Coh had used to smuggle Cwelanas secretly away. He slammed the trapdoor shut and spun around. Perhaps Coh used it to escape, too, he thought.

Teldin turned and walked over to the decorated box. Its edges were trimmed with gold, and its handle was studded with sapphires. He reached for the hinged door on the front and opened it.

He stepped back, his mouth open in horror.

The head that watched him had once been that of a human. The gray skin was stretched across its skull like ancient parchment, and, as Teldin watched, the sunken eyes blinked open. It saw Teldin and spoke to him with a soft voice tinged with both regret and ancient anger.

"I serve he whom you seek. He has taken the woman into the elven veins, and you will not find her."

"The veins," Teldin said. "You mean the warrens?"

"Give him the cloak, or all you love will die."

Teldin raised his sword. "Why does he want it so? If he gains the cloak, then *everyone* will die during the Dark Times."

"You are just as much a fool as my master predicted. This has nothing to do with the Dark Times. The cloak is the key! The cloak is what drew mage B'Laath'a to the Wanderer!

"The cloak is power incarnate! It is the *Spelljammer* itself! The Fool has promised—"

"The Fool?" Teldin shouted. "Coh is in with the Fool? Where is Cwelanas? Tell me!"

The gray head turned its eyes away, realizing it had already given away too much.

Teldin shouted once again for answers, but the head would not speak. He screamed in rage. His sword flashed, and he thrust the blade through the zombie's mouth so hard that the steel splintered through the back of the box. The zombie's dead eyes rolled up into its sockets. Then Teldin turned and strode out of the room.

The tower was theirs. As Teldin had defeated the cowering neogi in Coh's chambers, CassaRoc's warriors and the halfling fighters had overwhelmed the combined forces of the Beholder Alliance. Most of their enemies had escaped, probably to regroup later, but the beholders had done much of the humans' jobs for them, annihilating almost all of the neogi aboard the *Spelljammer*, even killing the great old master in its dank, bloody pit, along with its few premature hatchlings that had been nurtured inside its belly.

Teldin approached CassaRoc and Djan and sheathed his sword. "She's gone," Teldin said. "Coh has escaped, into the warr—"

He stopped suddenly, and his friends turned to watch. A hazy light was forming beside them, glowing reddish at the borders. The men took a step back, brandishing their weapons.

A shape formed inside the light and faced Teldin. Gaye Goldring appeared before them, still weak from her encounter with the Fool and the rats.

The warriors in the neogi tower stopped to see what was happening. Teldin walked toward her.

"Gaye," he said, unaware that her appearance was an astral projection, "are you really here?"

I must warn you, Teldin, she said suddenly, *of the Fool and his plans for the* Spelljammer. *He wants nothing less than complete control. He wants you—*

Her telepathic voice seemed to strangle, and the room became dimmer, as though the light were being absorbed.

Darkness flickered around her, and three gray shapes formed around her, swirling out from dark cyclones of smoke. The room grew cold, and the warriors covered their ears as a wind sprang from nowhere, chilling them with an unnatural wail.

The shapes floated toward Gaye, their dark arms outstretched, surrounding her. Simultaneously, another shape appeared behind her, swirling with gray smoke, howling a scream of undying pain and rage that made several warriors fall to their knees.

The humans covered their ears at the cold pain that flooded through them. Teldin immediately reached out for the kender.

At once, Gaye and the apparitions disappeared before his eyes, an expression of terror frozen on her face as the undead closed on her.

The room was silent as the screams faded around them.

"That—that was a banshee," Djan said. "Very, very bad."

Teldin stared at where the kender had vanished.

"Gaye," he said softly. "Gaye."

Chapter Nineteen

• • •

"*. . . And, lo, the loculus shall remain even though I be lost in the Red Chamber. My spells are powerful and will last far longer than I. The Historie will be available until the end of things, waiting for the Son of the Architects to claim it as his own. . . .*"
Neridox, librarian; journal 1009; reign of Jokarin.

The secret passageway the beholders had discovered in Coh's quarters led to a concealed exit across from the hulk tower. As the humans took the neogi tower and the fighting on the *Spelljammer* escalated between the races, the surviving beholders plunged into the tunnel and made their escape. The hidden exit opened near the beholder ruins, directly across from the neogi tower.

Once the beholders were inside, the monarch, Gray Eye, called for a war conference and quickly assessed the casualties. Two beholders had fallen: one to the four neogi, captured during the escape from the attacking humans, and the other, snapped in two by the powerful jaws of the neogi great old master as it thrashed mindlessly in hatred at its attackers. One beholder had lost an eyestalk to an umber hulk, and then, in anger, had ordered the ogre allies to dismember the hulk instantly.

Gray Eye's eyestalks twitched visibly in rage. The leader's *ioun* stones circled him crazily, reflecting his volcanic temper. "Our primary enemies are defeated," Gray Eye told the survivors. "We were victorious, and our alliance has served its purpose: to do our warring for us, with a minimum of casualties to the beholders.

"If they have not yet been defeated by the humans, they soon will be—or the survivors will live to return to their towers and lick their wounds."

Gray Eye floated quickly from side to side across his dais, as though he were pacing in thought. His teeth gnashed in anger. Then he faced his brethren and called to his second in command. "Blehal, go to our allies. Convince them that the war must continue, and to bring out their reserves. We will all meet here within the hour."

"But, Lord," Blehal said, "who shall I tell them we are attacking?"

Gray Eye smiled cruelly. His smaller eyestalks undulated like snakes above his milky great eye. "This war is far from over. The beholders must reign supreme, or we will be left for dead when the Dark Times arrive. The victors of this war will own the *Spelljammer*, and I intend for us to become the victors. As one mighty force, our alliance will prove deadly to our most despised enemies, the elves."

The beholders glared balefully at their leader, drinking in his murderous threats. "Soon we will toast our victory by drinking the blood of all our enemies." Gray Eye spun to face Blehal. "Go! Tell them to arm themselves for war!"

Blehal bobbed once in servitude and floated out of the room, two fellow beholders following closely behind him as protection. Gray Eye dismissed the others and floated silently above his dais, his mind filled with glorious dreams of victory and conquest.

It was not simply the Dark Times, though that was an unmatched impetus for his brethren to do his bidding. His purpose was more profound, for he knew the true nature of Teldin's cloak, and he wanted it for himself. *Let the Dark Times come. What will it matter? I will have all the power I will ever need to survive—to rule over the universe! The* Spelljammer *will be my ultimate weapon.*

In the beholder ruins, Gray Eye laughed softly to himself. His enemies would soon fall, and the cloak would be his.

He could already taste the sweetness of elf flesh on his tongue.

Chapter Twenty

• • •

". . . All things, in time, age. All things, in time, become corrupt. The Wanderer is timeless, yet lives still on our physical plane and is subject to both physical and magical laws. Like all things, the Wanderer must change with time, and in no place is this aging more evident than in the areas known as the Warrens. Where once, legend tells us, flowed rivers of magic, now only cold winds blow like the breath of fiends, and men who explore there seldom return. . . ."

Davibruc, cleric, whose son was lost in the warrens; reign of Bender the Weaver.

Darkness materialized around her. The warm glow that emanated from her astral body flickered on the walls around her. It was a tunnel, and Gaye felt the chill of the warrens permeate her soul.

Shapes began to form in the air around her, and the sound of the banshee's plaintive moan rang through her, filling her with a nameless dread, a loneliness that she had never known. She felt herself weaken more as the spirits became more tangible, and then the specters and the banshee had her surrounded. The fear they engendered was almost palpable, and their cloud of terror enveloped her, pulling her astral form away from Teldin just as he had reached for her.

Gaye felt the claustrophobic darkness of the warrens become solid around her. She had been transported to the warrens, where the banshee's powers would not be weakened by the light of the phlogiston. Beyond, in the darkness that owned the warrens, she caught a vague glimpse of a neogi master and its enslaved umber hulk, disappearing into the blackness. A woman screamed . . . then she heard the rattling laughter of the master lich.

The Fool, she thought. These are his agents . . . his slaves. She knew without thinking that they had been sent as the Fool's revenge.

The spirits numbered four. Three specters were the undead souls of humans who had been unlucky enough to explore the warrens years earlier and fall into the Fool's lair. The banshee was the soul of a tormented, undead elf who had been cursed by his guilt at helping the Fool unwittingly destroy a sector of the Elven High Command.

The banshee wailed, and its moan echoed through the chamber. Gaye shivered uncontrollably as numbness passed through her with a ripple of unimaginable coldness. The specters reached out. One's smoky hand touched her shoulder, another touched her head, and she was chilled, frozen immobile by their ephemeral touch.

The banshee's wail grew louder. She felt her breath constricting, her heart beating in frantic terror in response to the spirit's unholy wail.

Her mind raced for a strategy against the Fool's servants. Her psionic abilities, weakened as they were from the Fool's previous attack, seemed trivial against the spirits; nothing less than an exorcism would disperse these ethereal slaves of the Fool.

In desperation, she concentrated on warmth, on her own inner fires, to remove the paralysis the spirits had caused. Her fingers grew warm, and her hand erupted in a ball of golden energy.

The shades drew back abruptly, wailing in fear of her purifying light.

She knew she was too weak to summon again the brilliant fury of a nova, but perhaps there was another tactic that could save her, that would send these undead back to the Abyss.

Then she knew.

Paralyzed with fear, she focused inward. She visualized her latent energies as a flickering flame, suddenly growing in power. She imagined warmth creeping through her body, dispelling the paralysis with white heat.

The light at her fingertips was shrinking. The spirits crept closer toward Gaye, reaching for her with their spectral fingers. The banshee screamed, renewed by the encroaching darkness, and its howl was the sound of the wind singing through black trees and between tombstones, through the caverns of the dead.

Gaye swallowed her fear and sent her sight inward. She channeled her mental energies and visualized her powers in front of her, glowing beyond the surrounding circle of undead, in a tangible form outside of her body.

The spirits halted. The shimmering outline of a doorway appeared, a misty doorway through which she could pass to another world, even another ship.

But her purpose here was different, not a goal of escape, but one of defense. As the dimensional doorway materialized, which she had created as an opening to the sunlit world of Toril, the black chamber was flooded with warm daylight from Realmspace.

The banshee screamed in blazing pain. Its clawed hands of smoke went to its eyes. The spirits flickered weakly, silhouetted against the doorway, and the undead were blown away like wisps of black smoke on a torrential wind of light.

The banshee's wail died in her ears. Gaye sagged against the wall, drained of will and energy. The doorway dissipated and left her in darkness. Her astral form began to fade away.

Her last thought before she returned, unconscious, to her body in Herdspace was, I must warn Teldin.

Then she could think no more, and the warrens once again fell into shadow.

Chapter Twenty-One

• • •

". . . *Most answers are hidden in the riddles of the human heart, and in the conflicts that define a man's soul. . . .*"
Hanar Pasi, paladin; reign of Galor

Atop the neogi tower, two warriors hammered the tip of a broadsword into the roof. In the light breeze created by the *Spelljammer*'s movement through the flow, the makeshift flag that had been tied to the sword was a proud symbol of the humans' victory over evil. The outline of the *Spelljammer* had been drawn in purple paint on a white sheet, and was centered with a crude representation of Teldin's amulet. The designs were surrounded by stars, shooting from the amulet like *shurikens* of energy.

When their enemies had been routed, Teldin ordered the unhuman survivors to be chained and held in the prisoner's area, and the overflow in the pit of the great old master, surrounded by armed guards. With shovels and with their bare hands, the prisoners disposed of the master's corpse and those of its bludgeoned offspring, then were held deep within the pit for their eventual dispensation.

There was only a single neogi survivor; the others had been killed, if not by the Beholders Alliance, then in the surprise attack by the humans. About half of the minotaurs were dead, and two of the ogres had been killed defending the tower. The other unhumans had somehow escaped, fearful of the humans' far superior numbers.

A thorough search was made of the tower, and then it was gone over a second time. The rooms of the neogi were found deserted or strewn with neogi corpses, and no other escape tunnels were apparent.

During the second search, a guard called Teldin back to Coh's quarters. He lifted a shining shirt of chain mail and a dagger, which he had discovered in a corner. Teldin recognized them as CassaRoc entered the room. The Cloakmaster took them and tucked them in his belt. "She is without protection," he said angrily. "Coh has her, and she can't even defend herself." He lashed out and kicked a piece of ornamental statuary. The grotesque sculpture bounced off the wall and crashed into pieces on the floor.

"Coh is hiding somewhere in the warrens. You're right: he and the damned Fool are in this together somehow. And we don't even know how to get down there."

"Well, at least we've got the tower secured now," CassaRoc said. "You know, there might be someone who can help us out with this."

"Who?"

"Well, I've heard that some of our more adventurous halfling friends have ventured into the warrens. And then there's your mind flayer friend. He knows more about this ship than most. We could call for him."

"You won't have to." Na'Shee was at the door. Both Teldin and CassaRoc turned as she entered. "Estriss is here, asking to see you immediately. He almost got killed by our guards. They thought he was attacking them."

Teldin nodded. "Send him in immediately."

Djan came in a moment later, followed by the illithid. Estriss bore a heavy cloak, and a broadsword hung from his belt. Mind flayers usually disdained such human affectations as weapons, but Estriss had learned the ways of humans well, and those he could not fend off with his mental powers could be battled with steel. The mind flayer greeted Teldin and CassaRoc, then sat in one of the chairs that they had brought in to Master Coh's quarters.

There is a problem, Estriss said, *of which we must speak.*

Teldin brought another chair around. "Go ahead."

The illithids are preparing for something of which I want no part. I managed to escape the horned tower just before the attack was to begin.

"Attack?" Teldin interrupted. "What attack?"

The mind flayers and their goblin allies are attacking the elves as we speak, Estriss said. *They have long hated the elves, and have long desired more power here on the* Spelljammer. *They have decided that the time to strike is now.*

"So has every other race on board," CassaRoc said.

Indeed. The mind flayer leaned forward. *There could be trouble very soon*, Estriss said. His facial tentacles twitched. *That is the main reason I came over. I would have come sooner, but I could not escape the illithid tower without their notice.*

They are plotting to assassinate you, Teldin.

"How?"

I do not know. The general population was not privy to Trebek's plans.

"When?"

Again, I do not know, but Trebek wants you and the elves dead. That way—

A cry came from inside the tower. The men stood as Na'Shee came to the doorway. "It's the mind flayers and the elves. They've started fighting, too."

CassaRoc said, "Alert our men. Have them stand ready."

"For anything," Teldin added.

Na'Shee nodded once, then turned as the shouting increased in the hallway. They all heard the distant sound of metal clashing with metal.

"The war is escalating rapidly, Estriss," the Cloakmaster said. "We have trouble enough on the *Spelljammer* alone, and there is a score of ships closing on us from the flow. I need answers now."

What can I do? the illithid asked.

"Cwelanas is being held in the warrens by Master Coh and, I think, the Fool. I need to know how to get down there and rescue her."

Estriss shook his head slowly. His opaque eyes seemed moist, thoughtful. *I do not think I can help you, Cloakmaster. My research has uncovered mentions of the warrens on the* Spelljammer, *but I have not run across locations for entrances.*

I would guess that some have been sealed in the towers, for fear of what lurks there.

"There must be at least one open entrance," Teldin said, frustrated. "Coh had to find one somewhere."

Then Teldin spun around, his eyes wide. "What?"

CassaRoc looked at him, questioningly. "Cloakmaster? Are you all right?"

"I heard—" Teldin started. "I thought I heard—"

Then it came again, a whisper in his ears like the crashing of waves.

Only you can hear me, the voice of Gaye Goldring said softly to Teldin. *I am weak and have little time to speak.*

"Gaye. It's Gaye," Teldin said. "She's speaking to me."

Teldin, you are in more danger than you know. The Fool desires your cloak and your death. His goals are mad, and he wants the Spelljammer, *only so he can take it to its death. He will do anything to achieve his goals. Even now he has Cwelanas.*

"Cwelanas?" he said. "How?"

Coh is taking her to the Fool. The stakes have been raised.

He stood in wonderment at Gaye's seemingly magical abilities to discover hidden knowledge, to help protect him. "Gaye, how are you doing this? Where did you get these powers?"

She was silent for a moment, then an image sprang into his mind, of a sunlit day in Herdspace. *Here,* she said.

His head jerked back as his mind was washed with a series of images: of Gaye staying behind as Teldin sailed away from Herdspace; of fal One Six Nine accepting her as his student, and her beginning as a psionicist. He saw her first failed experiments in the psionic arts, then watched her steadily progress into a master psionicist. He saw the first time she used her clairvoyant abilities, and as she discovered that Teldin had finally reached the *Spelljammer.* And would need her help.

He saw this all in a single instant.

It took him a few seconds to interpret her message. Her voice grew weaker. *I must go now. Answer the call, Teldin. Do not delay.*

He blinked and called out to her, "You can't go! How do I

get down into the warrens? How do you know—"

Her voice was a whisper, fading away like her form. He made out one word as her voice trailed away: *library.*

He stood silently, surrounded by his warriors.

"You were talking to your friend Gaye?" CassaRoc asked.

"Yes." Teldin stared away for a moment, then turned to look Estriss and CassaRoc in the eyes. "Something is calling me, though it may not be the *adytum* of which Estriss has told us. Gaye mentioned it just now, as you did earlier, CassaRoc. And if I've learned anything on this quest, it is to follow my hunches and trust in fate."

Teldin looked at Na'Shee. "Perhaps you should come, too. I think we'll need all the help we can get."

"Where are we going?" Na'Shee said.

"The library," Teldin said.

* * * * *

In the eternal darkness that was the warrens, Cwelanas struggled against the behemoth that clasped her tightly within its massive arms.

They had taken her dagger and her mail back in the neogi tower, and now Cwelanas was helpless against the walking horrors that held her captive.

The neogi was huge, the largest she had ever seen. Master Coh was resplendent to his race, tattooed and painted in a spectrum of colors that covered his body. On his forehead was his trademark, a symbol made of interlocked circles that signified his name, his status, and was the brand on his slaves.

The umber hulk that held Cwelanas wore Coh's brand on his forehead as well. Orik was proud to be Master Coh's personal slave, even going so far as to try to learn the Common tongue to please his master. His attempts were barely successful, sounding more like the guttural grunts of apes, but he frequently managed to make relatively clear sentences.

"Silent be!" Orik commanded her. He would have said "Be quiet," but he always had trouble with the "Q" sound, and long ago he had given up even trying to sound it out.

Master Coh was a neogi with an inborn magical talent. In the lead, he concentrated steadily, finding their path using his magical senses to blaze a trail through the darkness. His sharp claws clacked against the floor as they made their way deeper into the warrens, toward his ally, the Fool.

Here, he knew he would receive asylum. Here, the ransom for the meat would be made and the Cloak of the First Pilot would be his. His friend, the Fool, would, of course, choose him. Did not the next one have to be a magician such as he? Would not the Fool reward him for bringing victory to the neogi?

He laughed to himself. The elf would be his key to succession.

He led them down a narrow tunnel, then into another, even tighter and darker. Orik had to crouch as he walked through the tunnel, dragging Cwelanas behind him.

The air grew colder, and the walls around them gradually opened into a chamber, swirling with a black mist that reeked of something rotten. Coh grinned. Venom dripped off his long fangs. He could feel the Fool's dark presence in the chamber around them.

A blue glow appeared. Coh blinked at the light, forming at the end of the Fool's wand of conjuration, then he grinned. The light blossomed, and the shrouded form of the Fool appeared. His piercing eyes watched Coh, almost burning into his brain.

"Fool," Coh said, "it is I, Coh, master of the neogi."

"Yes," said the Fool.

"Fool, I have a hostage. With this meat, my claim to the *Spelljammer* will be assured, if only you will—"

The blue light suddenly burst from the Fool's wand and flared out, encircling Orik's neck like a living thing, a twisting rope of glowing ectoplasm. The umber hulk's head erupted with an azure glow, and he reached up to grab his head.

Cwelanas fell heavily to the floor, scrabbled away, and huddled in a corner. Orik clawed at his face as the blue light quickly spread to engulf his body. He screamed once and spun in pain, searching for the master he knew would protect him. "Maaaa-ster . . ."

Coh turned his narrowed eyes toward the Fool. "What have you done? Are we not allies? Have I not—"

The Fool reached within his cloak of blackness and pulled a

broadsword from an ancient, jeweled scabbard. Its sharp blade was serrated wickedly, and the metal was dark, pockmarked with age and corruption. The Fool whispered a single word that seemed to vibrate within the walls of its lair.

With a low chuckle, he flipped the sword effortlessly into the air. At once, the blade came alive, twisted in midair, and aimed its black point at the heart of Master Coh.

Coh backed away, raising his claws in defense. But the blade sliced through them effortlessly and sank deep into his chest, drinking deeply the life force from his black heart.

The neogi collapsed to the floor, side by side with the charred corpse of his faithful servant.

The Fool gestured with a bony hand. One claw of Master Coh's twitched.

Cwelanas watched in terror as the Fool turned and came toward her, focusing his white-hot eyes at her and rasping low in his throat.

The Fool smiled.

* * * * *

In a connecting tunnel, protected in a tightly woven spell of invisibility, the neogi mage B'Laath'a watched as the blood seeped from Coh's mortal wound and as the master's limbs twitched in undead response to the Fool's spell.

His eyes gleamed with hatred. He had never trusted Coh, but had simply needed the master's resources to keep Cwelanas enslaved and close to the humans.

It was the Cloakmaster B'Laath'a had wanted, ever since his deathspiders had traced the ancient cloak to the reigar craft on Krynn so long ago. The plan had been his, and the cloak would soon have been his, if Coh had not lusted after its power himself.

Now undead master is, B'Laath'a thought. Plans now effect put into must I. Mine cloak will be! Traced to Krynn, did I, and cloak only mine will be!

Surrounded by his shield of invisibility, B'Laath'a backed softly away up the tunnel, toward the light.

Chapter Twenty-Two

• • •

"*. . . And the vessels of evil shall converge on the Sphere Wanderer. As the Progenitor was in the beginning, so shall be its offspring at the end . . .*"

Grimstone Shadow, mage; *The Tapestry of Margeaux*; reign of Shiwan.

A squadron of ten of CassaRoc's warriors charged from the neogi tower and formed a half-circle around the entrance. Immediately, Teldin's party ran through the door and was encircled by the warriors as they started their run to the library tower.

The fighting was steadily increasing across the *Spelljammer*, as the fear of the Dark Times swelled unreasonably and chaos took sway. Goblins and elves battled ferociously near the minotaur tower, which had been abandoned since the alliance of the minotaurs with the eye tyrants. Behind them, near the beholder ruins, the humans watched as a group of halflings beat back a trio of giants that had cornered them near the minotaur quarters.

From all corners of the *Spelljammer*, the clash of steel rang through the streets and alleys, punctuated by the wails of the dying and the war screams of the victors.

The warriors pushed their tightly knit wedge through the elf-goblin battle, scattering the unhumans with a minimum of bloodshed. The fighting was rapidly disintegrating into a free-for-all, and Teldin had organized this protective wedge to get his party through the nearest bottleneck of fighters, so that they could make a run past the goblin quarters for the library.

Past the minotaur tower, where they easily cut through a halfhearted gauntlet of ragged goblin fighters, the human wedge split apart and doubled back to the neogi tower. Teldin, CassaRoc, Chaladar, Estriss, Djan, and Na'Shee quickened their pace and bolted across a wide expanse of open deck for the library tower, situated alongside the captain's tower. Here, the ship was free of fighting and bloodshed. Teldin afforded a quick glance up, into the flow, and his pace slowed momentarily. The fleets encroaching on the *Spelljammer* were almost there. Teldin quickly gauged the distance to the closest vessel, a wasp ship, and decided it would be within ballista distance within half an hour.

"We see them!" Chaladar shouted. "Come on, Cloakmaster! We can do no good out here!"

They turned at the corner of the goblin quarters. The library tower, across the avenue, had been tightly sealed years ago, and the interior had never been seen since. The library's double doors were barricaded with brick and mortar, probably thick enough to withstand a battering ram, Teldin guessed.

"What now?" CassaRoc asked. He idly scratched his thickly bearded chin.

"I know you told me the tower had been sealed, but I had no idea it was *this* fortified," Teldin said.

Chaladar offered, "We should have brought a battering ram."

They had talked about a ram before, in the neogi tower, but the neogi had no use for battering rams, and the humans did not want to take a chance fighting their way across to the Tower of Thought. Too many lives could be lost.

Teldin stared at his objective and sighed angrily. There were no windows, no other doors, nothing.

"Damn."

Teldin felt himself staring at the sealed doors, and without realizing it at first, his arms began to sizzle with the familiar embrace of his cloak's energy. He heard CassaRoc say something, but the words seemed sluggish, barely understandable.

The muscles in his arms burned with fire. The energy flowed through him, embodying his frustration, his anger. Time slowed around him; the edge of his vision was a blur, and all he could see was the stone and mortar blocking him from his goal.

His mind swam, and, with certainty, he felt *I'm supposed to be here.*

He slid his sword from its scabbard. The energy that fluctuated through him shot out of his hands. As though it were encased in an aura, the energies of the cloak infused his steel and lit the metal from within, burning with a light that was pure and radiant, explosive.

A scream echoed in his ears, then Teldin realized it was a cry from his own mouth as he leaped up the short flight of steps and swung the sword into the stone barrier.

The sword broke through rock with a clap of thunder. His steel was invulnerable, alive, biting through the stone as though it were bread. Mortar and rock and brick flew out from the onslaught of the Cloakmaster's powerful blade, and he attacked the barrier again, relentlessly, heedless of the chalk and dust that surrounded him in a pale cloud.

The others stood frozen as the Cloakmaster disappeared in the cloud of dust, a raging berserker against a wall of rock. "Teldin!" CassaRoc shouted. "Are you all right?"

Chunks of brick and stone rained to the deck. There was a final cry, then the dust settled slowly and Teldin stood before a gaping hole in the barrier, untouched by the dust that had surrounded him. The wooden doors inside had been no match for the sharp power of Teldin's blade. The Cloakmaster had splintered a wide hole through the doors, and the darkness inside beckoned them with mystery.

He turned to face his companions. The power still pulsed through him; they could see the lines of rage and inner strength mapped like pulsating veins across his face. Then he sagged as the power of the cloak flooded out of him. At once, the sword began to vibrate in his hand, and, with a loud snap that echoed off the tower walls, the sword shattered into bent pieces of battered steel and clanged to his feet.

The warriors joined Teldin at the top of the stairs. Chaladar handed him a spare sword from his belt. "Good work," the paladin said understatedly.

Teldin was silent. He pointed his new sword toward the ragged gap in the door. "Let's go," he said, then he crawled through.

Once inside, he stared up into the blackness, waiting as the warriors each came through and stopped behind him. Na'Shee reached into a pouch on her belt and pulled out one of the *Spelljammer*'s smaller light rods, which was essentially a hand-sized crystal of the same luminescent material that made up the ship's light panels. Djan did the same, and the library was lit with a dim, bluish glow that barely reached the edge of the second floor.

They stood in a meager foyer, and tall pillars stretched up into the darkness to some point high above. The pillars were cracked, blackened with the fiery evidence of the destruction that had gone on here years before.

Around them, bookshelves stretched away into the shadows, but the shelves were bare except for thick black drifts of ash that fluttered in the breeze singing through the doors. The shelves themselves were but blackened skeletons of their former selves; the ladders that led up to them were charred and useless.

"What went on here?" Djan mused, turning to take in all the destruction.

Chaladar spoke reverently. The thick smell of smoke and soot hung on everything like a shroud. "It was during the time of Jokarin the Bold, or so the legend goes. Neridox, a mad wizard, was supposed to have sealed himself up here in the tower. As to the fire that obviously raged through here, I have no clue. This is not part of the tale."

The group slowly spread out on the lower floor. At the rear of the building, a flight of stone steps led up into the balconies that made up the second floor. The floor was covered with layers of ash and soot and lay undisturbed by the passage of time or by previous visitors.

Teldin stopped at a bookcase and reached out. He pulled a chunk of blackened leather from a mound of ash and wiped it off with his fingers. He could read part of a title written in gold:

ok
f the
ere
derer

He tossed it to the black floor. "There is nothing here," he said to himself, "nothing here at all."

"All these books," Djan said. "Gone. What good does it do to burn a book?"

"It is the evil that men do," Chaladar said softly, "that must be cleansed, not the wisdom that can lead them out of the darkness and into light."

There is a another level, Estriss said in Teldin's mind. The others heard the mind flayer as well, and they turned toward the Cloakmaster.

Teldin took the first step, and the group made its way up the stairs to the balconies. Here, the situation was the same as below: long walls of nothing but ash, grim testimony to the wisdom that had been ignored by the madness of long-forgotten violence.

Together they walked along the port gallery and stopped at a spiral staircase in the corner. Na'Shee held up her light and took a few steps down. "Nothing," she said. "It looks like it was a storage room of some sort."

Teldin nodded. Na'Shee came up beside him and gasped at the sight behind him.

The others turned. Djan held up his light rod.

The body they found was little more than a skeleton, mummified in its own blackened flesh. It was seated behind a desk between two spiral staircases. Its mouth gaped open in a soundless, eternal cry, and the dagger that had killed the man was still stuck in the dried skin between his ribs.

"Who was he?" Djan inquired.

CassaRoc whispered, "Probably the mage Neridox, murdered." He swallowed. "So much for his vengeful spirit. This is not part of the legend either."

The desk crumbled apart at their touch, and afterward they explored the second level and the storage room under the starboard staircase. They met below, after their searches on both floors had turned up nothing salvageable.

"There has to be something here," CassaRoc said.

"No," Chaladar said. "I've been looking for secret doors or rooms. All I found was a sealed door, probably leading into the captain's quarters. There is nothing left."

"I can feel it," Teldin said. He absently touched his amulet.

He staggered back, blinking.

"Cloakmaster, what is it?" Na'Shee asked, reaching for him.

He moved her hand away. "Light," he said. "I touched my amulet, and my eyes were filled with a bright—"

Teldin's chest grew warm in a surge of unbidden power, and light blazed forth from his amulet in a cone of pure brilliance. Chaladar threw his arm across his eyes. "What are you doing?" he shouted.

"I don't know!" The energy of the light sizzled in Teldin's ears. He turned, and the beam of light pierced the darkness of the library, dispelling its secret shadows as Teldin cast it over the walls of shelves. "It's never done anything like this before!"

He passed it over CassaRoc and Estriss, who spun away from its blinding white glow. It picked out the far corners with a circle of white light, then Teldin turned, and the beam of light moved across the pillars and toward the staircase.

Teldin stopped suddenly and let the light focus in the center of the room, between the support pillars. The others gathered around him and stared. "Do you see that?"

The others stood transfixed, silent.

Exposed in the beam of the amulet's arcane light, an ornate, oblong mirror floated above the floor. The mirror was full-length, floating on end inches above the floor. In the mirror's image Teldin saw the library.

The books were many, he could see, and the library was lit by torches and candlelight. Wildspace, he thought, then realized that it did not matter. It's a reflection, perhaps of a time long past.

Or, perhaps of a time . . . a time that is forever.

A smile crossed his lips, and he reached out for the mirror.

"Wait, Teldin!" Djan yelled.

Djan's voice seemed far behind him. Teldin's fingertips touched the surface of the looking glass, and he stepped in as though the glass were a liquid rippling around him.

* * * * *

Silence. Complete, utter silence. The amulet flickered once, and the beam of light disappeared like the light of a snuffed candle flame.

Teldin looked around. The books reached to the ceiling, on all the balconies, stacked in piles in the corners, on the desk of Neridox or someone nameless who came long before him. The titles gleamed in gold and silver, along bindings of brown leather and black: A Right and True Telling of the Creation of All That Is... The Sky God and its Children... The Magic of Imagination, Life and the Magic that is Existence... Spelljammer: A Historie, by one so Honored to be an Observer.

In the center of the library, as in the library he had just left in reality, Teldin found an artifact, floating above the floor in a timeless spell created by magic unimaginable to him. It was a globe of black crystal, like the Broken Sphere outside, shimmering with an iridescence, an energy, that shone from within. It spun rapidly, flickering light across his face with millisecond images of times long past, of events long forgotten—battles alongside the giff's tower—a cry of triumph as an orc ship exploded in a sea of wildspace—the singing of the Spelljammer *as it communed with an undersea beast of Harraka.*

The obsidian globe floated at arm level above the floor, crackling silently with energies he could feel in his fingers as he reached for it, energies he knew were the burning fires of the collected knowledge of the wanderer known as the Spelljammer . . .

—And he became one . . .

* * * * *

"Where is he?" Chaladar shouted.

"The mirror," Djan surmised, taking a step toward it. He reached out as though to touch it, then drew back his hand. "How . . . ?"

Wait, Estriss said in their minds. *Look inside. See if the Cloakmaster is well.*

Djan glanced into the mirror and saw only a reflection of the library as it had seemingly appeared an unknown time ago: filled with books, well-lit, ready to be used. "He is not there," he said. "No one is there."

"Well, where is he?" CassaRoc asked.

He is there, the mind flayer said. *Give him a chance. He will return.*

"This is nonsense," Chaladar said. "This is evil. The Cloakmaster must be returned—"

Then, almost with an audible sigh, the surface of the mirror shimmered, rippled, and Teldin, the Cloakmaster, leaped from inside it. The mirror faded away, back into its former state of invisibility.

CassaRoc gripped Teldin's arm. "Speak to me, Teldin. Are you all right?"

Slowly, the Cloakmaster looked up. He smiled weakly, and his eyes seemed filled with an inner peace that he had never before known.

"Yes. Yes, I am fine."

"What happened in there?" Na'Shee asked.

Estriss hung back. Teldin glanced up and saw the mind flayer looking his way.

"I have found my destiny," Teldin said. "Some of my answers are clear."

Estriss sucked in a breath. His facial tentacles twitched in agreement. *Yes, Cloakmaster. I should have suspected . . . You have seen the person you are to be.*

"Tell us," CassaRoc said. "What happened?"

They all stared silently at the Cloakmaster. Estriss bowed his head unknowingly.

"The wisdom of the *Spelljammer* is in there, inside the loculus," Teldin said, "hidden for ages. I touched it, briefly. I became one with it."

"And?" Chaladar said.

"I know my destiny now. I know why the cloak called to me. I know why it came to me, why I left Krynn to seek my fate among the spheres."

The others watched him curiously, waiting. "Djan, you call it *verenthestae.* I don't know what to call it, but I am supposed to be here. I am supposed to be on the *Spelljammer.* This is what my life has been all about, and I never even realized." He held up a length of his cloak. "This is the Cloak of the First Pilot—the first pilot of the *Spelljammer* itself. It is an ultimate helm . . . it is the Ultimate Helm, created at the same time as the *Spelljammer* and somehow eternally intertwined with its destiny. It is the helm of the first pilot, and—" He stopped. "It is my helm.

His voice grew lower, more determined. "This is mine, truly mine—and with it, I have to accept my destiny.

"No more war. No more blood, no more hate. This is a chance for life, for me. And I—"

He paused, looking at each one of them in turn. "I never dared to believe it. I'm not sure I believe it even now, even though I know it in here." He placed his hand over his heart, over the amulet.

Softly, the Cloakmaster told them. "I . . . am to be the next pilot of the *Spelljammer.* This is my destiny.

"I am to be the next—"

His words were forgotten as two events occurred simultaneously. The *Spelljammer* shuddered violently beneath their feet, and the thunderous sound of some collision with the *Spelljammer* echoed through the hole in the doors.

"It seems the war has finally come to us," Teldin said. "The fleets have arrived."

He started toward the doors, then halted abruptly. He bent over in silent pain, and the warriors rushed to him as he sank to his knees.

They watched as Teldin opened his arms. The amulet glowed from within, and his chest pulsated with an inner light, casting a warm glow upon the ashen floor. He clutched his hand to the amulet. "Not now," he said. "Not now."

Cloakmaster? Estriss inquired.

Teldin looked up. Their eyes met, and Teldin's pain was reflected in the mind flayer's silence.

His chest sizzled with inner fire. He looked down. The insignia, the design that was his link to the *Spelljammer*, was glowing again on his chest.

The sign . . . Estriss said. He clasped Teldin's arm. *It's calling you again. You will have to answer the Compass soon, or it will consume you.* Estriss paused to catch his breath. *You must follow its feelings, its strengths. It will lead you to the* adytum.

The *Spelljammer* shook again. Ash fell upon the party from the tower's tallest shelves.

"The war for the *Spelljammer* begins in earnest now," Teldin began to rail. "Cwelanas must be rescued. And now I must answer the *Spelljammer*'s summons. This is more than one man can do!"

"Teldin," Djan said calmly. "This is your destiny. Like it or not, you are the Cloakmaster, and you must choose—soon."

Teldin knew he could not abandon Cwelanas. He had come too far to lose his love, his faith, without fighting for her as hard as he could. He took a deep breath and tried to concentrate. Where is she? How do I find her?

A voice rang in his ears, and he saw a face—a head—speaking to him tonelessly. . . . *He has taken the woman into the elven veins, and you will not find her* . . .

"The warrens," he said. The burning in his chest throbbed with the beating of his heart. "There is an entrance to the warrens somewhere in the Elven High Command."

He stood and started slowly for the door. "Damn the war. Cwelanas comes first. The *Spelljammer* can defend itself for the moment. Cwelanas needs my help more than—"

He spun around as though he had been kicked. His chest glowed with a hot fire, and the amulet seemed to be a brand, searing itself into his flesh. The pattern blazed through his tunic, shining with the light of an ancient, three-pointed star.

Then he pitched forward onto the blackened floor.

CassaRoc rolled him over. "Teldin!" he shouted. "Teldin!"

But Teldin could hear only the call of the *Spelljammer*.

The call came to him powerfully, overriding all neural synapses and conscious thought in one immeasurable burst of energy. It came to him in images and in bits of words. Sounds. Emotions. Sensations that resembled taste and touch and smell.

Above all, there was the yearning, the need.

—*Lonely!*

He wanted to shake his head, to deny his guilt. He had not meant to ignore the call, but it was all happening so fast, and Cwelanas needed him, and he didn't know—

—*Where are you?*

Here! he shouted in his mind. *Here!*

—*Come*, it said, tugging at his mind, his emotions, his very being.

Where? he implored. *Where?*

In a blaze of light, it showed him.

He stood naked in the shadow of the *Spelljammer*'s great tail. He smelled the stench of death from the neogi tower, then saw the light from the flow play like gold fire along the towers across the *Spelljammer*'s back. It concentrated in a yellow pinpoint within the stem of the ship's tail, above the Dark Tower. The glow pulsated like a beating heart, like the burning tattoo upon his chest, and he realized the route he must take to achieve his ultimate destiny.

—*Worthy?* he felt.

Yes, he said.

—*Need!* it cried, and a part of him cried out with it.

—*Finish!*

—*Complete!*

—*Create . . . !*

His eyes blinked and adjusted to the real time inside the neogi tower. CassaRoc had slapped him. "What happened?" he wondered aloud.

"You passed out," Djan said.

"I know," Teldin said. "I know." He clasped Djan's arm. "Don't you understand? Now I know. *I know.* I know how to get to the *adytum.* I know what I must do."

They helped him stand. He placed his hands upon CassaRoc's and Na'Shee's shoulders. "The *Spelljammer* is calling me. It needs me."

He looked into their eyes, almost pleading. He did not want to go. Cwelanas was trapped in a hideaway of Coh, or the Fool, and her life depended on him.

But the amulet—no, the ship—was calling, and part of him answered willingly, as though he belonged here. And he knew he had no choice.

"The war is going to have to wait. I have to get to the *adytum.* May the gods forgive me, but I must answer the *Spelljammer*'s summons . . . now. I pray that Cwelanas will not be lost to me again."

Chapter Twenty-Three

• • •

". . . The call will be stronger than that of even the sirens. It will burn in the challenger's heart, answering the challenger's own need with a call of its own.

"Their need, in reality, is one . . ."

Bh'obb, the Mad Thinker; scribe; reign of the Two Who Are As One.

The *Spelljammer* was a landscape of battle, of splattered blood and clashing steel. The beholders and their allies had commenced fighting across the mighty vessel, engaging their foes in surprise attacks that left the decks slick with fresh blood. But their enemies were faster than they, and the beholders found themselves on the defensive, slowly being beaten back by humans and unhumans alike.

In the swirling haze of the flow, fleets had begun to close on the *Spelljammer* in a deadly swarm. The closest vessel, a deathspider, attacked with simultaneous firings of its forward ballistae. A rain of heavy boulders fell upon one edge of the minotaur tower, causing the starboard wall to cave in and sending a ripple of impact through the ship.

The deathspider banked and fired a second time. The roof of the neogi tower exploded under the onslaught of stone shot, burying a dozen warriors from the Tower of Thought under a ton of rubble. The hand-drawn flag of the Cloakmaster lay torn and forgotten beneath a layer of rock and stone wall.

Teldin and his companions knew it had started as they climbed from the hole in the library doors. The flow was peppered with the dark silhouettes of vessels creeping toward them like hungry carrion, and the sound of hand-to-hand combat echoed from every corner of the *Spelljammer*.

The war had indeed begun.

The weave of the amulet stung like fire through Teldin's chest. With each passing second, the pattern's energy seemed to grow hotter, more urgent, spreading deeper and deeper toward his heart. He knew he should be thinking of Cwelanas, held prisoner by Coh and the Fool. He knew he should be sitting at the table in the neogi tower with CassaRoc and Djan and Chaladar, drawing up detailed strategies for the war against the unhumans. He knew he had duties to protect his friends and allies.

But the Call was upon him, buzzing in his head like a swarm of furious insects. With every step, every action, he was driven to turn and run toward the great ship's tail. The psychic pull was inexorable and could not be ignored.

He needed to go now.

"I cannot wait any longer," Teldin told the group. "It's calling me, burning inside me. You can see it for yourself." He opened his tunic. His chest glowed from within, a yellow pattern of light burning just beneath the skin.

"Teldin, what of the war?" CassaRoc asked.

"Damn the war! It's all because of me anyway," Teldin said. Anger shone like a light in his eyes. "If I'd gone after the *adytum* when I first arrived, we might not be having this war. If we leave now, the war will be over all the sooner."

Djan folded his arms. "Agreed, my friend, but we're still going to have to deal with the war when we try to leave the tower. Where are we going to go?"

Teldin thought back and visualized his route in his head. The sigil on his chest seemed to spark, and words and images came to him unbidden.

"The *adytum* is located within the *Spelljammer*'s tail." He grimaced in pain as the sign on his chest burned. "I must somehow get to the Elven High Command, and go from there—perhaps through the Old Elvish Academy—then into the ship's memory, then through the Dark Tower."

"Memory? What are you talking about?" Djan asked.

Teldin concentrated, and images came to him of a spiraled hall of statues, of row upon row of miniature vessels arranged throughout the rooms. The burning in his chest became cooler, under some control.

Teldin sighed and relaxed. The more he acknowledged the *Spelljammer*'s call, the less pain he felt inside. "I meant the Armory," Teldin said.

CassaRoc laughed. "Dream on, Cloakmaster. The Armory and the Dark Tower? The shivaks won't let you get into one of them, let alone both. I suggest you think of something else."

"What else can I do?" Teldin appealed. "It's calling me. I'm not sure where I have to go, but I still have to try."

Djan nodded. Na'Shee was already securing her weapons. CassaRoc shook his head. "All right, all right. We go out and cut through the war as quickly as possible. We make it to the Elven High Command. Then what?"

Djan said, "The treaty with the elves. They should help us get through the tower. Surely they must know of passages connecting at least the elven towers together."

"We can go across the battlement, for what that's worth," CassaRoc said, "and cross above the academy. We can go straight into the Armory there."

"The Armory will be well protected," Na'Shee said. "Those shivaks are hard to kill."

"Perhaps the elves will loan us a few warriors when we get there. I think we should leave our people here, to help out the allies," Teldin said. "A small band would work better inside the towers anyway."

CassaRoc nodded. "Just ourselves, then?"

"Just ourselves," Teldin said, "and whoever the elves can spare."

"And what of Cwelanas?" Na'Shee inquired suddenly. She adjusted her crossbow, a sword, a dagger, and a heavy, double-headed flail that hung from her belt. The weapon's pointed, cast-iron spheres depended from heavy chains, attached to a thick club.

Teldin looked away. "The call is upon me. The *Spelljammer* is giving me no choice."

They ran down the steps of the library toward the goblin quarters. At the corner, they saw a small amount of fighting going on toward the bow, but most of the battles were restricted to the central and aft portions of the *Spelljammer*, directly in their path. There the fighting was fiercer than they had imagined. Without hesitation, the group dove into the fray, their shields raised and their swords unsheathed. Within mere seconds, Teldin was attacked by one of ShiCaga's towering ogres, and together Teldin and CassaRoc felled the unhuman, hacking at its ribs and legs. CassaRoc delivered the death blow through the ogre's heart.

At one point, an ogre wizard leaped toward them from the shadows of the minotaur tower. A spell played like dancing light around his hands, and he pointed them toward the Cloakmaster. But Estriss, the mind flayer, shoved Teldin aside and thrust out toward the mage with the power of his mind. The wizard reeled in dim comprehension as the world went black and he crumpled to the combatants' feet under the unimaginable weight of Estriss's mind blast.

He is big. He will survive, Estriss said to no one in particular.

"Too bad," CassaRoc said.

Na'Shee took the lead and plowed through the fighting, screaming a war cry with every swing of her blade. By the time the warriors passed the ruins of the beholders and the blasted neogi tower, their blades were wet with the blood of their enemies, and their hearts were cold with the fear that their comrades inside the tower were dead.

At the Elven High Command, the guards recognized Teldin as the Cloakmaster, but raised their swords in hatred as CassaRoc shoved Estriss toward the entrance. The leader of the guard, a tall elf bearing a thick white moustache, approached the mind flayer and said haughtily, "This thing cannot enter! We are at war with its kind!"

The doors opened, and Lothian Stardawn strode out to greet the warriors. The captain of the guard turned to him. "Lord Stardawn—"

"Colonel Suchbench, this is a valuable ally of ours," Stardawn said. "He is illithid, yes, but he is not a servant of Trebek. He is of the alliance, and he is a friend of the Cloakmaster."

The colonel brushed back his wide moustache and considered the illithid. "I don't like it, my lord, not at all, but you're in charge here. Pass, mind flayer," he said. He leaned closer and whispered, "but I'll see you dead if harm comes to any elf."

The warriors were led to an expansive entrance chamber. The walls were hung with ornate draperies and decorated with pale, ancient statuary that reflected the history and art of the elves.

"Cloakmaster," Lothian Stardawn said, stopping in front of Teldin. "What can the Empire of the Elves do for you?"

"Stardawn," Teldin said, "I am being summoned by the ship—" he pulled open the top of his shirt "—and I can no longer resist. The time is now."

Stardawn's eyes widened at the sight of the glowing pattern in the Cloakmaster's chest. For an instant, he considered that this situation might be more complex than he had thought, that perhaps this human truly was destined to be the heir to the *Spelljammer*'s helm. Then he dismissed the idea as unbecoming for an elf of his stature.

The *Spelljammer* will soon belong to the elves, to me, he mused.

"What can we do for you?" Stardawn asked.

"I have discerned the location of the ship's *adytum*," Teldin said. "The answers to my quest will be found there. I need your help in getting there."

Stardawn's eyes narrowed. "And where is this *adytum*?"

Teldin pointed with his sword. "It's hidden within the ship's tail. To get there, we need passage into the Armory, and from there into the Dark Tower. We can do this by crossing the battlement over to the Armory."

"You'll never get inside," Stardawn said. "Many of us have tried. No one is ever killed, but the guardian shivaks beat our warriors senseless, then throw them back out. You cannot defeat the shivaks. They are like . . ." he searched for the words ". . . like beings of stone."

"That's why we need your help," Teldin said. "If you could spare some of your fighters to accompany us, perhaps we could make it past the shivaks and gain entrance to the Dark Tower."

Stardawn considered this. "Let me take this up with the commanders," he said. "I shall return shortly. Until then . . . Guard!" he cried. "Bring our guests refreshment and whatever else they desire." He turned to Teldin. "Cloakmaster, please make yourself at home."

Stardawn disappeared behind a huge tapestry hung against the far wall. There he entered a small antechamber and sat at an ancient desk decorated with silver and gold.

He sat quietly and waited, staring blankly at the top of the desk. Time was short, he knew, if the Cloakmaster was this close to his goal. The Armory would be impassable without the elves' help, and Teldin would never achieve the captaincy. The shivaks were too strong and too numerous. Had he not tried to enter the Armory twice himself?

No, the Cloakmaster could not proceed.

Stardawn wasted time for several minutes, deciding what he should tell them, then strode purposefully into the audience chamber, where Teldin and his group waited. He stopped as Teldin rose from his chair.

"I'm sorry, Cloakmaster," Stardawn said with all due reverence. "The high command has decided that the elven empire shall not assist you."

"But what of our treaty?" CassaRoc inquired angrily. "You promised your help."

"And the command shall help you, as it is spelled out in our agreement. The battles you anticipate are against the shivaks, and have nothing to do with protecting the elves. As such, the high command refuses to aid you. I am truly sorry, Cloakmaster."

By this time, all in the group had risen from their chairs and were staring at Teldin. He absently toyed with his bronze amulet. " 'I'm sorry.' That's all the elves can say?"

Stardawn was silent. If Teldin had been paying attention, he would have noticed the anger smoldering inside the elf's eyes at the human's temerity to mock an elven commander.

Teldin said suddenly, "Then we go anyway."

The spell was broken. Na'Shee smiled and adjusted her heavy belt, hung with weaponry. CassaRoc stood prouder and nodded once. "There we go," he said.

"Wait," Stardawn said. "Your courage is admirable," he said

quickly, "but you cannot defeat the shivaks. I've been in there myself, exploring," he said quickly. "I've fought them and lost. For every man you have, two or three shivaks will appear. You have no chance."

It was Djan's turn to speak. "We have the Cloakmaster. It is his destiny to seek the *adytum.* We will be victorious. We must be."

This was not working properly, Stardawn knew. They were supposed to turn back, facing unbeatable opponents. Of course, he could let them go on and face defeat, but what if, just what if they were to beat the shivaks?

Then the cloak would never be his. And the *Spelljammer* would be denied to the elves, the natural rulers of the universe, and, most importantly, to him.

"Then," Stardawn said carefully, with just enough theatrics to make them believe him, "the high command be damned. I will go with you. If," he added, "you'll have me."

CassaRoc watched Teldin cautiously. The Cloakmaster smiled and looked into Stardawn's eyes. His hand was held to his chest, as though he were gaining warmth from the glowing symbol. "You are welcome to accompany us, Stardawn. We can certainly use your expertise."

Stardawn turned. "I will prepare myself for battle," he said. "I'll return shortly."

The group watched him go.

"I'm not sure that elf can be trusted," CassaRoc confided.

Teldin said slowly, "I'm sure he cannot." The pattern on his chest glowed even brighter. Teldin stared into the shadows where Stardawn had disappeared. "But this is the way it was meant to be. One of us will not return."

The silence lay heavy in the antechamber while the warriors pondered Teldin's prediction.

"Would you be kind enough to explain that?" CassaRoc finally asked.

"I wish I could. Stardawn is supposed to be with us, this I know. And . . . we must accept the decree of fate."

They watched him without commenting, then stood silently until Stardawn returned, well armed and suited for battle. He led them from the audience chamber to a small door off a central corridor. Other elves were busy there, hardly noticing the humans. They carried their brethren, wounded and bloody from the battles outside, on stretchers and in their arms.

Stardawn unlocked a wooden door with an ancient iron key, and the door slowly creaked open. Beyond, a staircase covered with dust led down into the darkness. "No one goes through here much," Stardawn admitted. "I was the last that I know of, almost a year ago."

The group entered the stairwell, and the elf closed the door. He took a light rod from a shelf. "First we go down. This leads to the lowest level, and that leads to a staircase up to the battlement. We won't need the lights outside. Besides, from what I saw, the Armory is lit by the *Spelljammer*'s light panels. We'll have no trouble seeing once we get inside."

They filed down the narrow staircase and gathered at the bottom. Stardawn unlocked the door and led them into an old storage area.

"This way," Stardawn said, and he led them between piles of dusty crates and casks of murky liquids to an ancient hidden door. He unlocked this one with another iron key and ushered them through. The chamber beyond also was used for storage, but the boxes and urns stacked across one wall seemed forgotten and were layered with a thick patina of dust. In one corner, a spiral staircase twisted up into darkness. Stardawn held up the light rod. "Not very far," he smiled, "only twenty five floors to go."

Teldin paused. This level, this room, of the elven command seemed familiar to him, though he had never been here. The smell of ancient dust, the feel of the wooden door, the sound of the lock being opened—I know this, he thought. He cocked his head and turned his thoughts inward. How do I know this place?

Stardawn took the first step onto the staircase, then stopped as a subtle noise echoed from somewhere behind them. As one, the warriors turned.

"Just a rat," Stardawn said. "The ship is infested with them."

"CassaRoc said warily, "A rat? A living rat?"

"Not a rat," Teldin insisted, "alive or dead." He started toward the wall hidden by crates. The decapitated head's message! he thought suddenly. He gritted his teeth. The entrance to the warrens is here!

"Help me with these crates," he told them.

His friends shrugged and started forward. Stardawn came over, anger flaring on his pale elven face. "Why do you want to find a rat?"

"It is not a rat I seek," the Cloakmaster said. "There is something more here. And it was no rat we heard."

They piled the boxes against the opposite wall. Some were so old that the wood had rotted through, and they fell into dust and splinters when held too tightly. Finally, near the floor, Teldin spied what he had hoped would be here. "Yes," he said, "it is here."

With a flurry of energy, Teldin shoved the other crates and jars aside. He stood and stared for a moment as the others crowded around him.

The doors in the floor were wooden, sealing a circular entrance of some sort. Heavy boxes had been placed atop it some time in the dim past.

" 'In the elven warrens,' the thing told me." Teldin glanced over his shoulder. His friends had not seen Coh's zombie slave. "In Coh's quarters. He had a zombie head that told me Coh had come here."

"No one has been through this door for a long time," Stardawn again admitted.

"No, but he is close, in a lair near here. Can you not feel his evil?" Teldin opened the doors.

The others said nothing. Chaladar grunted, for he could feel the coldness on his arms and smell it emanating from the entrance. "Aye, I feel it."

Na'Shee shivered. Estriss said, *There is powerful magic down there.*

The amulet glowed again, and Teldin felt its warmth ripple through his chest. The entrance to the warrens beckoned darkly, and he thought of Cwelanas, her soft laughter, the sadness behind her eyes.

No longer. She has been through too much.

"I'm going to get her."

Stardawn came up beside Chaladar and asked him what all this was about. Chaladar quickly, quietly explained about Cwelanas's kidnapping. Stardawn remained silent, but inside he felt joyous. If the Cloakmaster were to die in the warrens, then he could never make it to his precious *adytum* with his cloak.

"What are we going to do?" Stardawn asked, his tone level. "We shouldn't leave her with the Fool . . ."

"Cloakmaster," Na'Shee said, "I know you care for her, but if you find the *adytum*, there is no telling what might happen."

"True," Teldin said, "but the Fool still works his dark magic, and his undead still roam the ship. Maybe the *Spelljammer* can't do anything about the Fool's evil. Perhaps its up to me. Perhaps I have no choice."

"Perhaps *we* have no choice," Stardawn said. "If you go to find her, I'm coming with you."

"As will I," Na'Shee said.

Djan and CassaRoc agreed. Teldin pointed at the tunnel with his sword. "They're somewhere down there, down in the warrens. Are you sure you still want to go with me?"

CassaRoc answered. "We have lights. We have weapons. What more could we ask for?"

"Less powerful enemies," Teldin said.

"There is that," CassaRoc conceded.

Stardawn left the room, then came back shortly with a light rod for each of them. They all stood silently, staring into the hidden entrance to the warrens.

The amulet burned against Teldin's flesh, pulling part of him away, toward an unknown fate that had called to him from across the universe. But down there was the woman he loved. With an inner conflict that threatened to tear his psyche apart, Teldin squelched his yearning to explore the *Spelljammer* and concentrated on the hole leading into darkness.

He crouched and peered inside. His voice echoed softly through the tunnel. "Be ready for anything," he said.

He disappeared, down into the twilight darkness that was the warrens.

Chapter Twenty-Four

• • •

"*. . . Virtually overnight, our problem with the vermin running wild throughout the citadel has disappeared. Even our mages are hard put to explain where all the rats have gone. . . .*"

Barlow, scribe of the Chalice tower; letter to the Council, following the reign of Romar.

Blehal, the beholder, approached the dais of Gray Eye, the leader of the eye tyrants. His eyestalks wavered nervously as the leader turned to face him with his clouded great eye. Gray Eye focused all his eyes on his second in command. His huge mouth curled in a grotesque grimace.

"How goes the war?" Gray Eye asked.

Blehal floated forward, casting his gaze to the floor. With the approach of the vessels that now surrounded the *Spelljammer*, skirmishes had broken out all across the vessel and the beholders were hard pressed by all the races on the ship that hated the beholders.

Blehal's usually gruff voice seemed softer, almost in shame. "The war goes badly, lord. Even with our superior magic, the numbers are too great, and our allies are falling. The humans and the giff have joined the war, and I fear—" The beholder hesitated. "I fear we will soon be defeated."

Gray Eye laughed, the sound of bones being gnashed between his ragged teeth. "*Defeat.* You are insignificant, Blehal. You underestimate our power. The beholders will never see defeat—not with the kasharin in our control."

"The k—kasharin?" Blehal stammered, barely able to believe the leader's words.

Gray Eye faced away from him and stared off in serene contemplation. "The kasharin. Who else could bring total victory to the beholders? Who else on the *Spelljammer* has such . . . unimaginable power?"

Blehal floated back a few feet, shocked. His eyestalks stared at Gray Eye with horror. "But, lord, can we trust them to be released? They will kill without thinking. They will probably even try to kill us."

"They can be controlled," Gray Eye said, spinning around furiously. "They must be controlled." He glared at Blehal, his opaque eye pulsing with rage. "The surviving beholders must be called back. Only together can we charm the kasharin into obeying us. Only with them can our victory be assured."

He raised his voice. "Recall the beholders, Blehal! Now we prepare to destroy our enemies without quarter! And the unholy kasharin shall be our secret weapon!"

* * * * *

On a circular platform near one of the walls of his lair, the Fool kept Cwelanas chained with heavy iron manacles, so that he could torment her at any moment he pleased.

Blood ran in small trickles down her ankles, where the Fool had ordered his undead rats to snap at her flesh. Bruises ran up and down her arms, where the undead Coh had taunted her, in the ethereal voice of the Fool, with promises of his love, and how he could not wait to take her in his claws and show her the meaning of passion.

Occasionally the lair's carpet of black smoke curled up in wisps before her and figures took shape, almost like afterthoughts from the Fool's diseased mind. Several times the smoke took the shape of the cloak, billowing out and waving as though it were alive, calling the Fool into its embrace. Once it formed the shape of the *Spelljammer*, towered over by the Fool's silhouette, thrusting into the vessel with his black, serrated long sword. She wondered where the shapes came from, if they were unconscious manifestations projected by the Fool, . . . and if the Fool even knew they were being formed.

The Fool sat in his ivory throne of bones, his burning eyes flickering as he stared into his *orb of sight.* Occasionally a finger or arm would twitch nervously, or a low moan would escape from the Fool's cavernous mouth.

Cwelanas watched him. One skeletal hand was wrapped protectively around his heavy amulet, and she strained her eyes to get a better look.

The amulet was ornate, made of delicate gold that curled in on itself to create patterns and shapes as the amulet was twirled in the Fool's fingers. The crimson stone in the center seemed to burn with an inner fire. She had seen the Fool toying with the amulet once before, while he was pacing his chamber, worrying aloud that the *Spelljammer* might never be his to command, and that his plans to destroy the ship might fail. Then the Fool laughed with the false bravado of the evil dead, refusing to acknowledge such a possibility.

She was startled by a scream of both laughter and rage from the Fool as he stirred on his throne. He held the amulet of bloodfire in one hand as he rose and approached her. His eyes shone with bright, unnatural light.

"Your lover is on his way, little elf," the Fool croaked in his dry, brittle voice. "None of your magic can save him. He is coming for you, and he will give me exactly what I want, or you—and he—will die."

The Fool rasped an evil laugh. "You will die anyway. No matter. No matter. Your precious Cloakmaster is on his way here. And the cloak will be all mine."

He laughed, returning to rest upon his throne. Cwelanas focused on the amulet and wondered why the Fool held the jewel so tightly when she could tell he was afraid. Perhaps, in his obsession with the *Spelljammer*'s death, he no longer controlled his subconscious, hence the shapes from his mind formed in the chamber's dark air, he twitched nervously, and moaned unconsciously while peering into his orb.

He held the amulet and laughed and laughed.

"This is very good," he said, chuckling. "He's following my lures. He has discovered the entrance in the elven tower.

"Oh, he's on his way. The *Spelljammer* soon will die."

The Fool laughed. "Who is the fool now?" he cackled. "Who is the fool now?"

Chapter Twenty-Five

• • •

". . . I have had the same dream now for seven nights. In each, I walk to the head of the Spelljammer *and call out into the air. The birds are singing a pretty song, even though we have no birds. My husband appears from underneath the bow. His eyes are black.*

"In my last dream, he held out a ring for me to take. I woke and found the ring on my finger.

"I am doomed.

"My husband disappeared three years ago.

"The ring will not come off. . . ."

The Dream of the White Horse, a tale by Anonymous; reign of Jokarin.

The illumination from the warrior band's light rods cast a warm glow upon the pale, purplish walls of the warrens. The walls felt spongy, almost warm to the touch, and Teldin understood why the warrens were sometimes called the veins, for they spread throughout the *Spelljammer*'s body in a series of seemingly endless tunnels, twisting as though they were meant for lifeblood to course through them.

The tunnels widened once the warriors had made their way deeper into the ship, and they walked side by side, their weapons at the ready. Splotches of phosphorescent moonwort on the walls absorbed the light from their rods and glowed steadily after they had passed. Teldin, in the lead, paused occasionally at intersections, trying to peer as far as he could down the joining tunnels.

"How do you know where you're going?" Djan asked.

"I don't. I'm just trying to follow whatever trail I can find," Teldin said. "He's been down here a long time. I'm just looking for, well, a trail of darkness, I suppose."

"So you're going on instinct," CassaRoc offered.

"That's what I said."

"Do you feel anything from your amulet?"

Teldin caught CassaRoc's gaze and looked down. The glow from the amulet had ceased once they had passed into the warrens, and Teldin could feel nothing from it, as though its powers were muted down here. "No, nothing," Teldin said, "nothing at all."

Stardawn concentrated. Magic ran through his elven veins, and he reached out with a minor spell of detection. He pointed with his sword down a tunnel. "Farther in that direction. The taint comes from there."

They proceeded farther down. At one intersection, Teldin caught a wisp of black smoke curling in the distance, and he led the warriors toward it. At another intersection, each connecting tunnel except one was thickly layered with phosphorescent lichen. He chose the dark tunnel.

The Fool had designed his trap very well.

Teldin led them down the tunnel, his light rod held high. The lichen here glowed red and brown, as though diseased. The tunnel walls seemed to close in, tapering so that the warriors could walk only in single file. The light from the rods seemed to grow dimmer, as though the brightness were being absorbed by the lining of the walls, or countered with a lasting spell of darkness.

"I don't like this," Djan said behind Teldin. "I don't like this at all."

"You think I—" Then Teldin clutched his chest and staggered against the wall. His mind went cold. Pinpricks of ice tingled across his chest. "Cold," he said weakly. "It—it's calling me, and it can't . . . *sense* me here in the warrens. It is searching for me, but it *hurts*!"

The group stopped and waited while Teldin relaxed and the pain of the *Spelljammer*'s summons faded. Then they started forward again as Teldin regained his composure, and they trudged steadily deeper.

Teldin knew they were close when he saw a thin layer of black mist curling around his feet. He stopped the group and warned them. "Can you feel that?" he asked. The air was chill and reeked of rotting flesh. "We're near his lair, I'm sure. Be ready for anything."

He stepped into the mist. It curled coldly up his legs as he led the party in, then it rose higher with every step, until it was so thick that they could not see before them.

Teldin's senses told him that they had stepped out of a tunnel and into some kind of chamber. He tensed, his ears alert. In the darkness, the light from the rods was practically insignificant, swallowed by the black mist, and he heard rustling, almost like the soft, shuffling footsteps of others, from somewhere deep in the mist around them.

He felt the rustle of a breeze on his arms, then the mist swirled and eddied around them, borne on a cold wind that sprang from some unknown source. Their light rods spread warm, yellow light upon nests of crumbling blankets and broken bones, into the narrow entrances of other tunnels, and upon weapons and chests and leather pouches heaped against the far wall. Teldin picked up a pair of discarded short swords and looked them over.

"Well, we've found something," CassaRoc said, staring at the wooden chest. He stepped forward cautiously and kneeled. He opened a chest, and the light from his rod was reflected in a million sparkles upon his face.

"Gold," he said softly. "Gold."

The chest was packed with gold and silver coins, with necklaces and amulets, brooches and bracelets. He plucked out a gold ring boasting an opaque green stone that bore a diamond-shaped carving, with angles emanating from two points. He smiled and pocketed the ring, then lifted out a dazzling necklace encrusted with rubies and emeralds. In the center, a silver disk had been engraved with symbols and jewels, and CassaRoc held it up to the light.

Teldin noticed the warrior's uncustomary frown. "What is it?" he queried.

"I know this necklace," CassaRoc said. "This used to belong to a fighter of mine."

"Damn!" Na'Shee shouted behind them. "That's Chel's! I know her!"

CassaRoc turned. "Knew her. She died when you arrived here, Teldin."

Teldin said nothing.

CassaRoc gave Na'Shee the necklace, while Stardawn and Djan looked through the chest. CassaRoc waved his sword around. "What is this place?" he asked.

"I don't know," Teldin said. "It looks like someone has been staying here." He picked up one of the bones on the floor. "I don't like their eating habits, though. This is a human bone."

They all heard them then, closing in from the intersecting tunnels. The gold and silver and jewels were forgotten in the rush to bring weapons to bear, to arrange themselves defensively in a circle as their assailants shambled in from the tunnels around them.

"The undead," CassaRoc announced.

The warriors were quickly surrounded by a score of the undead. Most were human; two were elves, and three were halflings. Some bore swords and daggers, ready to use them, albeit awkwardly, with a semblance of living memory. Most just stared hungrily at the intruders, ready to kill by tooth and jagged bone.

"This was a trap," Na'Shee said. "We were suckered in."

Then one shape stepped from the farthest tunnel and stood in the entrance. Its teeth gleamed wickedly in the yellow light as it hissed with sadistic laughter. Its fur was mottled with blood, with the colors of the spectrum layered in dizzying patterns across its obscene body. An intricate series of circles was painted on its forehead.

"Trapped," the undead Coh said, snapping at them with his sharp yellow teeth. "Compliments of the Fool."

The zombie neogi turned then and plunged into the surrounding wall of mist.

The undead swarmed upon them.

The living sliced their way through the ranks of the undead with incredible ferocity. CassaRoc swore constantly as his sword cleaved through bone and dead flesh, severing heads and arms without conscious thought. He recognized two of the zombies, his own warriors who had died protecting Teldin from the neogi hordes: Chel, who once owned the jewel-studded necklace, and Gar, a fighter and merchant from the open market. He grimaced and killed them as mercifully as he could, staring at their long-dead faces as they lay together on the floor. "Sorry, my friends," he said.

Na'Shee left her crossbow hung at her waist and depended instead on the swiftness of her steel. She cut a swath through the undead forces, then spun around and came back, finishing off those who were still mobile with clean thrusts into their soft skulls or necks. When she was finished, she looked upon their peaceful faces and realized that she had sent friends of hers to their final, true deaths: K'aald, once a guard of CassaRoc's, and Jenn, from the Academy of Human Knowledge.

Na'Shee looked up and saw CassaRoc staring at his own dead compatriots on the floor, and wondered if undeath would happen to her as it had to their friends, . . . if the Fool were successful in his plans.

Djan was attacked by seven undead, who grappled with him and tore his sword from his hands. Stardawn saw the half-elf's plight and dispatched his own assailants with relative ease. He picked up an axe from the stack of weapons by the treasure chest and leaped into the fight, chopping through spinal columns and skulls as though they were made of twigs. Djan finally picked up his sword and, back to back, he and Stardawn fought off the zombies until most of the undead were a heap of bloody limbs jumbled at their feet.

Stardawn's last assailant was particularly strong and single-minded, virtually ignoring Stardawn's blows as one would the sting of a gnat. The elf was pressed against the wall, and the zombie's fetid hand was reaching for his neck when Stardawn realized that physical force would not be enough to finish the creature off. As the undead's fingers closed around his flesh, Stardawn whispered an ancient elven spell. The zombie's eyes rolled back in surprise. Within seconds, it loosened its grip on the elf as its body shook with a thin, papery rustling sound. The undead screamed once, and it fell to the floor in a cloud of black dust, decomposed instantly from the inside.

Teldin was an angry, elemental force against his unnatural enemies. He realized he had finally taken enough from this foe that he had never seen, and he attacked the Fool's undead with a short sword in each hand, whirling through their ranks, slicing indiscriminately with all his might. Black blood spattered his armor, his legs, but his cloak remained unstained. A head dangled from dead flesh on his right; on his left, a zombie dropped with a clean, powerful cut through its collarbone and heart. Teldin's hair was sticky with sweat and blood, and his eyes blazed with rage, framed by his taut, blood-spattered face.

He felt the power of the cloak blazing through him, pulsating through his veins with unheard of energy. His blades were silver arcs whistling through the air. His foes fell back, defenseless, maimed by the speed and strength of his swords. The cloak, useless against the nature of the undead, still filled Teldin with power, enhancing and amplifying his own strength and will.

The Cloakmaster's final foe plopped to the floor, sliced in two at the waist. Teldin stopped, panting, and felt the powers of the cloak flow out of him. The remains of the undead were all around him, and he stood in a putrid sea of their corrupt, oily blood.

His friends stared at him in shock. The warriors then cleaned their blades, and Teldin took a deep breath, relaxing. CassaRoc cast a wary glance at him. "We thought you went berserk," he finally said.

Teldin shook his head. "No, the cloak was . . . giving me energy."

He raised his sword and pointed into the black mist that surrounded them. "That way," he said. "Coh went through there."

"It's probably just another trap," Djan warned.

"Of course it's a trap," Teldin said. "What do you expect? He's trying to lead us to the Fool."

Stardawn said, "You plan to walk right into it?"

Teldin grinned and wiped his sword on the body of a zombie. He stood at the threshold of darkness, then stepped through. Reluctantly, the others followed.

In the dim light, framed by his blood-stained features, Teldin's smile was that of a hungry shark. "We're going to get him right where he wants us."

"You *are* right where I want you," came a mocking voice

from beyond. The darkness swirled away and dissipated, as though it had been absorbed back into its source, and the full size of the new chamber was revealed.

They were in the lair of the Fool.

Tunnels branched off from each side, and the roof of the cavern was lost in the shadows. The chamber was a natural formation, almost organic, diseased with tumors of black fungi and the stench of the dead.

The undead Coh greeted them. His eyes were blazing pin-pricks of light. He smiled, beckoning with his black claws, and Teldin lunged and drove his sword straight into Coh's mocking face. The undead neogi collapsed to the floor, spurting gouts of foul blood.

Laughter erupted from the far wall of the dimly lit chamber. Behind gauzy draperies of spiderwebs, the Fool waited for them, perched upon his throne of bones. Cwelanas kneeled before him, his skeletal hand tight on a heavy chain shackled to her slim neck.

"*Welcome, Cloakmaster,*" the Fool said. His voice sent shivers down Teldin's back. It was a death rattle, a breath from the grave.

The Fool stood, jerking Cwelanas's chain tight. The iron shackle dug deep into her throat as she struggled to retain her balance. The Fool slid his black long sword from its ancient scabbard and rested its sharp point against the back of Cwelanas's neck. He slung the heavy chain across her shoulders, and she cried out as the iron links pounded her vulnerable skin. With the other hand the Fool idly toyed with his scarlet amulet.

Teldin's friends arranged themselves around him protectively and faced the dais. Teldin nodded at Cwelanas, questioning with his eyes. "I'm all right," she said.

"*Silence!*" the Fool yelled with a hiss. The point of his blade drew a drop of blood from her flesh. The sword, tensing for more, for the blood and the life force of the elf, hummed in the Fool's hand.

"The deathblade hungers," the Fool said to Teldin. He laughed. "It has far less patience than I. It yearns to drink deeply of your lovely friend's soul. Shall I let it, Teldin Cloakmaster? Shall I drive my blade deep into her heart, so that my thirsty steel may drink?"

Teldin took a step forward. "If you harm her—" he started, but the Fool interrupted him.

"*What will you do, Cloakmaster*?" the Fool asked. "What do you think you really can do? You know nothing of my powers. You are but a whelp, a dispensable pawn who chanced on an instrument of power. Your meager determination brought you here, human, simply to see everyone you've ever loved die.

"Is that what you want, Cloakma—"

The Fool stopped suddenly as a glimmer of golden light appeared at Teldin's shoulder. It flickered like a flame, growing into a ball of light that coalesced into the astral form of Gaye Goldring. Her robes flowed about her, glowing with her own psionic energies. She spied the Fool upon his dais and quickly positioned her hands into a defensive posture.

"Ah, my little kender friend," the Fool mocked, "back for your final punishment? I am no shade or banshee to dispel with light, kender. You are nothing more than an insect to me. I will see you die today."

The Fool turned to Teldin.

"Understand this, human. The elf's blood will be spilled, O great Cloakmaster, unless you are prepared to bargain . . ."

"Bargain." It was Teldin's turn to laugh. "You don't want to bargain, Fool," he said. "You want only to kill."

The Spelljammer*, Teldin*, Gaye said. *His goal is to destroy the* Spelljammer *and everyone aboard, for revenge of when he was captain.*

"Captain?" said Chaladar.

The Fool glowered at them in contempt.

"I know you better than you realize," Teldin said. You're everything I ever fought against. You're everything I've ever hated: arrogance, hatred, war, murder, corruption, death.

"Look around. Do you know what this chamber was?"

The Fool seemed to shrink in upon himself. The warriors turned to observe their surroundings.

"This is the heart, Fool. This is the heart of the *Spelljammer*, and it is your evil that has corrupted it."

Teldin's friends stood there awestruck, deep within the body of the *Spelljammer* itself, the great ship's very heart.

"It is a living thing, more powerful and important than you will ever be!" Teldin shouted. "It is far more than a vessel or a city. It is a myth come to life."

The Fool bowed slightly. "If that is all you know, then, Cloakmaster, you know nothing."

"Nothing," Teldin said. "That's all you are, Fool, nothing. You've got all these empty powers, and all you want is to see your obsession come true. 'Death to the *Spelljammer.*' All because you lacked the discipline to be a worthy captain . . . or a worthy man."

The Fool flinched in anger. He was not used to humans talking back to him. "The *Spelljammer* deserves to die after what it did to me!" he shouted. "I was the captain, the best captain. I dared to use the *Spelljammer* to rule the spheres, and it committed mutiny to destroy me, to imprison me in the Dark Tower with the others. I had other plans."

The Fool's grip tightened on his ruby amulet. "I carefully made . . . arrangements for my escape. Plans for my revenge. And your damned cloak is destined to be the instrument of the *Spelljammer*'s death!"

"Can you think of nothing else?" Teldin challenged. "Did you sell your mind as well as your soul? You have the ship's population tricked into thinking you're an all powerful wizard, or a foul demigod, who secretly rules the *Spelljammer.*" Teldin raised his arms and gestured. "Look around you. You are surrounded by nothingness, darkness, emptiness. You are a ruler of nothing but the dead. You're nothing but a zombie yourself."

"The dead are excellent servants," the Fool said, "as you and your little whore will be soon, if you do not give me the Cloak of the First Pilot."

Teldin pointed his sword at the Fool. "The cloak is mine." He braced his legs defiantly. "The cloak cannot be removed unless I'm dead. If you want the cloak, you're going to have to take care of me first."

The Fool grimaced in what amounted to a smile. "I do so love a challenge," he said.

The blazing pinpricks in his eyes flickered momentarily, then around the warriors the moaning began. They gathered together and formed a tight circle.

The chamber filled with the shambling undead. Elves, humans, dwarves, even a long-undead k'r'r'r, surrounded them, fifty or so swarming in from warrens hidden deep in the shadows of the Fool's lair. Above their constant moaning, the Fool laughed.

"The decision is yours, Cloakmaster," he said. "Give up the cloak, or all of you will die, and your precious Cwelanas will come to love my embrace . . . in undeath."

"We've taken our chances before, Fool," Teldin said. "We'll take them now."

The Fool's eyes flickered once, and the undead attacked. The blades of the humans whistled through the air, slicing through dead bone with a fury for life that only the desperate can muster. The warriors' battle cries echoed through the chamber, drowning out the low moans of undead agony.

But the undead had them surrounded in numbers far superior to their own, and it was only a matter of time before they were overpowered. Chaladar was the first to be wounded, bitten in the leg by the yellow teeth of an undead neogi. Cassa-Roc, despite the mighty swings of his battle-axe, was grabbed from behind by an undead umber hulk. Teldin and the others were busy defending themselves. His sword sliced through three undead before he was overtaken by their sheer numbers. His cloak was impotent, useless; it hung to the floor without power.

The light in the room suddenly brightened, and the Cloakmaster realized the glow was emanating from Gaye. She floated inches above the floor, her eyes closed as if in sleep, her hands crossed over her chest. Her voice echoed like a sibilant whisper in his mind. *Protect the others.*

"Protect? How?"

The light that was her life force shone brighter. The undead flinched at her radiance, then continued on as the Fool screamed at them, "*Kill them! Kill them all!*"

Teldin felt Gaye's power flicker over his bare arms. Instinctively, he shouted "Come here!" to the others. "Quickly! We haven't much time!"

The warriors doubled their energies and pummeled away at the undead. Then they were lined around him, weapons ready, enveloped in Gaye's warm glow.

Her eyes snapped open. Her energy suddenly hummed in their ears like a powerful inhalation of breath. Teldin gasped, and he knew.

His body was flooded with the icefire of the cloak's power, and the cloak billowed out, stretching impossibly to encircle the warriors and pull them into a tight group. They all felt the cloak's energies then, tingling along their skin, raising the hairs on their arms and necks with a ripple of cold.

The cloak tightened around them, concealing them from Gaye's powers.

And the light from Gaye was expelled from her astral body in an explosion of heat and energy and psionic power, an ultrapowerful blast of mental energy that burned through the undead and knocked them to the floor, reeling in pain as their bodies resonated with purifying energy.

The undead collapsed upon themselves, all semblance of their minds burned away with the blast of Gaye's life force. She flickered weakly and floated to the floor, where her aura faded to a dim glow.

Teldin willed the cloak to unfurl, and he and his warriors rushed to her. She was weak, but she smiled bravely.

The chamber was littered with the bodies of the dead, and Teldin jumped through them toward the Fool's dais.

"*You may stop the undead,*" the Fool yelled, "*but you will never stop me!*"

The Cloakmaster reached the dais in one leap. He coiled and swung at the Fool with his sword, but the blade cleaved harmlessly through the image of the Fool as though it were smoke.

Teldin stepped back. "Cwelanas?" he said.

Her image wavered, then swirled away, a spell of illusion blown on the dark winds of the Fool's chamber. The image of the Fool seemed to smile in glee as it blew apart on a cold breeze. Over it all Teldin heard the Fool's laughter, from wherever his place of concealment was.

"*One chance more, you have, Cloakmaster,*" the Fool's voice echoed throughout the chamber. "*The cloak for the woman. This will be her only hope.*"

His voice faded, echoing with cackles of laughter, and Teldin spun on the dais to face his friends.

"All this for nothing! We walked straight into it."

"It had to be done," CassaRoc said. "We had the chance to find her. We would do it again."

Teldin nodded grimly.

Without warning, the *Spelljammer* shuddered violently from the pounding of ballistae up on deck. The Cloakmaster steadied himself, then went over to the others as the shaking ceased.

Gaye knelt over Chaladar, who grimaced in pain at the burning sensation of the undead neogi's bite. *I can heal this easily,* Gaye assured.

"What about yourself?" said Teldin.

She forced a smile. "I am weak but well, not too weak to help your friends."

Gaye placed her hands above Chaladar's wound and relaxed, willing herself deep into a healing trance. Her aura merged with that of the paladin, and she could feel his unconsciousness as though it were a sweet, cold narcotic, washing through her, tempting her to release her hold on wakefulness and fall into blissful darkness. Then the pain in Chaladar's leg flared an angry scarlet in Gaye's own leg, and she willed the pain away.

Heat flowed through Gaye's hands, enveloping the paladin's injury and permeating his skin to settle deep into the bone. Her hands burned with her psionic healing powers, and her mind flooded with cold, like a night breeze. She wavered as dark unconsciousness washed over her, brought on by both the intense strain of healing and the stress of using her psionic abilities so much in so short a time.

Within minutes, Chaladar's wound was healed and the paladin stood, stretching his leg as though nothing had happened. Gaye seemed to sag with weariness, and her glow dimmed.

We must leave this place, Estriss remarked. *Cwelanas is still missing, and the Cloakmaster must seek the* adytum. *If he does not reach it soon, the* Spelljammer *may be lost.*

"We must leave," Teldin agreed. "This farce of the Fool's has wasted enough time."

Gaye smiled thinly at him. *I must leave to renew my energy. You will need me in the time to come. But I have the strength to do one thing more to help you on your quest.*

"What?" Teldin asked.

Gaye raised her astral arms and concentrated. Slowly, the group began to shimmer with her own golden energy, and they found themselves shimmering into existence on deck, materializing in the center of a group of warring elves and mind flayers.

The unhumans' swords were raised in combat. Their bloody skirmish stopped suddenly as the warriors appeared in their midst, cries of surprise echoing around them.

Then, screaming their angry battle cries, the unhumans attacked.

And in the sudden melee, no one considered that, in their last moments in the Fool's lair, the body of the undead Master Coh was nowhere to be seen.

Chapter Twenty-Six

• • •

"*. . . The beholders claim that a stranger will come to bring darkness upon us all. The dwarves claim that a weapon will be forged that will both destroy and create. The elves claim that the past will become the present.*

"*Ancient legends, all, that have circulated for a thousand years. My own scrying has revealed but one thing: all are one and the same. . . .*"

Marias, fortune-teller of the market; reign of Bentley the Fearless.

The unhuman screams were of rage and anger and hatred, of an unquenchable bloodlust that spanned the races.

The battle for the cloak spread like an unstoppable fire. The beholders battled the mind flayers; the Shou fought the humanoids; the mind flayers engaged the elves. The decks ran red with the blood of humans and unhumans alike, mingling together for the first time . . . in death, in eternal peace.

The *Spelljammer* was ablaze with the fires of war.

Above, in the Rainbow Ocean, uncounted vessels converged on the Broken Sphere. Even at this distance, Teldin could tell that several were fighting with other ships, casting grappling hooks and firing light ballistae at their enemies. Larger ships loomed behind them, aiming for the vicinity of the *Spelljammer*. They followed me here, Teldin knew. They followed the cloak and its powers, all to gain control of the spheres. All to wage war and enslave others and rape the universe of all its innate good.

He swore to himself. Never. Not If I have something to do about it.

He knew that his time to gain the *adytum* was running short.

He and his companions found themselves surrounded by unhumans near the tower of the Tenth Pit, Teldin realized. He faced the *Spelljammer*'s thick tail, and to his right, towering above a corner of the beholder ruins, stood the proud tower of the elves.

"We have to make it back to the elven command!" Teldin shouted, pointing his sword. Then a shrill unhuman cry broke out around him, and Teldin spun around to meet his attackers, his shield and sword raised high in defense. Arranged beside him, the other warriors all prepared to defend against the battling unhuman hordes, to help the Cloakmaster achieve his destiny.

Teldin lurched forward, his chest tight with the hot, constricting pain that was the call of the *Spelljammer*. Outside of the warrens, the call was more intense, more urgent, and the heat that crackled through him was fiery, insistent. Cwelanas was all but forgotten in the heat of the call, and he spun around and screamed in mindless agony as the *Spelljammer* summoned him.

"I will come!" he shouted. "I will come!"

A group of illithids was the first to attack, recognizing the Cloakmaster easily and momentarily forgetting their hatred of the elves. CassaRoc leaped in front of Teldin and engaged two of them as Teldin struggled to keep the call under control. CassaRoc knocked one mind flayer's outstretched claws away with a powerful swing of his sword, then pierced the other illithid straight through. He pulled his sword free and laughed loudly. "Come on, mind flayers!" he cried. "The only brains you'll feed on today will be those of your own dead and dying!"

The elves saw their chance as they realized the illithids had turned their attention toward the humans. As a group, they viciously attacked the mind flayers from behind and cut through their forces without mercy. Stardawn rushed to the elves' aid, keeping close enough to Teldin to protect him from both the mind flayers and his elven brethren, who knew nothing of his pretended alliance with the Cloakmaster. He wanted Teldin to die at his own hands and give him the secret of the cloak.

Na'Shee and Djan together took on three mind flayers, fighting furiously with shield and steel. The illithids fought back even harder with their mental powers, finally backing the pair up against one cracked pillar outside the beholder ruins.

Djan was lucky. One haphazard thrust of his sword pierced an illithid's eye. It stumbled as its hand went up to protect its face. Djan saw his opportunity and thrust his blade straight through the mind flayer's heart. With a cry of horror and pain, the illithid dropped to its knees. Djan jerked out his sword. Blood spurted from the mind flayer's mortal wound, spraying Djan's boots. Then the mind flayer keeled over with a thump, its facial tentacles twitching once in a spreading pool of its own blood.

Na'Shee kept the others at bay with a flashy display of swordsmanship that easily broke through the mind flayers' meager physical defenses. Blood oozed from half a dozen shallow wounds across their limbs as the woman effortlessly deflected their sword thrusts and turned away their virgin steel. She flicked out her blade, and an illithid dropped to her feet, its hand neatly severed at the wrist. The mind flayer dropped back, and its partner closed in. She dispatched it with relative ease, hammering away its blade with her shield, then running her sword through its chest. As the illithid fell, she reached for the long dagger tucked in its belt and hurled it expertly at the wounded illithid, now limping away with its bleeding stump. The dagger caught the mind flayer squarely between its shoulders, and the unhuman fell forward, flat onto its tentacled face.

Teldin was attacked by three mind flayers, shouting, *Beware his powers!* and *The cloak will be ours!* His blade lashed out faster than the mind flayers could comprehend, drawing a long line of scarlet down one illithid's arm and driving deep into another's unprotected neck to sever an artery in a great fountain of blood.

Teldin had never fought so fast or so furiously. His strength, his being, was noticeably different. The tingle of cold energy from the cloak no longer seemed to be present. Teldin's sense of perception was not distorted in any way either; time did not slow for him as he protected himself with his steel, and his strong frame did not shiver with the energies of the cloak. He knew that he alone could not fight as furiously as this, and he wondered if the cloak's apparent lack of power was the cause.

He felt it on his shoulders; he knew the cloak was there, was always there, flowing around him as though he had been born with it. He felt it with him like one feels the hair on one's head, as though it belonged.

Teldin knew instinctively, as his sword whipped out to meet his assailants' pitiful physical offense, that now the cloak and he were one. It was no longer a tool that he should try to control, nor had it ever really been. In the short time since the attack of the Fool's undead, the cloak's energies had become his own. The cloak had become nothing less than a second skin, a sentient, protective limb that worked with him, not for him, and had been waiting until Teldin's need had driven it to bond with him.

Five illithids charged through the skirmish, armed with nothing but their innate mental powers. The group parted, and the leader of the mind flayers stepped through. Behind the Cloakmaster, Estriss screamed, *Beware! Lord Trebek wants you dead!*

Trebek stood before the Cloakmaster in regal black robes and hissed angrily at him. His tentacles quivered in hatred. *It is my honor to destroy you,* Trebek said. The mind flayer stood tall, and Teldin could see his concentration turn inward, focusing his mental power.

Teldin's mind reeled with a shout of *Nooooo!* as Estriss levitated across the deck and landed between them. Estriss turned to Lord Trebek and held up his hands, warning the illithid away. *Do not do this, Trebek. This is more complex than you can imagine.*

Trebek glared at him. The leader's opaque eyes narrowed. *You are a traitor to your own race,* phlbasta. *You consort with food, with humans. Have you no pride in your race at all?*

Trebek's eyes became slits. Estriss suddenly felt a pinpoint of hot pain blossom in his mind, and he staggered back, moaning under the attack.

You are not a true illithid! Trebek nearly screamed. *Our brethren die bleeding under the onslaught of the elves, and you chase after humans as though you were their pet or a goblin slave!*

Estriss's head jerked back as a powerful mind blast from Trebek sent him reeling. He shook his head, trying to clear the haze that had fallen across his eyes. Dimly he saw Trebek's silhouette nearing him. He focused his thoughts and cast out with his innate mental blast. He heard Trebek grunt loudly, then his eyes cleared and he watched the illithid leader stagger back, hands on his head.

Trebek, his eyes narrowed and red, stared at him, and it seemed as though a lightning bolt of sizzling energy shot into Estriss's mind and exploded in his brain.

Estriss fell to his knees, his head ringing with fire. His thoughts would not hold together, and he knew he needed time to regroup and concentrate properly.

You are the enemy! Trebek screamed in his mind. *I knew I should have killed you when you first arrived! I smelled even then the taint of human influence on you!*

Trebek's tentacles wrapped around his head. He felt the illithid's ragged teeth scrape his scalp, and Estriss lashed out instinctively, defensively, with a blast stronger than any he could conceive. Trebek's eyes widened as a jolt of fire flared in his mind; then Estriss pulled himself from Trebek's grasp, and he concentrated, levitating swiftly above the leader and across to his other side.

Trebek spun around, his hands again to his head. *Coward! Face your superior like a true illithid!*

I am not a true illithid, as you already said. In blood, yes. But I believe in life. And I believe in honesty. You believe in nothing but your own hunger, and your own self-interest.

Estriss stared Trebek in the eyes. They met in the center of the room. Their powers were great, evenly matched, but Estriss had less of a stomach for fighting, for hatred, and Trebek had staked his claim on the *Spelljammer* with his uncompromising skill as an illithid warrior, and as a very smooth diplomat.

Trebek knew that he would win.

Estriss tired easily under Trebek's mental onslaught. The physical plane was forgotten as their mental powers hammered at each other with blows of electric pain. Estriss lost ground as Trebek pressed hard against him, and found himself cornered against a line of Trebek's warriors.

He knew that all was lost if he could not reach within himself and fight as he should. He was a researcher, a scholar. He was an anomaly, a friend, an individual.

He knew what the battle was really about. It was not about mind flayers and humans, or the cloak, or the Dark Times. It was about hatred, about the fear and hatred that many have for those who are different.

He was the first illithid to know the meaning of friendship. And he was the first to throw off the mantle of group identity and rejoice in his individuality.

He brought himself up. Shaking, focusing his powers, Estriss felt his mind harness all his reserves for one last burst of mental energy. His muscles stood out under his purple skin, and he tensed, seeing only Trebek's evil face in his eyes. He pushed with his mind until he felt as though his brain would snap under the strain, and he reeled as the power flowed out of him in a single, concentrated bolt of energy.

Trebek screamed and fell to his knees. His mind was a white blur of stabbing pain, exploding, spreading across his field of vision, hammering behind his eyes with needles of ice.

Estriss doubled over and gasped, his focus released. Trebek swayed, then forced itself up on one knee. He hissed weakly, defiantly at his nemesis. Estriss shambled over, sword in hand, and casually slapped Trebek across the face with the flat of his blade. He lowered his sword to a point between the leader's eyes.

Surrender, Estriss said mentally.

Trebek grabbed the illithid's ankle.

Estriss flicked the point of his sword into Trebek's tentacles. The mind flayer snapped back his head and tightened his grip on Estriss's ankle.

Surrender, Trebek.

You use the weapon . . . of a human, the fallen leader said. *I will never surrender . . . to a traitor.*

Trebek shook with the strain of toppling Estriss, but the illithid stood firm and slashed his sword across the side of Trebek's purple face.

I do not want to kill you. What would you have me do? We have no real quarrel. You have shown me hospitality. You are my brother.

Trebek's answer was an angry grunt as he tried to stand. Estriss shoved him down with one hand upon his head.

Then Trebek's voice shouted in Estriss's mind. *Then act like a true mind flayer, brother, . . . not like a human!*

Estriss nodded slowly. He threw down his sword. His tentacles tightened around Trebek's head, and his teeth sank deep into the leader's thick skull.

The warriors around them stepped back. Chaladar and CassaRoc sprang to Estriss's sides as Trebek's limp body fell to the deck. Blood oozed from the round orifice concealed under Estriss' tentacles, and he slurped the last of Trebek's brains into his mouth.

He picked up his sword and took a deep breath. His head swam with the invigorating taste of Trebek's memories, his desires. Then Estriss's eyes cleared and he saw his companions and the enemy mind flayers. They stared at the blood dripping down his tentacles, down the front of his tunic.

Trebek is dead, Estriss said to the illithid warriors. *The mantle of leadership is now mine.*

The mind flayers shifted uneasily. *Go now,* Estriss commanded. *Destroy the enemies of the illithids, but leave the Cloakmaster to me. Go!*

The illithids turned and trotted away toward their tower. Estriss looked over at the Cloakmaster. *They will not harm us now,* he said, though he was not truly sure of that. *We must leave as well.*

A hand clapped the Cloakmaster on the shoulder, and Teldin spun around angrily, his sword raised. CassaRoc stepped back. "Whoa!" he said. "Are you all right?"

Teldin turned around. His opponents were all laid out in a bloody heap before him, killed by his own hand while he had been thinking about the cloak. "What happened?"

Stardawn came over, sheathing his sword. "I've never seen anybody fight like that before. You cut through them like they were ghosts."

Teldin thought out loud. "It's the cloak. It has . . . merged with me in some way. I can't control it—I guess I never could—but now I've somehow absorbed its powers." He stood up straight. "I feel better and stronger than I've ever felt before, and the cloak feels as if I never should have been without it."

The warriors stared at him. Djan smiled and whispered under his breath, "*Verenthestae.*"

"Where do you think Gaye is?" CassaRoc inquired.

"Gaye is no fool," Teldin said. "Apparently she's more powerful than I ever knew. I don't know much about psionics, but I'd guess that she could transport us using her abilities, but not transport herself at the same time."

"That sounds right," Na'Shee said.

They paused for a moment and looked around them, surrounded by the bodies of their foes. Sounds of battle came from all sides: the screams of the dying, the clangs of steel against steel. The *Spelljammer* was covered with puddles of blood, and the many towers seemed fragile, vulnerable.

"It's irreversible now," Teldin said softly. "The war lust has started. This isn't just about me and the cloak anymore. This is about hatred. Each race thinks that it is superior to the others, and no one will be satisfied until all the others are dead."

Stardawn watched him solemnly. The elves *are* superior, he thought, and I will soon be dancing upon all of your graves.

"We should go," Djan said to Teldin.

The Cloakmaster nodded. "Yes, I know," he said. "I just hope there's something left of the *Spelljammer* after I reach the *adytum.*"

They broke into a run and headed around the corner of the beholder ruins toward the elf tower. The deck was strewn with the bodies of minotaurs, of a few mind flayers and elves and humans. Fighting was going on here between the ruins and the elf tower. A huge hill giant pummeled his way through the ranks of elves and illithids, who fought among themselves with bloodlust in their eyes. One dying beholder lay gasping against a cracked pillar of the ruins. Its great eye widened as it spied them, and it screamed out a loud, shrill cry that grated like the soulless clawing of fingernails across slate.

A beholder floated out of the ruins, followed by two of its scaly kinsmen. They spied the Cloakmaster and his group. One beholder hurried back to the doorway, and a beam of light lanced out from one of its wavering eyestalks with a hiss of burning air. It shouted, "The Cloakmaster has come! Attack him! Attack!"

The doorway of the beholder ruins darkened. Ragged shadows floated from the entrance, bobbing unsteadily above the deck, as though light, and the outdoors, were unnatural to them. The beholders spread out and away from the dark shapes emerging from the ruins. Their enslaved minotaurs raced from the ruins, their horrified gazes focused on the things escaping from the ruins. Several minotaurs broke ranks and ran toward the relative safety of the war elsewhere on the *Spelljammer*. They knew that unholy death had been unleashed, and that escape was their only prayer.

"Why are they running?" CassaRoc asked. He turned then and saw a few of the dark shapes floating toward him.

Djan helped support Na'Shee, who touched her forehead tenderly. They stared toward the ruins.

"By the Dark Queen," Teldin said. He had his sword ready in his hand. "What in the Abyss are they?"

They floated out, bobbing drunkenly, as though drugged, barely aware of their surroundings. Their great eyes blinked at the light from the chaotic flow. Teldin heard Na'Shee gasp in horror. "They're . . . they're so . . ."

CassaRoc said, "Ugly."

"Obscene," offered Chaladar.

The things clearly had been beholders, but they were true beholders no longer. Their great, round bodies were blackened, malformed, as though burned from the inside out, and wrapped with stained and moldy bandages. There were thirteen of them, and each of their ten eyestalks hung shriveled, withered, and blind upon their crowns. Their long, gnarly mouths were pulled back in endless pain, exposing rotting, ragged teeth, and their great red eyes blinked slowly, taking in their surroundings as though they were but a dim memory.

Djan said, "They look undead."

"Mummies," Stardawn guessed.

One of the floating monsters came nearer to the humans. It focused on a beholder floating beyond them, closer to the elf tower. Its mouth drew back in a cry of fury, and a scarlet bolt of power burst from the thing's central eye. The air sizzled with its heat. The ray found its target, and the beholder screamed as its scales blistered away. The eye tyrant imploded in a burst of crimson energy.

The kasharin, Estriss said. *I had thought they were only rumor, legend. They're the survivors of the Blinding Rot.*

"We've got to get clear," CassaRoc said. "What can we do against death magic like that?"

The death rays of the kasharin lanced out at foes and beholders alike. The kasharin's hatred for the living—especially the other beholders, it seemed to Teldin—was boundless, and all were considered potential targets. The air was filled with the sound of death rays blazing from the beholder mummies and the wails of the dying.

Minotaurs, screaming in agony, burst into red flame. A hill giant ran up to a kasharin, its immense battle-axe raised for the kill. The kasharin twisted toward it and blasted out with its magic. The beam burned through the giant's shield, and the creature was engulfed in scarlet flame as its skin smoldered and blackened. Rays of blazing energy shot forth from its eyes and mouth as it burned away from the inside. The axe clattered to the deck.

The kasharin turned toward Teldin and grimaced.

Red energy flickered behind its great eye as its orb swelled with power.

Teldin raised his shield and sword. He thought briefly of hurling himself toward the thing, driving his sword into its eye as they both died, the mummy in its own blood, he, a charred corpse.

The kasharin shook as its energies built up inside it. The great eye flared red. The death ray shot toward him, a blazing beam that seared the air.

Teldin threw up his shield protectively, knowing it was useless. Then he was hammered from the side by a heavy weight, and the death beam licked across his shoulder and found a minotaur standing beyond the humans.

Teldin fell to the deck, his left arm trapped beneath him. The weight blocked his view as the minotaur imploded. Teldin twisted his head and looked up. All he saw was plaid.

"I couldn't let it kill you, sir," Emil said.

The Cloakmaster looked behind the small warrior. Others from the Tower of Thought were rushing their way, firing crossbow bolts and tossing spears at the unhumans and the kasharin.

Teldin smiled and reached for his sword as Emil stood up. "Just in time," Teldin said. Then he looked up as a round shadow fell across him, from behind his savior's shoulder. "Paladine's blood!" Teldin shouted. "Watch out, Emil!"

The little fighter turned. A kasharin had floated within a few feet of him, and its great eye flared an angry red as it stared solely at Emil.

The fighter took a step back and fumbled under his cloak for his slingshot, but the air hummed with the power of the kasharin's death ray. Emil was blown back, his skin blistered and smoking with the power of the kasharin's fury.

Teldin leaped up. Emil twisted in agony as the kasharin's death magic burned within him. "*Spelljammer*—" Emil had time to say. "Save . . . the *Spelljammer*—"

Then Emil died in a gout of red-hot energy that was as bright to Teldin as the light of a thousand suns.

He had had enough. Teldin screamed into the flow, at the fighting, the senselessness of it all. He screamed at the treachery of the races, at the friends who had betrayed him in his quest across the spheres, at the friends and lovers who had died, at their murderers and their selfish desires.

At the death.

He reached down and gripped a huge battle-axe that a minotaur had dropped while fleeing the ruins. He spun and screamed aloud, raising the axe high above his head, and he drove it deep into the kasharin's great eye. Energy flickered around the steel as Teldin pulled it out, then swung it hard into the kasharin's crusted body. Scales split as the axe cleaved through the mummy's dead flesh. Thin black blood sprayed Teldin's arms and burned like acid. Teldin screamed as he jerked the axe out of the kasharin and plunged it deep into its crimson eye.

He screamed as the kasharin plopped lifeless to the deck. He screamed as he chopped into its body until all that was left were pieces of blackened scales and diseased flesh.

He screamed as he felt hands on him, pulling him toward the elf tower and away from the beholders' murder machines. *Teldin*, he heard Estriss say dimly, as though at a distance, *Teldin, we must hurry.*

Teldin jerked his shoulder away. The warriors watched him as Estriss approached slowly, his hands held peaceably before him. *Teldin, you must listen . . .*

The Cloakmaster's glazed eyes slowly focused on the mind flayer. *We have to leave here*, Estriss said. *The* Spelljammer *needs you.*

The warriors broke into a run, Teldin at the rear, lost in thought. He looked up briefly as he felt pebbles fall across his shoulder, then a corner of the beholder ruins collapsed under a heavy rain of boulders and iron shot from a ship in the flow. The war was on in full force, and in the heat of senseless violence, the *Spelljammer* had become less an object of conquest than an enemy to be destroyed.

Stardawn led them to the heavily guarded entrance of the Elven High Command. The guards stopped them and formed a protective shield around them while the battles with the kasharin widened and the beholder-mummies spread between the towers.

Then Stardawn led them through the entrance chamber and the audience gallery to the darkened, spiral staircase at the lower level. They started up, twisting toward the battlements, and wound their way slowly to the top, climbing single file up the narrow staircase. At the uppermost landing, Stardawn took a heavy key from his belt and opened the door to the battlements. Here the air of the *Spelljammer*'s protective bubble seemed thinner, and their cloaks and hair waved in a slight breeze. They hurried across the stone battlement and stopped at the sealed entrance of the Armory.

The sky was filled with vessels battling among themselves or twisting down toward the *Spelljammer* with their weapons armed. Teldin shook his head. All this . . . for what?

My destiny.

The warriors took positions around Teldin, who turned to face the double doors into the Armory. The doors were sealed with a disk of metal that gleamed like silver, bronze, and gold all at once. A three-pointed star was molded into its surface.

"Have people tried to get in this way before?" Teldin asked Stardawn.

The elf nodded. "The seal can be broken with the right weapon, but after our people have gone inside, they've been tossed out, unconscious or dead, and the thing seals up again."

Teldin nodded and stood squarely in front of the door. The seal was exactly the size of his amulet, he saw, and bore the sign of the Juna. He smiled and instinctively closed his eyes.

He felt the breeze flow between his outstretched fingers, through his hair. The cloak flapped softly against him. Its energies billowed through his body like a cool-warm breeze, and the three-pointed star shone in his mind's eye as a focal point for his powers.

Then his amulet glowed from within. The sign of the star was revealed in white-hot light and crackling bolts of energy flew between the two disks, flowing along the contours of the amulet's pattern like a maze to be solved, as though the pattern were a combination to a lock.

The amulet flared a brilliant blue-white, and the metal seal melted away from the doors with a final bolt of energy from Teldin's amulet. The doors burst open by themselves, and the darkness of the Armory greeted them. The molten droplets that had been the armory's seal fluttered on the floor as though they were alive, and they trickled silently into the shadows ahead of the warriors.

"This is what you were meant to do," Djan said. "This is what it has all led up to."

Teldin smiled at his friends. "Let's go in."

A series of twin explosions echoed off the surrounding towers. The warriors turned as the ship rocked with the impact. "There!" Na'Shee shouted, as a great ball of flame erupted from the giff tower.

"What is happening here?" Teldin said to himself. "This has to come to an end." He touched his amulet protectively and closed his eyes. "This must all end soon."

Chapter Twenty-Seven

• • •

"*. . . The Armory and the Dark Tower are mysteries waiting to be solved. Adventurers have sought their secrets, only to be rudely dispatched by the Nameless Servants. Rumors abound, chief among them that the enemies of the* Spelljammer *are imprisoned in the holds of the Dark Tower, and that the Armory bears weapons and treasures unimaginable and very well protected. . . .*"

Rambergius, cleric of the Tower of Thought; reign of Coronas.

The number of ships that Teldin and CassaRoc had originally seen through CassaRoc's spyglass had now almost quadrupled, dotting the flow with vicious shapes that were speeding dead on for the *Spelljammer*. There were seventy-one of them now—tsunamis, tyrants, wasps, deathspiders, scorpions, eelships, and more—swarming through the flow like black, furious insects, grappling each other with their hooks and lines, battling among themselves with their catapults and powerful ballistae.

Many aboard those ships had touched the cloak; many knew of magic spells to trace the cloak and the warrior who had claimed it. They came from all across the spheres to rendezvous here, where their crystals and spells and philters and psionic powers had told them they would find the legendary *Spelljammer* and its ultimate helm, the Cloak of the First Pilot. Behind the ships, mere specks against the chaotic phlogiston, more ships followed—twenty five warships, in a fleet as yet unidentified, racing toward the *Spelljammer* recklessly.

All were converging in a dance that had started an eon before, a dance that played on amid the music of death and violence.

The ships battled ferociously in their zeal to both defeat their enemies and reach the *Spelljammer* first, to assume command of the godlike vessel. A specially outfitted wasp dove straight for a nautiloid and rammed straight through the side of its shell-like hull. Immediately, a score of warriors swarmed over the grappling ram and through the great rent in the nautiloid, attacking its crew upon sight.

Below the *Spelljammer*, a squid ship and a hammership battled it out at medium range. Iron-tipped missiles were shot from the three ballistae on board the squid, and two of the projectiles tore through the underbelly of the hammership. The other shot went wild and bounced harmlessly off the underside of the *Spelljammer*'s port wing.

The hammership dipped precariously, losing speed and altitude. The captain refused to give up, and she responded to the squid ship's attack by banking and aiming the catapults at the body of the squid. Boulders were sent hurtling through the flow to crash into the squidship's top deck and straight through the bottom. The broken bodies of mind flayers floated out, twisted and bloody, to be swallowed into the cold, lifeless flow.

The hammership listed to port and started spiraling down. Within seconds, the wounded ship spun out of control. Its downward gyre suddenly slowed. For a moment, it looked as if the hammership was straightening, slowing its momentum. Then the ship veered wildly off course and took off on an erratic path straight for the black wall of the Broken Sphere, where it crashed helplessly into the impervious crystal wall, spitting bodies and splinters of wood and metal into the emptiness.

Above the *Spelljammer*, two dragonflies swooped down to overtake a slow-moving Shou dragonship. Warriors aboard the swifter dragonflies stood ready on the main deck, their bows and crossbows cocked and armed. Each dragonfly closed in on one side of the Shou craft, and as they sailed past, the dragonflies' arrows arced through the flow like birds flying in formation. Most of the Shou warriors on the dragonship's deck were at the ship's three large weapons and were left unable to protect themselves from the bolts that suddenly appeared from the sky, blindly nailing their brothers in their chests and heads.

The survivors on deck wasted no time and quickly shot their catapults and ballistae at the dragonflies as they swooped past. But the Shou weapons were too slow, and their boulders were sent harmlessly into the phlogiston. The missile shot from a Shou ballista hissed just feet past a speeding dragonfly, and found a target in the hull of an elven man-o-war that had been descending on the *Spelljammer*.

The elven ship suddenly changed course, the missile protruding from its side like an oversized spear. The Shou watched as the ship banked and turned straight for them, seemingly on a suicide run. As the vengeful elves on the deck readied their catapults and ballistae, elves at the bow were aiming at the dragon ship with their hand-held weapons.

The man-o-war closed in. At the last second, the elven warriors simultaneously let loose their fire. The dragonship rocked under the onslaught of granite boulders that battered the decks and crushed Shou under their weight. The black waves of arrows and bolts from the elves skewered the Shou on deck, and the iron-shafted ballistae impaled the dragonship's hull as though it were made of paper.

The man-o-war swept gracefully up and over the Shou craft so that its hull passed inches from the tip of the dragonship's sail. The elven ship was up and away, gaining distance between itself and the battle and providing time to repair the Shou's ballista damage. The dragonship lurched far to starboard, and Shou warriors slid across the angled deck to grasp futilely for handholds along the sides of the ship. Some were able to grab hold of staves along the main deck; most, though, spilled into the flow, to float there with the bodies of the dead.

Across the vista of the Rainbow Ocean, sidewheelers and shrike ships, a whaleship, even a dwarven citadel sculpted from an asteroid, assaulted one another with their weapons of wood and steel and magic. Catapults twanged, reverberating through the flow as their stone shot was sent careening into the hulls of other vessels. The war for the *Spelljammer* had become a free-for-all, one more battle in a second Unhuman War—a war that would very likely produce no clear victor, except for the bloodthirsty warrior known as Death.

The *Spelljammer* quietly sailed in orbit around the Broken Sphere. Its mighty wings swept through fields of insignificant debris that had once been enemy ships. All of the doors of all its primary towers had been opened, and the peoples of the *Spelljammer* were abandoning their battles with the ship's other inhabitants and were preparing to defend their ship—and take the last invading orc or neogi with them.

Mages upon several tower roofs sent their arcane spells into the flow. Rays of light and power emanated toward the attacking ships and blew holes into their hulls. Upon the roof of the Guild tower, Leoster and his most accomplished wizards stood in a circle, chanting their individual spells and focusing the powers of the magical plane through their bodies. Rings of scarlet light and energy emanated from their hands and were blown toward the enemy fleets like the smoke rings of giants. They encircled a pirate hammership in a concentric cage, and the vessel crumbled under the feet of the crew, its planks and nails and hull falling apart, disintegrating like brittle, ancient plaster.

Crimson lightning shot from the eyes of an elven mage upon the tower of the Armory, and an illithid ship exploded in the phlogiston in a flash of ethereal red fire, which, for some reason, did not ignite the volatile flow.

A sleek vipership angled up toward an octopus and increased its speed. Its piercing ram gleamed in the light of the flow as the distance between them grew smaller. The octopus saw the viper immediately and fired its heavy ballistae at too close a distance. The missiles hummed past the viper and disappeared into the flow. The viper impaled the octopus through its bulbous hull, erupting into the chart room and captain's quarters. Then the decks of the viper ran busy with its crew, shooting grappling lines across the gap between the ship. Weapons sang out and swords clashed as the octopus was quickly boarded and taken.

The two ships were then surrounded in a bubble of green

light, cast from a coordinated group of psionicists upon one of the *Spelljammer*'s main batteries. The two ships quivered, then shook apart, fluttering into dust and chips of wood, to be blown forever on the winds and eddies of the flow.

Five thousand feet off the *Spelljammer*'s bow, two bee-class wasps furiously engaged an angelship. The wasps fired six ballistae straight into the hull and wings of the angelship. Then one wasp disengaged while the other grappled the angelship and boarded it. The wasp flitted around, as though it didn't know what ship to attack next, then it homed in on the *Spelljammer* and sped forward in a graceful, descending arc.

Laughter came from the top of the giff tower. Lord High Gunsman Rexan "Diamondtip" Hojson had spied the wasp in the corner of his eye, and he instantly decided that this was the perfect test for his quadruple bombard. He shouted the order to lower the tower's sides to reveal the weapon. The walls slid open, and the light of the flow played gloriously off the surface of the giff's explosive bombard.

Diamondtip kept the wasp in his sights and carefully plotted the ship's planned trajectory. He shouted orders to his gunnery crew, outfitted in thick, protective helmets that fully covered their heads. Their uniforms were heavily padded and woven with an elven material that would not catch fire.

The giff's secret weapon swiveled smoothly around on its platform, and one of its four bombards was aimed precisely according to Diamondtip's orders. The other bombards were loaded and ready to fire, should the first bombard miss its target.

The wasp flew closer and closer, buzzing almost like its insect counterpart. As it made its approach to the *Spelljammer*, Diamondtip could see the wasp's extra ballistae being loaded for a close run.

Then the wasp was inside the *Spelljammer*'s air envelope, and Diamondtip screamed, "Fire!"

The bombard's recoil shook the giff tower as the sound of the explosion reverberated through Diamondtip's thick skull. At the same time, the phlogiston-permeated air in the tower burst into flame. Diamondtip was thrown into a wall by the shock wave, and the giff strapped to the bombard seats struggled to regain their composure, shaking off the effects of the phlogiston. Luckily, their uniforms, scorched as they were, kept back the heat of the explosion.

Above the *Spelljammer*, the wasp was engulfed in a ball of flame that bounced across the landing field to scatter into flaming shards of debris. Where the burning wasp skipped, a wake of explosions followed as the phlogiston ignited.

The gunner who fired turned to Diamondtip and raised his hand in salute. Then the giff tower rang with low, hearty laughter, the sound of victory. The ride had been a little rough, but the quadruple bombard worked. The tower, Diamondtip estimated, could take perhaps a score or more explosions before it would threaten to collapse beneath them, and definitely less if they used all four bombards simultaneously.

To die in an explosion . . .

Diamondtip congratulated his gunners, then pointed into the flow. "I see our next target!" he shouted happily. The gunners turned to their bombards, and Diamondtip rejoiced in the exhilaration of an explosive, honorable death, which only a giff could appreciate.

Chapter Twenty-Eight

• • •

"*. . . Fear can take many forms and can affect people in many ways. Jokarin the Bold, fearless in all endeavors and champion of Reorx, would not disclose to me what occurred in the place he calls the* adytum.

"*Even the bravest of us all can sometimes have a shadow fall across his heart. . .*"

Namu, philosopher of the Guild; journal

Na'Shee was the last to pass through the great doorway, and as she crossed the threshold into the Armory, the double doors behind her closed by themselves. She spun as she heard the doors slam against the door frame, and she grasped the handles and twisted hard. The doors were shut solidly. "Locked," she said. "We're locked in."

Teldin turned slowly. His eyes seemed blank, glazed over. "Don't worry. It's just a precaution so others cannot enter. The doors will open when it's necessary."

"What exactly does that mean?" CassaRoc asked.

Teldin smiled as he heard voices and saw images that were his alone. They seemed to come easier now, since he had touched the globe in the library's loculus. "It means that I will take care of it."

They stood in a dark, circular hall, surrounded by tables and cases and shelves bearing dim, rectangular shapes. The warriors took a few steps, spreading out to explore, and the light panels in the ceiling winked on automatically, casting dim, bluish light throughout the cavernous hall.

This is amazing, said Estriss, his eyes wide with wonder at the assortment of items spread throughout the long gallery. *Absolutely amazing. The history, the things we could learn here . . .*

The chamber seemed larger now that they were inside, far larger than was apparent from the outside. The tall walls and rows upon rows of tables were crowded with transparent cases made of an impervious glasslike material. Inside them, protected against the elements and any potential thieves or glory-seekers, were hundreds of objects of both mundane and exotic design. Some were clearly of recent make; others were obviously ancient, showing signs of disuse and age. Many other objects were so obscure that Teldin and his allies could not discern exactly what they were, or what their functions were.

One portion of the hall boasted an enormous collection of walking sticks and staffs, even two scepters of long-forgotten kings. Another section contained more jewelry and precious gems than the warriors had ever imagined in one place. The light gleamed off the jewels as if they were alive, seething with untapped powers. The gold appeared so pure, so warm, that it might melt in one's hand. One particular metal coin hummed inside its case. Other cases held strange vestments and articles of clothing: a pair of boots with silver wings; a tunic that seemed to glow a vibrant green, then red in the *Spelljammer*'s pale light.

A portion of one wall held within it a large library of books and scrolls and bound yellow manuscripts. One tome bore the title *Tomb of Torture*, written in Elvish script. Estriss ran his scholar's hand across some of the titles: *The Epistle of Lord JaykEl of the Blue Order of the* Spelljammer; *The Helmsman's Companion* by Gorg Blasterbeam, Once Scribe of Humptown. Another read *The Star Quest of Bryn* and promised "A Ribald Adventure of Treachery and Untold Perverse Delights."

Estriss hissed in wonder and drew back his hand. He had found a strange book bound in a brittle, flesh-colored leather. Its ancient cover was tattooed with designs and sigils that made the humans nauseated to look too long at them. Estriss looked up. *You do not want to know*, he said.

"What is this place?" Na'Shee wondered aloud. Her voice echoed hollowly through the gallery.

Teldin stood frozen in the center of the room. His voice seemed far away when he answered. "This whole tower is the *Spelljammer*'s . . ." He concentrated, letting the knowledge wash over him in a soothing wave. "This is the *Spelljammer*'s memory, containing all its experiences and adventures throughout the spheres, collected here in physical form. This room holds . . ." He paused, seemingly searching for the words. "These are most of the magical items that have ever come aboard the *Spelljammer*. Their owners are long dead, and they wait here as individual memories, of events that mostly occurred long before any of us were born."

"How can the *Spelljammer* have a memory?" Chaladar asked.

Teldin smiled as he turned slowly, taking in all of the chamber. "The *Spelljammer* is more than a city sailing between the spheres, or a vessel that can be owned by whoever has the most men and weapons. The *Spelljammer* is . . . alive."

"Alive?" Chaladar said. "I don't understand. How can that be?"

"It is alive, and it is sentient," Teldin told them. "And it has brought me here because I bear the Ultimate Helm, because it needs me to fulfill its own destiny, just as its destiny is my own."

"Can we take them?" CassaRoc asked. He had not listened to Teldin's revelation. He was standing over a case containing a metallic vest, shimmering with all the colors of the spectrum.

Teldin grinned slightly. He slipped his sword out of its scabbard. "You may try. Be ready, everyone."

The others quickly pulled out their blades. "Be ready for what?" Djan asked.

"You'll see," Teldin said. Then, "CassaRoc, go ahead."

CassaRoc examined the case and could not find a lock. He brought the hilt of his sword down hard upon the case, and his arm reverberated with the impact.

It happened so fast that no one had time to see where the creatures had come from. There were six of them: huge, lumbering gray shapes that at first seemed amorphous at their approach. Then the warriors could make out individual features: strangely shaped arms that ended in whiplike hands, and pale, fleshy bodies that resembled neogi and beholders and centaurs.

The guardian shivaks converged on the humans, ready to protect the Armory and the ship's collection of memories. Faceless, composed entirely of a thick, leathery flesh, and without internal organs, the shivaks served the ship and tirelessly defended its secrets. The warriors were simply intruders to them, and were to be dealt with as any intruder would be dealt with: first apprehended, then defeated and rendered unconscious, then returned outside to the decks of the *Spelljammer.*

Djan was knocked to the floor by the huge arm of a centaurian shivak. It pulled back a great, curled fist, and sent its arm in a downward swing toward Djan's head.

In the instant before impact, Teldin shouted "*No!*"

His voice echoed impossibly loud throughout the chamber and carried with it a tone of authority, which the shivaks dully recognized as a sign of the Helmbearer. Each shivak halted in its tracks. One shivak had Estriss clasped within its three curled arms. Another tightly clasped Stardawn's wrist within its thick hand, ready to pummel the elf into unconsciousness.

Light blazed out from Teldin's ancient amulet and flickered into the eyes of each shivak, casting the image of a three-pointed star across each face. Teldin turned instinctively, letting the light pass over each shivak in turn. As though it were a message, or a command stimulated by the amulet's intrinsic magical energies, the shivaks released their holds on the humans. The amulet ceased its flashes of light, and the shivaks stood immobile where they had stopped.

"We will meet no more resistance," Teldin said.

"Will you please tell me what in the Nine Hells just happened?" said CassaRoc, sputtering.

"They have recognized the sign of the *Spelljammer,*" Teldin said. "They listen to no other command. We now have unlimited passage through the Armory, and no shivak will try to stop us."

A shadowed spiral staircase against the far wall led Teldin and his friends down to the next level of the Armory. Djan whistled as light panels in the wall winked on as the warriors proceeded down to the next floor. "How does the *Spelljammer* know we're here?"

Teldin did not answer. He took each stair confidently, as though he had walked these steps before.

Then the stairs ended, and the group found themselves in another huge gallery. The light panels above them brightened as Chaladar brought up the rear, and they stood silently as they gazed upon a chamber filled from wall to wall with display cases of various sizes, arranged in orderly rows that seemed to go on into infinity.

Estriss immediately approached the closest case. *Amazing,* the mind flayer said. *Teldin, come here and look. The detail on this is amazing.*

The others surrounded Estriss and peered into the case, then eagerly spread out to examine the other cases throughout the gallery.

Like the chamber above, the walls and tables were covered with uncounted displays, but these cases did not contain magical items like those above.

Estriss pointed with one blunt, purplish finger. *Look there. The rigging is perfect. Whoever built these is a remarkable craftsman. The markings, the decorations—the craftsmanship is incredibly delicate.*

Inside each case was a scale model of a different ship: squidships, deathspiders, battle dolphins, illithid dreadnoughts, wasp ships, hammerships, elven man-o-wars and flitters, a gnomish sidewheeler, beholder tyrants, damselflies, dragonflies, Shou dragonships, viperships, scorpion ships, lampreys, deathglories, an elven armada, and more. Each case held a different scale model, the types of which stretched the known spheres, and not a few were completely unknown to Teldin and his allies.

Na'Shee shouted from far across the gallery. "Teldin, you better come here! I think you ought to see this!"

They hurried over to Na'Shee, where she stood above one rectangular case. Inside was a scale model of a nautiloid, gleaming in perfect condition.

"So?" Stardawn said.

"Read the name," Na'Shee invited.

CassaRoc bent down to look, then he stood up abruptly and

stared at Teldin. "What's going on here?"

Estriss said, *What is it?*

"The name painted on the bow," Chaladar said, "says it's the *Julia*."

"That's our ship," Djan said. "We crashed the nautiloid when we came on board."

Who built these, Teldin? Estriss asked. *Who could build these so perfectly, so fast?*

Teldin shook his head slowly and indicated all the ships contained in the cases throughout the room. He gathered his breath, letting the information flow into him. "These are not models," he said. "These are actual ships, all the ships that have ever reached the *Spelljammer* during its voyages across the universe. Thousands of them have been shrunk, rebuilt, if needed, and kept as memories. The ship did this." He peered into the case at his own nautiloid. "I can feel the magical power as well. All the spelljamming helms are intact."

CassaRoc said, "Can they ever be used again?"

Teldin looked at him curiously. "I don't know," he said.

The floor below was identical to the ones above it, containing cases of swords and daggers. "All magical, in one way or another," Teldin told them. He examined one sword of ancient make, its blade gleaming in the gallery's cold light. Mystic runes had been hammered into the steel below a crude design depicting a circle of standing stones. "Some of them are legendary."

The gallery below held cases of axes and maces and warhammers. Na'Shee lingered long, staring at a particularly handsome double-headed flail that gleamed inside its case. Teldin pulled her away. "Perhaps later," he said as he led her to the stairs.

"How far down does this go?" Stardawn asked Teldin.

The Cloakmaster watched him. The elf seemed anxious, perhaps a little nervous. His hand kept straying to the hilt of his sword, and his eyes seemed to wander, warily keeping track of his surroundings.

"The lower floors hold weaponry and ammunition, enough to arm the entire population of the *Spelljammer*." Teldin led them down the stairs to the next level. "Stones for the catapults, ballista bolts, replacement parts for the weapons, even smoke powder. The *Spelljammer* knows when these things are needed, and the armory will open below when the occasion arises."

The light panels blinked on in the next gallery, and the company walked through, examining the cases of arrows and spears and crossbow bolts.

"Magical?" CassaRoc said.

Teldin nodded.

They proceeded to the level below. The light panels came on, and they stood silently, staring at the tall cases standing in long rows down the hall.

Djan gasped involuntarily. Na'Shee reached for the hilt of a sword.

"Are they alive?" Na'Shee asked Teldin.

He shook his head.

The cases seemed more like transparent coffins, for each contained the preserved bodies, both male and female, of examples of every race that had ever boarded the *Spelljammer*. Human, illithid, gnome, k'r'r'r, arcane, beholder, dracon—all who had traveled the Rainbow Ocean to find the *Spelljammer*. They found three cases that had been shattered. Jagged fragments of glass had sprayed across the floor, and the bodies that had been inside had sometime been removed by thieves—or rescuers—unknown.

The next staircase was long and winding, leading down into darkness. Teldin took the lead and finally brought the warriors to a great golden door at the base of the stairs, where a single light crystal in a golden sconce bloomed at their approach. He placed his hand upon it, and the door silently opened inward at the Cloakmaster's touch.

The chamber was huge and appeared to be a vault of some kind with an immense, domed ceiling high above. The light inside was dim, a pale blue, and the hall was encircled by a narrow, angled ledge about three feet off the floor. The ledge was studded with brilliant diamonds, shining with their own inner, crystalline fires.

CassaRoc stroked his beard and stared at the jewels. "These jewels are worth a king's ransom. Do you know what we could do with this wealth?"

"These are worth far more than ordinary gems," Teldin said,

reaching out to touch a blue diamond.

Instantly, above them, the domed vault was filled with the interior image of a crystal sphere. Planets swam in orbit around a miniature sun, and stars glittered around them like jewels, seemingly close enough to take in their hands and hold like fireflies. The planets glowed vibrantly with color, and the sun cast its yellow light upon their astonished, upturned faces.

"Every sphere the *Spelljammer* has ever visited is remembered here," Teldin said reverently. His voice echoed solemnly through the room. "All the spheres, and more than you could imagine. Over two thousand of them, all watched over by the *Spelljammer*, their protector—"

He stopped, scarcely believing his own words. But he knew they were true; he could see the words, the images in his mind. The sign of the amulet pounded warmly in his chest, a soothing reminder of his destiny and the truth of what he saw.

"The *Spelljammer*," Teldin said. "It has been here almost since the beginning of time—not this *Spelljammer*—this is but the last of many. Its sentience holds the memories of the others, memories of its birth . . . and of the Broken Sphere."

His friends watched him silently, unable to comprehend what he had told them.

Teldin thought for a moment. "I—I'm getting images, or messages, from the *Spelljammer*. It's not telling me everything. I am seeing little pieces at a time." He paused in thought. "The One Egg, the Broken Sphere, was an original sphere, a natural sphere far larger than those we know. Then it was destroyed—I can't see it all yet—and the *Spelljammer* has tried to somehow replace it, I think, ever since. Or . . . *atone* for it."

"The story is incredible," Stardawn said. There was a hint of anger in his eyes. "Could this ship be that powerful?"

"Yes. It is more powerful, more primal, than we know."

And who created the Spelljammer? Estriss repeated. *The Juna?*

"The Juna," Teldin said, "yes, among many others. The *Spelljammer* was less created than . . . conceived."

Teldin touched the diamond again, and the image of the sphere flickered away. He looked up, sadly, where the spherescape had been. "We must go below."

The stairs leading to the next floor were in the center of the room, a wide, stone stairway that spiraled down into darkness and seemed, to them, to go far beyond the dimensions of the tower. *The* Spelljammer *is distorting our senses,* Estriss said. *This tower cannot be this tall.*

"Or this wide," said CassaRoc. "I noticed that as soon as we set foot in the first chamber. It is a magical illusion."

"Perhaps," Teldin said. "Perhaps."

The group had just completed the first turn in the stairway when lights, hidden in the floors, came on, illuminating the domed ceiling and the stairway's entrance above. At first, the companions thought they were surrounded by warriors, black silhouettes backlighted with pale lighting, then the entire staircase became illuminated, and the humans saw who they faced: a line of statues, spiraling down alongside the stairs. The base of each statue was embedded with a diamond.

The statue at the top was clearly the most ancient, pockmarked by age and coated in layers of gray dust. The figure was that of a man, square-jawed and stocky, bearing a long cloak and a circular amulet.

That's your amulet, Teldin, Estriss said.

"Yes," Teldin acknowledged, looking closer. The pattern on the amulet was the same, as was the barely discernable pattern on the inside of the cloak, a pattern of three-pointed stars. "And that is the cloak I bear. You are looking upon the First Pilot, the first captain of the *Spelljammer.*"

"Who was he?" Djan asked. "What can you tell us?"

Teldin thought, then shook his head. "As I said, I don't understand it all myself."

CassaRoc said, "If this is the First Pilot, then all these statues must be—"

"—statues of all the *Spelljammer*'s captains," Teldin said automatically. "And the diamonds—"

"—are memory crystals, like in the vault above," Na'Shee said.

"Yes, displaying the life histories of the captains and their reigns aboard the *Spelljammer.*"

They continued down the Rotunda of the Captains. Teldin stopped once and pointed at the stairs. They were covered with dust, but thin, straight trails were visible, as though something had recently passed this way. "The seal," Teldin said. "The droplets from the melted seal on the door outside. They came this way."

They followed the thin trail past more than 150 statues, male and female, even one of a beholder. As the warriors made their descent, the statues appeared more recently constructed, less dusty. Teldin recognized the face of Romar, the captain who eventually became the Fool. Then, finally, they realized they were nearing the bottom of the stairs. The last statue was on the right, standing to the side of a huge door. Another, smaller spiral staircase led even farther down.

"Look," Teldin said.

The metal droplets had traveled down the staircase and up the body of the last statue, to collect and transform into a shiny disk at the statue's neck. The statue bore a long cloak and stood proudly among the others, the last in a long line of both heroes and rogues.

The statue was featureless, with only a blank template for a face, but Estriss saw immediately who the statue was to resemble. As he looked around, he realized the others did as well. Even Stardawn seemed moved, frozen as he stared at the raw, unformed stone.

Teldin stared at the statue. "I understand now. I know now why the *Spelljammer* has called me." He turned to his friends. "I was once told of my destiny by a fal, and I did not believe it. But he was right, and that is why I am here."

He took a breath and ran his hand up the statue's cloak.

"This is me," he said. "I am to be the next captain of the *Spelljammer*."

Chapter Twenty-Nine

• • •

". . . *The creature was of the stuff that made up the shivaks, but was so fearsome in its aspect that I had but scarce time to examine it. This shivak was immense, a grotesque simulacrum of a beholder, guarding the throne of the legendary* adytum *against all usurpers. As soon as it spied me, it attacked. . . .*"
Jokarin the Bold, private log

"The captain?" Chaladar said, incredulous. "How long have you known this?"

"I tried to tell you in the library tower, when I experienced the orb inside the loculus, but the *Spelljammer* was attacked, and we rushed outside before I could finish."

Estriss said, *It is no wonder that all the races want you dead, and the cloak for themselves. The Ultimate Helm will grant any bearer the captaincy of the* Spelljammer.

"And the *Spelljammer* would become the ultimate weapon of destruction," Chaladar reasoned. "Chaos would spread across the spheres like a plague."

"I don't know about that," Teldin said. "The Fool was once the captain, and he was rejected for his actions against life and peace."

"That may be true," Djan interjected, "but the ones who want the *Spelljammer* have probably never been aboard. They probably know nothing of the *Spelljammer*'s sentience. Even the populace knows nothing of it."

Stardawn was silent throughout the discussion, frozen with

anger. He knew all he needed now. He had known for a long time, since he had bought his information from the mad arcane, that a magical item was the key to becoming the *Spelljammer*'s captain. But the item now was Teldin's cloak, and he would let Teldin lead him to the *adytum*, where he then would take the cloak for himself, and take the captaincy with it.

Teldin turned away from the discussion and opened a great door. A narrow set of ten stairs led down from the Armory to the roof of the Dark Tower. He started down, then waited below for the rest of the party to file out.

Teldin took the group across the roof of the Dark Tower to stand in the shadow of the *Spelljammer*'s mammoth tail. The ship's body was laid out before them as though they were its lords. From here they could see bodies on the decks, the rubble caused by barrages from above. Screams and angry cries came from below, and they heard the twang of coiled springs as ballistae were fired at the vessels in the flow around the ship.

The Cloakmaster reached out and ran his hand along the tail's broad, purplish surface, searching. His hand found a point at eye level, then Teldin stepped back and motioned for the others to follow. He pointed to a mottled area on the side of the tail. "There," he said, and he stood facing the tail, his arms outstretched.

The amulet at his neck pulsated with crackles of electricity, then cast out a coruscating burst of energy that bathed the tail in its blinding glow. In immediate response, the mottled area of the tail changed color, transforming from a speckled purple into a swirl of red and blue. The surface then twisted impossibly, as though its very flesh were transforming into liquid. It rippled away in a miasmic whirlpool of color, exposing a shifting, formless opening. Within, a staircase twisted organically, like a vein, stretching up into the tail.

Teldin crawled into the opening, crouched inside, and looked around. He moved to let in the others, and they started slowly up the narrow, chaotic staircase in single file. The stairs were translucent, unevenly formed of a chitinous, weblike material that seemed to be one long structure spiraling up through the tail. The silence inside seemed palpable, almost holy, and they went steadily up the staircase without talking, feeling the weight of their search pressing on them.

The staircase opened at a bubblelike landing, an organic ovoid deep inside the *Spelljammer*'s skin. In the wall before them was a roughly circular object. Folds of the *Spelljammer*'s tough flesh pressed together into a doorway that appeared more like a closed wound than an entrance.

Teldin appraised the entrance and willed instinctively. His amulet flared once and shone the sign of the Juna upon the doorway. The folds of flesh peeled back as the doorway slowly dilated open in an invitation to the Cloakmaster.

The warriors gathered behind Teldin and looked inside. The iris opened onto a short entrance hall, then the hall widened into a hollow, organic pocket, the *Spelljammer*'s *adytum*. Rough-hewn light crystals embedded in the walls flickered on silently. Three rough steps led to an uneven dais, upon which sat a simple, unadorned throne made of the *Spelljammer*'s stony flesh.

This is it, Teldin thought. This is what my quest has been about.

Teldin stared at the throne for a few seconds, then took his first, tremulous step through the opening and stopped just inside the *adytum*.

A great shape suddenly blocked his view of the dais, and a huge hand slammed hard against the side of his head and sent him reeling across the room.

Teldin had just enough time to sit up on one arm. His head swam from the blow and images came to him, flashes of insight that showed him what he must do. "Stay outside!" he shouted to the others.

CassaRoc yelled at him angrily. "You can't fight this thing alone!"

"No!" Teldin said. "You must stay there! You won't be attacked outside the *adytum*! This is my fight! You can do nothing for me!"

Then the Cloakmaster was lifted high above the floor and flung across the room. He collided heavily against the throne.

His head swam under the impact, and his side flared with bright pain. He reached up for the arm of the throne and hauled himself off the floor.

His eyes widened.

The guardian that lumbered toward him was the largest shivak he had seen. It had taken the form of an impossibly huge illithid. Where most mind flayers stood no more than seven feet tall, this shivak was fully fifteen. Its gray, leathery hide was stretched tight, like muscle, across its chest and down its powerful arms, and its tentacled face seemed frozen in a horrifying grimace of pure, unreasoning hatred.

This had been the last captain's greatest fear, Teldin realized, and he wondered what form the guardian shivak would take if there were to be a captain after him.

Understanding blossomed in the Cloakmaster's mind. This was the *Spelljammer*'s final test of worthiness. All potential captains had to defeat the guardian of the *adytum*, a monstrous shivak in the form of the previous captain's worst fear, before they could claim the ship as their own. The last captain's face flickered behind his eyes, and Teldin saw Jokarin the Bold battling a shivak whose form was that of a huge, misshapen beholder. He saw the moment of bonding then, when the shivak was defeated by Jokarin's cunning use of a magical gauntlet and Jokarin took the throne. He saw Jokarin and the *Spelljammer* become, briefly, as one, and saw the seed from Jokarin's mind enter the consciousness of the *Spelljammer* and lay dormant, waiting, for the next challenger to come.

Then Teldin had no more time to think. The shivak, all the more threatening because it attacked in silence, reached out to take him between its enormous arms. Desperately, Teldin swung out blindly with his sword. One long finger of the shivak's right hand was severed and sent spinning to the floor.

The shivak held Teldin tightly in its iron grasp and lifted his feet from the floor. The sword dropped from his useless hand. The thing's tentacles, perhaps in a dim remembrance of a true mind flayer's need for human brains, twisted hungrily as it brought Teldin's face toward its obscene mouth.

He twisted in the shivak's arms and hammered its thick body with powerful kicks. He grunted with the effort, concentrating on coiling all his strength in his legs. He felt his feet pummel the shivak's stomach, then he managed to twist free one arm. He reached out and grabbed one tentacle from the monster's face and twisted it. The shivak stumbled in pain, then Teldin's other arm was free and he was pushing back on the shivak's head, trying to break its neck.

The thing's grip around his waist tightened. Teldin cried out, then gritted his teeth and pounded his fist repeatedly into the shivak's face. His fist sank once into its flesh as it yielded to Teldin's strength, and then he was free, dropping to the shivak's feet.

Teldin's sword was already in his hand when he leaped again; he swung it into the shivak's side. The blade thunked into the thing's leathery hide and carved a bloodless gouge into its waist. Then Teldin spun and chopped the sword into the shivak's chest and stomach. One gray tentacle went flying as Teldin's sword sliced across its face. Teldin brought his sword high and swung it down in a deadly arc, toward the shivak's heart. The thing moved in a blur and caught the blade between its huge hands. It bent back the polished steel until the sword snapped in half, then it cast the ragged metal shards to the floor and advanced on Teldin, destruction smoldering in its deep-set eyes.

In the entrance hall, Na'Shee fitted a bolt to her crossbow and took aim. CassaRoc held up his hand and pushed down the crossbow so that it pointed to the floor. "No," he said, "Teldin's right. He has to defeat that thing by himself. I don't think anything we could do would help him anyway. It's his fight now."

Stardawn overheard and smiled inwardly. The human had no chance against the shivak, anyone could see that. The monster was huge, a juggernaut of single-minded destruction. Good. He wanted this over, and the less help, the better. Then he could take the cloak from Teldin's bloody, battered body and take command of the *Spelljammer* himself.

The shivak walloped the Cloakmaster with a stony fist to his stomach. He flew back and hit the throne, stumbling to the floor. He pushed himself up, and the shivak halted, focusing its blank eyes at him fixedly.

Then pain was a living thing, growing like the fires of a star inside Teldin's mind, filling his sight with electric, blinding nothingness. Teldin fell to his knees, gasping. The guardian shivak was more powerful than he had known, imbued not just with the form, but the magical abilities of the being it emulated. The shivak strode toward him as his mind rang with the force of an illithid mind blast, capable of crippling, even killing, normal human victims.

Through clouded vision, he saw his friends at the entrance, watching the battle with fear in their eyes. He knew that the important things—friendship, love, and life—stood before him. He forced himself to his feet and balled his fists. His pain was unimportant. It was their pain, and their possible deaths, that he had to worry about, and he stared at the monstrous shivak as it came for him, ready to depose the would-be captain.

He felt himself grow calm, felt his skin tingle with a hidden reserve of serenity, of inner strength. It was the cloak, he knew; still, it was himself also. The powers they now shared depended on determination, on a zeal for life and preservation over the forces of evil, and the cloak had become merely an amplifier of his own abilities, his own inner fires.

Perhaps that was all it had ever been.

The shivak swung a mighty fist, and Teldin ducked under the swing to deliver a rapid series of solid punches to the shivak's torso. It brought its balled fists down on Teldin's shoulders, and he dropped to his knees, throbbing. Impulsively, he reached out for the thing's ankle and lifted it off the floor, then stood quickly and shoved the shivak away.

It rolled and hopped up, its speed disguised by its great bulk, and lunged for him. Teldin ran for it and jumped into the air, lashing out with all the power his legs could muster. His feet slammed into the shivak's chest, and the monster went sprawling back into the wall.

Teldin landed on his feet. The shivak stood unsteadily, and Teldin dove in with a left-right-left series of punches to the shivak's ugly face. He pounded his fists into the thing's stomach repeatedly until the shivak doubled over. Then he felt his anger burning within him, his strength cording like steel, and he brought his right hand up in a dizzying blur that slammed into the shivak's weakened jaw and knocked the thing's feet inches off the floor.

The shivak collapsed. It struggled to its knees, lowering its head for a final, spiteful mind blast toward its antagonist.

The Cloakmaster felt it between them then: their energies, flickering like heat waves in the air between them, around them. The power of the cloak was *his*, and he raised his hands, feeling his skin shimmer with invisible energies, with powers unimaginable.

The shivak tensed, ready to destroy the interloper with the force of its mind; but the Cloakmaster felt the power building in the air between them, and he channeled his own energies through the cloak and cast out with his mind.

The cloak billowed out, filled with a cold breeze from arcane planes unexplored by human travelers. The lining shimmered, became a deep blue, and was filled with specks of light whirling like galaxies deep within.

The shivak stumbled as the coldness of the ethereal planes tore from the cloak in winds and gusts that would have felled trees and toppled houses. It struggled forward, taking one uncertain step toward the Cloakmaster, then darkness flooded from the cloak, enveloping the shivak in a cyclone of night.

The shivak howled in fear as the winds of darkness raged around it. It sank to its knees and faced the Cloakmaster, holding out its hands in subservience.

Teldin felt the power building in him, through him. He screamed, feeling his need for the *Spelljammer*, the end of his quest, become real in his heart. He could not hear his cry over the wail of the cold, empty winds. At once, the stony shivak, frozen by the coldness, the soullessness of the extraplanar winds, exploded with the force of Teldin's being. The shivak shattered into pieces, and jagged chunks of its thick hide hurtled across the *adytum*, embedding into the floor and walls.

Teldin sank to his knees, the strength flooding out of him in a wave. The shivak's remains collapsed in upon themselves, as though being sucked away from the inside. The stony fragments of its flesh were absorbed into the floor and walls.

On the dais, two round pedestals grew out of the floor at the arms of the throne.

Silence fell within the *adytum*. CassaRoc and the others were inside, congratulating the Cloakmaster. He stood, and the cloak shrank to its normal size, draping his shoulder as though it had always belonged there.

CassaRoc indicated the throne. "I think that's for you," he

said, smiling.

They stepped aside to let Teldin step upon the dais. He stood before the throne and stared down at it. "You better get away," Teldin said. "I don't know what will happen."

They all stepped a few feet away. Stardawn, hesitating, stood directly in front of Teldin, a step ahead of the others. His hand was on the hilt of his sword.

Teldin sat in the throne. Unsure, he placed one hand on the top of one pedestal, then the other.

Instantly, he felt warm. A golden glow appeared at his hands that quickly spread throughout his body. His cloak shivered, flapped in an invisible breeze. He felt it wriggle around him, then lose its feel, its texture. It fell apart around him into thin shreds, then it disintegrated into the material of the throne. The amulet seared into Teldin's flesh, glowing below his neck, and he felt only the peaceful glow of the bonding, the warmth of his own life force.

"*Yes*," Teldin said, and his eyes focused far away on some dreamlike vista only he could see. The bonding had begun, and he was filled with the life, the history, the song, and being of the *Spelljammer*, the herald of his destiny. "*Yes*," he said. "*This is what it was all about.*"

His eyes were filled with visions, and his mouth hung slack as his mind struggled to absorb it all. Then he suddenly focused his gaze at his friends. "*I know. Now I know. Estriss, Djan, CassaRoc . . . Now I know it all. Now I—*"

Stardawn screamed a foul curse in Elvish and leaped upon the dais. His sword flashed wickedly in the light of Teldin's golden aura.

The others shouted and moved to intercept him, but the elf was too fast, and with a mighty lunge, he thrust his elven sword deep into Teldin's chest.

Blood pooled around the point of the sword, embedded deep into Teldin's heart. The Cloakmaster stood slowly and stared down at the sword in his chest. He looked then into Stardawn's eyes and smiled.

"*You have done nothing*," Teldin announced, his eyes misty with the *Spelljammer*'s fires. "*I am still the captain*."

And Teldin fell back onto the throne.

He sagged against the chair, his still hands upon the

pedestals. His eyes flickered shut, and his head hung lifeless on his chest.

Na'Shee cried, "Nooooo!" but Teldin, the Cloakmaster, the new captain of the *Spelljammer*, was no more.

The air shimmered in a corner of the *adytum*. The light seemed to dim, as though it were being muted, absorbed, and the *adytum* sparkled as the energies of a spell were dispersed. Then the Fool was revealed, standing where his powerful spells of invisibility and concealment had protected him from all notice, even from the guardian shivak and the *Spelljammer* itself. At his feet, shackled at the neck, huddled Cwelanas.

The Fool lifted a skeletal hand and pointed a bony finger at Stardawn. He took a step. Stardawn gurgled, feeling the power behind the Fool's glaring eyes close around his neck like a vise.

"The Cloakmaster was mine, insect!" the Fool shouted. "The *Spelljammer* was to be mine! Mine alone!"

The Fool released Cwelanas's chains and stepped toward Stardawn. "*Now, elf lord*," he said, "*you shall pay*."

Chapter Thirty

• • •

"*. . . Death is but a gateway. We all hold the key.*
"*Shall I open the door for you? . . .*"
Surturrus, Lord of the Tenth Pit; reign of Noj the Heavy

Teldin floated. The universe was a sea of twilight, of grayness broken only by lightning veins of white and yellow that crackled in the distance.

His body was gone, invisible, yet he felt. *He was cool and warm, hot and cold, real and unreal at the same time. He felt separate from himself, stolen from his body, yet he was more comfortable and more complete, more whole, than he had ever felt before. He stretched out one finger and felt the universe shift around him instinctively. He opened his eyes, and suns were born. He breathed, and the flow shifted its currents around a score of spheres.*

He was planets. He was stars. He was spheres, suns, systems, memories, races long dead.

He was all.

His sight, his senses, were filled with a panoramic vista of the flow, of the oneness of each sphere with its obsidian counterparts scattered like pebbles across the universe.

He thought of himself. He felt his being pull back, into the reality of the Spelljammer, *and his mind saw and felt the unhuman fleets converging on the* Spelljammer. *Elves, neogi, humans, giff—their ships promised bloodshed and war, and the stench of death followed in their wake.*

—Who? *he thought.* —Where?

The answer rang through him with a force unimaginable, a force that had seen stars being born, seen planets die, seen whole spheres bubble into existence and slowly solidify, a thousand years witnessed within a second. It was a word, yet not a word, more a feeling that was sound and sight and touch and smell and taste, all at once.

—Here, *was the answer.*

—Live.

—See.

—Feel.

—Hear.

—Die.

—Experience.

—Know.

—All.

Then:

—We are not the first.

And the universe was a sphere, a single, wondrous black jewel floating in the empty, endless wastes of the chaotic phlogiston. Alone, perhaps; at least unknown by the beings from any other sphere.

—Ouiyan.

Eighteen worlds swung in slow, graceful arcs around Aeyenna, the eternal sun. Eighteen worlds—blue, green, vibrant with a variety of life unknown today. There, among the worlds, life had evolved, reaching out from mother oceans to stare transfixed into the skies. Empires flourished and were destroyed, then were rebuilt upon ancient foundations. Myth gave way to science, then magic, and humanity learned to coexist peacefully with the animals that shared the worlds. Children swam with the great beasts of the sea; mages and scholars shared philosophies with wolves and whales.

Most unique among the worlds of Ouiyan were the spaakiil.

Alone among all the beasts of the One Sphere, the spaakiil *sailed through wildspace and atmospheres alike, great mantas that sang and frolicked among the stars, swam along the boundaries of magic and reality. To each world they brought wonder. To each world they brought the joys of life and diver-*

sity. To each world they brought peace. To each world they brought their songs of greeting from other worlds, and the knowledge that granted humanity the skills to break the cage of gravity and sail the first spelljammers into space.

To each world, the spaakiil *were considered holy: gods to one world; messengers to another; brothers to a third.*

To each world—except one—they were considered friends.

The outermost planet was unknown to the others, circling Aeyenna in an orbit so far distant that the sunlight never shone brighter than dark twilight. The eighteenth world was a cold rock, where vegetable life was limited to black scrubs and thick, dark flowers that cried plaintively as the pinpoint that was the sun teased the sky.

It was from here that evil came and spread across the sphere.

They called themselves the Sh'tarrgh, and for years, the Sh'tarrgh waged war against humanity, the Stealers of the Sun. The grotesque gray humanoids fed on the blood and fear of their chosen enemies. They attacked first the seventeenth world and spread from there to claim the sphere as their own. For years cities were leveled by their weapons of destruction, their mages of darkness. The oceans of Resanel boiled under the heat weapons of the Sh'tarrgh. The Citadel of Kiril, housing four thousand men and women, was reduced to rubble in a day. Worlds died as armies were enveloped in clouds of magic, and nothing but bones and armor were left when the clouds dispersed.

The worlds burned at the Sh'tarrgh's departure, and the One Sphere echoed with the screams of the innocent and the dying.

The Sh'tarrgh wanted nothing but the worlds that orbited peacefully in the glow of the sun. They cared not at all for life; they simply wanted, and wanted. They wanted what before they could not have . . . the sacred, blessed sunlight, and their lust for power fueled their evil.

The leaders of the sphere met only days before Ouiyan was to become but a memory, a legend. The war had gone on too long, for almost a century of mindless death. Already BedevanSov and Ladria had been taken by the Sh'tarrgh, and Ondora was about to fall. Politicians and kings, wizards and priests, knew that the sphere would not hold much longer. It was decided, then, to devise a plan that could save those who were left.

Days later, magic users and kings converged secretly on Irryan, the forest moon of Colurranur, to organize one last attempt to win back their worlds.

The sky above Irryan darkened, and they knew that all was lost—the Sh'tarrgh were attacking.

Then they looked up and rejoiced, for the sky was filled with the triangular shapes of the spaakiil, *circling silently, filling the survivors with awe at their graceful omnipresence.*

The numbers of the spaakiil *had dwindled under the ceaseless attacks of the Sh'tarrgh; but they selflessly offered humanity one last chance to defeat the Sh'tarrgh, one last chance for life.*

The humans listened to the idea of the spaakiil, *and rejected it. No one should sacrifice so much for others, but the* spaakiil *were insistent, and the threat of the Sh'tarrgh was overwhelming.*

Word was soon sent throughout the sphere to all the mages on all the worlds. On the island of Terah, in the sea of Gelaan, the spaakiil *and wizards from all the races of Ouiyan together wove their spells. The skies swirled with dark clouds and danced with lightning. On the other side of the planet, tornadoes cut swaths across the countryside, and strange lights played in the sky.*

Then it was over. A thousand mages had come to Terah, but fewer than two hundred survived the stress of what they had done.

The spaakiil, *the wild singers of the stars, were gone.*

In the sky, blotting the sun, swam a single, impossibly large spaakiil.

No longer alive, as humans knew life, the first Spelljammer, *Egrestarrian, swam above Colurranur, a gleaming, sprawling city spread out upon its back for the refugees of the original, forgotten Unhuman War—the people who would be known in later ages as the Lovokei, the Kutalla, the Broul, and the Juna. Egrestarrian sailed to every world of the One Sphere and took on all who wished to escape the Sh'tarrgh.*

Many stayed to fight, to defend their homes. Some were held prisoner by the Sh'tarrgh; others felt that escape was cowardly and simply wished to die.

The virginal ship sailed through wildspace and defended itself with its stinger, a powerful weapon of annihilation, while the humans built the first spaceborne ballistae and catapults to destroy their evil enemies.

The armadas of the Sh'tarrgh came together as the Spelljammer *left the orbit of the innermost world, laden with the refugees and survivors of the unhuman wars. Sh'tarrgh battleships numbered six score and converged on the ship from all sides.*

The Spelljammer *was built to preserve life, and was not conceived as an offensive weapon. Its only defenses were natural: speed, maneuverability, and its magical nature. In the Sh'tarrgh Convergence—an attack that lasted only seconds—the people of the* Spelljammer *learned a valuable lesson: that to defend, even peaceable peoples need defensive weapons.*

Against the combined might of the Sh'tarrgh, the Spelljammer *was impotent. Its only hope—the only hope of thousands—was to escape, to explore.*

Escape lay on the other side of the black, crystalline wall of the One Sphere.

The survivors knew nothing of what awaited them beyond the barrier. The Spelljammer *knew only that escape was their only hope, and that the means to flee this sphere were inborn with the ship, a natural talent of the* spaakiil, *carried over to their legacy.*

The people in the citadel waited, and Egrestarrian sang.

Its song reverberated off the sphere, and its simple beauty cast fear into the hearts of the demonic Sh'tarrgh.

Then, near Aeyenna, between the Spelljammer *and the fleets of the Sh'tarrgh, opened a portal.*

The Spelljammer *sang. The portal widened, and the great ship sailed to freedom through the gateway, into the endless, eternal Rainbow Ocean.*

But no one had ever before been outside, into the phlogiston. No one knew that if the gateway were left open too wide for too long, the phlogiston would pour inside, into wildspace, and be sucked into the sun, there to explode.

The Spelljammer *was only minutes outside Ouiyan when the crystal shell exploded. The ship screamed and wept at the same time as it felt the worlds, the peoples, of its birth die in an all-consuming blast that cracked the crystal sphere and sent black shards hurtling into the flow.*

The phlogiston's destructive force sent the Spelljammer *tum-*

bling helplessly. In seconds, the surfaces of the worlds were blown to black cinders, and the peoples, along with their deadly enemies, the Sh'targh, became memories, forever mourned by the Spelljammer.

For the Spelljammer *was created to preserve life, not destroy it.*

The Spelljammer *wept in shame for centuries. The* Spelljammer *sailed on. Children were born; families were raised; old people died. The* Spelljammer *sailed on. Communities were built. New spheres were discovered. War was started, for one insignificant reason or another.*

In time, the Spelljammer *found purpose in the tragedy that had borne it.*

Untold worlds awaited the Wanderer. The One Sphere was not the only sphere, as humanity soon learned. The Spelljammer *sailed on to explore the spheres and their worlds, to discover, to learn; and left behind a sense of wonder, a sense of purpose, of the quest that pulled humanity out of the spheres to explore. . . .*

And the Spelljammer *sailed on.*

Egrestarrian, the Spelljammer, *died.*

Drestarin, the Spelljammer, *was born.*

The Spelljammer *died.*

Wrycanion, the Spelljammer, *sailed on.*

Finally, Creannon, the Spelljammer *of the Cloakmaster, was born, with all its precursors' memories—and guilt—intact.*

Like the blinding instant when a sun is born, all this the Cloakmaster experienced in a moment that lasted for eternity.

Teldin, at one with the Spelljammer, *knew that time at the Broken Sphere had become dangerously short. The ferocity of the unhumans was unstoppable, and he realized instinctively that only one thing could prevent the* Spelljammer*'s own needless death and the conquest of evil throughout the spheres.*

That one thing would destroy everything and everyone within range.

—Not again, *Teldin said.*

—*Verenthestae, the ship responded.* —The circles close once again. As one dies, one is born.

—There have been too many deaths already.

—Murderers embrace death, worship death. Are they not one with death, as we are one with life?

—Death can be cheated.

—Destiny cannot.

—But there may be choices . . .

—Destiny demands fulfillment. Murder demands atonement.

—There may be a way.

—Our destiny is clear.

—Why me? *Teldin asked.*

His universe was the amulet, glowing with white heat as it was when it was forged upon an anvil at the base of the Spelljammer*'s captain's tower millennia ago. It blazed from within with the power of the three-pointed star, the idealized symbol that was to represent Ouiyan's long-lost sun. The points represented the powers that created the* Spelljammer*: the merging of the* spaakiil, *of humans, and of magic. Its light, its power, represented the eternal light of hope, of life.*

Attached with a golden chain to the original ultimate helm, the cloak, together they formed a single, inseparable device: the helm created for the First Pilot to command the ship, the amulet to help guide the captain—and the Spelljammer*—to their twin destinies.*

Years later, they were separated, forced to wait for destiny to once again bring them together. Without the amulet, the Spelljammer *was captained haphazardly by other captains with other helms—such was the nature of spelljamming. The true helm, the Ultimate Helm, the creators knew, eventually would find its way back to the true captain, perhaps many centuries after they had been forgotten. The cloak and the amulet would be joined again, and the Last Pilot would sail the* Spelljammer *to its ultimate fate.*

—Why me? *Teldin said again.* —Who am I?

—You are the Last Pilot.

—Why?

—You are the Son of the Architect.

—Who? Who am I?

—This is the purpose for which you have sought. It was foreordained for you to find your destiny here, where it began millennia ago. Only you are the Chosen. Only you have the courage and the Helm and the Compass and the need. You are the Last Pilot.

—There have been too many deaths already, *Teldin said.* —Something else must be done.

—It is our destiny to end and begin again, to renew, to punish, to rejoice, to live.

They were silent. The Cloakmaster thought for a minute, perhaps a year, as the Spelljammer *knew time. Then he spoke.*

—Tell me. What happens when a *Spelljammer* dies?

They spoke together then, for a long time, . . . minutes, perhaps, or years.

Then they were decided, and for the first time since the coming of the Cloakmaster, the Spelljammer *sang out joyously, spreading the colors of hope upon the eddies of the flow. The* Spelljammer *cast forth a seed of being, of pure, magical energies, that shot through Teldin's awareness and across the universe, and he felt it explode against its target, permeating ancient metal with its dormant energies.*

Teldin waited until the Spelljammer*'s song was finished, then he spoke.*

—I need one last thing, *he said.* —For me.

—For . . . life . . .

The two agreed as one, for the destiny that Teldin sought was the destiny that had always been.

The Spelljammer *sang with a song of Teldin. In Herdspace, a kender, lost in a healing, meditative trance, woke suddenly and heard the song. Music filled with latent energies and inner fires coursed through her, and she answered with a thought that knew no physical boundaries.*

The Cloakmaster heard, and he opened his eyes.

Chapter Thirty-One

• • •

". . . The statues could only be those of the ship's captains. The weapons, the artifacts, the vessels under glass—all must have some purpose that I have not yet fathomed.

"The secrets of this accursed ship will soon be mine, I vow. I know the nature of the helms, and I know of the magic that each person here unwittingly breathes. This prison is intolerable! I wonder if any of the items in the Armory are actually helms, and if they can help me escape. . . ."

The journal of Arcane; following the reign of Jokarin

Na'Shee was the first to react. She leaped upon Stardawn and hurled him to the floor. Her hand went up, ready to smash into the elf's face, but the elf threw a powerful right jab into her jaw.

She was knocked across him. Stardawn scrambled up and jerked the sword from the Cloakmaster's lifeless chest. He angled the blade toward the dark shape of the Fool. "The Cloakmaster is dead, now, Fool!" the elf shouted. "I shall be captain now, as it always should have been!"

He placed his hand on one of the throne's pedestals, then stared down, waiting for the trickle of energy to flow up his arm, bonding him to the *Spelljammer.*

The Fool laughed.

"*You killed the captain, elf,*" the Fool said. "*You killed my plans for the* Spelljammer. *The helm is gone with the Bonding, and you have only your own, pitiful delusions to live for.*"

The others in the party pulled out their weapons as the Fool approached. He lifted a hand, and an invisible wave of force sent the warriors sprawling into the walls. Djan's head collided with the wall, and the world went dark around him.

The Fool spun on Stardawn. To the elf lord it was as if the Fool suddenly sailed from the floor to stand before him upon the dais. Two skeletal hands clasped tightly around Stardawn's throat.

The Fool's eyes glimmered brightly, blazing into Stardawn's eyes. He felt the strength wash out of him, felt his legs go limp, and the Fool clasped him high in the air with one hand around his neck.

"*Mine . . .*" the Fool said, as though to himself. "*You have ruined it all . . . and you shall pay.*"

Stardawn's eyes went wide with terror. The dried, brittle skull that was the Fool's face seemed to open in a smile. Stardawn shuddered in the Fool's grasp, his limbs twitching in an uncontrollable paroxysm of fear. The Fool covered the elf's face, his mouth and nose, with his hand. Two fingertips of bone touched the elf's eyes gently, like a lover's embrace.

Stardawn screamed. He flailed violently in the Fool's cold grasp, and his life force was sucked from his body like smoke, consumed hungrily like a sweet morsel, and the Fool laughed at his meal.

He flung the elf's body to the floor at the warriors' feet. CassaRoc stood uneasily, half-dazed, and the others brought themselves around as the Fool crept toward them.

"*All shall pay,*" the Fool said softly. "*All shall pay for stealing my revenge.*"

The master lich halted suddenly. A sphere of light formed around the warriors, a protective bubble of force. Inside the shield, a glow appeared, and the astral form of Gaye Goldring materialized, burning with a strength the Fool had never conceived. The lich spoke a chant, and the shield shuddered as his spell flickered at its edges, ineffective against the kender's psionic strength.

"How?" he asked.

Inside the shield, the warriors turned away from the Fool and gasped, staring behind him.

Then the Fool felt himself levitated, held in a grip of power that spun him around to face his assailant. His black, shining eyes dimmed in uncomprehending fear.

The Cloakmaster stood before him, holding the Fool in midair with the forces of his new life with the *Spelljammer*. He willed the Fool closer, and his vision, filled with dreamscapes and worlds beyond imagining, focused on the dead face of the master lich.

"*No more*," the Cloakmaster said.

The Fool struggled against the forces that held him. He gestured with his hands, and the Cloakmaster was slammed back into his throne by a fist formed from the air. The Fool dropped and jumped off the dais, summoning his strength. He pulled his deathblade from its rotted scabbard. "*You have died once already, Cloakmaster. I believe you can die again.*"

The air swirled between them, coalescing with flares of magic. An aura formed in the air, took shape, and the Cloakmaster reached out and plucked the spell from the air.

The energies flickered in his hand, outlining a blade of power, pulsating with his own life force. He leaped, and the blades met between the two enemies, death and life, sparks flying from their swords.

Inside the shield, the warriors could feel the thick tension in the *adytum*, the two primal forces battling for supremacy of the *Spelljammer*. Estriss looked after the unconscious Djan, and the others stood ready, weapons out, to join in the fray.

The Cloakmaster and the Fool were behemoths of raw power, battling around the chamber in a ballet that would only lead to death. Their blades collided and rang, were knocked to carve deep wounds into the *Spelljammer*'s walls. The Fool drew first blood, slipping under the Cloakmaster's guard to slice deep into his forearm. But blood did not flow from the wound, and the Cloakmaster battled on, heedless, seething with power.

Forgotten, alone in the corner, was Cwelanas.

She pulled her iron chains from the floor and wrapped them around one arm. The Fool was concentrating solely on the fight. He had forgotten all about her, and she could finally move.

Teldin fought with the strength and speed of a storm, but the Fool's powers were considerable, and she knew that there was little she could do to help Teldin defeat the creature, unarmed as she was.

But there was something she could take. . . .

The Fool was a lich of some kind, she knew, though she had never seen or heard of a lich quite like this one. She thought back, trying to remember what she knew of their weaknesses, their fears. She looked up, saw the Fool's eyes blazing with evil fire, and she realized what had been bothering her all along.

The Fool did have a weakness.

It was called a phylactery, a container of some kind in which the lich stored its life force in exchange for powers granted by the gods or otherworldly forces of darkness.

Usually these phylacteries were heavily guarded by the lich, hidden in some secret place, for if the phylactery were ever destroyed, the lich would be destroyed, its life force claimed by the entity that originally had granted its dark powers.

What if a lich, or a different, more powerful type of lich, had become so arrogant that it no longer guarded its phylactery? What if this master lich, in its egotistical sense of invulnerability, even wore its phylactery, say, as an ornament, a piece of jewelry, out in the open for all to desire?

Cwelanas knew then what she must do.

The others stayed protected behind the kender's psionic shield. Cwelanas took a deep breath and gathered all her strength, giving form to all the rage and frustration she had felt, helpless in the Fool's grasp.

Then, in one swift lunge, Cwelanas leaped to her feet. Her heavy chain uncoiled and she flung herself between the combatants, swinging the chain in the air. With the snap of brittle bones, the chain whipped around the Fool's head.

One bony hand shot up and grasped her wrist. The Fool laughed in her face, his skull splintered above its right, dead eye. "*You cannot hurt me, woman. You—*"

Then its eyes seemed to widen in fear. Her other hand had found the Fool's amulet and gripped it tightly in one fist. She yanked hard once. A golden link shot away from the necklace, and the amulet came loose from the Fool's neck.

"*No*!" it screamed. "*No*! *Give me that*!"

Cwelanas shoved the Fool away. It staggered back a step,

then rushed for her, fury blazing in its hollow eyes.

But her arm was back. She put all her strength behind the throw, and suddenly the amulet was sent flying across the chamber, to be plucked from the air effortlessly by the Cloakmaster.

"Destroy it!" Cwelanas screamed. "Destroy it now!"

The Cloakmaster dropped it to the floor, and he brought the heavy heel of his boot down upon it, shattering the ruby facets.

With an explosion of scarlet energies, the amulet burst. The Cloakmaster stepped away as crimson smoke erupted in a widening circle in the floor. A storm of orange and black smoke, streams of magical fire and raw power, shone through the widening circle of light to cast its deep red glow upon the Fool's horrified countenance.

The circle of flame fluctuated, widened, flaring brilliantly with extraplanar energies, then a great shadow eclipsed the light blazing from the fiery, otherworldly plane. One great, clawed hand reached out from somewhere unreal, somewhere unimagined on the plane of the groundlings, and into our universe from its own.

The Fool screamed, "*Noooooooo!*"

The fiendish being was more than twice Teldin's size, and it stepped from its own funereal plane into the *adytum*, glowing, scarlet smoke trailing in its wake. It gestured with its four arms, two ending in powerfully clawed hands, the others with sharp pincers that could disembowel a man with one casual swipe. The fangs in its shaggy canine head were jagged and sharp, and it snarled ferally at the shielded warriors who backed away from it. Its blank eyes burned an angry red, and it moved to stare first at the Cloakmaster, then Cwelanas, then finally on the skeletal form of the Fool.

Its laughter echoed like thunder throughout the chamber, reverberating off the walls so loudly that the fighters could feel it in their feet. *I KNOW WHY I HAVE BEEN SUMMONED!* The words boomed through their heads as the thing spoke telepathically.

The thing roared ferociously, moving slowly toward the Fool. The lich lifted Cwelanas before him and used her as a shield, backing as far away as possible.

It was one of the tanar'ri, a dark god of the Abyss. The shaggy glabrezu stomped across the *adytum* and looked down at the quivering Fool.

ROMAR, THE FOOL! The tanar'ri lord roared its demonic laughter. Smoke curled from its lips and nostrils.

With the swipe of one impossibly large hand, the glabrezu knocked Cwelanas from the Fool's grasp and sent her hurtling against the kender's shield. Cwelanas had time to cry out once as her bones shattered against the impenetrable shield, then she fell to the bubble's base, unconscious.

Blood pooled around her head. Her face was scarred with gashes from the glabrezu's claws. Gaye instantly enlarged the bubble to take in Cwelanas, and CassaRoc bent to examine the elf's wounds.

All felt the glabrezu's voice pounding in their minds. *ROMAR! YOUR TIME HAS COME!* The Fool cowered behind the Cloakmaster's throne. His bony hands were crossed protectively in front of him. *OUR CONTRACT IS CONCLUDED! YOUR SOUL IS MINE!*

The glabrezu reached out with one of its pincers. The Fool shrank down to his knees, and the long pincer raked across the Fool's cheek, drawing a line of thin black blood. The Fool raised his puny hands in supplication to the tanar'ri.

"Lord Mowg, no, I beseech you—the phylactery, that one broke it, there—" The Fool pointed at the unconscious Cwelanas. "It was not meant—"

The glabrezu's other pincer lashed out and grasped the Fool by the neck. Lord Mowg lifted the Fool to face him. The other pincer came up, and the glabrezu plunged the sharp points deep into the Fool's hollow eyes.

The Fool jerked electrically in the tanar'ri's grasp. Bolts of blue energy—the Fool's ill-spent life force—shimmered through Mowg's pincers and into his monstrous body. The Fool's already shrunken body seemed to tighten in on itself. The glabrezu smiled with contentment, lapping at the Fool's dark force, flicking its tongue at the lifeless husk that was the Fool.

With a final, convulsive shudder, the Fool found true death in Lord Mowg's blistering grip. The glabrezu's mouth gaped wide, and it stuffed the Fool's body between his jaws, impossibly accommodating the lich's girth as though it were but a morsel. It swallowed, growling, its evil power resonating off the walls like a low hum.

Then Mowg faced the humans.

It lashed out at the shield. Gaye's image grimaced as the glabrezu's blow hammered at the barrier, and she concentrated, letting the shield grow stronger in her mind.

Lord Mowg stepped back and swiped a claw through the air. The fiend roared with amusement, filling the *adytum* with its raucous, barking laughter.

The tanar'ri placed one clawed foot into the ring of power and climbed inside. The glabrezu sank through the doorway of fire, laughing. The gate closed with a final explosion of fire, and Mowg, a lord of the tanar'ri, was gone from the Prime Material plane.

The Cloakmaster stepped off the dais. Gaye dropped her psionic shield, and the Cloakmaster stepped over to Cwelanas and placed his hands upon her head.

She glowed from within, infused with the combined energies of the Cloakmaster and the *Spelljammer*. He felt her wounds, the flow of her blood, and, with a thought, his energies healed the glabrezu's damage and pulled her up from the bliss of unconsciousness.

Djan woke with but a single, healing touch. The Cloakmaster kept his hand on the half-elf's head. He jerked once as a spark of power opened his mind.

"What was that?" Djan asked.

The Cloakmaster went to each of the warriors in turn, finishing with Estriss, then he helped Cwelanas to her feet and touched her head as well. Her forehead glowed at the touch of his fingertips.

"*The* Spelljammer *has magic of its own*," the Cloakmaster said. "*I have released you from its spell, a spell of protection that all aboard have fallen under. Now you may leave.*"

"Leave?" Chaladar said. "We cannot. The *Spelljammer* needs our protection."

The Cloakmaster held up a hand. "*I do not have much time like this*," he said. "*Much must be done, and there is much to explain.*"

"Teldin," Cwelanas said, looking at the wound in his chest, "are you . . . ?"

He nodded. "*I am one with the Spelljammer now. I am not as I was before. I know what has to be done. I know how our destinies have been intertwined. I know what our purpose is.*"

"Your quest, then?" CassaRoc inquired. "You have found your answers?"

Teldin nodded. "*To questions I never knew existed.*"

Cwelanas went to him and stared into his glowing eyes. "Is it you? Is it really you, Teldin? Or is it the *Spelljammer*?"

As she watched, the glow in his eyes faded, and his eyes returned to normal. He smiled down at her. "It is I, Cwelanas. It's still me."

Djan said, "Now what? What happens next?"

"The *Spelljammer* is being surrounded by the fleets of our enemies. Even though they are also fighting among themselves, their forces are great and we may not survive their attack." The Cloakmaster paused. "In fact, I'm sure of it."

"You couldn't have become captain of the ship just to see it destroyed," CassaRoc said. "There must be a reason."

"Oh, there is," The Cloakmaster said, "but it's far more complicated than that. Soon the *Spelljammer* will be no longer—at least, not as we know it. We are giving you a chance to live."

"Oh, no," CassaRoc said loudly. "We didn't come all this way to see you sacrifice yourself to save us. No, we're staying with you."

"You have it wrong," the Cloakmaster said. "There will be no sacrifice, CassaRoc, not really. Things simply will be . . . very different. You have to trust me."

"What's going to happen?" Na'Shee asked.

Teldin placed his hands on Cwelanas's arms. "I have bonded with the ship. We are one. The *Spelljammer*'s life cycle is beginning anew, and in the gardens you will find the only means to your survival. By the time you get there, a smalljammer will have been created.

"There is time enough to create only a single ship. It is essential that you escape on board the smalljammer. You must protect it at all costs. It may be this universe's only chance to create life . . . if this Unhuman War is lost."

"Create life?" Cwelanas said. "Teldin, I don't want to leave you. I can't just—"

"Cwelanas," Teldin said softly, "in time, you will understand. You and the smalljammer have a purpose, a common destiny. I give the ship to you. You must sail to freedom, to life."

The Cloakmaster reached into his belt and held out the shirt of chain mail that he had found in the neogi tower. "Your mail," he said. "With the *Spelljammer*'s help, I have granted your mail the power of an ultimate helm and more. Wear this. Take the smalljammer and sail to safety. It is your only hope."

Cwelanas took the mail from the Cloakmaster's hands. Instantly, she felt the amulet's power surge through her, through the mail.

"Is this how it felt to you?" she asked.

"Yes. You now bear the smalljammer's ultimate helm." Her mouth hung open. "You are now the First Pilot of your smalljammer," Teldin said, "and you must go where the winds of destiny take you."

And you, Teldin? Estriss inquired. *What will happen to you?*

"My destiny has been written. I brought to the *Spelljammer* the Cloak of the First Pilot. I am the *Spelljammer*'s last."

"I don't understand what that means," Djan said.

"You must go. I have a duty to perform, one that has waited for a thousand centuries. You . . . you must live."

Teldin placed his hands around Gaye's astral form, and she glowed fiercer, more brightly than ever before. "I will need your help," he said.

"Does it have to happen this way?" Cwelanas asked. Her eyes pleaded with him. "Teldin, we need you. I need you."

"You know what you must do," the Cloakmaster said gently. "*Verenthestae*."

She nodded reluctantly. "But you . . . ?"

The Cloakmaster looked up and smiled at each of his friends in turn. "You have all been great friends. Djan, Chaladar, Na'Shee, go in peace, and learn. CassaRoc, be well. You are a great warrior for good, though you may not know it. And Estriss . . . may you find your answers, as I have found mine."

He looked down into Cwelanas's eyes. Slowly he bent to kiss her. Their lips met. Cwelanas tasted her own tears on her tongue. She knew it was the last kiss that she and Teldin would share.

The Cloakmaster pulled away and stepped onto the dais. "Go now. Live." He lifted Stardawn's body with one hand and threw it to them. "Cast it from the roof of the Armory. Let the races know that the new captain has come." He sat upon the throne.

Gaye floated over to wait beside the Cloakmaster's shoulder. The warriors filed slowly out of the chamber, Stardawn's body hefted over CassaRoc's shoulder, and they disappeared down the entrance hall. Cwelanas was the last to go. She nodded once, wept silently, then ran from the room.

Behind her, in the *adytum*, the eyes of the Cloakmaster glowed with an inner light, and the mark of the Compass burned fiercely inside his flesh. The opening to the chamber closed in upon itself.

—*We are done*, he said, and his body slowly began to fade away.

—*My friends will survive. Many humans will be saved.*

—*That is good.*

—*Gaye will help.*

—*That is good.*

—*But the unhumans . . .*

—*Perhaps . . . that is also good.*

—*But we were destined to preserve, not destroy.*

—*The children of the Sh'tarrgh are the antithesis of life. To preserve, we must destroy.*

Teldin thought quietly, then decided.

—*That is good.*

Gaye began to fade, following the Cloakmaster's unspoken commands. In a few moments, the only thing left in the *adytum* was the captain's throne. Smoke curled up from the back of the chair, where the pattern of the Compass had been seared into the stone.

Chapter Thirty-Two

• • •

"*. . . The One Egg shattered from the inside, and its shell was cast out upon the flow like seeds in the wind.*

"*Only one thing survived, that which bears its curse even today, and will one day be punished for its sins against the gods and man . . .*"

The Old Book, handed down through legend; recorded in the reign of Night Walker.

The flow was a battleground, a sea of fighting.

Ships swooped past the *Spelljammer*, grappled together in their thick ropes and firing ballistae at each other mercilessly. A hammership banked just outside the *Spelljammer*'s air envelope and fired its catapults toward the ship. Most of the boulders missed completely, passing harmlessly though the air bubble to fall toward the Broken Sphere on the other side of the ship, but one load of boulders hurtled toward the *Spelljammer* and thundered into the Elven High Command, sending heavy chunks of stone to the deck far below. The top floors of the command stood shattered, like a broken chimney, and the golden dragon standard that had flown at the pinnacle of the tower lay in a hundred twisted pieces across the roofs of the dwarven citadel and the Communal Church of Wildspace. Rubble littered the streets, and the elves unlucky enough to have been stationed on the roof fell to their deaths and splattered on the deck.

The warring between the races had stopped suddenly, as

soon as the intercepting ships had begun firing at the *Spelljammer*. The warring factions on the ship had realized that the *Spelljammer* needed to be defended. The fighters had all disengaged and raced to their respective communities, where weapons such as catapults and ballistae were armed and readied for retaliation against the newcomers from the flow.

The streets of the *Spelljammer* lay empty, save for debris and the bodies of the dead and slowly dying. Blood was spattered on the walls of the ship's towers and collected in wide puddles in the uneven streets. The warring now went on high above the towers and would soon be joined by the natural defenses of the legendary *Spelljammer*.

Deep within the entity, the Cloakmaster felt all and saw all through the *Spelljammer*'s magical senses. It was as though his arms were the *Spelljammer*'s wings; his feet, its tail; its eyes, his eyes. As they slowly circled the Broken Sphere and swept aside the debris of broken ships, he felt splintered wood and cracked shell brush harmlessly along his wings like minuscule insects. He shuddered as the giff's bombard rang out upon the *Spelljammer*'s back. He blinked as a wasp ship exploded in front of his eyes. He felt warmth as the peoples spread out across his back came together in his defense, almost becoming one with the purpose of the ship.

He watched and heard and felt the other ships around him. Their movement through the phlogiston was like wind rushing between his fingers. Boulders hurtled by catapults felt to him like gentle rain, and the missiles that rushed past him were less than a light breeze. The ships that exploded, or were destroyed by spells, were nothing more than gusts of heat upon his face.

So many races were represented: Shou, elves, illithids, neogi, humans, giff, halflings, dwarves, orcs and scro, beholders, minotaurs . . . He felt them all, from B'Laath'a, the cunning neogi that had tortured Cwelanas, to the asteroid of dwarves who had allied themselves with the halflings. They were ready to die, either in defense of themselves or their friends, or in a futile attempt to take the *Spelljammer*. The Cloakmaster realized that, to them, it just did not matter. It was the beginning of a war that had been long in coming, and the unhumans would not stop until they overran the universe with their war machines and humanity was enslaved or extinguished.

—*How many more must die?* Teldin asked.

—*Only those whose deaths are decreed by destiny, and by their own twisted desires.*

—*How many?*

The *Spelljammer* paused. —*Most.*

—*Must we . . . ?*

—*It has been ordained. The cycle must begin anew. What was, will be again.*

The Cloakmaster watched as the universe around him seemed to run black with death, like the rats that had attacked him in the Tower of Thought.

A tradesman and a nautiloid seemed to join as the nautiloid swung close enough to scrape the tradesman's side in a shearing attack that ripped off its starboard wings and shaved its mainmast into a mere splinter. Then the tradesman's deck became crowded with its halfling crew, shooting flaming arrows through the conjoined air envelopes to ignite inside the nautiloid's chambered hull. Black smoke joined the phlogiston in its endless swirl. Small explosions broke out as the arrows ignited the flow, sending shockwaves across the small ships' decks.

Off to port, an illithid dreadnought turned and aimed its weapons at the *Spelljammer.* Ten ballistae fired from the *Spelljammer*'s port batteries, then ten more from starboard. Then the dreadnought was torn by seven unyielding missiles. The ship spun crazily above the *Spelljammer*, looking more like a pin cushion than a fearsome illithid vessel.

To the Cloakmaster, it was as though someone had flung open the gates of the Abyss to let the fiendish lords run free.

—*Don't they realize that the captain has come? Don't they realize that the ship cannot be theirs?*

—*Some know, some don't, but it no longer matters. They fight because it is their way. Their song is one of conquest. Our song is one of peace.*

And the *Spelljammer* sang.

Finally, in his soul, he understood the *Spelljammer*'s high, sweet song. It was soft in his ears, flooding his entire being with soothing tranquility. Around the Broken Sphere, none could hear the *Spelljammer*'s song, but battles became less intense, and hatred and anger were momentarily dispelled.

The Cloakmaster was here because his path was true. Death had always been his enemy. Even in the War of the Lance, he had hated himself for the atrocities he had witnessed across the battlefields, and for what he had had to do. Yes, he had killed in self-defense. He had killed in defense of others. He had killed for an ideal that he would have died for, a purpose that had been far more important than a lone groundling named Moore.

And his purpose with the *Spelljammer*, he knew, was even greater.

He hesitated, had deliberately put it off, but his destiny could wait no longer, and his fight for life was the only thing that could save the universe from becoming enslaved by the unhumans.

This universe must survive, he thought. He knew that it was his duty to survive this war at the Broken Sphere, no matter how strong the enemy. Survive—that was all the *Spelljammer* had to do. Fight, defend, destroy, if necessary, but . . . survive. That was all.

Until the time was right.

Teldin knew the *Spelljammer* could survive only so long . . . and that there would be no escape from its final destiny.

—*Life*, he sang, and his own song merged with that of the *Spelljammer*.

—*Life*, they sang.

The great *spaakiil*, whose legacy had been forgotten by all who lived, turned its tail to the Broken Sphere and swam toward the war.

The *Spelljammer*'s change of course was noticed immediately. Some ships disengaged their enemies to veer away and wait to see what the *Spelljammer* was up to. Others ignored the great ship and pressed harder with their attacks against the smaller ships in an effort to defeat their enemies first.

Their concerns were unimportant. Their movements around the *Spelljammer* were nothing to the Cloakmaster, who looked upon the massed fleets as insignificant in the larger scheme of things.

Then the *Spelljammer* was in the thick of battle. Missiles

shot from its towers to rend great holes in the ships fleeing before it. The *Spelljammer* tore through the mass of ships effortlessly, a juggernaut against the puny warships.

Three lampreys had engaged a single battle dolphin, firing upon it in a concentrated attack with their ballistae. The shadow of the *Spelljammer* fell across them like the specter of death, and the ships were torn asunder as the great ship plowed through them as if they were gnats. The battle dolphin was torn in half as the neogi tower caught it under the lower hull. Then the two halves of the dolphin separated, one to tumble across the starboard wing and into the endless flow, the other to spin out of control and collide with one of the fleeing lampreys. The remaining lampreys fell apart like sticks when the turning *Spelljammer* caught them from behind and shattered their hulls against the edge of its port wing.

The great battle began anew, and the *Spelljammer* no longer stayed out of the fight. In a wide, sweeping arc that cut through the enemy fleets, the *Spelljammer* was deliberate and careful, staying steadily on its planned course with its main objective always in clear focus. Wasp battled mosquito; nautiloid fought deathglory—the *Spelljammer* tore through them all without hesitation, raining missiles and boulders, arrows and bolts, upon its outclassed enemies.

Teldin winced within the *Spelljammer*'s being. A eye tyrant ship had rammed the *Spelljammer* from below, carving a great gouge in the chitinous hull that had withstood brushes with comets and the deep cold of Icespace. He could feel the beholder crew disgorging through the ship's hollow boarding ram, and he dropped the *Spelljammer* so that its underbelly scraped the top and starboard side of a dwarven citadel. The stone ship left a long scrape along the *Spelljammer*'s belly, but the rock cracked and shattered the tyrant out of the *Spelljammer*'s hull, to send it floating helplessly in the great ship's wake. The citadel went spinning like a top, and the dwarves inside were hurled against the outer walls from the ship's centrifugal force.

Single ships attacked the *Spelljammer* fruitlessly and were quickly dealt with by the crews manning the ship's complement of ninety ballistae and sixty catapults. The Armory doors were wide open on the main deck, and the population was taking supplies and building extra weapons for all the towers, both human and unhuman. Ammunition was plentiful and was shared by all the communities.

Then the Cloakmaster felt the ships around the *Spelljammer* separating in some semblance of organization. There were two squadrons of ships closing in: four hammerships, arranged in a classic diamond attack formation, and the six deathspiders, hexagonally flanking the command mindspider.

Teldin moved his arm. The ship banked to port and turned to stare down the approaching hammerships.

He took a deep breath and felt the energy well up in him, around him, through him, pulsing with a heartbeat of thunder and fire.

He shivered as the energy traveled hot up his spine.

High above the decks of the *Spelljammer*, its great tail tensed, quivering imperceptibly to the humans below. It glowed white hot for an instant, then a flaming bubble of incredible energy shot out of its tip and absorbed the hammerships.

The explosion took out seven other ships that had been stupid enough to stray near the attack. First there was blinding white light that blotted everything from view, then the fires of the *Spelljammer*'s annihilation weapon spread throughout the phlogiston, which instantly erupted for a radius of more than two thousand feet. The *Spelljammer* rocked as the flow exploded in its path. Parts of vessels—a splintered mast, half of a light ballista, brass fittings—shot through the *Spelljammer*'s air envelope to embed deeply in tower walls.

The *Spelljammer* made a sudden turn to starboard, faster than anyone had expected the great ship could ever make. The Cloakmaster focused all his enhanced senses on the remaining squadron of ships in his path, the neogi deathspiders.

He thought of Cwelanas, whom he knew was racing for the safety of her smalljammer. He thought of the tattoo with which the neogi B'Laath'a had branded her. He thought of the simple words that had drawn him from his home so long ago.

Keep it from the neogi. Take it to the creators.

The neogi deathspiders were closing. *The neogi.*

He felt the energy tingling up his spine.

Cwelanas, he thought.

Energy flared from the *Spelljammer*'s tail in a comet of raw white power. The sphere hurtled down at the onrushing deathspiders and exploded in a nova that created a new, temporary sun in the flow.

The deathspiders exploded, burned, and melted in the coldness of the flow, and what was left was but charred dust, molecules of waste that had once been evil, breathing neogi and their weapons of senseless destruction.

The *Spelljammer* sailed through the fine debris of the neogi squadron and twisted deliberately to point toward the Broken Sphere.

Around the vessel, the remaining fleets watched, turned, prepared for one final assault against the legendary ship.

The Cloakmaster smiled grimly.

The *Spelljammer* sang.

As one, the *Spelljammer* and the fleets behind it headed for the Broken Sphere.

Chapter Thirty-Three

• • •

"*. . . What is this reality, this existence, that we ourselves have not made? . . .*"

Kai Tato, Shou wizard; "Dance of the Eons"; reign of Gran Aurora

The warriors made it to the bottom floor of the Armory without encountering the senseless shivaks. "Why aren't they stopping us?" CassaRoc asked as they hurried through an immense warehouse of weapons and supplies.

"I don't know," Cwelanas said. "Either Teldin has ordered them to let us pass, or it's because I now bear an ultimate helm."

The doors swung inward upon their approach, and they blinked at the bright light of the phlogiston. CassaRoc hefted Stardawn's body and tossed it unceremoniously under the battlements behind the Old Elvish Academy. "There." He wiped his hands on his chest. "On this side, we're closer to the garden doors to port," CassaRoc said. "We ought to cut between the Shou tower and the dwarven citadel."

Cwelanas nodded. The *Spelljammer* shifted then, and they watched as the ship sped deliberately toward a mass of enemy fleets.

"What's going to happen?" Djan asked.

Cwelanas stared at him and shook her head sadly. Estriss answered him, knowingly. *Teldin is giving us a chance to live . . . and I believe he will try to make this as even a battle as he can.*

The enemy ships appeared considerably closer, more formidable. "Bah," CassaRoc said. "He will destroy himself and the *Spelljammer*, just like I said before."

"No," Cwelanas said, "it's more than that. Teldin . . ." She stared off, as though her helm were letting her see visions of a future to come. "Believe me, he will be fine."

They looked at her strangely, then CassaRoc said, "I suppose we have to trust you, too."

She smiled. "Yes, I guess you do."

They broke into a run, Na'Shee taking the rear, and started past the Shou tower toward the entrance to the gardens, where the Cloakmaster had told them the smalljammer waited. The *Spelljammer*'s port wing was relatively clear of fighting; most of the battles were being fought in towers, by the communities protecting the ship from the oncoming enemies.

The gardens were located in a cavernous chamber beneath the city. In reality, the chamber was an immense hangar, with huge, louvered doors located on each side, behind the *Spelljammer*'s massive gills. The doors were barely open, and closing even more, when the party arrived. The warriors lowered themselves to the deck and crawled underneath the port door. "The Dark Times have come," Cwelanas told them. "It was not just a legend. The Bonding brings with it a time of birth, the Dark Times, when the gardens must be closed to nurture the smalljammers . . ."

She trailed off, unable to take in the immensity of the gardens. The landscape stretched off into fields of grain, into seeming forests of jamberry trees and other plants cultivated from across the spheres. The ceiling of the gardens stood about 150 feet above her head and was lined by countless light panels that provided cycles of both day and night to the crops and plants that made up the ship's primary food supply.

"Where?" Cwelanas wondered.

Chaladar pointed beyond a vegetable garden to the circular forest of jamberry trees. "Teldin is smart. I would bet that he hid the smalljammer there, in order to keep it hidden from view."

Cwelanas plunged into the wood. The ground was littered with leaves and fallen jamberries, and she rushed between the trees to discover a dirt path that rounded through the wood.

On the far side of the path, at the edge of a grove encircled by the path, she stopped. The others gathered around her.

The smalljammer gleamed in the light, untouched and fresh, like a newborn child. Like the *Spelljammer*, the smalljammer was manta-shaped and made of a chitinous substance that was shaded from light blue to light purple. On its back was an organically constructed cabin comprising two decks and a jewellike observation deck on top. Its eyes were windows to the control cabin, and its tail, identical to that of its parent, hung over its body. Its wingspan stretched more than 140 feet, and the ship sat silently, serenely, waiting for the gentle touch of its first pilot.

Cwelanas carefully swung up onto a wing and entered the cabin through the open door on the wing deck. Most of the inside deck was open space, more than enough for a fair amount of cargo or passengers. The innermost cabins were unfurnished rooms, ready to be made habitable. The bulbous forward cabin contained only a seat for the ship's captain. Hatchways from there led to the upper deck and the roof. The upper deck contained several more personal cabins, the galley, and a storage room.

Cwelanas ran her hand down the side of the chair, then she sat slowly, stiffly in the throne. For a moment, the palms of her hands grew hot as energy seemingly transferred from the ship into her, then back again. She shivered, as though a breath had been blown on the back of her neck. She felt strong, refreshed, and even the throne seemed softer.

Estriss hissed calmly, an expression of contentment. *You are now the ship's captain*, the mind flayer said.

Cwelanas sat blinking, astonished. The throne had changed shape, conforming to her size and posture. No chair had ever felt so comfortable. "The captain . . . me. I'm the new—"

The hangar door outside the ship rang with a deafening impact, and the door thudded inward, bowing under some great mass that had collided against it from the outside. The *Spelljammer* rocked unsteadily, sending the warriors reeling to the side of the smalljammer.

Cwelanas sprang from the captain's chair and climbed up the hatchway to stand at the pinnacle of the observation cabin. "Damn," she said. "Not this."

The door had been bent and fractured inward, and she could make out the basic outline of a small ship's bow imprinted in the door. From outside she could hear the sounds of screams and fighting. "We're not going to get out that way," she said out loud.

The group clambered out the hatchway and jumped off the smalljammer's wing.

The hangar doors were made of organic material as strong as steel, but were pliable, like aluminum. The door was veined with cracks in some areas, but was primarily bent inward, and Cwelanas realized that there was no way this door was ever going to recede into the ceiling again.

"Damn it!" she said, pounding her fist against her thigh. "Damn them! Damn them all!"

Without warning, a heavy weight crashed into her from behind, sending her sprawling to the ground. She tasted dirt on her tongue and gritted her teeth. Above her, someone laughed coarsely.

She rolled over and winced in the artificial daylight from the ceiling, then a shadow eclipsed the light, and she stared into a sleek black face that was split wide with an evil yellow grin.

She scrabbled backward involuntarily until her back was pressed hard against the crumpled door. She reached for the sword at her side. Her companions stood silently only ten feet away from her, staring blankly, and she saw that they had been rendered immobile with some sort of spell.

Two eyes looked down at her, two eyes filled with black, undead fire.

"Master Coh," she whispered.

Another neogi crept up on her other side.

"You," she hissed. "You."

B'Laath'a, the new master of the undead Coh, smiled.

Chapter Thirty-Four

• • •

"*. . . The catastrophe that brought us will return to deliver us. Our mortal beings will not remember, but we shall remember in the inner cores of our hearts. The sights that await us on the other side will frighten us with all that we have ever dared to imagine. . . .*"

Miral, priestess; *Legend of the Beyond*; reign of Hawk

The enemy fire increased from all sides almost as soon as the *Spelljammer* turned and increased its speed toward the Broken Sphere. The enemies knew now just how dangerous the vessel was, and it seemed to the Cloakmaster that there was no way the fleets would ever let the *Spelljammer* survive.

They came for him, for the *Spelljammer*, in a black swarm of violence.

A small mosquito ship dove into the *Spelljammer*'s air envelope and banked in a determined suicide run toward the captain's tower. As it swung in above the bow, between the *Spelljammer*'s long rams, the mosquito was hit by a single ballista shot from the dwarven citadel. It tumbled out of control and fell to starboard, colliding heavily into the *Spelljammer*'s hangar door.

A hurricane ship catapulted a large shot of stone and iron balls into the library tower. The upper floors disintegrated in a cloud of ancient dust and rubble, which rained upon the warriors massed atop the captain's tower and killed one of them instantly. Then huge ballistae bolts from two shrikes and a crabship speared through the top floors of the dracon tower, and a forgotten store of smoke powder inside went up in a great gout of flame, jolting the *Spelljammer* with a resulting explosion of the surrounding phlogiston.

Bombards spun crazily atop the giff tower, and iron shot hurtled toward a dozen different ships simultaneously. A side of the crabship blew out as a shot hit it squarely in its carapace, and the ship spun into a dive toward the *Spelljammer.* What was left of the library tower and the captain's tower was destroyed with the impact. The explosion rolled the great ship five degrees to port, and debris spewed out into the flow.

The Cloakmaster screamed, feeling the ship's pain as buildings exploded, as it bled its life force over the fleets of its enemies. Still, there was irony in the *Spelljammer*'s injuries, for most of the damage to the ship was located on its starboard wing, and it was the coming of the Cloakmaster, upon the starboard wing, that had initiated the war in the first place.

He could feel the ship's life force ebbing, weakening with each attack on it. He had trouble banking the ship, then steeled himself and forced the ship down and to port. The Broken Sphere was spinning in a slow, eternal rotation, and the jagged gap in the crystal sphere now lay straight ahead, the gap that the *Spelljammer* had created a thousand lifetimes ago.

The ship slowed enough to keep the enemy ships interested. Let them think we're helpless, the Cloakmaster thought. Let them think they have us, then . . .

It had to be soon, Teldin knew. Time was short, and he thought fleetingly of Cwelanas and the others, trapped in the gardens with the smalljammer.

He reached out with the *Spelljammer*'s senses and willed the hangar doors to open. They worked in tandem, opening and closing together, but the damage done in the collision with the mosquito had jammed the starboard door, and neither would open.

The *Spelljammer* shook under its enemies' attack.

She has to get free! the Cloakmaster shouted in his mind. They may be the universe's only hope!

He concentrated. He felt tendrils of energy snake through the hull of the ship and sparkle in the nerve endings around the hangar doors, but it was no good. The damage to the hangar door was too extensive, and the starboard door would move up only a few inches.

—*Perhaps . . .* the *Spelljammer* started, sadly.

—*No! I will not think that. She must be freed! She is too . . .*

—*Life is all important, is it not?*

—*Yes. Cwelanas . . . Life . . .*

—*Yes . . . Then . . . there will come a way.*

—*Yes.*

The *Spelljammer* was being hammered on all sides. Wasps dove in for quick shots, then sped quickly out of the great ship's way. Boulders from the catapults of an elven man-o-war ruptured the walls of the great ship's Elven High Command. Ballistae missiles aimed for the *Spelljammer*'s eyes thunked deep into the soft grass of the landing field and into the ship's skin. The great ship's dwarven battery was destroyed under a catapult assault from five leaf ships.

The Cloakmaster felt the ship's injuries as though they were his own. His view of space became momentarily blurred, indistinct. His being grew cold, and the sounds around him, of the battle, of ships exploding in the phlogiston, became muted.

Then he heard voices. They called him, beckoning, echoing softly from a distance in the white haze. He reached toward them and felt coldness chill him to his soul. He was falling, falling in a sea of blue, but the voices called. . . .

He shook himself, and the *Spelljammer* quivered as it sailed toward the sphere.

The voices grew louder, then their speakers appeared from the mists: his father, Amdar; his grandfather; and a woman he dimly recognized from when he was a child.

—*Mother?*

He held his hands up to ward them away.

—*No,* he said. They were dead—had been dead for so long now. Another voice came, a high, querulous voice with a peculiar laugh, who called to him as a friend: Emil. Emil the Fierce.

Teldin screamed to himself and shook himself out of the darkness. He reached out, feeling the energies of the flow around him, the increasing strength of the *Spelljammer*. He shook himself and flexed his hands and arms, feeling his life force flowing through him, through the *Spelljammer*, spreading warmth through their bodies. The gates to death had been opened wide, calling to him, beckoning for him. And the *Spelljammer* had almost sailed straight through.

But they were alive. And he could not let the ship die, neither it nor Cwelanas; they were not ready for that, not yet.

The only ones who would die today would be the ones who worshipped war and death.

He focused on himself, the ship, and felt the strong, distinctive life forces of CassaRoc, Estriss, Djan, and Na'Shee, of Chaladar the paladin, whose life force glowed with the white light of honor and inner strength. They were waiting in the gardens, and there, he knew, they would find their means to escape, their means to lead humanity to a universe of freedom and peace.

—*Yes*, Teldin said. —*Something must be done.*

—*Yes*, the *Spelljammer* said.

They were alive. They were on course.

The gap in the Broken Sphere lay only a few short miles ahead.

The Cloakmaster gasped. The *Spelljammer* involuntarily shuddered, as though with fear.

The path toward the Broken Sphere was blocked. The jagged gap lay ahead, directly behind a twisting, squirming Shou tsunami, a mammoth elven armada, and a wolflike battlewagon of the scro.

All were converging on him, directly in the *Spelljammer*'s path.

Chapter Thirty-Five

• • •

"*. . . It is said that the conflagration will be great, and that all who committed evil will perish in the fires of creation. . . .*"
Leoster I, *A Journey Out of the Fire*; reign of Kel the Marked

The undead Coh spread his wide mouth in a hungry smile. Bits of dead meat hung between his needlelike teeth. Droplets of bloody saliva oozed from his fangs. His master, B'Laath'a, moved behind him, leering. "Meeeaatt . . ." he spoke slowly at Cwelanas. "Know do I you. Cloakmeat the whore you were of. Mark of mine wear you. Meat for me, now will you be."

Cwelanas struggled weakly off the garden floor and yanked a short sword from her belt. She glared at the neogi defiantly with her golden elven eyes. "Did you mean for that to rhyme, or did it just work out that way?"

The grin collapsed across B'Laath'a's eellike face. His eyes grew dark with hatred. He struggled with his syntax, each word dripping with venom. "Prepare . . . to . . . die," he said clearly. B'Laath'a raised one claw in a gesture, and Coh lurched forward like a grotesque marionette, his lower jaw hanging loose from Teldin's assault in the Fool's lair.

"Can we not talk this over?" Cwelanas said, stalling. The smalljammer seemed too far for her to make a run for it, and she wasn't sure that she alone, with just a short sword and a tiny dagger, could do much against the nastiest neogi she had ever met—much less the nastiest undead neogi.

Coh crouched for a spring, then leaped toward her, growling deep in his throat. Cwelanas was faster. She had anticipated the move and dove to the ground. Coh collapsed behind her and scrabbled quickly around, just in time to see Cwelanas leap up and run toward the relative protection of the smalljammer.

Together B'Laath'a and the undead Coh scrambled after her on their black, spidery legs. She could hear their hissing breath as the distance between them began to close. The smalljammer was still too far away, and her friends were still frozen in B'Laath'a's spell of immobility. She glanced hurriedly out of the corner of her eye to see if—to hope that—the hangar door had somehow opened.

It had not.

B'Laath'a had been spying on Cwelanas through a servant of his own, an undead rat that he had secreted in the Fool's lair. Coh had been under his control only seconds after being felled by the Cloakmaster, and he had waited until he knew the outcome of the Fool's plans before he had put his own into action: to take Cwelanas again and bargain with the Cloakmaster for control of the ship.

B'Laath'a grinned wickedly. The elf had no chance.

Coh tackled her from behind. Blood pooled along her arm where his sharp claws raked her pale flesh, and her face went down into the dirt. She twisted under him, kicking up with her knee. It sank harmless into his bulbous stomach. One long leg of his slapped her across the face. His pointed claw dug a shallow gouge straight across her cheeks and nose.

Cwelanas jerked her arm free from Coh's grasp and swung her sword toward him. At that awkward angle, the sword could do little more than chop, but the blade went into his side and took out a chunk of his painted flesh. Black blood spattered her chain mail and tunic. Coh raised his serpentine head and howled a scream of pain and infinite rage. His undead anger glimmered like crimson sparks in his black, dead eyes, and he focused on the elf with a smoldering hatred that only the undead could have for the living.

Coh's drooling lips spread wide. His jaws stretched open, and rows of teeth glinted a diseased yellow in the *Spelljammer*'s artificial light. His head twisted slowly, almost instinctively, coiling back and preparing to strike. Then his teeth flashed and his head snapped toward her, and he plunged his needle-sharp fangs into her shoulder.

Cwelanas heard one dead fang snap off as the neogi bit through her chain mail, then her flesh seemed to rupture and catch fire, burning coldly as Coh's neogi venom entered her bloodstream. He twisted his head and pulled her up, trying to rip out a chunk of her flesh. Blood streamed hot down her side, and she pounded her fists against his head. Dimly she noticed the slits that were his ears on the side of his head, and she hammered them repeatedly.

Coh jerked his head up, releasing her. Blood spilled over her from sixteen round puncture wounds in the flesh of her shoulder. The wounds rang with intense pain. She covered them with her hand and kicked up between the neogi's legs.

He grunted once and shifted his weight upon her. Then Cwelanas realized she had a little room to move, and she pulled her legs up into a tight ball and flattened her feet into his chest. She braced her arms and almost screamed at the tearing fire in her shoulder, then gathered her strength and shoved. Coh went flying and tumbled to the deck more than ten feet away.

Cwelanas pushed herself off the floor and picked up her sword. She tasted her blood, dripping down her face, and her left arm dangled uselessly at her side. She could barely wiggle her fingers. Her breath came in short, ragged gasps. She knew the neogi bite injected a victim with a slowing poison, but she felt cold paralysis spreading through her side. The only answer she could come up with was that Coh's poison was somehow changed with him when he had become undead.

B'Laath'a hung back and watched as Coh shambled up and came for her again. She swung her sword in a deadly arc that missed his face by an inch. He advanced slowly, snapping at her with his venomous teeth, though one long fang was very obviously missing in the front. She backed away, sweeping the sword in front of her as protection.

He lunged for her. She swung the sword out, and Coh slipped behind the swing and slashed down with a claw. The sword fell to the deck. Blood streamed from a wound across the back of her hand. Coh picked up her sword and tossed it blindly into the forest of jamberry trees.

"Now *th*eee how you are good no *th*ting with," Coh said, lisping.

He snapped up one of his forelegs and scraped her hard again in the face. Her head snapped back. Blood spattered the ground.

He coiled back his head for one lightning-quick lunge that would have shredded the flesh from Cwelanas's neck, but the elf ducked, feeling Coh's yellow teeth snap just inches away, where her face had been. She leaped straight between his black legs and wrapped her arm around his neck.

The pain in her arm and shoulder was like white fire as she kept Coh's reptilian head tight against her shoulder. Her other arm shot up with her dagger clasped in her fist, and she plunged the blade deep between his ribs, into his lungs, in his side, in his neck.

The undead neogi squirmed against her, squealing in pain as each thrust brought him closer to true death. Cwelanas's arm and body dripped slick with Coh's tainted blood. His claws raked her back and legs, but did no damage to her chain mail vest.

She felt the anger in her building as she plunged the dagger deep into his body repeatedly, and still the damned thing would not die. He thrashed against her, wriggling his head in a vain effort to tear loose from her stranglehold. He managed to bring her around in front.

Cwelanas then kicked out hard and connected a powerful knee into his belly. The air blew out of him, and as he was momentarily stunned, she slipped the dagger under his spiderlike legs and plunged it up into his heart. His blood spurted onto her like hot oil, and she pulled out the blade and drove it straight into one of his black, undead eyes.

He squealed like a fiend from the Abyss. His head thrashed madly, and with both hands she thrust the dagger deeper into the eye socket, then heaved until she felt the steel crack through bone and plunge directly into the reptile's soft, unliving brain.

The neogi jerked once, spasmodically, then Coh slid limp to her feet. His jaws snapped once in an involuntary effort to close around his quarry's flesh. His head fell back, onto the ground, the hilt of the dagger deep in his eye socket. Blood oozed from between his dead lips.

Cwelanas put her arm to her stomach, suddenly nauseated. The world spun around her. She put out an arm to maintain her balance, but her feet would not move properly. The smalljammer loomed ahead in the trees, but she realized that she was not moving. Somewhere she heard claws scraping through the leaves of the gardens. From somewhere, a dim thought came to her: B'Laath'a.

Her shoulder burned, flaring bright with pain, and B'Laath'a attacked from the side, throwing himself upon her and snapping with his dripping teeth.

She held back his slithering head with her good arm. It was all too much, the killing, the ceaseless attacks by Teldin's enemies. She felt her anger burning hot inside her, building like a furnace, then she realized that it was her vest of chain mail that seemed to burn, emanating with power.

It is more than a helm, she realized. It has the powers of Teldin's cloak!

She relaxed inside, still keeping the vengeful neogi at bay, and concentrated on the blossom of heat that she felt pulsing in her heart. B'Laath'a stopped his attack and stared at her, then his eyes widened, and she clasped him to her in an embrace from which he could not escape.

Power coursed through her with the heat of molten steel. The chain mail glowed, and in a burst of energy, B'Laath'a was flung away with the force of a ballista and sent hurtling into the light panels in the ceiling high above.

The neogi crashed into a crystal panel. Cwelanas dimly heard his bones crack upon impact. Then the mage fell from the ceiling and landed with a dull, sickening crunch near the smalljammer. Blood oozed from a score of breaks and lacerations across his body. His eyes, empty, devoid of their innate, unhuman evil, stared blankly at her.

The elf tried to stand, then fell to the ground, her side aching with cold fire from the undead neogi's bite. She thought she heard a cry, but the world was nothing but a blur around her, and she let herself fall deep into the sweet sleep of unconsciousness.

Chapter Thirty-Six

• • •

". . . *No warrior stands alone, least of all he chosen by fate to deliver some higher meaning to his actions.*

"*Each champion who has come here has had two things in common: a blind drive to succeed at his individual goals, and a charisma that pulls to him warriors who will stand ready to see his destiny through.*

"*In so doing, these warriors may find their own wondrous destinies. . . .*"

Seversen, scribe, *Book of the Rushing Rapids*; reign of Tomsun the Drinker

The rainbow lights of the phlogiston glittered off the Broken Sphere's cracked shell, flickering as though to the beat of some secret symphony. The sphere seemed less the shattered remnant of an eons-old disaster than a giant backdrop, an empty theater where an act of the second Unhuman War was being played out for the ghosts of the dead.

From port came an elven armada, the largest ship of the elven fleet. With a wingspan of three hundred feet, the armada was a hundred tons of death bearing a hundred elves, fourteen heavy weapons, and three explosive bombards. As the Cloakmaster watched through the eyes of the *Spelljammer*, hatches opened on the sides and belly of the butterfly-shaped armada, and a swarm of smaller attack flitters was deployed, buzzing speedily toward the *Spelljammer*.

From the bow came the smallest of the attacking vessels. A

sleek scro battlewagon, shaped like an attacking wild boar, hurtled toward the *Spelljammer.* One hundred and fifty feet long, the battlewagon, proudly christened *Eviscerator,* seemed almost as dangerous as the armada, for it carried fourteen medium weapons, a ram, and four bombards. In addition, it was equipped with a wildfire projector, which could spew a highly pressurized stream of fire, the way fountains spewed water. The ship was crewed by 160 ferocious scro fighters, reared, like their ancestors, the orcs, on a diet of hatred and blood.

From starboard came a Shou tsunami, second only to the *Spelljammer* in length. Like an impossible centipede, the massive vessel squirmed through space as if it were alive, three times the length of the armada's wingspan. Its segmented hull held two hundred Shou warriors, and its powerful defenses consisted of twenty-two heavy weapons, six bombards, and three jettisons. Hatches above each of the ship's legs held individual locust ships, which, when released en masse, would create a swarm that could wreak destruction on their enemies. The locusts were each equipped with a single light weapon, but were more often used in suicide dives against other craft and were sometimes filled with smoke powder, in order to blow the enemy into the gods' embrace.

The scro warriors upon the flat, outer decks of the battlewagon were engaged in small arms combat with the armada, the ship of their most hated enemies, the elves. Arrows from the scro archers arced through the flow in showers, skewering the elves unlucky enough to pull duty on unprotected decks. Three elves manning a ballista fell under the scro onslaught, one elf tumbling over a rail to fall into the phlogiston like a limp doll.

As the *Spelljammer* increased its speed and the fleets of its enemies followed toward the gap in the Broken Sphere, the scro halted their battle with the elves and turned to concentrate on the great ship bearing down on them.

The Cloakmaster watched as the scro scrambled across the decks of the battlewagon to prepare for the attack, then the first wave of flitters from the elven armada penetrated the *Spelljammer*'s air envelope and buzzed the decks. Archers hidden inside each flitter aimed their bows and crossbows toward the emplacements in the *Spelljammer*'s towers. The elves shot on sight, killing a dwarf who was notching a crossbow on the Chalice tower and injuring eight other warriors on the Tower of Thought and the wing batteries.

The *Spelljammer* shook as a trio of boulders crashed into the roof of the ship's stores and into the open market, now abandoned. The battlewagon had loaded its eight catapults and was already sending two more heavy shots toward the *Spelljammer*. Dust and rubble slammed into the streets as boulders tore through the walls of the council chambers. A load of iron shot hurtled over the towers in an ever-spreading cone, weakening battlements as they crashed into stone and crushing the skulls and bones of warriors under their weight.

Pain erupted throughout the Cloakmaster's body as each new injury wounded the *Spelljammer*. He winced as flitters shot arrows toward the ship's great eyes. He screamed as a heavy ballista bolt shot from the armada and the steel-tipped missile pierced the roof of the Armory. He felt himself weakening, the *Spelljammer* slowing as the Broken Sphere grew larger in his eyes.

—*No!* he screamed. —*We're too close to give up! We can't!*

The *Spelljammer* was silent, or perhaps his voice was the voice of the *Spelljammer* itself, screaming as one, sharing pain, sharing senses, sharing death.

—*No!*

He began to grow warm and thought that he felt a light touch upon his being. He instantly felt stronger, flooded with an energy that he recognized as his own, a reserve he did not know he had.

Then Gaye Goldring's face, translucent, glowing, floated before him.

"*I'm here,*" she said. "*You have not given up yet. You can't.*"

—*So close*, he said.

"*Yes, you're close. Look . . .*"

The *Spelljammer* was so close now that the immense gap in the Broken Sphere was no longer visible, even though it was more than a hundred miles distant. The Cloakmaster could clearly see the darkness inside, the cold rocks that had once been the first planets, and the fiery remnant of the star, Aeyenna, flaring as errant swirls of phlogiston were sucked into the core.

"You have the strength, Teldin. You've got it inside you. I'll be with you to help you reach the sphere. I'll do everything I can."

Gaye faded from his sight. He knew she had already helped him, bringing forth his own strength with merely a touch of her empathic powers. He barely heard her finish with, "*I'll be out there . . .*"

Then the *Spelljammer* lurched forward, increasing its speed. The Cloakmaster moved, and the *Spelljammer*'s huge wings moved in unison, sucking in a thick stream of phlogiston and pulling it in its wake.

The enemy fleets followed behind, occasionally firing their catapults and ballistae, but generally content, for now, to allow the three larger ships to do their work for them. Together, the fleets all sailed for the Broken Sphere.

The decks of the *Spelljammer* rang with explosions from the giff bombards, from the twang of the ship's powerful catapults as loads were shot toward the attacking vessels. Lord Diamondtip, his ponderous ears protected by a helmet layered with thick cloth, laughed every time a ship was hit by his smoke powder weapons. A beholder tyrant ship came just a bit too close and shot an ineffective volley of stone and iron shot toward the giff tower. Diamondback ordered his soldiers to "Rotate and fire at will!" and the four-bombard platform was rotated twice, each gun firing in turn until the beholder ship was hammered into chunks. Finally, the tyrant exploded in the phlogiston, and the towers of the *Spelljammer* vibrated with the resultant explosion as the flow ignited in a ball of glorious fire.

Diamondtip patted the wall of the giff tower. The surface was blackened with the force of the explosions, the immediate ignitions of the surrounding flow, but the tower still held. "Stay with me," Lord Diamondtip said to the tower. "Stay with me."

The elven flitters that had disgorged from the armada swooped down at the *Spelljammer* and through its streets like deadly wraiths. The light craft were built for speed, and the archers cramped inside whittled away at the *Spelljammer*'s defenses with the sting of an insect. Some flitters even carried elven mages, who cast their spells of shadow or invisible force with a single, rapid pass.

The weaponry atop the dwarven citadel proved invaluable against a heavily outfitted nautiloid that seemed to swoop in from nowhere. The nautiloid shot four heavy ballistae and four heavy catapults simultaneously at the starboard wing batteries. Some of the shot went high and took out a portion of the roof of the Shou tower; but the weapons had been carefully aimed and destroyed the top floors of the human and elven batteries. The elven battery then caught fire, and a huge explosion ripped through the building and blasted stone chunks in a wide fan across the tail and the aft towers.

The starboard batteries responded quickly with their heavy weapons, but the dwarves directly beneath the nautiloid had the advantage of proximity. As the shadow of the nautiloid passed over their heads, Lord Agate Ironlord Kova ordered his troops to return fire. In the adjoining tower, Vagner Firespitter, as well, shouted to his dwarves to "Fire until we blow the scum right out of the flow!"

The nautiloid was sandwiched between the assaults of the dwarven communities and battered mercilessly with loads of iron shot until a final missile from one of Firespitter's light ballistae pierced the chambered hull. The ship burst into a ball of flame. It fell in a flaming arc upon the beholder ruins and rolled off the stern of the *Spelljammer*, leaving a trail of exploding phlogiston as it fell from the deck.

The dwarven communities shouted and cheered. In seconds, the *Spelljammer* and its air envelope had left the nautiloid behind, exposing the flaming ship to the flow, and the phlogiston ignited again with a huge explosion that was momentarily blinding.

As the flitters from the armada ducked between the *Spelljammer*'s towers to shoot and run, the Shou tsunami came steadily forward. The scro battlewagon never let up its onslaught, banking so that the tsunami was temporarily blocked from view as it swept closer and closer to the great ship's bow and attacked. Three ballistae and four catapults fired from the battlewagon's port side. Iron shot and missiles were black blurs as they hurtled toward the *Spelljammer* and crashed into the walls of the ship's stores and the Tower of Trade. A gaping hole was blown into the tower's lower levels, and the whole building collapsed upon itself in a shudder that shook the ship.

Then the first wave of missiles and boulders rained upon the *Spelljammer* from the approaching elven armada. Most of the missiles went short, passing harmlessly in front of the ship. A few boulders dug deep trenches into the landing field, and one steel missile embedded itself in the *Spelljammer*'s port ram.

The scro battlewagon continued on its downward dive toward the ship. Ballistae and catapults from both sides of the boar fell upon the towers in a deadly hail of stone and metal debris. Archers along the sides targeted the *Spelljammer*'s warriors in the upper ruins of the captain's tower and atop the Guild tower. Seven Guild warriors dropped dead on the tower roof, the ill-made arrows of scro protruding from their bodies. The fighters in the captain's tower profited from better cover in the ruins, and most of the scro arrows bounced off the stone walls. The archers there returned fire, and three scro fighters staggered away from the rails of the battlewagon, arrows quivering in their chests and necks.

The dwarves under Lord Kova had their ballistae ready and aimed toward the onrushing battlewagon. As the fearsome prow of the boar ship *Eviscerator* sailed over the decks, Kova screamed "Fire!" and the dwarves' ballistae shot their missiles simultaneously. One missed completely, arcing over the battlewagon and passing into the flow. Two others impaled the hull, but did not drive deep enough to inflict significant damage to the ship or its crew.

The last missile collided with the scro ship just as it started a sweeping turn to move away and then come back on another run. The missile angled into the boar's prow and chipped off most of its starboard face. The missile and the face dropped to the great ship's deck, bounced off the captain's tower, and landed between the library and illithid towers.

The *Spelljammer*'s fighters soon came to understand the attack strategies of the elven flitters, and quickly learned how to fight back against their swiftest opponents. Light catapults were used to the best advantage, and soon flitters were falling to the decks all around and crumpling like paper, battered and torn by the rock storms that shot from the towers. One flitter was hit by a hail of iron shot from the Chalice tower and sailed directly into the roof, crushing the warriors who had shot it.

The number of elven flitters was soon cut down in half. By that time, the armada had come well within range to bear its heavy weapons, and the scro battlewagon had turned itself around to stare down the *Spelljammer* once again and begin another attack run.

High above the decks, directly below the *Spelljammer*'s triangular stinger tail, a glowing ball of light appeared, which transformed in the figure of Gaye Goldring. Arms outstretched, floating above the towers like a spirit of the winds, she summoned power to her and concentrated, molding the wild energies of her mind, the energies with which Teldin had fortified her, and focusing on the approaching ships. Energy flickered around her in a golden cloud of lightning, of swirling, formless power.

In the lower hull of the elven armada, a pinprick of golden light blossomed. It spread slowly, glowing bright with Gaye's psionic energy. The glow faded as it spread across the hull in an expanding circle, and where the light had burned, the hull became discolored and appeared warped or weakened.

Gaye floated there, concentrating on her target, while the armada attacked, while missiles rained death upon the *Spelljammer* and its crew. The minotaur tower was felled by a barrage of both stone and missiles. Immediately, the *Spelljammer*'s weapons shot back from the hulk and giant towers. One missile punctured one of the armada's great wings and continued past. Another was shot straight into the armada's lower hull.

The elven ship shuddered as the missile pierced the hull easily, like a sewing needle through fabric. Gaye's molecular manipulation had transformed the armada's thick, chitinous hull into a material no stronger than parchment. The crew of the *Spelljammer* quickly assessed the armada's weakness, and weapons across the ship were aimed at the discolored, vulnerable patch that now had grown to cover the armada's entire underside.

Within minutes, the armada fluttered drunkenly across the flow, a dozen missiles sticking out of its underbelly like stubby legs. Its wings were broken and bent, tattered into shreds by the shots from the *Spelljammer*'s catapults.

The armada managed one last, fitful assault against the *Spelljammer.* One missile found its target in the uppermost chamber of the illithid tower. Trebek's books and scrolls exploded out of the tower and showered the decks below.

Then the armada shook as chambers inside ruptured, fires broke out, and explosions rolled in a chain reaction throughout the ship. The elven flagship blew apart and sent the shattered hull scattering in all directions. Blackened bodies spun into the flow; then the phlogiston ignited around the wrecked ship, and the sky blazed.

The *Spelljammer* was buffeted by the storm of heat and turbulence. The scro battlewagon shook and was tossed sideways by the blast. The Shou tsunami appeared unbothered; only its frontal antennae were slightly scorched as it sailed harmlessly through the last of the explosion.

The *Spelljammer* adjusted its course and accelerated. Its starboard wing swung up, over the scro battlewagon, which could not recover fast enough from the explosion to fire at the *Spelljammer*'s lower hull. The battlewagon's helmsman realized his mistake and quickly turned the ship around in pursuit.

The tsunami fired its heavy weapons as the *Spelljammer* passed directly in front of it. Boulders fell into the walls of the Long Fangs' tower and the beholder ruins, then the *Spelljammer*'s crew retaliated individually, firing indiscriminately at the beautiful Shou ship as it wriggled through the flow. One of the tsunami's long antennae cracked and was sent spinning away by a hail of iron shot.

The *Spelljammer* flew straight through the gap in the Broken Sphere, heedless of its enemies. It was swallowed by the darkness, by the enormous weight of its ancient, forgotten birth. Behind it, clouds of phlogiston roiled into the sphere, kicked up by the *Spelljammer*'s wings and sucked in by its wake.

The battlewagon fired from behind and to starboard, clipping the mast of a galleon with a ballista missile, then the wildfire projector was readied on the *Eviscerator*'s upper firing platform. The boar ship sped forward, close enough to the galleon to see the surprised look in the pirates' eyes as the scro on deck aimed their arrows and killed eight warriors in a single pass.

The scro ship penetrated the *Spelljammer*'s air envelope. One missile, shot from atop the Armory, impaled one of the ship's great forelegs. The battlewagon rocked with the impact of a heavy load of iron shot.

Then the scro aimed the wildfire projector, and the top of the Dark Tower was engulfed in flames that licked up the *Spelljammer*'s tail. The scro hopped and laughed on the deck of the *Eviscerator* and aimed again. Fire splattered the base of the Armory in a wide swath that blazed through the Old Elvish Academy and the Academy of Human Knowledge. The flames spread from roof to roof, and soon the Long Fangs' tower and the beholder ruins were eaten by fire. Phlogiston exploded chaotically, raining rubble down upon the decks.

Missiles from the *Spelljammer* embedded into the battlewagon like spears. The scro ship twisted evasively, ignoring most of the *Spelljammer*'s attacks by staying far to starboard, off the wing. Inside the control cabin, the scro helmsman sweated copiously in a struggle to keep the ship out of danger, yet still in a position where it could dive in easily and whittle away at the *Spelljammer*'s defenses . . . and kill as many hells-spawned elves as possible.

Concentrating on the scene outside, transmitted to him by the *Eviscerator*'s helm, the helmsman did not notice a golden glow appear at his side. He did not notice the shape of a woman materialize and beckon to him, her fingers stretched at strange angles, her gaze fixed upon his face. He jerked once, violently, struggling in his mind as a superior force battled with his subconscious. He suddenly stood and awkwardly faced her.

His eyes were wide with fear as first one of his arms went up into the air, then another. He watched helplessly as his right leg came up involuntarily, and he started hopping. The battlewagon began to slow. It listed to port as the helmsman's mind strayed from controlling the ship's course and speed. Gaye could hear shouts from the decks above as the ship continued to list.

"What are you doing?" he screamed in the Common tongue.

"Stop this! Stop this now! You'll kill us all!"

Gaye stopped. Instead, she concentrated. The scro pulled a short sword from his scabbard. His eyes widened even more. "No!" he shouted. "No!"

He brought the point of his sword to his unprotected chest. The sharp point dug into his flesh. Blood welled in a shiny, thick drop. "You can't do this to me! You can't!"

Then he gasped, as his body was flung against a wall and the impact pushed the sword into his heart. He fell to his knees, then pitched over.

"*Yes, I can,*" Gaye said calmly.

The battered battlewagon listed dangerously to port and began its descent. The door to the cabin burst open, and a contingent of scro warriors charged in, their weapons drawn.

Gaye concentrated and felt the psionic energies building inside her, unstoppable. She looked down. Her hand was glowing white-hot with the power of her own life force.

Life, she thought, for Teldin, for the *Spelljammer*. Let destiny be served.

She was stronger, more powerful, than she had ever felt before. The scro warriors came to a halt only a few feet from her. Her powers flickered around her like a thing alive, blistering their orclike faces with the heat of a star. They scrambled to get away, but Gaye let the feeling of purity, of heat, rush over her, and then she was one—one with Teldin, one with the *Spelljammer*, seeing their united, eternal destiny in a flare of energy that lit the phlogiston like a blazing star.

The *Eviscerator*'s foredeck blew apart in a single burst of stellar fire. When the phlogiston exploded in a blazing sphere, half the battlewagon was ruptured, shattered and torn apart into shreds and splinters, its hull blackened and blistered. It arced down like a dying comet, down through the flow . . . on a collision course with the *Spelljammer*.

Chapter Thirty-Seven

• • •

"*. . . It is all forgotten. I leave all my collected knowledge here in the Orb, for I fear that great harm will come to the library, and the wisdom of man and the gods will be stolen from the Wanderer.*

"*The Orb will wait here for those with the courage and the insight to find it and use it. I cannot leave this place, and so cannot share my strange tales of adventure with others but in this small way. Here I leave the history of the spheres, the secrets of the Bonding, and here I leave the key to Creannon, and the map of its future, far beyond this mortal plane. . . .*"

Neridox, librarian; journal 1701; reign of Jokarin.

They could do nothing but watch helplessly, frozen, as Cwelanas battled the neogi. They had been caught unawares as Cwelanas ran to check the hangar door. B'Laath'a, waiting in the cover of the jamberry trees, had stepped out and cast a spell at them, holding them immobile where they stood.

They watched as Cwelanas killed Coh and the mage leaped to take his place. Then B'Laath'a was destroyed with the power of her chain mail. Cwelanas fell to the ground. The spell holding the warriors was broken with B'Laath'a's death, and they jumped to help the elf.

She was barely awake, shivering as though with intense cold. CassaRoc knew a bad fever when he saw one, and this one was the worst he had ever seen. "You'll be all right. We need to get you a healer. Can you take the helm like this?"

She tried to shrug. "It doesn't matter," she said. Her voice was barely above a whisper. "I have to, don't I?"

CassaRoc pushed back a strand of hair. The wounds in her shoulder were angry and red, puckered like craters and surrounded by yellow and blue bruises. "Are you sure?"

Cwelanas smiled through her pain. She felt her body shiver with a reserve of energy, and her pain began to slowly recede. The chain mail Teldin had given her played its power through her like a healing flow of energy. "I think I will be fine. Teldin has taken care of that. We must go."

In the smalljammer's control room, CassaRoc helped Cwelanas take her seat. Instantly, she felt better, at peace, as the ship warmed to her touch. Its energies flowed through her, giving her strength. "We still have to get out of the gardens," she observed.

The others looked at her, confused. They had never caught up with her to examine the hangar doors. "What do you mean?" Djan asked. I thought Teldin told us to sail away from here."

"Yes," she said, "but to cast off we must first get out of the gardens, and neither of the doors will open."

CassaRoc shook his head sadly and rubbed the bridge of his nose. "Damn," he said. "Damn."

The ship was pounded from above, and the collision reverberated like thunder above their heads. The *Spelljammer* shook as though it were being slammed by a giant hammer. The warriors sprawled to the cabin deck. The hammering came closer, closer, rolling heavily like a bouncing boulder, and the ship shook with its thudding impact.

The wall of the gardens exploded inward in a hail debris from the *Spelljammer*'s thick hull. Rubble slammed against the smalljammer, then pattered like hard rain as the echo of the explosion died away.

Cwelanas looked up, coughing as she inhaled dust. The others stood around her.

"Look!" Na'Shee said, pointing.

Chapter Thirty-Eight

• • •

". . . The Architects looked far into Egrestarrian's future and saw the day that a courageous warrior would lead the Offspring to its time of Rebirth. This warrior, they knew, would hold in his heart the strength of peace, a hatred of death, and a quest for a higher existence than that of his own plane.

"It is these noble desires with which they seeded Egrestarrian, the Compass, and the Cloak of the First Pilot; for they knew that the currents of destiny would lead these things to the Son of the Architects, who held these concepts dear in his soul, and would die for his ideals as the Last Pilot. . . ."

The Mage of the Owls, journal; reign of Velina, the second Pilot.

The Cloakmaster saw it with the *Spelljammer*'s eyes. The scro battlewagon was listing dangerously, descending toward the *Spelljammer* at incredible speed.

He reached out with his senses and felt Gaye. He felt her warm, golden glow, distant, weak, but still alive and, without words, he knew that all was right. Then he reached out and touched the battlewagon, looking ahead with one of the *Spelljammer*'s innate senses that transcended understanding and human explanation.

He asked a question.

He saw a ship, a star, a broken sphere.

He understood, and it was good.

The *Eviscerator* plummeted down from the flow. A ballista

missile from the Tower of Trade unexpectedly hit the ship's wildfire projector, and the stern of the scro battlewagon erupted into flames that trailed the ship like a cape of fire.

Teldin willed the ship to move, and the *Spelljammer* turned gracefully. The starboard wing lay spread out before the hurtling battlewagon to act as a landing field, but the *Eviscerator* was sailing in from starboard. And the centaur tower lay directly in its fiery path.

The maimed face of the battlewagon met the stonework of the centaur tower head on. It crashed through the tower, then bounced once, twice, and started rolling as flying chunks of stone rained all around it. A trail of flaming wildfire followed, quickly spreading across the starboard wing as quick as liquid fire, igniting the flow in a series of explosions.

The fiery substance burned through the outer hull to catch fire inside the ship's porous body. The scro battlewagon careened over the wing and spun blindly into the starboard door of the gardens, tearing a huge, jagged hole in it before bouncing off the *Spelljammer*'s bow and tumbling into the phlogiston.

The explosion at the bow hurled the *Spelljammer* up and shot the jagged remains of the battlewagon into the ship's underbelly. The Cloakmaster reeled under the explosive force, then sought out the *Spelljammer*'s consciousness, felt the cold wildspace of the Broken Sphere surrounding him, and he again became one with the ship. He straightened their course toward the remnant of the star.

He reached out and saw Cwelanas and CassaRoc, Djan and Estriss, Na'Shee and Chaladar safe in the smalljammer, and he touched their souls in a final farewell gesture. Cwelanas shook herself; CassaRoc got up from the floor and placed a hand on her uninjured shoulder, wondering why he was suddenly thinking of Teldin.

—*You must go now,* Teldin told Cwelanas. —*This may be your last chance.*

She did not hear him, but she felt the meaning of his words in her soul. She nodded to herself, and the smalljammer levitated inches above the earthen floor of the gardens and angled toward the rent in the door.

The battlewagon's wildfire spread quickly into the gardens,

choking the air with oily black smoke. Teldin felt part of his soul, the *Spelljammer*'s soul, lift then. In a minute, as the Shou tsunami and its plague of locusts, twice as dangerous as the elven flitters, descended upon the *Spelljammer*, he watched as the smalljammer flew from the wound in the door and accelerated, turning sharply past the great ship's rams and shooting past, flying like a missile out through the gap in the Broken Sphere, and into the endless void.

—*Good*, Teldin said.

—*Good*, the *Spelljammer* said.

And their voices were one.

The *Spelljammer* increased its speed.

The locusts that fell upon the *Spelljammer* from the tsunami were all armed with light weapons. They flew through the streets and between towers crazily, their missiles and catapults reaching places that the *Spelljammer*'s crew originally thought were safe. Some locusts were loaded with smoke powder and deliberately rammed into the most heavily fortified towers, committing fiery suicides that were designed to burn out the enemy.

Selura Killcrow, crushed beneath a load of medium boulders shot toward a group of her fighters, died under the onslaught.

Korvok the Fell, who had proudly boasted that he was the foulest man in all the spheres, died as a Shou mage from the tsunami targeted the Tenth Pit with a spell of detonation and the walls themselves exploded with their own latent energy.

Arvanon, the lizard priest of the *Spelljammer*, died as the wildfire from the wrecked battlewagon filled the gardens with a roiling fireball.

Kaba Danel, the leader of the dracons, died as a wave of arrows from some unseen vessel spilled across the top of the dracon tower and found a target in his chest.

The forgotten captains imprisoned in the Dark Tower—Jokarin, Theorx, and Miark—all died true deaths under the weight of the tower's rubble.

Unholy fires broke out across the *Spelljammer*. The roof and upper floors of the dwarven citadel exploded in flame as a pair of locusts slammed into it, killing more than a hundred dwarves in a single blow. A squadron of locusts swarmed over the port towers and stormed them with lightning bolts of pointed steel. Ogres died under tons of rubble. The kasharin butchered themselves with their death rays for lack of living targets. The towers of Trade and Thought fell under the locusts' assault, to become nothing but a pile of rubble and shattered bones.

The tsunami itself came on then. Missiles and boulders, iron shot and jettisons, flew through the flow unerringly, piercing the *Spelljammer*'s eyes, shattering the buildings arranged behind the bow, destroying what was left of the dracon tower. The giff tower fired its quadruple bombard, and the top of the tower exploded in a huge gout of orange flame. The phlogiston around it burst into a cascade of fire, and the Cloakmaster knew—*felt*—that Diamondtip and the giff were gone.

He felt hot anger surge through him as his people died, as the beauty, the wonder, of the *Spelljammer*'s existence was obliterated by the wolves of war. His fury accelerated up his spine, collecting in his tail with the force of a nova.

The tail blazed white with the light of a thousand stars, and a shimmering torpedo of energy shot like a comet straight into the bow of the Shou tsunami. The sky lit up with the purifying light of vengeance.

The *Spelljammer* sped up and tore through the dust cloud that had been the tsunami. Cold black planets shot past. The ships that had been following disappeared behind him, becoming specks against the ragged outline of the flow. A trail of phlogiston followed the *Spelljammer* as though the ship were dragging a fiery leash. Teldin reached out with his mind and touched the souls of the ship's survivors. He exerted his will, and the air envelope was filled with a sweet narcotic that brought peace to the ship's remaining inhabitants.

—*Understand*, he implored, and he showed them what must be done.

And they understood.

Aeyenna was a broken star, still active, but not whole, clearly dying a slow death. It grew in Teldin's eyes, blossomed like a brilliant, shining promise.

He gauged the ship's impossible speed of thought through wildspace, and the distance between he and the stellar remnant. Energy flickered teasingly along his spine and burned hot in the tip of his tail.

—*Aeyenna*, he sang loudly, *the First Sun*.

He focused on the remnant burning in wildspace before him.

—*Be strong. Be pure.*

—*Be renewed.*

At the last instant, before he expelled the *Spelljammer*'s final, explosive star, Teldin thought —*Cwelanas, . . . I do love you*.

Then the globe of energy shot out toward its target inexorably, perfectly, without mercy . . . into the *Spelljammer* itself.

The great ship exploded, its rubble and fragments and bodies and the shards of its hull becoming fire, spreading out through the Broken Sphere in a million blazing meteors.

For an instant, against the black wall of the sphere, the ship became a firebird, outlined in light and flame.

But the *Spelljammer* lived.

Its core, its soul, shone in the black Broken Sphere with the light of a nova.

The soul of the *spaakiil* merged with the surviving fragment of Aeyenna.

The explosion was exultant, holy.

The *Spelljammer*'s wake of phlogiston ignited immediately, merging in flame with the ship's soul, with the swirling, living matter of the *Spelljammer* and the star it had killed.

He could feel the great ship's enemies dying instantly, like a candle snuffed out with a single, powerful breath. He felt his own people die, then merge together, like butterflies on the wind. He felt the locusts and their helmsmen burn away, without pain, to transform into pure energy. He felt the foul flesh of B'Laath'a, of the Fool, see true light for the first time, and he hoped their souls knew peace.

His energies exploded outward and vibrated against the wall of the cracked sphere. The energies, merging with the chaotic matter of the flow, reshaped, reformed. They swirled, condensed, creating a new inner shell for the Broken Sphere. Fractures were filled, made whole with the energies from the *Spelljammer*'s sacrifice. With each explosion of matter, with each resultant expulsion of raw energy, the immeasurable gap in the sphere slowly closed.

* * * * *

Cwelanas watched, screaming, with the mental view from her ship's helm. The flow before the smalljammer was spotted with a large fleet of vessels, all bearing down upon her. She knew she could not defeat them. She knew she could not get into even a single battle, for the smalljammer had no weapons aboard.

Then, in her mind's eye she saw the Broken Sphere, behind her, light up impossibly from inside. She felt people die in a single blaze of pure white light. She felt the *Spelljammer* . . .

No! she thought. *TELDIN!*

She spun the smalljammer about and desperately headed for the sphere. She broke out in a cold sweat and felt the cabin waver dizzily around her. CassaRoc and Chaladar shouted at her, but she could not hear them for the thunderous beating in her own ears.

In the instant before she passed out, she heard—felt—a voice, a soul.

Yes, it was Teldin, one last time.

She felt a song, his song, echo through her very being. It was an ancient song, one of fate, of wonder, a song of life.

She halted the smalljammer's movement, and the ship sat silently in the flow while her friends gathered around her and she wept.

Chapter Thirty-Nine

• • •

". . . And it is written that the Cloak of the First Pilot will deliver the Last Pilot to the throne of Creannon, the Destined One.

"And the Last Pilot shall sow the seeds of Creannon's destiny, and shall rejoice in the budding of new life.

"For that which was lost will be restored; and that which will be lost shall be restored. . . ."

Sargathus, librarian; reign of the Third Pilot

The fleet surrounded the smalljammer without incident. It was a fleet of sidewheelers, all gnomish make, and two elven armadas, and she recognized the military bearing of the fleet's leader instantly.

Herphan Gomja, the giff who had befriended Teldin at the start of his quest, wept openly at news of the Cloakmaster's death. He and the ships under Vallus Leafbower's command had arrived too late to defend the *Spelljammer*, but Gomja saw new purpose in the deliverance of Cwelanas and the *Spelljammer*'s progeny.

They stayed for a day in orbit around the Broken Sphere, and they marveled at the ebony crystalline wall that stretched before them, blotting out the horizon. The shell was perfectly intact, and it glowed as though with an inner life, energy flickering through the shell like thoughts: generating, regenerating, creating.

The Broken Sphere was no more, for it had been renewed.

The warriors aboard the smalljammer were offered posts on the ships of the gnomish-elven fleet. No one wanted to decide on anything just yet, preferring to stay with Cwelanas for this leg, the first leg, of her own quest throughout the spheres. This war was over, and each person had seen all too much of battle since the Cloakmaster's arrival. The mind flayer stayed with Cwelanas as well, and he studied the sphere while they lingered in orbit.

With the War for the *Spelljammer* over, the ships turned away from the sphere, the *Spelljammer* Sphere, as Estriss was calling it, and headed deeper into the flow.

Cwelanas found her friends outside, on the observation deck, staring behind them at the slowly receding black sphere. They turned at her approach. Djan put a hand on her shoulder. "*Verenthestae*," he said. "All is as it should be."

She nodded, wishing it were otherwise. They all watched the sphere in silence for a time, then the mind flayer looked up.

My observations are not complete, but I have discovered something interesting, he said.

Na'Shee brushed back her hair and turned. CassaRoc leaned forward on the rail and tried to look farther into the flow, as though he were searching for something.

"What have you found?" Cwelanas asked.

Estriss gestured toward the *Spelljammer* Sphere. *The sphere is somehow locked from entrance. We could not open portals to sail inside, even if we tried.*

"I know," she said.

The mind flayer nodded. *But there are thin parts in the crystal, where the shell is still forming. It is not opaque at those points.*

"What is it, Estriss? What did you see?"

His eyes crinkled happily, as though he had witnessed all the wonders of the universe.

A new birth. A new beginning. A sun, Estriss said. *I believe I saw a new sun.*

Epilogue

• • •

"*Here begins the log of Creannon, the* Spelljammer, *and the Last Pilot, who is now the First. . . .*"

Cloakmaster, the Chosen Pilot; day one

The eternal blackness of cold, empty space, a void of nothingness, was momentarily dispelled. First an almost infinitesimal glimmer of light appeared where before there had been nothing, then an immeasurable expulsion of pure, blinding power ripped the contours of space and time and spewed energy—pebbles, trails, streams of raw power—across the black, eternal, timeless sea.

In the center of the explosion, a shape, a living thing, feeding off the fires of creation, began to coalesce inside the raw, swirling phlogiston.

It glowed from within, magic and energy pulsing like rivers of fire through the veins that had once been called warrens.

Creannon, the *Spelljammer*, sailed from the doorway its own death had created and spread its great wings into wildspace. The nova of its birth dissipated. The *Spelljammer* sang into a cold, sunless night that it had never before experienced in the forever light of the flow.

—*The universe*, the *Spelljammer* said, *is ours.*

—*It is reborn.*

The soul of Teldin marveled at the emptiness of this universe. Here the powers and the matter of the flow had been transformed into raw, untamed energy, and he could feel through the *Spelljammer*'s senses that the universe was spread out before them like a blanket, unbounded as far as he could see. This universe seemed to be entirely wildspace: cold, empty, mostly devoid of life. Here suns burned in space while the planets around them slowly evolved, and rarely did the processes of life naturally occur.

—*This will change*, the Cloakmaster said.

—*Yes. Our destiny is to create. Life is all-important.*

—*And the universe we have left behind . . . What of it?*

—*That is closed to us now. We must look forward, not behind.*

—*What of the Broken Sphere? What have we left behind?*

There was a pause. Then: —*Here is but one of their possible futures . . .*

Destiny appeared before them, a view of the Broken Sphere that seemed to envelop them as though they were there.

They watched. Seconds became years, then decades.

The sphere of phlogiston solidified to become a black crystalline wall that seemed to take up all of existence. Inside, the phlogiston swirled and condensed. The flaming shards that had been the *Spelljammer*'s hull had embedded in the inside layer of the reforming sphere. There the latent magical energies imbued within the phlogiston merged with the *Spelljammer*'s soul. The shards transformed into crystals, glowing with power. The memories of the *Spelljammer* became the stars that generations of as yet unborn humans would look up to and dream about, create myths around, make love under, and reach for.

The swirling phlogiston inside the sphere was a roiling firestorm. In time, the energies separated, and the forces of magic condensed the spinning balls of phlogiston into a glorious, brilliant sun and worlds—eighteen of them, perhaps more, perhaps less. The sphere would be reborn—not identical to Ouiyan, but in honor of the sacrifice the sphere had made millennia in the past.

—*Its destiny*, the *Spelljammer* sang, *is unlike ours. It waits to write itself, where our destiny is and always has been written for us.*

A thousand years later, the worlds teemed with life. Eight-legged horses roamed the ocher plains of Thoris. The seas of

Hedriana swam with orange fish that changed color with the hours of the day. On Elias, even the smallest field mice had the innate ability to summon magic. And on the recreated worlds that had once been Colurranur, BedevanSov, Ondora, Ladria, Asveleyn, and Resanel, life reappeared. Species that had been destroyed millennia ago were renewed, reshaped, on new worlds formed from the molecules of the old, and they shared their worlds with new forms of life that celebrated the variety of existence and the wonder of being.

And into the animal kingdom came humanity, which brought with it fire. Humanoids brought with them intelligence and evolving languages. They brought myth and wonder, fear and awe. They told tales of legend, of how the night eats the sky, of how the gods look upon them from the eyes in the night. They learned the ways of magic, and they learned how to fly.

Humanity learned, and once again lived in peace. Like their forgotten forerunners, they lived peacefully with the other life forms of their worlds, learned how to speak with the beasts of the sea, how to respect life in all its forms, and how to play games of skill with the denizens of the trees...

... and every year, as they migrated from planet to planet, as they returned to teach humanity how to sing into the stars and imagine worlds and places undreamed of, swarms of reborn *spaakiil*, the last legacy of the *Spelljammer*, filled the skies.

—*This is the future*, the *Spelljammer* said, *a future unwritten, merely shaped by the darkness of future past, one of millions of realities that have yet to unfold, waiting to take shape in the Sphere That Once Was. In a thousand years or so, when all this has come to pass—or has not—and perhaps the known spheres will have found peace, Ouiyan Reborn will once again be open for all vessels from all spheres. Here all may learn, orcs and humans, mind flayers and beholders. All may learn . . . together. Songs of joy will be sung throughout the spheres, the races will live and evolve together, and the Spelljammer will lead the fleets of war and death into a universe of eternal light.*

—*And when they reach the stars?* Teldin asked.

—*Then nothing will be impossible.*

The Reborn Egg vanished from view, and Teldin's vista was filled with darkness. He reached out with the senses of the

Spelljammer, and in the wildspace around him he felt only emptiness, the cold wastes that stretched without the spherical boundaries that he knew. He knew not where they were; but the universe belonged to them.

—*And us? What are we to create?*

—*We are changed*, the *Spelljammer* sang, and the Cloakmaster reached out to examine . . . himself.

The *Spelljammer* was larger, sleeker. Its mantalike body had retained its basic shape, but its flesh was translucent, flickering like blue crystal, and the warrens had become veins that pulsated with the immense power of its life force.

The city on its back gleamed with the fires from the *Spelljammer's* body. Its towers were taller, more ornate; built of gold and silver, of polished, vibrant crystal, and a shimmering metallic stone that was brighter than any substance the Cloakmaster had ever seen.

It was the *Spelljammer*, reborn into a pure, untouched universe, formed by an unknown set of physical laws. Perhaps it was a new dimension. Perhaps the *Spelljammer* had reappeared in a sphere far larger than any other in the known universe. Perhaps . . .

The Cloakmaster felt himself smile, though he was ethereal now, his body one with that of the *Spelljammer*. Wherever they were, this was their universe, their creation, a broad plain of wildspace that stretched out before them, beckoning to be explored. Out there, on the fringes of his senses, he felt something waiting for them, singing its own song in this place of discovery. There were magnificent cities—there had to be; he could touch them with his soul—floating between suns. Swimmers sailed the seas of space, basking in the warmth of stars. Minds called to him with their need, their yearning, to dream.

There was life.

The Cloakmaster understood it all then, the purpose of the *Spelljammer* and the interweaving of so many destinies: the *Spelljammer* creating life; the new life spreading out and creating its own wonders, finding its own dreams, creating its own *Spelljammers*, its own realities, spreading magic and wonder of life everywhere.

Its purpose, written by the Architects when the universe

was young, was clear: The *Spelljammer* must not pay penance for its innocent crime, but find purpose in life, its own life.

To create, discover, teach, show, renew, restore, and live.

The simple life he had known before was long gone. The past was past, and the universe of his birth was just a dim vision in a spyglass, forever too distant for him to reach. This place, this universe . . . this was untouched, virginal, he felt. This was his to explore, his to create. Part of him sang with joy at his new birth, at the wonder of his destiny; and part of him wept at the worlds that were now forever lost.

—Verenthestae, the *Spelljammer* said. *—It means far more than the interweaving of destiny. It is a concept that has survived the millennia, originating from an ancient tongue from the Broken Sphere.* Tru'vaer. *It means also . . .*

The *Spelljammer* sang into the void. Its new, crystalline body glowed with the light of innocence. Its veins flowed with the power of galaxies, and its song rang through his heart, unwrapping the now useless layers of humanity that Teldin Moore, the Cloakmaster, had held onto like precious gems, and exposing the blinding light of his soul.

And in the bearing of his soul, he felt what *verenthestae* meant, though words could only approximate its true meaning.

—Let the light of the soul shine forth and be revealed.

—Let the song of the soul spread truth into darkness.

—Let those apart be brought together.

—Know thyself.

—Seek . . .

—Love . . .

—Cherish life . . .

—And do not yield.

He blazed with the light of a star. The heart of the *Spelljammer* burned with Teldin's soul, and their song was absorbed into the fires of a newly created sun.

The *Spelljammer* banked lazily, away from the spiraling system of dust clouds and gases. The emptiness of the void stretched far ahead, into eternity, and the *Spelljammer* sang into it, waiting for the distant day that its song of life would finally be answered and the wonders that it had seen across the void would be shared.

About the Author

Russ T. Howard has written for *Premiere*, *Omni*, *Gauntlet*, *The Stephen King Companion*, and *Censorship in America*. He lives in Virginia and Florida with his wife, and occasionally may be found at the Adventurer's Club on Walt Disney World's Pleasure Island.